WICKED GAMES

Angela Knight

BERKLEY BOOKS, NEW YORK

THE BERKLEY PUBLISHING GROUP
Published by the Penguin Group
Penguin Group (USA) LLC
375 Hudson Street, New York, New York 10014

USA • Canada • UK • Ireland • Australia • New Zealand • India • South Africa • China

penguin.com

A Penguin Random House Company

This book is an original publication of The Berkley Publishing Group.

Berkley Books are published by The Berkley Publishing Group.
BERKLEY® is a registered trademark of Penguin Group (USA) LLC.
The "B" design is a trademark of Penguin Group (USA) LLC.

Library of Congress Cataloging-in-Publication Data

Knight, Angela.
[Short stories. Selections]
Wicked games / Angela Knight.
pages cm
ISBN 978-0-425-21565-4 (pbk.)
I. Title.
PS3611.N557A6 2014
813'.6–dc23   2013047662

PUBLISHING HISTORY
Berkley trade paperback edition / April 2014

PRINTED IN THE UNITED STATES OF AMERICA

10 9 8 7 6 5 4 3 2 1

Cover photo of Muscular Man Embracing Woman in Bra and Garter Belt © Ocean / Corbis.
Cover design by Rita Frangie.
Interior text design by Laura K. Corless.

ACKNOWLEDGMENTS

This book is dedicated to the ladies who helped me make sure it doesn't suck. Or if it does, it's certainly not their fault.

One of those is my new writing goddess, Joey W. Hill, who writes the best erotic romance I have ever read—and I've read a lot of good erotic romance. Joey gave me a wonderful, detailed critique, analyzing everything from logic to sentence structure, and she made a lot of great suggestions about how to resolve the problems she saw.

Then, of course, the happy gang of writers and beta readers who have been helping me with my books for years now: Shelby Morgen, Kate Douglas, Diane Whiteside, Camille Anthony, and Marteeka Karland.

Last but not least is my Bookdragon, Virginia Ettel, who, with Diane, also moderates my Yahoo loop. They're all dear friends.

And as always, I want to thank my editor, Cindy Hwang, her assistant, Kristine Swartz, and Berkley's production team.

CONTENTS

FOREWORD

Consider yourself warned: if you're one of those people who thinks my Mageverse books are too sexy, put *Wicked Games* down and back slowly away.

It's *nasty*.

Spankings. Bondage. Assorted sex toys, magical and otherwise. Blow jobs, cunnilingus, anal sex. And then they get down to bid'ness.

Like I said, nasty.

Before you think, "Okay, AK's ripping off Fifty Shades of Pervy Billionaire," nope. I wrote two of the stories in 1990, both to learn how to write and for my own kinky enjoyment. This was five years before I was published in erotic romance. (And possibly before some of you were born. If so, and you run into me somewhere, don't tell me as much. Seriously. Just don't.) I published them in 2001 as part of an e-book called *Bodice Rippers*, under the name Anastasia Day. The problem was, the two stories together weren't long enough, so I needed a novel-length story.

That ended up being the prequel of my Mageverse series, which, for those who don't know, deals with the Knights of the Round Table.

Only in my version, Arthur and his knights are vampires, while Queen Guinevere and her ladies are witches.

"The Once and Future Lover" is Gwen and Arthur's book, the story of how Merlin gave them their powers. It also answers the question of what *did* happen with Lancelot anyway.

For those who aren't familiar with my books but are familiar with Arthurian legend, I deviate considerably from the usual accounts. In my universe, Arthur didn't become king by pulling the sword from the stone, and he wasn't raised by Merlin. He was raised by his father, Uther Pendragon, until he became king when his father was assassinated. However, as was the custom during the Middle Ages, he spent several years during his childhood being fostered by Kay's family. Merlin doesn't appear until the events here.

I did this because historians believe most Arthurian legends are inventions by poets and troubadours. Little is known of the period, so I decided to model much of the setting in terms of architecture, armor, and clothing on ancient Rome. My reasoning was that though Arthur and his people were Celts, Rome occupied southern England for almost four hundred years, from the initial invasion in 43 CE to 409 CE. This story is set around 500 CE or so, so I felt that though there would have been changes, you'd still be able to see the Roman influences.

You'll also note I never use the word "vampire" in this story. That's because it's not a word they'd be using in this period. Also note these folks don't really speak English at this point; they'd be speaking Celtic British, which would have sounded a bit like Welsh. But since you probably don't speak Welsh—and God knows I don't—I provided us all with a translation.

Now, when I started work on "The Once and Future Lover," I thought I knew those characters. After all, Arthur and Gwen have been in every one of the thirteen Mageverse novels and novellas.

I didn't know jack.

I've always written Arthur as, well, a little bit goofy. Yeah, he's an immortal vampire king who wields Excalibur, but he also loves Elvis and *Monty Python and the Holy Grail*. He may be gorgeous and heroic, but he's still the kind of borderline nerd who'll recite the Dead Parrot Sketch at the drop of a long sword.

Jack? Didn't know it. Or him. Or whatever.

This book has taught me that Arthur is the scariest bastard I have ever written.

Still with me?

As I said, the other two stories, "Bondage, Beauty and the Beast" and "A Question of Pleasure" were first published as part of an e-book anthology, *Bodice Rippers*. At the end of the book, you'll also find an excerpt from Morgana's book, "Oath of Service." You'll find it in *Love Bites*, a forthcoming anthology of my vampire erotic romance fiction.

First, a little background. I started reading the genre with eighties romances, which were called bodice rippers because at some point during the story, the hero ripped the heroine's bodice open and seduced her, not always with her consent.

Why the hell we thought rape was acceptable behavior in a hero is a good question. For years, the usual explanation has been that this was the early days of the sexual revolution. Back then, the only reason a Good Girl would have premarital sex was if somebody made her. And since the only other somebody around was the hero, well . . .

There's an element of truth to that.

It's also very true that rape is not heroic behavior. Any bastard who'd take a woman against her will needs to have a bullet put tenderly into his brain stem. I spent ten years as a reporter, and two-thirds of the murders I covered were committed by some creep who'd told his victim he loved her.

So why did so many of us adore bodice rippers?

I'd been thinking about that while writing "The Once and Future Lover." I suspect there was an unconscious element of domination and submission going on, but of course, in real-life BDSM, nobody plays any game until everybody consents to whatever happens. I just know I found those books hot, even though I should have known better.

Another factor is something millions of readers already know: Alpha Males are sexy.

But *why?*

Well, before iPhones, before Fifth Avenue penthouses, before indoor plumbing—hell, before agriculture—men were men and women were women.

And women didn't move real damned fast when nine months pregnant.

A girl needed somebody quick, strong, and ferociously protective to make sure she and the kiddies had enough for lunch without *becoming* lunch for some saber-toothed kitty cat. If you survived, there was a good chance it was because you were sleeping with an aggressive son of a bitch who was handy with a club.

A couple of hundred thousand years later, we're still looking for aggressive—if loving—SOBs.

Sometimes this bites us on the ass. One can easily mistake *mean as hell* for heroic and dominant, especially in a bar. (Which is why the "loving" part is just as important as the dominant-SOB part.)

But still.

For some of us (*Oooh! Me, me!*), there's something about being tied up and banged like a kettle drum by a guy who looks like The Rock. It makes our inner cave girl sit up and say, "Oi, what's this, then?"

So if I haven't managed to scare you off, I hope you enjoy my *Wicked Games.*

WICKED GAMES

THE ONCE
AND FUTURE
LOVER

ONE

Gwen dreamed of death, of blood and terror and grief. She jolted awake. In her panic, she almost shot from the bed, but her husband's brawny arm was wrapped around her waist. She stilled, his breath warming her nape.

Arthur Pendragon slept as he so often did, curled around her, surrounding her in his swordsman's hard strength.

He's not dead. It was only a nightmare. Going limp as a soaked rag in her relief, Gwen turned her head to press her cheek against his broad bare chest. His heart thudded in her ear, steady and strong and comforting. Like Arthur himself.

As her dream panic drained away, she heard the deep voices of the guards out on the balustrade murmur something to each other. They sounded unusually tense.

Reality hit Gwen like an armored fist. Today was the day Arthur would fight to the death.

Against Mordred. His son, heir, and enemy.

Her stomach curled into a sour knot. She had to pace, do *something*, or she was going to start screaming. What if this morning's dream had been more than a nightmare? What if it had been a vision?

Slowly, carefully, she eased Arthur's warm, muscled forearm from around her waist, swung her feet to the stone floor, and rose, trying not to wake him. They'd been up late last night, making love out of desperation as much as desire. Arthur needed to sleep every minute he could.

A cooling breeze poured through the open shutters of the chamber's sole window, which overlooked the courtyard where he and Mordred would do battle in a few hours' time. A shaft of blue dawn light spilled in, illuminating her husband as he sprawled in tanned, brawny nudity across their bed.

Arthur was not a tall man, though Gwen suspected he was actually more muscular at thirty-seven than the nineteen-year-old she'd married, back when they'd called him the Princeling King. He still drilled with his knights every morning, going full out with sword and shield. Whenever she pointed out the likelihood of being hurt in such practice, he'd snort. *"I'll not grow too soft to sit a horse."*

Her beautiful man. Her handsome king.

Responsibility more than age had salted Arthur's hair with gray. More pewter threaded the beard that framed his lushly sensual mouth, and sprinkled the soft, dark thatch that covered his powerful chest. Still, the hair on his groin was as dark as ever, a sable ruff surrounding the long cock she'd always adored, the heavy balls she loved to cradle in her palm.

If he dies, I might as well crawl into the grave with him.

Gwen had seen too many battles over seventeen years as Arthur's queen. She knew what happened when an older man fought a big brute nineteen years younger, and it wasn't pretty.

The wizard Merlin had promised power to the winner of today's battle. Arthur wanted that power to better protect his people from the invading Saxons, not to mention a Celtic warlord named Varn who had been a thorn in his side for the past two years. Then there was the collection of former rulers whose kingdoms Arthur had conquered more than a decade before, any one of whom would love to topple the High King.

As for Mordred . . . Well, he just wanted an acceptable excuse to kill his father. Anything more was just gravy on the goose as far as he was concerned.

Arthur deserved better than a bastard son who hated him. Unfortunately, Gwen had been unable to give her king that successor—and God knew she'd tried.

Three pregnancies. Three miscarriages.

A familiar bitter sting gathered behind her eyelids, and she clenched her jaw, blinking hard, forcing her twisted features to smooth. *You will not cry. You will show only smiling confidence. You will not make Arthur doubt himself.*

Doubt can kill a man in a fight like this.

Mordred had enough advantages as it was. Gwen wasn't going to hand him another arrow for his assassin's quiver.

Wheeling, she paced naked across the chamber. All too soon, they'd have to walk out into the courtyard below to face the prince's challenge. Gwen only hoped Mordred didn't win. Not only would his victory be a catastrophe for her and Arthur, it would be a disaster for Britain.

Her mind flashed back to a night months before, when Mordred had tried to convince Arthur to declare war on the Saxons. The king had refused.

"War always sounds like a good idea to those who've never fought," Arthur said. The knights, ladies, and courtiers seated at the Round Table fell silent over their trenchers, watching the interplay between their liege and his son. "Believe me, the enthusiasm dims when you're knee-deep in mud, blood, and someone else's intestines."

"But isn't conquest the right of the strong, Father," Mordred argued, "Proof of God's favor?"

"Unless you lose, in which case it's proof God doesn't favor you as much as you thought." Arthur cut a slice of venison and fed it to Gwen, giving her one of his wickedly sensual smiles. "Then it's too damned late, and those you love are getting butchered for your arrogance."

The prince started to retort, but Arthur cut him off. "I'm not declaring war on Hengrid and his Saxons, Mordred. Their raids may eventually push me into it, but I'd rather wait until our people get in the harvest and survive the winter. This is the longest stretch of peace we've had in thirty years. Let the peasants savor it a little longer."

"Peasants." The prince speared a bite of mutton on the tip of his dagger and ate it with a wolfish snap. His green eyes glinted with growing temper over the curl of his lip. "What do we care for the opinion of peasants?"

Arthur studied him. Everyone else held their collective breath, Gwen included, wondering if they were about to witness another explosive row. Mordred was a bit too much like his father, right down to the infamous Pendragon temper. Unfortunately, he lacked Arthur's iron self-control. "Peasants, my son, are the ones who do the worst of the dying in war. Marching armies too often murder peasant children, rape peasant wives, and burn peasant crops, leaving the survivors to starve. Never forget, a good king doesn't declare war unless he has no choice."

Mordred dipped his head in grudging acquiescence. "Aye, Father."

Arthur turned away as Lord Kay said something Gwen didn't catch. She was immobilized by the sight of rage and malice flashing across Mordred's face, there and gone so quickly she wasn't even sure she'd seen it. *Maybe I didn't. Maybe it was naught but too much imagination and too many bad memories. Dear God, let that be all.*

Mordred's rage and impulsiveness had grown throughout his childhood, reaching a bitter pitch in his teens that had made all their lives unbearable. Yet in the past year, that storminess had seemed to abate. Gwen, Arthur, and Mordred's mother, Morgana, had begun to hope the worst was over, that he'd finally learned to control his anger.

But staring at his expressionless profile, she wondered uneasily if he'd just gotten better at hiding his darkness . . .

Now Gwen squeezed her eyes closed. With a queen's ruthless discipline, she concentrated on making her mind as smooth as a frozen lake, feeling no fear. No doubt. No pain. Feeling nothing.

"You know," a deep voice purred in her ear, "you do have the most beautiful rump I've ever seen." Arthur's big hands cupped both her bare cheeks. "I made you queen for this arse."

But there are better things to feel than nothing. She turned her head to smile up into her husband's wicked grin. If he was working just a little too hard at it, she'd do them both the favor of refusing to notice. *He's not dead yet. And neither am I.* "At the time," she drawled, "you told me it was my eyes that won you. Or perhaps my mouth."

"And so they were. You're a woman of many parts." He slid his arms around her and leaned down to take her lips in a kiss so passionate, it made a fine distraction. She opened her mouth with a sigh and leaned into his warm strength. His tongue slipped inside her lips, explored sensitive flesh, teased with gentle strokes. Heat gathered between them everywhere they touched, dancing along the surface of her skin, coiling in the tips of her breasts and between her thighs.

Arthur's arms curled around her, tracing the naked rise of her hip before sliding down to cup her between her thighs. One finger stroked her sex with an exquisitely gentle touch that brought heat rushing to her core.

As delicious as that felt, though, she knew they would be interrupted. "My maid and the servants are due . . ."

"We'll send them away."

". . . and you did order Lancelot to attend you for new orders."

"He can damned well wait with the servants. None of them will begrudge us whatever moments we can steal."

She considered arguing, but Arthur's free hand distracted her as it traced a leisurely path up her torso, his swordsman's callused palm a little rough. The erotic scrape of his skin along hers made Gwen squirm.

The thought of the duel tried to surface again, but she thrust it down hard. Arthur was right. *If this is to be the last time, let's make a memory to keep me warm through all the lonely winters. Everyone else can wait.*

Especially Mordred.

Arthur found her nipple, twisted it with the perfect pressure. He knew just how hard she liked his touch, when she liked it, and where.

Throwing her head back on his shoulder, Gwen rolled her rump against his erection. "Mmm," she purred. "You're very, very . . . tempting."

"I could say the same to you." The hand teasing her sex parted her innermost lips to stroke the delicate flesh. "Sweet as cream, and just as wet."

Guinevere turned her head and smiled up into his dark, hot gaze. "As I said, tempting." She let her body relax, let all her fear and tension go. It was a trick she'd learned years ago, before other battles, other wars.

Arthur gave her nipple a harder tug, drawing it out to the edge where pain and pleasure met, simultaneously letting her feel the bite of his nails. The sharp sting made her moan. He chuckled at the sound, switching his attention to the other nipple and tormenting it just as skillfully. The fingers in her sex found her clit, pinched hard, making her writhe.

Gwen groaned in delight. It had taken her years to convince him to be even slightly rough with her. His instinct was to treat her as if she had no more heft than a cobweb, easily shredded by careless hands. She loved her husband's bone-deep, instinctive chivalry, yet she'd always found his rare moments of passionate violence unbearably arousing. Perhaps it was because they were so out of character for him. Or perhaps they simply served some need of her own she couldn't explain. He gave her clit another scissoring pinch, then let go to delve deeper into her pussy, two fingers pumping until she shuddered as her knees grew weak. "Oh, you do like that, don't you, wife?"

When she could do nothing but moan, he tightened his grip on her nipple, ripping a yelp of aroused protest from her lips. "Your king asked you a question, girl."

"Yes!" she whispered. "Saints, Arthur, oh, God, it feels so . . ." She twisted in his arms, rolling her hips back against his blade-hard cock until it slid deliciously along the valley between her cheeks.

He groaned in arousal and gave her a hard, involuntary thrust before he stilled with an obvious effort. "Watch it, woman. You'll make me spill."

"I'll take that chance," she panted.

"I won't." He pulled his fingers from her delightfully stinging flesh, caught her by the shoulders, and spun her to face him. She went into his arms with an eager moan. His mouth covered hers, hot and wet and fierce. She kissed him back, starving, loving the feel of his hands cupping her arse, the hard length of his erection. His fingers dug in with a bruising grip, skillfully adding tinder to her already blazing arousal.

His tongue slipped into her mouth, and she chased it with her own, suckling and circling it as if it were his cock. He growled against her mouth and lifted her off her feet, cradling her arse in broad, strong hands. With a groan, Gwen wrapped her legs around his waist and hooked one heel over the opposite ankle. She started to lift herself with her horsewoman's strong thighs, meaning to impale her sex on Arthur's shaft.

"No, I don't think so." Turning to the bed, he spilled her onto her back across the mattress. Before she knew what he intended, he dropped to his knees beside the bed, spread her thighs wide, and buried his face between them. The first long lick tugged at her inner labia, but didn't touch her clit. Not quite.

"Arthurrrr," Gwen moaned. "God, Arthur, let me suck you. I need to . . ."

He lifted his head long enough to growl. "I think not. I've other plans." His tongue swirled a lazy circle around her clit before slipping up one inner lip and down the other, then up again to her clit for another maddening circuit. Around and around until her empty cunt clenched, craving his thick cock, making her whimper with the hot desperation of her need.

Closing his mouth over her clit at last, he suckled, almost catapulting her into orgasm, until he backed off at the last possible instant. When Gwen spat a truly filthy curse she'd learned from Arthur himself, he laughed like a devil and sought out that exquisitely sensitive spot between her pussy and anus. His tongue pressed hard, swirling with surprising force, triggering a tingling jolt of delight. Wrapping her legs around his broad back, Gwen hunched against his face, maddened by the climax dangling just out of reach.

Rumbling approval, Arthur slid two fingers into her pussy and pumped until she twisted in delight, unable to keep still.

"You're so wet," he growled, his voice deep and dark and rough. "You really want my cock, don't you?"

"Jesu, yes! Please, Arthur . . ."

The king grinned, hungry as a fox contemplating a helpless hen. "No." And thrust one finger up her arse.

The sheer unexpected kick of wicked pleasure ripped a gasp from her mouth. The gasp turned into a groan when he began tonguing swirling patterns around her clit, not quite touching the hard little nub, until she jerked with wracking pleasure. All the while, he pumped his finger in and out of her anus. The storm of sensation grew into a gale when he added a second digit and a wicked little fillip of pain. She cried out and started begging for his cock in a stream of incoherent pleas.

"One day I'm going to fuck you here," he told her, scissoring his fingers apart, intensifying the ache. "I'm going to make you scream as I dig my big dick in. You'll beg me to stop, but that will only make me harder, hungrier. I'll fuck and fuck and fuck until you come shrieking. Then I'll blow, flooding your little arse with so much come, you'll leak it from your sore hole all day long. Sitting at the Round Table with all my knights. They'll go mad wondering about the secret smile on your face."

She shivered. "Now. Do it *now*." *There may not be a later.*

"No." His black eyes watched her face with dark male hunger. "No, I think I'll save it for a special occasion."

Before she could wail a protest, his mouth covered her clit and sucked so hard, his cheeks hollowed. Gwen's climax hit in a storm of fiery sparks that bowed her spine and ripped a scream from her lips. Never mind the servants who probably heard; for once, she didn't care.

"Fuck me, Arthur." Gwen gasped, writhing, desperate. Lost. "However you want it, *do* it. Jesu, please!"

With a low, bestial growl, Arthur surged to his feet and grabbed her behind her knees. A hard tug dragged her to the edge of the bed. He snatched up a pillow and shoved it under her backside, angling her pussy for his use. One big hand gripped the ruddy jut of his cock and presented it to her opening.

His gaze met hers, hunger stark in his dark warrior's eyes as he reared over her, broad-shouldered and massive from hours swinging sword and shield.

Arthur entered slowly as he always did, making sure she was ready for him. *As if I could be anything else.* Gwen tightened her inner muscles, loving the sensation of that thick, meaty cock stuffing her by hot inches.

"Jesu, you feel delectable." Groaning, he brushed his thumb over her clit, first circling it with his thumb, then teasing the inner lips stretched tight around his shaft. He seemed to know every point on her body where he could trigger pleasure. Gwen moaned helplessly as he filled her deeper and deeper, until every inch of that thick member was inside her. Slowly, he rolled his hips, rocking, grinding. "So tight. So hot and slick."

It took Gwen almost a minute to manage speech. "You are so . . ." He circled his hips, and her mind went blank. "Good." That last word emerged as a whimper.

Arthur laughed, low and wolfish. "As are you, my lady."

His cock . . . *Angels and devils, his cock!* Each stroke seared her with distilled pleasure, goading her into rolling her hips against his.

Arthur grabbed her behind the knees. Knowing what he wanted, she rested her heels on his broad shoulders, a pose that tightened her, heightening the sensation for both of them.

Pleasure pealed through her in bell-like reverberations. Reaching up her body with his free hand, he caught the peak of one breast, knowing just how to pull and tug the way she liked it best. Sensation piled on sensation with every hard thrust, until she hurtled into pleasure, the deep, hard pulses bowing her spine. Gwen screamed in delight, barely aware as her king drove to the balls, head thrown back with an orgasmic roar.

Arthur collapsed on the bed beside Gwen, breathing hard, his heart pounding, his skin sweat-slick. For a moment he was content to simply listen to her pant. "Why are you breathing . . . so . . . hard . . . ?" he joked. "I did all the work."

"I . . . offered," she gasped. "You . . . turned me . . . down."

"Good point." Scooping one arm under her, Arthur hauled her over on top of him and tucked her blond head under his chin.

"I've got . . . an . . . idea," she panted, her heart thundering against his chest. "Let's . . . just stay . . . right here. All day."

"Tempting . . ." He managed to catch his breath, at least enough for a feeble attempt at a joke. "But I'd hate to disappoint the boy."

"Fuck him." The violence in her snarl made him blink. "You have given him quite enough as it is."

"Apparently he doesn't think so," Arthur said, keeping his voice light despite the desolation he felt. "And he is my son."

"But he isn't *mine*." As he blinked, startled, she gestured wearily. "Forgive me."

"Nothing to forgive." But he frowned, for her outburst was telling. She had never reproached him about siring Mordred; for one thing, he and Gwen had yet to meet when he'd slept with the boy's beautiful mother. He'd been a callow seventeen then, fresh from his first major battlefield victory. Morgana, a year older, black-haired and beautiful, had been summoned to use her Druid healer's skills to save his best friend's life. Lancelot had lived, and the young king had celebrated his victory between the pretty healer's thighs.

What neither Morgana nor Arthur had known back then was that they were actually half siblings. Evidently, Arthur's father, King Uther Pendragon, had fathered Morgana during an assault on her Druid mother. They'd only learned the truth last week, when the wizard Merlin had sensed the incestuous connection and informed them of the shocking news.

At the time, Arthur hadn't even known he'd become a father. Mordred was ten years old before Morgana brought the child to court while seeking the position of Camelot's healer.

Gwen had known Mordred was Arthur's son the moment she saw him. His mouth, his blade-straight nose, the shape of his broad, sculpted jaw all bore the Pendragon stamp. Most other women would have been outraged at being presented with a husband's by-blow, no matter when he'd been sired. Instead, Gwen had greeted boy and mother with joy. From then on, she treated Mordred as her own.

For all the good it had done. Arthur sighed, absently caressing his wife's bare shoulder. "I would I knew what happened. Where I went wrong."

"My queen?" Gwen's maid called through the door. "It's time. We have the water for your bath . . ."

"Come, husband. I'll let you wash my back." Gwen gave him a warm, lingering kiss before pulling out of his arms to pad toward the dressing chamber.

"Which, as motivations go, is a damned good one." He rose and reached for his robe. "Certainly better than the chance to drink from some wretched cup."

The king groaned in pleasure as he sank into the huge bronze tub that required a team of servants to fill. The water was pleasantly cool despite the building June heat. "God's balls, that feels good."

Gwen dropped her robe and stepped into the water between his knees, then settled down opposite him with a sigh of appreciation. "This tub has to be the most wonderful gift you've ever given me."

"Including the emeralds?"

She considered the question, head tilted, expression judicious. "Those were truly beautiful . . ." Her smile turned wicked. "But I do believe the view from here is even better."

"I can say the same of you, though honesty compels me to admit that necklace was as much a gift for me as for you. I do love the sight of those stones against your pale, pretty breasts."

"And here I thought you were just generous."

"Oh, I am." He grinned at her. "I've also been fascinated by those lovely tits since the day I met you."

Gwen gave herself a glance far more critical than the view deserved. "They are not as firm as they were when I was sixteen."

"Those were a girl's breasts, my dear. Now they are a woman's. Don't underestimate the attractions of a lover who knows what he's about."

Gwen laughed. "Flatterer."

"You know better than that. I've never had the patience to think of pretty lies. The truth is so much easier to remember."

He smiled, relishing her return smile of appreciation. Her oval face looked soft and lovely, her large blue eyes smoky over full lips. Her maid had used combs to secure her hair atop her head in a messy pile of blond curls. If there was any silver among that gold, he'd never found it. Her body was still as lithe as a girl's, her breasts pert, her legs long, lovely, and strong.

His one regret in seventeen years of marriage was that he'd never been able to give her the child she'd wanted. And now, of course, it was too late.

We're left with Mordred, unless I can contrive to kill him.

The thought made his gut coil into a sick knot of guilt and pain. When he was growing up, his own father's love had seemed as unreachable as the moon; he'd been determined to serve his son better. *I should have saved myself the effort.*

Mordred had grown up to be as big a cold-blooded bastard as Uther. More so.

At least Uther hadn't wanted Arthur dead.

Knotting the thick leather belt around his waist, Arthur strode into the sleeping chamber, his chain mail hauberk ringing softly. As he closed the door behind him, he could hear women's voices as the maid dressed Gwen's hair.

Knuckles banged the balustrade door in a decisive knock. "My liege?"

"Enter, Lance." He sat down on the bed and began pulling on his boots.

His dearest friend strode in, dressed in a mail shirt almost as finely made as Arthur's, his helm tucked under one arm. At thirty-nine, he was a big, dark-haired man, hard-eyed and steady. He was also the best swordsman Arthur had ever known—and the king had known many fine warriors over the years.

"My lord Lancelot." Arthur gave him a formal nod and dropped into one of the chairs sitting beside the cold fireplace.

Lance had never been slow at picking up on cues. He promptly dropped to one knee and bent his head, though as boyhood friends, they weren't normally so formal. "My liege, how may I serve you?"

"Be seated." Arthur waved him toward the high-backed wooden chair Gwen normally occupied. "I would give you your orders before I begin this day's work."

"Of course." Lancelot rose to his feet as easily as if he wore wool rather than chain mail. The knight's expression was coolly attentive, but there was a certain tension around his eyes that suggested some strong emotion roiled beneath his courtier's mask.

Arthur could make a pretty good guess what he was thinking. "You have my permission to speak, Sir Knight."

Lance paused as if choosing his words carefully. "Am I still your champion, my liege?"

Arthur lifted a brow. "Have I told you you're not?"

"I wondered if I had given some offense. It *is* a champion's honor to fight for his liege. Unless you don't believe I can win?"

"Unfortunately, that's not the point. Merlin made it clear I must prove myself worthy to drink from this enchanted cup of his. If I refuse the challenge, none of my court will be allowed to attempt it. Given the political situation, we can't afford to spurn any advantage."

"That cup's still not worth your life, sire."

He grimaced. "Don't assume the rest of the court shares your opinion."

"Most of them do. Arthur, your subjects love you. You are fair, quick to rein in abusive lords even when it costs you politically, and generous with those who need it, whether noble or peasant." He believed every word he said, too; Lance had never stooped to flattery.

The king grunted. "My father was a stone-hearted bastard, but on one subject he was absolutely correct: if God grants you a crown, He expects you to serve as much as you're served. Which is why I cannot allow myself to be branded a coward before my entire court."

Restless, he rose and began to pace the chamber, his mail ringing. "Another thing—what if I refuse? Merlin said he needs powerful champions for this great mission of his, whatever that should prove to be. What if he decides to repeat his offer to someone else, who then moves against us for whatever reason? I have no desire to face unkillable warriors with the strength of ten."

"So you believe Merlin's cup can do what he claims?"

"You don't?" Arthur leaned a shoulder against the wall and eyed his friend.

"Merlin has worked some impressive magic," Lance admitted. "But so did that magician who came to court two summers ago, the one who claimed he could bring the dead to life. Him you sent packing with a boot in the arse."

"Merlin is not some simple trickster."

He'd proved that last week.

They'd been in the midst of the evening meal in the Table Chamber when Arthur looked past Gwen's shoulder to see a circle of air ripple like a pool of clear water disturbed by a tossed pebble. The ripples stilled, revealing a moonlit wood, as if he looked through a window.

Gasps sounded. As they all stared in astonishment, a boy stepped through the opening to look around with cool interest. Tall and slender, he was perhaps fifteen, with a long, intelligent face framed by black hair that fell around his narrow shoulders. He wore a blue tunic of fine embroidered linen that matched his leggings and knee-high leather boots.

A girl stepped through the impossible opening, which vanished with a silent burst of sparks. A delicate nymph of a maid, she wore a thin silk gown in verdant green, her hair a tumble of blond curls that cascaded to her waist. Her enormous black eyes were set aslant in her heart-shaped face, and her mouth was small and pink, with lips that brought rosebuds to mind.

Where in the name of all the saints had the pair come from?

A sword licked out in a bright arc, stopping a fraction from the lad's throat. "Who are you," snarled Lancelot, "and how the hell did you do that?" Silent and lethal, the knight had risen from the Table to challenge the pair.

There was a reason Arthur had named Lance the royal champion—his personal defender and bodyguard.

The strange boy glanced down at the blade so close to his Adam's apple, lifting a brow in an expression of cool interest. He looked up the weapon's length to meet Lance's deadly gaze.

The champion's eyes widened. He actually backed up a pace before he caught himself and brought his sword to bear again. "What. Are. You?"

Steel whispered on leather as every knight sitting at the Round Table rose and drew his sword. Arthur, too, held his blade at the ready as he moved closer to the trio.

The boy looked around at the lethal weapons, but there was no fear at all in his black gaze. "I am Merlin." His voice rumbled, far too deep and resonant to come from that young mouth. "I am a Magus." He gestured at the girl. "This is my companion, the Maja Nimue. We come to your court seeking warriors to fight in a just cause."

Arthur could have had the pair killed—or at least tried to; given what he knew now, he doubted it would have been that simple. Instead, he'd watched in fascination as Merlin conjured a silver cup filled with a glowing liquid he'd said had the ability to grant superhuman strength and speed to the champions he sought. When Lord Kay had scoffed, the boy wizard opened a magical doorway to the Channel, and invited them all to step through.

Now the king shook his head in remembered awe. "From Camelot to the English Channel—leagues traveled in a heartbeat. You were as wonderstruck as I."

Lance braced his elbows on his knees, his expression troubled. "But what if it was some sort of illusion . . . ?"

"We all stepped through that gate, Lance. We smelled the sea, heard the boom of the surf. That shell Gwen brought back is right here. Still smells of the ocean." Flipping open the jewel chest that sat on the mantel, Arthur grabbed the oyster shell and held it up. "Is this some fairy trinket, spun of air and moonlight?"

Lance being Lance, he didn't back down. "No, sire. But even if Merlin does work magic, that does not mean he isn't playing some deep and lethal game. We cannot afford to lose you. I don't want to bend my knee to Mordred."

"Do you think I'm that easy to defeat?" He tossed the shell back in the jewel chest.

"No, but I do think Mordred is three inches taller, at least a stone heavier, and nineteen years younger. Any one of those things you could overcome, but all?" He shrugged.

"Lance, I've been making war since I was fifteen. Hell, you were there, fighting beside me. Mordred may be built like a bull, but I can scheme rings around him."

"You can *strategize* rings around him. Don't underestimate his talent for scheming. And if he does kill you, what happens to the rest of us?" His lips tightened. "Especially Queen Guinevere."

TWO

Remembering that night, Arthur clenched his hand around the hilt of his sword. "So you saw Mordred look at Gwen like a war-camp whore?"

"Aye, and I gave serious thought to calling him out on the spot." Lancelot hesitated before admitting, "I also saw the way he smirked when he realized you'd caught him at it."

"It was like finding the contents of the cesspit in my ale." Any other man would have looked guilty or fearful of his king's reaction. Mordred's gaze hadn't even dropped. And what was worse, he'd grinned. Grinned the way a man grinned at some fool he'd gulled, knowing his victim had finally realized how utterly he'd been deceived.

"When Merlin announced we were to duel, I intended to tell him where to put his cup." Arthur shook his head. "But when I saw the anticipation on Mordred's face, the way he looked at Gwen . . . When I realized my heir thought he could mock the High King of Britain like a half-wit dwarf . . ." He ground his teeth in fury. "I'll either kill that bastard or die."

"Why not just banish him? Throw him in gaol? I'd be delighted to put him there." Lance bared his own teeth. "Especially if he resists."

"You know why, Lance. Half the court would whisper I did it out of fear."

"But if you told the court why . . ."

"And expose Gwen to that kind of gossip? Everyone would whisper he'd cuckolded me." Realizing he'd half drawn his sword, Arthur slid the weapon home and relaxed his white-knuckled grip. "I won't have my queen made the butt of wagging tongues."

"My liege, no one will slander Queen Guinevere in my presence," Lancelot told him quietly. "And I know I speak for all your knights."

"Lance, did *you* know I'd raised a viper?"

"I'd have warned you if I had." The knight frowned. "Though Galahad did tell me once Mordred has a reputation of being someone you had to watch if you didn't want a dirk in the ribs." The youngest of the Round Table's knights, Lancelot's son had grown to manhood beside Mordred. "At the time, I thought, 'Well, what prince doesn't have that reputation?'" Lance grinned. "Present company excepted, of course."

Arthur snorted. "My father really *did* believe he'd raised a viper. He accused me of plotting treason on more than one occasion."

"Usually when he was drunk. I don't think he ever truly believed it, save when he was in his cups."

"Either way, every time I had doubts about Mordred, I told myself that paranoia about one's own children must be a hazard of kingship." Arthur raked a hand through his hair and sighed. "Deep down, I knew what he was, but I always told myself I could fix him. If I only showed him enough love, enough understanding, gave him enough training, he'd become the man I wanted him to be."

For once, there was no deference in Lancelot's stare, only a friend's honest compassion. "Arthur, you did everything you could for that boy."

"Except the one thing that would have made a difference—keeping him safe from that bastard priest."

Soon after he acknowledged Mordred as his son, Morgana had told him and Gwen that when the boy was only five, the village priest had named her a heretic for being Druid. Morgana had believed his antipathy had more to do with her bad judgment in healing a sick child when Father Bennett's attempt at a miracle failed. Bennett apparently did not appreciate being shown up; he'd claimed Mordred was the product of Morgana's fornication with the devil.

While Morgana tried to defend herself against the village's outraged elders, Bennett had taken the child away, saying he would cast out Mordred's demons. Afterward, the boy would never say exactly what he did, but for years he'd wake screaming from nightmares he had far too often.

The priest was lucky he'd been dead of plague by the time Arthur heard the story, or he'd have learned what hell was like at the king's own hand.

Arthur had always felt that experience had been the thing to warp his son. It was why he and Gwen had been so patient for so long in the face of Mordred's rages, the reason they made so many excuses for the inexcusable.

"For God's sake, Arthur!" Frustration tightened Lance's mouth into a tight line. "At the time, you didn't even know the boy existed! How the hell could you have possibly protected him?"

"By making sure everyone in the kingdom knew I won't tolerate that kind of treatment of any child, mine or not."

"Men like that donkey's prick don't care about laws—not even those of God. Why do you think he'd listen to you if he wouldn't listen to Christ?"

"Good point." Arthur threw himself down on his bed with a grunt. "It's too bloody late now, in any case. Mordred is the vicious little prick he is. Which brings me to the reason I sent for you."

Lancelot bowed his head in submission. "I am honored to serve you in whatever way I can."

"Protect Gwen." He picked up the gauntlets he'd left on the bed and began to tug them on. "If it becomes evident I'm losing, take the rest of the Round Table and get her to safety."

"We will, of course, guard Queen Guinevere with our lives."

Arthur met his eyes, letting him see the gratitude he felt. "I know you will. From the time we were boys, you always served me with complete dedication."

"Then you shouldn't send him from your side." Gwen swept into the room, looking regal in an overtunic of imported blue silk embroidered with silver thread. Its short hem revealed the thin white linen underskirt swirling around her sandaled feet. A thin white veil concealed her bright hair, secured by a golden circlet inset with sapphires. She looked lovely—and furious, flags of color flaming on her cheeks. "If you want me protected, let the Table knights remain where they belong: at your back."

Arthur sighed and moved to take her in his arms. She refused to relax against him, instead glowering rebelliously up into his eyes. "How can I keep my mind on winning if I'm wondering whether you'll be picked off by some assassin's arrow? If anything happened to you, it would gut me. Don't you think such an advantage would tempt Mordred?"

"Even Mordred would not dare have me assassinated in front of all the court."

"Perhaps, but I'd as soon not test him. I've had all the unpleasant surprises I care to have from that quarter."

"At least keep eight Table knights to protect you. That will leave me with three." Correctly interpreting his expression, she bargained, "Lance, Galahad, and Tristan, rounded out with a dozen soldiers."

"Plus Gawain, Percival, Marrok, and Cador. I want more of my elite fighters with you, Gwen."

"What if you need them? Even if Mordred dies, he may already have persuaded your more treacherous lords to join Varn and his bandits in rebellion." He opened his mouth to refuse, only hesitating at the pleading in her eyes. "Please, Arthur."

He sighed and drew her close. "I'll keep five. You take the rest."

She let her head fall against his chest. "Thank you."

Arthur glanced up at Lancelot. "But tell all your fellow Table knights

to have their fastest mounts ready in case I'm killed outright. You'll probably have to fight your way past Mordred and his men. Kill every last one
of them you can, the prince included. Take her to Lord Bohort at Corn-
ouaille." Bohort was her sister's husband, and as formidable as he was
loyal. Turning back to Gwen, he added, "Tell your maid to pack only
what you'll most need."

Guinevere nodded decisively. "My jewels." When he lifted a brow,
she growled, "I hear good assassins are expensive. If you fall, that young
viper will not have long to gloat." She turned and strode from the room,
calling for her maid.

The two men watched her go. "If she doesn't want to leave, pick her
up and carry her," Arthur told Lancelot. "I don't want her at my bastard's mercy."

Arthur's great-grandfather Bicoir had built Camelot as a cross
between a Roman fortress and the villas he'd seen as a young
man. After the Romans pulled out of Britain, he became a war leader,
building a kingdom through a combination of conquest and savvy
alliances.

He'd taught his descendants the military tactics he'd learned from
the Romans, along with the construction techniques the Legion used
to construct fortifications.

The fortress was laid out in a great stone square around a central
courtyard that was open to the sky. A balustrade ran around the inside
of the two-story square, providing a way to move from room to room.

Soldiers and knights had been honing their skills in Camelot's huge
central courtyard ever since. Today, one of the old man's descendants
would probably die there.

Rows of wooden benches had been set up around the innermost
combat circle to accommodate those who wanted to watch. Now every
bench was packed with courtiers seated thigh to thigh. Those with lesser

status had crowded in along the courtyard walls, and more onlookers packed the second floor balustrade used to walk from room to room.

A pair of chairs had been set up for the royal couple under a bright red canvas awning draped over a wooden frame. Merlin and Nimue stood waiting beneath it, looking deceptively young, like children playing dress-up in tunics of embroidered silk. The pair bowed deeply to the king and queen.

Chattering courtiers fell silent and rose in acknowledgment as Gwen and Arthur entered the courtyard. Catching Merlin's gaze, the king dipped his chin in a nod of acknowledgment.

To Gwen's grim pleasure, most of the onlookers appeared worried as they watched him stride onto the field. Mordred's followers wore expressions of anticipation, as did four lords Arthur had defeated in the battles that followed Uther's assassination. Gwen made mental note of them, in case she needed revenge later.

She was not in the mood to turn the other cheek.

The kingdom's elite Knights of the Round Table had gathered in a tense knot off to one side of the awning: Galahad, Bors, Gawain, Tristan, Percival, Marrok, Kay, Cador, Bedivere, and Baldulf. Like Arthur and Lancelot, they were dressed for war in helm and hauberk, shields on their arms and swords hanging at their belts. Mordred stood stonily at the head of his own eleven, though his followers included at least another twenty, most of them the sons of the wealthy. His resemblance to his sire was uncanny, save for his greater height—and the green eyes, as pale and feral as a cat's.

"Is it my imagination, or does Mordred and his pack of dogs look entirely too confident?" Gwen murmured to Arthur.

"You're not imagining anything," he growled. "They expect me to lose. I won't. Too much rides on this." His gaze lingered on her face in a way that told her he was talking about her more than his throne.

Gwen stared up at him, struck by the savage determination in his eyes. She'd always known Arthur loved her, of course, but on some level she'd thought he loved his country and his knights at least as much. It was startling to realize he held her dearer than any of it.

His knights started toward them. Arthur and Lancelot advanced to meet them, with Gwen trailing. She broke step as her attention fell on one particular face among those seated around the courtyard.

Gwen and Morgana Le Fay had become unlikely friends soon after Arthur's former lover appeared at court with her young son. At the time, Gwen hadn't expected to like the woman, had only meant to pretend friendship as a way to quiet any rumors that Morgana and Arthur were still lovers.

And the ruse had worked. Gwen did not have a reputation as a pliant wife; the court reasoned that if she'd become friends with Morgana, there must be nothing to all those lewd whispers.

Yet if the friendship had started out as pretense, that soon changed when Gwen realized Morgana was as witty and bright as she was beautiful.

Best of all, she was loyal. Morgana had never tried to use their friendship to wheedle riches or favors as too many others did, and she never repeated anything the queen said to her. She quickly became the dearest friend Guinevere had ever had, the one person, other than Arthur himself, whom Gwen trusted without question.

Which was why Gwen worried for her friend now. Morgana's lovely face wasn't just pale, it was almost ghostly, and her green eyes looked huge with anxiety.

Gwen couldn't blame her. No matter what her own feelings were, Morgana would soon have to watch her son either die or kill his father. Another woman might imagine all the riches that would come her way as the mother of the new High King. The healer wasn't that woman. She was far too intelligent not to see the implications.

Her anguished gaze met Gwen's. The queen glanced at Arthur, now deep in conversation with his knights, then gestured Morgana over. Her friend shot off the bench and started toward her.

Gwen was so intent on the healer, she ignored the soft ring of approaching chain mail. She realized her mistake when Morgana's eyes widened in horror.

A male hand clamped over Gwen's right upper arm hard enough to bruise. Hot breath gusted against her ear as Mordred whispered, "After I've killed him, my sweet stepmother, I'll fuck you. In your cunt and your mouth. In your ar . . ."

She wheeled and slapped him with every ounce of her body weight behind her hand. As he released her in shock, she jerked the dagger from her jeweled belt sheath and plunged it toward the only unarmored part of him she could reach: the underside of his jaw.

Her knife wrist slapped into Mordred's palm. For all that he looked like a bullock, he was fast.

"You ungrateful cur!" Gwen raged. "I will die before I ever let you touch me!" She lunged at him, her sandaled feet thumping harmlessly on his booted shins, her free hand curling into claws as she went for his eyes. He grabbed her wrist and jerked her off her feet. He didn't even have to work at it. She was distantly aware of outraged male voices, drowned out by Arthur's furious bellow.

Gwen barely heard them. She was utterly focused on Mordred's face, so disturbingly like Arthur's—except for those cruel eyes. "If you kill my husband, by the womb of the Virgin, I'll see you dead. Get out of the habit of sleeping, *boy*. My assassins will come at you from behind every tapestry and column, every rock and hedgerow. You'll know every smiling friend could belong to me, just waiting to dig that viper's heart out of your . . ."

"Shut *up*, Gwen!" Morgana screamed.

Blinking, the queen realized her friend had both arms wrapped around Mordred's forearm as she desperately tried to keep him from hitting Gwen.

Then Lancelot was there, his fist slamming into Mordred's jaw so hard, the prince dropped Guinevere and staggered back. She hit the packed dirt of the training field, her head striking hard enough to send stars shooting behind her eyes.

A pair of booted feet came down on either side of her hips. She looked up woozily to see Arthur standing astride her, his sword raised to protect her. "By the Father, Son, and Holy Ghost, I am still High King of Britain! Any man who lays hand on my queen dies *now!*"

"She's gone barking mad!" Mordred spat. "I but spoke to her, and she tried to bury her dagger in my throat!"

"You threatened to rape me!" Gwen had just enough self-control not to screech the words loud enough for the entire court to hear. Above her, Arthur froze.

"Mordred!" Morgana cried in stricken betrayal. "Guinevere took us in, treated you like her own . . ."

"Because she knew she'd never give Arthur an heir," Mordred sneered. "That blond bitch is as barren as a salted field. Which is to the good, or she'd have surely presented our king with his champion's brat."

"You lying lickspittle cur!" Arthur launched himself at his son, sword aimed at the prince's throat. Mordred parried and retreated, his gaze icy with calculation.

Arthur's knights lunged at Mordred's followers with a chorused roar of outrage. The prince's men bellowed and drew their weapons. The air filled with clangs and curses as the two groups began to fight.

"Get up, Gwen, before you get trampled!" Morgana swooped down and helped her to her feet.

"Get the queen off the field!" Arthur bellowed at Lancelot, stalking his son with murder in his eyes.

Lance planted his palm against the small of Gwen's back, urging her toward the dubious shelter of the awning. "Move!" Galahad backed along behind them, keeping an eye out for would-be attackers as he brought up the rear.

"No!" Gwen set her feet, looking back at Arthur. "Protect your king! I'll go . . ."

Arthur's sword bounced off something invisible in a cascade of blue sparks.

"Enough!" Merlin's roar could not possibly have come from the throat of the beardless boy he appeared to be.

Both men flew off their feet as if dragged into the air by an invisible giant. It dropped them again to land, staggering. Everyone else froze in astonishment as Merlin stalked between the two groups of warriors. "You will cease!" the wizard snapped, "Or I will leave this little world of yours to drown in blood, as your vicious nature apparently dictates!"

"He threatened to rape my queen." Arthur glared at Mordred, who snarled back like a reflection in a demonic mirror. "I'll see him dead!"

"Kill him, then!" Merlin spat, stepping right against the king's chest with an expression so savage, the larger man retreated a step in sheer astonishment. "And then watch as humanity sinks into darkness because you lacked the strength of will to control your ugly temper."

"Who do you think you . . . ?" Arthur began.

Merlin talked right over him. "You are supposed to be High King of Britain, Arthur Pendragon. If you can't put the good of your people above your pricked ego, you are no good to me."

"A threat to my wife is not an ego prick." Arthur glared at Mordred. "Especially not when it's my own son who threatens her!"

"*I do not care!*" Merlin roared. "This is your test, Pendragon. *And you are failing it!*"

The sound of his voice was like being plunged into a frozen lake. Every hair rose on Gwen's body in atavistic terror. She wouldn't have been more astonished if the stripling wizard had turned into a dragon.

She wasn't alone, either. Every face she saw drained of blood in unison. Men as well as women cried out.

Gwen had never seen her husband retreat from anyone, including other kings, but he actually took a step back from Merlin. Even so, he didn't let his gaze drop as he curled a lip. "You've made your point. I might as well slay my bastard in ten minutes as now."

Catching Lance's gaze, he jerked a thumb at the pavilion and the chairs standing there. Lance dipped his head and sheathed his sword. "My queen?" He offered his arm.

Gwen schooled her face, concealing just how shaken she was behind her best regal air, and placed her hand in the crook of his arm. "Morgana, attend me."

Mordred's mother blinked once. "Of course, your majesty." She fell in behind them, all three of them ignoring the astounded stares of their audience in the stands.

Morgana dropped her voice low enough to reach no further than Gwen's ears. "My queen, this will look strange to the court. I am Mordred's mother, after all. Never mind that sometimes I fear . . ." She broke off.

Gwen shot her a grim glance. Recently there'd been bruises on the healer's lovely face she'd refused to explain. Gwen and Arthur had believed she had an abusive lover, but neither of them were able to ferret out who it was in order to put a stop to it. They both hated to see anyone victimized, woman, man, or child.

But what if there was no lover? Had *Mordred* been beating his mother? The thought made Gwen feel sick. He'd proven today that he was certainly capable of it. But his own mother . . .

Why did we fail with him? How did we go so wrong? Gwen had been just as involved in rearing him as Arthur and Morgana. She had to be; Arthur had often been called away by his duties, while Morgana was kept just as busy in her role as Camelot's healer and midwife. Gwen tried to fill in for them, reasoning that if she couldn't give birth to Arthur's heir, she could at least help raise him.

But I failed in that, too. With an effort of will, Gwen relaxed her tight fists. *We've got to deal with the man he is, not the man we tried to make him.*

They reached the awning's shade, and Lancelot conducted the queen to her chair. She gestured to one of the hovering servants. "Fetch a seat for my lady Morgana."

The man nodded and hurried away, returning a moment later with a low wooden bench. He positioned it beside the queen's chair, and Gwen motioned for her friend to seat herself.

The healer hesitated, frowning at the number of staring faces turned their way. "My queen . . ."

"I have been providing exercise for wagging court tongues since I married Arthur. I couldn't stop them wagging if I took religious orders. Sit *down*, Morgana."

Her friend obeyed, then leaned closer and dropped her voice. "I am so sorry! You've always been kind to both of us, even when few would have been. How could he treat you like this?"

Gwen reached over and rested a calming hand on the healer's, bunched in white-knuckled fists in her lap. "Morgana, your son is a man grown now. His sins are his own."

"I know, but he didn't have to be so bloody stupid about committing them. He's given Arthur no choice except to kill him." Her gaze went to Mordred's face. "He cannot be allowed to take the throne, or he'll plunge Britain into darkness."

"He's still your son. No mother could be thought disloyal for wanting her child to survive."

"I'm not speaking as a mother, but as a citizen of Britain. Mordred would be a disaster as king. He's too ruled by his appetites and passions rather than his head. Arthur feels just as deeply, but his sense of justice always balances his temper."

"Usually," Gwen murmured back. "But not always." Both women fell silent, watching warily as Merlin returned to Nimue in the pavilion's shade. Lancelot promptly moved to position himself between the pair and the queen, but they ignored his protective stance. Their shifting expressions suggested they were having some kind of intense discussion, but neither spoke. Not out loud, at least. Magically? There was no way to tell.

Arthur completed whatever consultation he'd been having with his knights. As he strode under the awning, Gwen and Morgana rose and sank into curtseys. Merlin and Nimue, too, bowed as their audience stood respectfully. The Knights of the Round Table knelt.

Mordred and his contingent did not.

Arthur swept a cold gaze over the crowd as he offered a hand to his wife. Gwen took it and let him draw her to her feet.

His hard stare reached Mordred and his men. He lifted an icy black brow. The prince promptly sank to one knee, his men following suit. No sooner had he done so than Mordred's expression turned sour, as if he'd belatedly realized he'd yielded a tactical point. Gwen suspected the habit of obeisance to his father's royal authority had kicked in automatically, despite his lethal ambitions. The king gave him an acidic half smile.

Don't play power games with Arthur, boy, Gwen thought. *He is far beyond your weight.*

"Today I do battle to the death with Mordred, son of Morgana Le Fay, before this day my heir," Arthur announced in a voice that rolled across the courtyard like a trumpet call.

Mordred gasped audibly in outrage at his summary disinheritance. Arthur shot him a cold glance that clearly said, *After the performance you just gave, what did you expect?*

The king turned to Merlin. "Now, wizard, if you would state the stakes of this combat." He sank onto his chair and lounged back with the chime of mail. His expression suggested he didn't give a damn one way or another.

Merlin eyed him a moment, then straightened and addressed the crowd. "The winner of this contest may win a sip from my enchanted Grail." The goblet appeared on his palm in a burst of golden sparks.

The audience murmured in awe. Gwen wasn't surprised; there was an overwhelming sense of power about that cup that was definitely no conjurer's trick.

"Be it known that though this is a duel to the death, I alone shall judge whether to award the Grail based on who fights not only with the most skill and courage, but with the greatest sense of honor." Merlin turned to Arthur and bowed, the cup vanishing from his hand. "Now, sire, if you and your opponent will enter the circle?"

His face set like stone, Arthur nodded coldly and rose to stride onto the field to meet the son he'd just disowned.

Feeling sick with anxiety, Gwen groped for Morgana's hand. Her friend's skin felt like ice even in the June heat.

Mordred moved toward his father, wearing an ugly grin of anticipation. Gwen longed to slap him.

The fighters stopped on opposite sides of the packed-earth circle. Merlin stepped between them. He looked about twelve compared to the two men, both of whom towered over him. The wizard spoke to them in a voice so low, it was impossible to hear what he said. Each man replied in the same low tones. Merlin nodded and stepped back out of the circle. "Begin," he said, and backed away.

Neither fighter moved. They only stared at each other, as if locked in some kind of mental combat. Which probably wasn't far off; Arthur often said that more battles were won or lost between a warrior's ears than by the strength of his sword arm. *"A giant can lose to a dwarf if he lets overconfidence blind him."* The trouble was, he'd taught Mordred the same strategies, including this one: *"A big man who keeps a cool head will win every time."*

For once, Gwen hoped her husband was wrong.

THREE

Arthur let his heartbeat slow, banishing both his fear for his wife and his rage that his son had dared threaten her. Instead he focused on taking deep breaths as he watched his opponent. *That's all he is,* he told himself. *Just another opponent, like all the others I've beaten since I killed my first man.*

He'd been only fifteen when he'd slain the assassin who murdered Uther Pendragon minutes before. The killer had obviously expected him to be too overcome with grief to defend himself. Instead, the bastard died with Arthur's dagger in his throat and astonishment in his eyes.

"I wonder," Mordred drawled, "if you have any idea how many times I barely kept from laughing in your face . . . ?" He grinned, cold green eyes empty of emotion: not humor, fear, or even rage. "Every time you told me you loved me, I longed to tell you you're nothing to me but an old man in my way. Now I can finally be rid of you, and everything you have will be mine." His humorless grin broadened into evil. "Including your wife."

Arthur laughed. Even to his ears, it sounded icy. "That was a trifle overplayed, boy. Do you really think you can manipulate the High King of Britain into stupidity with a few schoolboy taunts?"

"I don't see why not. I've never found it difficult to manipulate you before."

"I didn't know you were an enemy before." Arthur began to circle to Mordred's right. "You showed your hand a little too soon. If you'd gone on playing the dutiful son a bit longer, perhaps faked a little regret, you might have taken me by surprise. Instead, you went after Gwen and pissed me off. I always warned you your impulsivity would get you in trouble. Now, boy, it's going to be the death of you."

"I am not a boy!" Mordred roared, just as furious as Arthur had anticipated. "And I will be king!" Slamming his body against his father's, the prince drove him backward with his greater weight. His sword flashed toward Arthur's head. The king barely got his shield up in time to block.

As if frenzied, Mordred swung at him again and again until Arthur's shield clanged like an anvil under a smith's hammer. Fighting to keep his feet against those pounding blows, the king silently swore. He'd known Mordred was strong, known he was fast, but he hadn't realized how much the boy had been holding back during practice.

Arthur lunged, determined to power through Mordred's guard. The prince used his shield to knock his father's blade aside hard enough to rattle his teeth.

But in the process, he left himself open. Reversing his swing, Arthur drove his sword's pommel through the gap to smash into Mordred's jaw. The younger man staggered backward.

Catching Mordred's shield with his own, he levered it aside and thrust his blade into the gap, aiming for his opponent's throat. Mordred tried to dodge, but Arthur felt the familiar sensation of a blade parting flesh. Blood flew, but not enough for a deep wound. Not fatal. Close, but not quite.

Fear flashed through the green eyes revealed by the Y-shaped opening of Mordred's helm as his black brows knitted in pain.

Memory flashed through Arthur's consciousness: a young Mordred, that same expression on his face as Morgana stitched up his palm. He'd cut himself playing with Arthur's sword.

Pain twisted the king's heart. God's blood, he actually had to stop himself from asking if his son was all right.

Stop seeing him as your son, or he'll destroy everything you hold dear. Your kingdom. Your knights. Gwen.

Why didn't I realize what he is before we came to this? Am I that bloody blind? He tried to ignore the thought, knowing he couldn't afford the distraction.

Sure enough, the moment's distraction cost him as Mordred leaped into an attack. Arthur brought up his sword, only to miss the parry. The prince's blade clanged against his helm so hard, he saw stars and tasted blood. Reeling back a pace, Arthur caught himself before Mordred could take advantage of his disorientation with another attack. Steadying, he began circling his foe. *I've got to see this bastard as nothing more than armor, shield, and sword.*

Saints knew Mordred had no problem seeing him in that light; frigid green eyes watched him with a wolf's bloodthirst.

The two men settled into the familiar dance of combat. Attack followed block followed attack, swords licking in search of vulnerable flesh. Just as Lance had predicted, the prince's youth, strength, and longer reach soon began to tell as fatigue weighted Arthur's blade and dragged at his feet.

To make matters worse, Mordred knew Arthur's weaknesses as only a family member could, like that old hip injury that plagued him whenever it rained. The prince went after it at every opportunity with hammering attacks, harrying him until Arthur had to work not to favor that leg. *Damned if I'll give the little shit the satisfaction.*

It was hardly the first time the king had fought a man so much bigger. Or even so much faster, though it was rare to meet one who was both. It certainly didn't happen as often now as when they'd called Arthur the Princeling King. He'd won those early fights through strategy and cunning; he'd win this one the same way.

Ignoring his complaining hip and tiring muscles, Arthur focused on his foe. Mordred's mouth had gone tight and thin with either pain or building fatigue, until he abruptly broke away and retreated. Arthur, old wolf that he was, went after him, almost stepping on his toes with a long pace inside the prince's guard.

"You're old and slow and weak," Mordred spat, leaping back. "It's time to let a younger . . ." He attacked in midword, his shield ramming Arthur's into his chest. The prince's sword arched low around the locked shields to spear the king's aching hip.

Pain lanced up Arthur's spine in a scarlet thunderclap. He ignored it to muscle against Mordred's shield, forcing it down one finger width, then two . . .

The king struck, ramming his sword point into the protective leather gorget around his foe's throat. The blow sent the prince sprawling flat on his back, gagging in agony as his blade flew from his hand.

Arthur's foot landed squarely in the center of Mordred's chest, bearing down hard as the younger man struggled to breathe. Coolly, the king angled his sword against the bare skin on the underside of the prince's jaw. All he had to do was lean his weight against the blade to cut Mordred's throat. Instinctively, Arthur looked up, his gaze seeking his queen's face. Under the awning, Gwen and Morgana wore matching wide-eyed expressions of maternal horror.

Dammit, he threatened you!

He jerked his gaze downward as the prince dragged his helm off and fell back with his arms flung wide. Making a point of being no threat.

Calculation filled Mordred's green eyes as he tried to speak, only to break off in wracking coughs. Arthur's sword strike apparently hadn't crushed his larynx; he'd be dying now if it had. But the blow was definitely causing him considerable pain.

If I don't kill him now, he'll drown my kingdom in blood.

"Do it, Arthur," Gwen's voice rang across the field, over the silent crowd.

"Yes," Morgana said, though she had to know she had no say in this. "You must."

Mordred croaked a rasping sound of shock, presumably at his mother's endorsement of his execution.

Arthur set his weight and lifted the sword over his head. Green eyes widened in fear and disbelief.

Damn it, there came another memory: Mordred's smile as a boy, lighting his face with mischief, bright as sunrise. He hadn't smiled often, but when he did . . . Tears stung Arthur's eyes, but he braced to bring the blade down and end his child . . .

And realized he couldn't do it.

You fucking fool, he raged at himself, *he'll destroy everything you love! Gwen, the kingdom . . . My enemies will gather around him and drag us all into war!*

But though he could have slain Mordred in combat, the king simply didn't have it in him to slit the boy's throat. Blade still raised over his son's head, Arthur snarled, "Did I raise you to keep your word like heart's blood?"

Mordred's gaze didn't even flicker. "Yes . . . my . . . liege . . ." he croaked.

Lying little fuck. Fortunately there were ways to keep a man from finding followers. It might not be enough to satisfy Merlin, but it would have to do. Arthur used his best battleground roar. "Do you swear by your honor that you will make no attempt to incite rebellion against your king?"

"I . . . swear," Mordred croaked. Lying again.

"Do you swear that you will lead no men against mine, nor kill either me or my subjects, nor commit any other form of treason?"

Mordred swallowed as if trying to force his protesting larynx to cooperate. "I . . . so swear . . . on . . . on my honor."

Looking up, Arthur swept a cold glance over the crowd, searching out his most rebellious lords one by one. "Mordred has sworn on his honor to attempt no treason against me, my subjects, or my kingdom. If he violates that oath . . ."

Mordred jerked in protest under the booted foot still planted on his chest. Without looking down, Arthur pressed the point of his sword against his throat, spilling a bright, narrow stream of blood. The prince froze. ". . . If he violates that oath, any man who follows him is a fool. If he would break an oath to his own king—to his own *father*— why would anyone imagine his word is worth anything?"

Arthur lifted his foot and stepped back. "You are no longer my heir," he told Mordred, making sure his voice carried to everyone present. "You are no longer my son. And you are banished. Leave Camelot now. You have three days to get out of the country. If you ride hard, you can just do it. If you are caught in Britain on day four, you will hang. Now get out of my sight."

Pale as milk, Mordred struggled to his feet. He turned toward his pack of followers. As one, they looked away. He curled a lip bitterly, pivoted, and limped from the courtyard.

Arthur flicked a gaze at Percival, Cador, and Marrok. The three Knights of the Round Table could be trusted to make sure he left without yielding to the temptation to kill him. They were also a lethal combination on the battlefield.

The trio approached and braced to attention. "Watch him pack and escort him to the Channel. I want to make sure he actually leaves. And don't let him get himself killed between here and there."

"Aye, my king," Percival said, and turned to his partners. "Let's go." They trooped off.

Now I've got Merlin to deal with. The wizard would, of course, deny Arthur the Grail, which meant he now had to wonder which of his enemies would drink from it.

The king started toward the pavilion, forcing himself not to limp despite the pain lancing through his injured hip with every step.

Guinevere, bless her, had called for water. She stepped from beneath the awning and knelt to present the goblet to Arthur with regal elegance. He shot a glance toward the stands, but their watching audience had already dropped to their knees with a mass rustle and murmur. They all looked a bit stunned. Evidently very few of them had expected him to win.

I don't suppose I can blame them, considering I didn't expect to win, either. Lancelot, after all, had been right; the odds hadn't favored Arthur.

Thanking his wife, the king accepted the goblet and drank a gulping swallow for the sake of his dust-dry throat. After helping his queen to her feet, he led her back to the pavilion, seated her, and sank into his own chair. Crossing one knee over the other, Arthur lifted an insolent brow at Merlin. "Well?" He took another swallow.

"Well played, King Arthur. But then, I expected nothing less."

He damned near strangled on the water. "Didn't you?"

Merlin's voice dropped. "You could have killed him. Indeed, most men would have. Instead, you found a way to make it difficult for your enemies to use him."

Arthur's hand tightened on his goblet. "But not impossible."

"No. Not impossible." He gestured, and the Grail appeared in the wizard's hand, glowing even in the bright light of afternoon. "But very little *is* impossible."

"I thought our battle was to be to the death."

Merlin shrugged. "You could have killed him. You simply chose not to." He looked into Arthur's eyes, and the impact of his gaze was like a blow from a strong man's fist. "I was not attempting to discover if you are a powerful man, Arthur. You wouldn't be High King if you weren't. What I sought to determine was if you could be trusted to use power wisely, yet with mercy. Even mercy for one who betrayed you."

"You know so bloody much," Arthur growled. "Do you know if my kingdom will pay the price for my clemency?"

"If I could divine the future at will, would I have needed to test you?"

The king's lips twitched with reluctant humor. "I suppose not."

"However, there are things you need to know before you decide whether to drink from my cup," Merlin continued, raising the Grail as if in a toast. The cup vanished in a rain of sparks. "I suggest we adjourn to discuss this in more privacy."

Arthur nodded. "I have no objection." He rose, took his queen's hand, and limped off the field, aware of the crowd streaming after them.

The Table Chamber was the true heart of the fortress of Camelot. The massive oak Round Table dominated the impressive space that soared to a vaulted ceiling two stories overhead. Weapons glinted on the torchlit stone walls: swords, axes, lances, and shields captured from Arthur's foes. Between the clusters of arms, crimson banners hung from the vaulted ceiling two stories overhead, each glinting with the rampant dragon that symbolized the reign of the Pendragon line.

Twenty-four chairs surrounded the table, presently occupied by Arthur and his knights, Merlin, Nimue, Gwen, Morgana, and a number of others chosen by the two conjurers. Since the total was greater than the number the Table could accommodate, the rest sat at long tables around the walls. Gwen ordered food and wine for her guests, then dismissed the servants once it arrived.

Nimue studied Arthur with a frown. "It might help if I heal that injury before we begin this discussion."

"You're hurt?" Guinevere's gaze swept the length of his body in alarm.

"Mordred caught me in that old hip wound," Arthur explained, then turned to Nimue. "I would be grateful."

"I will need to touch you." When he nodded, she rose and knelt before him to rest fragile fingers on his dirty knee. Heat rolled up his thigh, followed an instant later by a blessed cool that surprised him into inhaling. An odd sensation followed, like something moving beneath his skin. He was still trying to figure out what the hell it was when Nimue took her hand away.

"The wound will trouble you no more."

Arthur flexed his leg, surprised when agony didn't shoot through his hip. "There's no pain at all." He laughed, surprised and gratified. "I've grown so used to the constant ache, it actually feels a bit strange."

As those at the Table murmured in astonishment—even Morgana looked impressed by the speed of the healing—Nimue frowned. "From the scarring, it must have given you a great deal of pain for a long time."

Still rubbing his hip in amazement, Arthur nodded absently. "Yes, I took an arrow during a siege of an enemy fortress fifteen years ago."

"He almost lost that leg." Gwen's wondering eyes appeared very wide and blue as she gazed at Nimue. A grin spread across her face, brilliant as dawn, and she caught the witch's hand. "Thank you! Thank you so much. I had feared it would always torment him. . . ."

"You're welcome, of course." Nimue smiled at the queen. "I'm glad I could help."

Arthur rubbed his thigh hard and grinned when the pain showed no sign of returning. "So," he said, reaching to carve a slice of suckling pig for Gwen, then putting it on the trencher they shared. "Tell me about this choice of yours, Merlin."

"To understand that, my king, you must first learn of the future I foresee for humanity if you decline my cup."

Arthur looked up from pouring Gwen a goblet of wine. "I thought you said you couldn't foresee the future."

"It's difficult for me to see any individual's future, but the fate of an entire people is a different matter," Merlin said. He paused as if to consider the best way to explain. "It's similar to the way it's easier to see something large than something very tiny."

Considering the point, the king nodded. "That does make sense."

"So." Leaning back in his seat on Arthur's left, the wizard took a sip of his wine as he flicked his free hand at the metal brazier in the center of the table.

Flames roared up, casting light across the watching faces in shades of blue and gold and crimson, yet radiating no heat. Those watching murmured or gasped at the brilliant display. "Now," said the boy wizard in his oddly resonant voice, "share my vision."

Towers appeared in the leaping flames, standing so breathtakingly tall, the people that bustled around them looked like ants. Hulking metal carts on fat black wheels rolled between the great structures, following streets paved not in stone, but a smooth black substance painted with lines of yellow and white.

One cart, yellow as a marigold, rolled up beside a tower. Arthur saw the same dazzled absorption on the faces of those around him that he felt himself.

"If that's a cart," Gwen murmured, puzzled, watching two people get out of it, "where's the horse?"

She was right. There wasn't a single horse anywhere in sight, despite the stream of carts flowing between the buildings, accompanied by arrhythmic trumpet blasts.

But as Arthur started to ask about that mystery, a rumble sounded, intensifying until he felt the reverberations in his bones.

All those surrounding the towers stopped to stare skyward in alarm.

And died.

Fire blossomed, blinding enough to make the noonday sun appear no more than a candle's flame. When the light died, the city was gone, save for blackened ruins clustered around an immense glass pit. There was no sign of anyone at all.

"What happened to them?" someone asked.

"They died," Merlin said grimly. "All of them. Instantly."

The image shifted, fleeing across the Earth like a bird on the wing. Miles away, the first carts appeared, melted into slag or blazing like torches. More miles passed before people appeared, staggering, so horribly burned, Gwen at first didn't realize they were people at all.

"Mankind will be extinct within three years." Merlin's voice sounded low and tight. "Dead of burns, starvation, exposure, or poison in the air and water."

"Surely this is the wrath of God?" Arthur turned a troubled gaze on the wizard. "His judgment for the sins of these people?"

Merlin snorted. "God did not do this, Arthur. Men did."

The king gaped at him. "Are they all magicians in this future of yours? How did they do this?"

"Not magic. Weapons." The wizard shook his head in sorrow. "Weapons you can't imagine. Your language doesn't have the words, even if I tried to explain." He turned a brooding gaze on the horrific scene. "And this is only one possible future. There are an endless number of ways and times and reasons humanity may wipe the earth bare of all life. You and your knights and ladies could serve as the balance. You could save your world."

"But if it's the will of God . . ." Arthur's spread his hands. He had never felt so helpless. "How is drinking from a cup supposed to give me the ability to change this?"

"If it's the will of God, it will happen no matter what you do. But what if it's only the will of sinful men?" The wizard leaned in until they were almost nose to nose. "What if you can save all those who would otherwise suffer and die?"

Arthur shook his head. "Merlin, I don't see how that would even be possible. It must have taken years to build that city. Decades. Perhaps centuries. I am only one mortal man. I'll be dust long before then."

"Not if you drink from the Grail. A sip from my cup will change you, allowing you to live centuries without aging a day. You could guide your race beyond those shoals."

"I don't see how even immortality could give me the ability to prevent something like that." He gestured at the brazier and the slagged city it portrayed.

"Immortality is only one of the gifts the cup will bestow."

"But why don't you do whatever it is you want done? Obviously, you have great power. Why must it be me?"

"Because this is a task for your kind, and I'm not one of you. What's more, yours is not the only people in danger. My task is to help those others gain the power to save themselves, just as you must."

"Again, how? As some kind of immortal tyrant? Always at war, always waiting for betrayal? I have been High King but two decades. I wouldn't care to bear such a weight for centuries."

"A tyrant is the last thing your people need." It seemed the night sky shone reflected in Merlin's eyes, a spiral of stars through darkness. "You would only guide, not order. In the end, humanity must choose its own way, just as all creatures must. But the choice will be better for your guidance."

Arthur studied him. "Do you see that, too, then, with this Sight of yours?"

"I see . . ." Merlin blinked and shook his head. "Not enough. Only that the paths to extinction become fewer if you drink. You, and the men and women I will choose from among your people."

"Men and women?" His brows lifted.

Merlin gestured at their listeners. "By drinking from my Grail, the men will become Magi, gaining physical speed and strength far beyond mortal abilities, while the women will become Majae, with magical skills like those Nimue and I have."

With a frown, Arthur studied the wizard. "I assume you don't intend my ladies to fight to the death? It would be no even contest, even assuming any knight of mine would fight a woman who has never held a blade."

"Obviously, I don't intend the men and women to fight, especially not to the death. The combat is only a way for me to judge which of your people is most worthy."

Nimue spoke up. "As to the women, the contest they face will not be fought with steel. Your queen and the others . . ."

"Wait . . . my queen?" Arthur glowered at Merlin's lover. "Queen Guinevere will *not* fight."

Guinevere turned from her husband to look at the young witch, who stared back at him with ruthless eyes. "Then are you willing to watch her die of old age or mortal disease, while you live on, looking a decade younger than you do now? For if you drink from the Grail and she does not, that is precisely what will happen." For all her blond delicacy, there was steel in the young witch, tempered and cold as a blade in a snowbank.

The kind of cold that burns, Gwen thought. Before her courage could fail her, she said the only thing she could. "I'll take your test."

Arthur caught her hand, worry in his eyes. "Gwen . . ."

"I will do whatever I must to keep you. I'll fight however they choose. And I'll not lose." She locked eyes with him. Gwen hadn't been married to Arthur Pendragon all these years without learning how to stare him down.

His gaze finally softened. "As you wish, my lady." He turned a level stare on Merlin. "I'll drink from your Grail—after my queen passes your test."

Merlin didn't even blink. "No."

Arthur had a way of seeming to grow larger and more dangerous when crossed. He used that trick now. "Then I'll not drink."

Merlin's voice dropped. "As you will. But be warned: if you decline my cup, others will not. It may be you will have cause to regret it."

A chill slid over him. "Are you threatening to offer it to Mordred?"

Merlin's head rocked back as he gave Arthur an impatient look. "Of course not, but someone will accept it, regardless of the cost. Especially if it means tasting their heart's dearest dreams."

Dearest dreams? Like an heir? Arthur thought, suddenly seeing a personal benefit to something that had begun to sound a lot like martyrdom without even the promise of heaven as a reward. Could Nimue heal whatever it was had caused his and Gwen's childlessness as easily as she had his hip?

Gwen's gaze met his, and he knew she was thinking the same thing. "If we drink from your Grail, would a child be possible?" he demanded. "Could we become parents?"

Merlin turned to the fire as if seeking an answer in its flames. After a long pause he said, "When you decide you want another son, there will be no difficulty."

"A child. *Our* child," Gwen whispered. She caught his hand. "Ours. I'd fight any battle to hold your son in my arms."

Arthur turned to Merlin. "I'll drink your potion."

"There is one more thing to consider, sire." Nimue frowned, looking from his face to Gwen's. "If she loses . . ."

"I will not lose." Gwen said stonily. She'd fight to her last breath for her chance at that cup, no matter what it cost her.

The witch gazed at her without blinking, without even appearing to breathe. Finally she looked at Merlin and tilted her chin ever so slightly.

As if she'd given him permission, Merlin turned to Arthur. "There is one thing more. The women who drink from the Grail will gain the power to work magic almost as great as Nimue's. The men, however, will become like the males of my race." He swept his black gaze around the room. "Those who whisper I don't eat are correct. I must drink the blood of my mate instead. It's her magic which sustains my life."

As everyone in the room gasped, cursed, or crossed themselves, one of the knights said exactly what Gwen was thinking. "You want our king to become a blood-drinker?"

"Oh, not damned likely," Lancelot snapped, before he turned to Arthur. Normally he deferred to the High King, but sometimes he acted like the childhood friend he was. "You can't mean to do this, sire. Not even to gain an heir."

"It could cost your soul," Kay agreed. "Not to mention your throne. You'd be handing your enemies a cause they could use to trigger a revolt."

Gwen's heart sank, knowing the two men had a point.

Arthur paused a moment before he said, "My knights are correct. I want a son or daughter, but not at the cost of plunging my kingdom into a civil war that could cost the lives of all I love—not to mention those of uncounted innocents."

"Rejecting my offer will not prevent such a war, my king," Merlin retorted. "Even now, the Saxons flood into your kingdom, hungry for land and conquest. Keeping them out would take more manpower than you can muster. It doesn't take a wizard's Sight to know they'll eventually march against you. Perhaps not this year, perhaps not even the next, but you will inevitably face them. When that day comes, you and your elite knights will be older, slower, and weaker, against a force that greatly outnumbers yours. They'll wipe you out, Arthur. Not just you personally, but your entire culture. All you've accomplished, all you've fought and bled for, will be lost to darkness."

"If you're correct," Arthur retorted, "we're going to have to deal with the Saxons regardless of whether we drink from your cup or not."

"True enough, but your ladies will have magical abilities almost the equal to mine, while no mere human will be able to best you and your knights in battle—you'll be too fast, with too much raw strength. You'd be more than a match for the Saxons."

Gwen frowned. "But did I understand that Arthur would have to drink your mate's blood?"

A blend of incredulity, anger, and pure male possessiveness flashed across Merlin's face. "Hardly. He'll have to get his own witch."

"It's not exactly a hardship to feed a Magus," Nimue put in. "It does me no harm. Indeed, if the day came when Merlin could not drink of me, my health truly would suffer, for the blood he takes keeps my body in balance."

One of Gwen's ladies burst out, "But . . . doesn't that hurt?"

The witch's lips curled into a smile more earthy than ethereal. "Only enough to be interesting." She and Merlin exchanged a wicked glance.

"How old are you?" Arthur demanded, wearing a tight expression of profound discomfort.

Merlin glanced at him, plainly puzzled. A moment later understanding filled his eyes. "Older than we look. Much older."

Arthur studied him, frowning. "This potion will not turn *us* into children?"

"You will appear younger, but not that much younger. The potion will adjust your age until you are at your physical prime." Merlin ran a hand through his hair, his expression growing harried. "Nimue and I miscalculated when we chose these forms. The first people we saw were a goose girl and a stripling shepherd. We didn't know how you judge age. If I had it to do over, I'd take the form of an old man with a gray beard halfway to my belt."

Take the form? Gwen wondered. *What in the name of all the saints are they?*

"But we have veered from the subject at hand—the choice you face." The cool glint in Merlin's gaze said he would not entertain questions. "If you drink from the Grail, you will become immortal, able to heal virtually any injury save decapitation. You will be many times stronger than you are now, with the speed to match . . ."

"Which would be damned handy on the battlefield," Arthur murmured.

"Yes, I rather think it would be. Like you, the eleven men who win their respective contests will have the opportunity to become something more than human. So will the twelve women who will likewise gain immortality, with the ability to work great feats of magic besides."

Arthur frowned. "What price will we pay for all this? It's been my experience that any boon exacts some equal cost."

Merlin glanced soberly at Guinevere. "As I said, you will have to drink blood as I do. Small amounts, true, no more than a goblet's worth, not enough to endanger those you drink from. The Majae, however, will need to give blood as badly as the Magi will need to receive it, for otherwise they'll risk illness, even death. If your wife fails her test, you will have to drink from a Maja—one of the new witches— or risk killing the queen. And for us, drinking from a woman is intensely sexual."

Arthur swallowed, aware that Gwen had frozen beside him, her eyes wide. "That . . . is a very high price, Merlin."

"Aye. You see why I said you must consider the choice carefully."

His immediate instinct was to refuse out of hand, but he could feel his wife's gaze on his face.

God help him, but he'd never found it easy to deny Gwen anything. Could he really refuse her the chance at the child she wanted so desperately?

Could he really turn away from the chance at a son who might become the king Britain so desperately needed, especially since he'd banished Mordred . . . ?

FOUR

Arthur knew there'd be political ramifications to becoming one of these Magi of Merlin's. In recent years, the church had taken to persecuting Druids with determined hostility. He wasn't looking forward to discovering the Pope's reaction to a blood-drinking king.

Which was why he needed to know all the implications, so he asked the next question that came to mind. "We'll be able to work magic, as you do?"

"The women will, but the males' magic will be limited to shape-shifting—the ability to take the form of wolves—and self-healing."

"Why? You don't have such a limit."

Merlin's expression darkened. "My people have found males with the full spectrum of power sometimes use it to abuse their females. It's best to ensure women have the advantage in order to protect themselves."

Arthur longed to protest that Gwen had nothing to fear from him, but he held his tongue. There was no guarantee the same would be true of everyone else who passed Merlin's test. Many men did subject their wives, lovers, and children to abuse, though Arthur dealt harshly with anyone he caught at it. If a man with the power Merlin had described turned on his wife, she'd be hard-pressed to survive, even with magical talents of her own.

Merlin gestured, and the Grail appeared in his hand once more. Mist bubbled from its contents, a glowing blue smoke that painted the wizard's young face with cerulean highlights and cobalt shadows. "You now know as much as you may about the task before you, the abilities this cup will bring, and the price it may exact. Make your choice, Arthur."

"If you will allow me to confer with my wife and my knights . . ."

Merlin nodded. "Of course." He and Nimue rose and walked from the room.

"You must do this, Arthur," Gwen told him after the door closed behind the pair. "If Mordred or the rebels come at you again, such abilities would save us."

"But, Gwen—what if you don't pass this test of Merlin's? I don't want to watch you grow old and die."

"And I don't want to watch some young fool run you through because age has stripped you of your abilities," Gwen shot back. "You defeated Mordred today through superior strategy and a quick blade hand. But I'll say one thing for that boy: he learns from his mistakes. When he breaks his oath—and he will—he won't rely on simply out-muscling you. He'll strike at you where you're most vulnerable: your sense of honor, and the father's love you try so hard to ignore."

Arthur snorted. "Then he's going to be sadly disappointed, because he killed that when he threatened you."

"He's alive now, isn't he?"

The king waved that point aside, though it was a damned good one. "Be that as it may, I'm more concerned with whether I should allow you to take Merlin's test."

Gwen's blond brows lifted. "Allow?"

"You're assuming Queen Guinevere will fail her challenge," Lancelot pointed out. When they both looked at him, the knight lifted his chin. "Forgive me, sire, but you're underestimating her. She is as strong a woman as you are a man."

"He's right," Kay agreed. "The queen may look the fragile female, but there's a core of steel running just beneath all that silk." A tall man, Arthur's foster brother had a broad, handsome face, a thick blond beard, and a gleaming mane of hair he refused to cut, though he had to braid it and coil it tightly under his helm when he fought. Combat disadvantage or not, women loved the hair, and Kay loved women. "But there is another concern."

"There always is," the king growled. "What's yours?"

"Your enemies will say you have been seduced by the powers of darkness." When Arthur snorted, the big man spread his hands. "Some will tell any lie that gains them a political advantage."

"And the gullible will believe their slander." The king grimaced, knowing he was right. "But if I don't drink from Merlin's Grail, my enemies will be just as quick to take it for themselves, should they get the chance at it. And even if they don't, Merlin's right about the Saxons. We don't have the manpower to keep them out as it is now."

"Nay, sire," Kay agreed. "We can't patrol every inch of coastline without leaving gaps they can slip through."

Arthur turned to Gwen. Whenever he faced a decision with as many cons as pros, he'd learned to listen to her opinion. Seventeen years of marriage had taught him his queen was more often right than wrong. Yet if she couldn't be by his side, what was the point? As if reading his mind, she spoke now. "Arthur," Gwen said softly. "You have always been willing to gamble on your own strength and wits, no matter how grim the odds. Be as willing to take a chance on me. I swear I will not fail you."

Arthur stilled, gazing into those clear, determined eyes. "You're right. You've never failed me, not in all our years of marriage. All right, I'll drink from the Grail."

"But what of the wagging tongues?" Kay asked.

The king bared his teeth. "We'll cut them out as needed." He turned to Galahad, the youngest of his knights. "Call them back in, if you please."

They waited until Nimue and Merlin were seated again. When the wizard's gaze met his in expectation, Arthur gave the man a decisive nod. "I'll drink from your cup."

Merlin looked pleased. "Ah, good." As if to forestall any second thoughts, he extended the Grail, his expression expectant.

Arthur took it. Ignoring the blue mist boiling from its surface, he tossed back its contents in one long swallow, then handed the cup back.

An instant later, fire raced across his skin and sizzled through his blood with pain so savage, it was all he could do not to howl at the agony. He shot to his feet, unable to remain sitting with such agony slicing through him, only to stagger as his knees buckled.

"Arthur!" Gwen gasped as Lancelot caught the king.

"'M fine," Arthur slurred, lifting his lolling head with an obvious effort. Beads of sweat broke out on his face as his skin took on a gray cast that sent terror shooting through Gwen's blood like pellets of sleet. "Jus' tired . . . Need to sleep." His head fell forward as Lancelot helped him back into his chair.

Steel slithered from eleven scabbards in a metallic chorus. Merlin lifted a brow at the ring of sword points aimed at him by grim-faced Knights of the Round Table. "Arthur will be fine." He sounded amused, despite the murderous intent in the warriors' eyes. "But he'll be unconscious for a day at least while his body completes its transformation. The spell in the potion is complex, and it takes time to do its work."

"Then let's get him into bed," Gwen told the knights.

"Shouldn't someone watch these two?" Kay asked, gesturing at Merlin and Nimue, his gaze hard.

She flicked a glance back at Merlin and Nimue, neither of whom looked at all intimidated. "Given their magic, what's the point? Besides, they have the king's confidence. Unless any of you doubt Arthur's judgment, we have more important things to focus on—like getting him to our chambers."

Kay inclined his head, conceding the point. She rose as Lancelot and Kay helped the barely conscious king to his feet.

As Gwen led the way from the room, she frowned in worry. What was the Grail doing to Arthur?

B y the time they helped the king out of his dusty, bloody armor, sweat streamed from his skin, and his eyes swept back and forth behind his closed lids as his lips moved with muttered, disjointed orders.

"He's feverish." Gwen turned toward Nimue, who had followed them to Gwen and Arthur's chambers. "Shouldn't we do something?"

"This fever won't hurt him. His body heats because Merlin's spell is transforming it."

"Is there something I can do to help?" Gwen sat on the mattress beside him and covered his nude body with a linen sheet. He didn't stir.

"Just give him your throat once he wakes. When he finishes his change, he's going to need a lot of blood."

Judging from the looks on the knights' faces, they didn't much like the idea, but they also knew it was far too late to complain.

Lance turned to Kay. "The rumor mill is no doubt hard at its grinding. I'll bet you a week's pay some barking-mad idiot has already decided Arthur has become a wizard puppet."

Kay grunted. "We'd better make sure we're patrolling the fortress and village in enough numbers to discourage would-be killers. If we roust all the soldiers out of the barracks and taverns, we'll have the manpower for the job."

"I suggest we use only the Round Table knights to guard this room," Lance said. "I trust us, but I'm not so sure about random barracks rats who might have a yen to assassinate King Arthur."

"Good point." Kay looked thoughtful. "I think I'll head down to the village, hit the pubs myself. Start a conversation or two with my boys before I roust them out to work." As seneschal of Camelot, he oversaw the fortress guards.

Lancelot's lips took on a cynical quirk. "While you're at it, make sure you squash any nasty rumors before they can take root."

"I'll do that." The big man left, silent as a ghost.

Lancelot turned to Gwen and bowed. "With your permission, we will go work out our watch schedule."

Gwen gestured. "Tend to it, then, Sir Knight."

He left, the rest of the Round Table filing out after him, probably off to work out the rest of the watch schedule. Nimue waited until the rumble of masculine voices had retreated down the hall. "I do have a more immediate topic we must discuss."

"Then let's not do it standing." Guinevere led the way to the pair of chairs before the cold hearth. As Nimue took the one opposite her, Gwen looked up to see Morgana through the chamber's open door, walking along the balustrade, her shoulders hunched wearily.

Deciding she could use some reinforcements for this conversation, Gwen called, "Morgana? Come in here, please. And close the door behind you." Her friend nodded and stepped inside. "Come sit down by me, darling. You look like you could use a goblet of wine."

"After what my son did?" Morgana grimaced. "It's going to take at least an entire bottle. Maybe two."

"Then we'll have to make sure you get it." Nimue gestured, conjuring a third chair as the shutters swung closed, leaving the three women in blessed dimness.

Morgana started as candles placed around the room burst into flame. After a moment, she sat down. Normally Gwen, too, would have flinched at this flamboyant display of magic, but after the kind of day she'd had, igniting a few candle flames didn't even rate a second glance. Not in the face of her singing relief.

Against all odds, she still had her husband. She'd find a way to deal with the rest of it. For the first time all day, her muscles began to relax.

"First you need to be aware that the sun disrupts magic, so Arthur will have to avoid direct sunlight," Nimue began. "Now that he's become a being of magic, he'll be more prone toward severe burns and sunstroke. What's more, he'll be unable to remain awake while the sun is up."

Gwen frowned, wondering why they were only hearing about this now. "That's a pretty serious weakness."

"True, but you—or in any case, the twelve Majae—won't have the same vulnerability. They'll be able to protect the men against daylight threats."

"But if there are only twelve of these Majae, that's not much of a force, even with the twelve Magi," Morgana pointed out. "How are we to protect ourselves with so few?"

"Eventually, there'll be more of you. Your children will inherit the potential to gain these powers as well. And since the Magekind will be immortal, your numbers will increase rapidly."

Gwen wanted to quiz the witch about just how the children would gain those powers, but her attention fell on her husband's sweating face. There would be plenty of time for questions later. Right now, her immediate concern was Arthur. "You said earlier you had something to tell me about the king."

Nimue gestured, conjuring a bottle and a trio of goblets. She filled the cups and handed two of them to Gwen and Morgana. "When he wakes, he will want blood—and sex. And he may be more forceful about getting them than he has been. Or will be afterward."

Was the woman trying to frighten her? "Come now, Nimue. I can't believe Arthur would ever hurt me, no matter how he's changed."

"He won't hurt you." She grinned, dark and knowing. "But he will be fairly demanding."

Gwen snorted. "He's demanding now."

"Not compared to this. When he first wakes, he won't recognize you—won't even be capable of real thought until you let him drink from you. And he'll be very, very aroused. Don't try to resist him, no matter how aggressive he is."

Gwen stared at Nimue, her mouth going dry as her imagination fired. Arthur, holding her down, taking her, drinking from her . . . She hoped the witch couldn't sense her growing arousal. "Just how much blood will he need?"

"Not enough to kill you, though I don't doubt it would be a serious problem if we weren't here. Have them send for me once he feeds. I'll heal you."

"How will he obtain this blood?"

"His teeth will be sharper. He will bite your throat and drink."

Morgana stared at the witch, her eyes wide. "Oh, my."

Nimue laughed. "Don't look so terrified, child. It's actually quite erotic."

The healer blinked. "You think being bitten is erotic?"

"Well, yes. Of course, it helps that I have a Truebond with Merlin."

"A what?" Gwen frowned. Sometimes talking to Merlin and Nimue could be incredibly frustrating. She found herself parroting half the things they said in sheer confusion.

"A Truebond. It's a kind of magical mental link. It allows me to feel what Merlin feels, share his thoughts, his needs. When we make love . . ." She smiled, the expression deeply sensual.

To actually feel how Arthur experienced passion—to feel what it would be like to have a cock . . . *Jesu, I'm growing wet.* "It sounds . . . intriguing."

"Oh, it is. But it's not for everyone, and it does have a darker side. For example, if one of us dies, the shock of the severed bond would kill the other. But it grants so many advantages, it's worth the risk."

"But how do you accomplish such a thing?" Morgana asked.

"Magic, of course. But the male must allow it. You can't force a Truebond on someone else; they must love and trust you enough to allow it. Otherwise they'll quickly learn to block you out. The consequences of forcing another person's mind can be ugly. Still, it's something you may want to remember, should you pass your own test."

"Frankly, I doubt Arthur would even permit it." Gwen sat back with a huff. "He's so protective, there are times I can't even get him to talk about whatever's bothering him. He certainly wouldn't allow me to read his mind."

"He may surprise you." Nimue studied Arthur as he twisted restlessly, muttering something about troop movements. "In the meantime, you may safely leave him sleeping, if with a contingent of guards. I would suggest seeing to whatever preparations you want to make for your own test."

"Who would I be fighting?"

"Why, me, of course."

Lovely. Gwen eyed her warily. "As much as it pains me to admit it, I know nothing of swords and combat."

"You'll learn," Nimue said a trifle grimly. "But in any case, you'll have no need of such knowledge for my challenge, for this won't be a physical contest. You need only will and intelligence."

"Those I have."

"So I've noticed."

"So when shall we do this?"

"Later." She gestured at Arthur as he lay sleeping. "There isn't time to test you and, should you succeed, accomplish your transformation before your husband wakes."

G wen slept poorly that night beside her comatose husband, dreams spinning through her brain in a frantic tumble of the day's events.

Mordred threatening her, the face of the boy she'd raised and loved now unrecognizable in its malicious hatred.

Arthur's pain. That icy moment when he'd raised his sword over his son's head.

Morgana, gripping Gwen's hand so hard, she'd thought the bones would break.

The dream warped, and it was Arthur helpless on the ground, Mordred standing over him, Mordred bringing his sword down in a bright, vicious arc . . .

Gwen screamed, jerking awake to find her husband lying next to her, still deep in the Grail sleep. She sat up and touched his chest, needing to feel his heart beating, make sure Merlin hadn't turned him into a monster . . .

Especially after the way Lancelot and the other knights had argued against her sleeping with Arthur, fearing his mental state when he woke. Gwen had overruled them, flatly refusing to believe her husband would ever hurt her, Grail or no Grail. Yet now, with her heart pounding in her ears, she found herself eyeing him anxiously.

But no, it was still Arthur, his face dear and familiar in a shaft of moonlight.

Wait. Gwen frowned. He did look a little different. She rose and found flint and steel, then fumbled with them until she got the hanging oil lamp lit. The wick hissed and spat as she turned to study her husband in the golden light it cast.

The gray was gone from his hair. His face looked younger, too; some of the familiar lines carved by more than two decades as king had vanished. Gwen glanced away, then looked back again.

But no, she wasn't imagining things. He did look younger, less than thirty. A warrior at the height of his strength.

Sweet Mother, he's beautiful. Her gaze traced the strong, narrow line of his nose, the width of his jaw, and the sensual curve of his wide mouth framed by his short, dark beard.

It reminded her of the first time she'd seen him. Barely nineteen, he'd already been king for four years, having only been fifteen at the time of his father's murder.

On hearing the story of Arthur's vengeance for Uther's death, Gwen's father had snorted. "After which the boy no doubt went right on with his dinner," Leodegraunce said. "Uther was a thoroughgoing bastard. Which is doubtless how the child learned to kill assassins over the fish course. The only surprise is that Uther didn't gut his own murderer himself."

At nineteen, Arthur hadn't looked like a killer, at least to Gwen's infatuated sixteen-year-old eyes. He'd been a head taller than she was even then, and brawnier than any other boy she knew, as one might expect of a man who'd spent the past four years fighting to survive. Somehow he'd managed not only to keep his father's kingdom, but also to expand it through conquest. Even as young as he'd been, bards were already singing of his exploits.

She'd taken one look into those velvety dark eyes and fallen deep into girlish love. But then, Arthur had been driving young girls into swoons for years.

The surprise was he'd fallen just as hard for her. Leodegraunce, cunning old fox that he'd been, had recognized the blooming attraction and wasted no time encouraging it. By the time Arthur left the family's holdings a week later, Gwen rode at his side, a new bride. A new queen.

He'd never appeared to regret his hasty choice, whether born of infatuation or true love. Yet however it had begun, the emotion between them had only deepened, growing richer and more powerful over the years, through battles, bitter arguments, and Mordred's stormy childhood. Even three heartbreaking miscarriages had only served to strengthen it.

It would survive Merlin and his Grail, too.

Realizing she'd lose her mind if she did nothing but watch Arthur sleep, Gwen dressed for the day, left his knights standing watch, and went about her duties.

Today that included watching Merlin test the male candidates he'd chosen, including Tristan, Gawain, and Galahad. To Gwen's pleasure, the three Round Table knights won, even after Merlin had each of them fight four and five opponents at once. But then, Arthur had chosen his elite with care, taking into account not only combat skills but also bravery, wit, and sense of honor. She suspected the remaining Table knights would pass Merlin's test as handily as the first three.

During the midday meal, the queen noticed something that worried her. Several of the lords who'd been present at Arthur's duel were missing. Gwen sent servants to check their lodgings in the surrounding town, only to learn all four had packed up their households and decamped the night before. Yet she knew Arthur had not given them permission to leave Camelot.

When she conferred with Lord Kay, the seneschal frowned deeply. "I didn't even notice they were gone," he admitted. "Too preoccupied with this bloody contest of Merlin's. Do you want me to send couriers after them, order them to turn around?"

Gwen didn't hesitate. "Yes. Arthur will want to deal with them when he wakes."

"Which should be sometime tonight, assuming Merlin's correct."

She glanced at the lowering sun. "I have much to see to before then. I'd best get to it."

Kay studied her with obvious concern. "If you need me . . ."

"I will definitely send for you."

"Good luck."

She gave him a carefully confident smile. "I won't need it." *Or at least, I certainly hope not.*

Kay didn't look as if he was fooled.

FIVE

G wen hurried along the balustrade in the light of her oil lamp to find Lancelot and Bors standing guard outside her and Arthur's chambers. Both men looked tense and grim-faced.

"He's awake," Lance told her.

"And growling," Bors added. "Literally. He sounds rather like a bear."

"We left the room when it became apparent our presence was agitating him."

Bors grimaced. "Agitate, hell. He was *stalking* us."

Gwen hesitated, considering the implications. "Then I'd better go in alone. We don't want him stirred up any more than he already is."

The two knights exchanged a concerned glance. "I don't think that's a good idea," Lance told her. "Bors and I will . . ."

"I appreciate your concern, but Arthur won't hurt me."

"Arthur wouldn't," Bors agreed. "But I'm not convinced that what's in there is Arthur."

Gwen frowned. "Nimue would have warned me if there was a possibility he'd be a real danger to me."

"Perhaps," Lancelot said darkly. "Unless they intended to turn the High King into a beast and trick us into feeding him the High Queen."

"Lord Lancelot, I think you've been standing guard too long with nothing to distract your bard's imagination," Gwen told him tartly. "Didn't your son just drink from the Grail?"

"Yes, my queen, but we're short-handed, what with three of the Table knights in this Grail sleep. I felt my place was guarding you and the king. Particularly since I can do Galahad no good anyway."

"Galahad will be fine. And so will I. Stand aside, my lords."

"At least consult Lord Kay . . ."

A growl sounded from the other side of the door, low and savage and distinctly feral.

Bors was right. He did sound like a bear.

The two men looked at her with identical expressions of deep doubt. Gwen's heart bounded into her throat, but she gave the pair her best regal stare. "My king needs me. Stand aside, gentlemen."

"My queen, the king wouldn't want you to . . ." Lance began.

"Stand. Aside," Gwen gritted.

Bors wavered in the face of her obvious anger, but Lance, stubborn as always, refused to back down. "What if he kills you?"

"Do you need a week in gaol to remind you to obey your queen's orders?"

For a moment she thought she was going to have to call the rest of the Round Table to physically remove them. That could easily have backfired, especially since the champion was right: Arthur wouldn't have wanted her to take the risk.

She watched them weigh their conflicting duties—obedience to the queen against protecting her, even from the king. Patience flying, Gwen lifted her voice in a roar she'd learned from Arthur. "Move!"

They stepped apart out of sheer reflex. Gwen sailed between them, jerked open the door, then slammed it behind her before they had time to recover.

* * *

Concealed behind a cloak of magic, Nimue turned to Merlin. "I told you she would make them obey."

Merlin grunted. "Let us see if her courage holds against Arthur."

Nimue only smiled. "She'll handle him. That one is steel to the marrow."

Despite the lamp she held, the room was dark as a crypt after the torchlit balustrade. Gwen fumbled to attach the lamp to the chain that hung from the ceiling.

When she turned around, Mordred loomed over her like a wall of muscle. Gwen froze in stark terror, unable to breathe, much less scream for help.

Until she realized his eyes were dark, not Mordred's icy green.

Arthur, she realized, and felt her heart lurch back into rhythm. *It's Arthur!* He didn't look quite as young as his son, though he could easily have been an older brother. "Christ's wounds, husband, you frightened me witless!"

He stepped against her, forcing her to retreat until her back hit the wall. Leaning down, he sucked in a deep huffing breath, as if scenting her.

"You're scaring me." Gwen struggled to regain control of her rising voice. "Give me a little room, please."

He didn't react, still breathing deeply bare inches from her throat. She planted both palms against his chest and shoved. "Step back, Arthur!"

He caught her wrists and lifted them over her head. Pinning her hands in one of his against the cool plaster, he leaned against her.

Gwen once had a horse she was grooming pin her by shifting his weight, trapping her between his shoulder and the stable wall. The animal hadn't applied any real pressure, but she'd found she couldn't move him no matter how she pushed and struggled. Point made, the gelding finally stepped aside and let her go.

Arthur's hold felt exactly like that. Not tight enough to hurt, but completely inescapable. He watched her, his expression patient, while she strained against his warm, immoveable strength. "Arthur, dammit, let me . . ."

"My queen?" Lancelot called through the door. "Do you need help?"

Arthur tensed and lifted his head, glaring toward the door. His lips peeled off his teeth.

Two of them were fangs.

"My queen? Are you all right?"

"I'm fine, Lance! He's not hurting me, he's just irritating the hell out of me. It's not the first time, and I assure you it won't be the last. Quit listening at the door before you hear something that will embarrass you as much as it does us."

There was a long, uncomfortable silence. "Excuse me, my queen. I was but concerned. You sound . . . breathless."

"Breathless or not, I'm in no danger." *I hope.* She had never been so intensely aware of her husband's size and strength, especially compared to her own far more delicate body. Was he actually bigger than he had been the day before, if not in height, then in sheer muscular breadth?

He looked down at her, his black stare hungry as he bared those fangs again. "Mine."

Gwen actually felt the word rumble from his chest to hers. "Yes, my king. Yours. Still. Always."

His snarl became a smile, sensual and hot. Gwen knew that smile. That was Arthur. The tension in her knotted shoulders began to relax.

Arthur lowered his head slowly, still watching her with that lupine intensity. The hand not holding her wrists reached up to cup one breast through her thin linen tunic. Pleasure unspooled along her nerves as she stared up into her husband's face, at the smile that looked both familiar and alien with the curve of his lips baring those white, white fangs. His cupping fingers curled to milk her nipple with exquisite delicacy, pinching and tugging with steadily increasing force. Delight grew with each stroke, given an extrawicked kick by the undercurrent of danger added by those fangs. She tried to squirm, but he didn't budge even the fraction he would have before. Instead he smiled, obviously well aware of her tangled emotions.

Then Arthur pounced.

She was in his arms before she even felt him move. He spun and dropped onto the bed, pinning her beneath his hot, hard strength as she yelped in alarm.

"Betterrrr," he growled, and smiled.

The dark satisfaction in his black eyes made her catch her breath. Her sex tightened in the kind of wet clench that usually followed a whole evening's worth of skilled, determined foreplay.

Arthur knew it, too. He leaned down and wrapped one big hand in the front of her gown. He did it slowly, giving her plenty of time to realize what he intended—and plenty of time to realize there was nothing she could do to stop him, even if she'd wanted to. Which she definitely did not.

Even so, Gwen gasped when he shredded the gown with one easy tug. The sound of ripping linen sounded incredibly loud—and just as erotic. "That was one of my favorite tunics," she told him. Which it was, though with such animal want pumping through her veins, she really didn't care about the tunic.

His lips curled in another fang-revealing smile. "Wet."

"Hard," she retorted. The hot length of him pressed against her belly. He was also naked, since they'd put him to bed that way. Normally, that wouldn't give her pause; Arthur slept nude on all but the coldest nights. Their running joke had always been that he had enough fur to keep him warm—and her, too, for that matter. The man radiated heat like a human hearth.

So it had been a very long time since Gwen had felt this kind of aching awareness of her husband's nudity. Yet now every last inch of him seemed branded on her quivering senses. Gwen found herself staring up at him in the lamp's flickering golden light, wide-eyed as a virgin.

He stared back, levering off her to look her up and down. Under that wolfish gaze, her nipples drew hard as cherry stones. Lowering his head, he took one rigid peak into his mouth.

And moaned.

The sound was deep, ragged, distilled male eroticism given voice. She found herself echoing him as he swirled his tongue over the peak, back and forth, around and around. Strong fingers found her breast, stroking and squeezing, increasing her arousal until Gwen found herself pressing her thighs together in an attempt to alleviate the ache between them. She groaned, rolling her hips against his thick length as she fisted her hands in the gleaming raw silk of his hair.

Feeling out of control, Gwen shivered, overwhelmed by Arthur's animal sensuality. So familiar, yet simultaneously so alien.

Suckling hard, he rumbled a rough, wordless sound that might have been warning or need. Or both. She gasped back at him, digging her nails into the thick muscle of his shoulders, feeling just as lost in incoherent hunger as he was.

Arthur transferred his mouth to the other breast, triggering another bright ping of delight. Wanting to give him the same kind of pleasure, Gwen reached between them. His cock felt huge, hot, insanely tempting as she curled shaking fingers around its meaty width. "In me, Arthur," she whispered. "Now. Please."

Instead he pulled out of her arms and backed down her body. Settling between her thighs, he nudged them apart as she whimpered in helpless longing.

He bent over her clitoris, his lips sealing the little nubbin inside his mouth's piercingly sweet hold. His tongue swirled around it, wet and maddening, before he tightened his lips and sucked so hard, she twisted like a woman in agony. Her entire body shuddered, her thigh muscles jerking as her sex pulsed in need.

Ecstasy shot up her sensitized body. "Arthur!" Gwen's spine arched as her hands flew to fist in his hair.

Staring down at him, she found him watching her face as his

tongue swirled and lapped and stabbed between her slick folds. His dark eyes narrowed, and she tensed, knowing that look. Sure enough, a beat later she felt the tips of his fangs against the sensitive inner lips. Not biting. Quite. But the erotic threat of it shot heat and fear and stark arousal through her blood. Jolting like a mare under a knight's spur, she ground her pussy against his mouth. Wanting. Burning.

She needed him. In her, as deep as she could get him. "Fuck me," she gasped. "Ohhhhhh, Arthur, my king, please . . . Fuck me!" Her hands tightened on his hair, barely resisting the need to pull. Goaded, she hooked one calf over his shoulder and dug her heel into his back. "Please, oh, please . . . Mary and Joseph, Arthur . . ."

He growled and reared, jerking out of her hold to grab the thin gold cord she'd used to tie her now-shredded tunic, still loosely in place around her bare waist. Big hands snapped it like thread.

"What are you . . . ?" she began, only to yelp as he flipped her over onto her belly. Dragging her hands down to the small of her back, he lashed her wrists together with a few efficient coils of cord. "Arthur, curse it, stop that! What do you think you're doing?"

"Fucking you. Like you want." He pulled her hips upward, positioned the smooth hot head of his cock against her, and drove to the balls in one merciless plunge. "Mine!" The word emerged from his chest wrapped in a feral growl as he withdrew and thrust again, then again and again, punctuating each word with deep, hard plunges. "Mine, mine, mine!"

If she hadn't been so wet, so insanely hot with need, being stuffed so savagely with his big rod would have hurt. Instead pleasure slashed her like a whip. "Arthuuuuuurrrrr!" she wailed, her voice high and breathless.

He growled back and began to fuck her in earnest, spearing her in long thrusts that crammed her with exactly what she needed. Convulsing, Gwen writhed as his plundering strokes hammered her in a searing erotic storm.

Her knees went out from under her. Arthur followed her down, not even breaking his rhythm, his hips pounding hers, his cock digging so deep, his balls swung against her sex. Gwen gasped, half-blind with pleasure. The movement of his pelvis hitting her rump ground his weight down on her pinned wrists, but before she could manage a protest, he was already rolling them both over. Fingers circling her clit, he fucked up into her from beneath.

Gwen cried out as the orgasm intensified, pulsing in time to his stroking fingers and driving cock. Fisting his free hand in her hair, he dragged her head back against his shoulder. And bit, sinking his fangs into her skin. Gwen screamed as the bright sting added to the sensation of his ramming thrusts. Growling against her skin, he drank, corkscrewing his hips in circles, grinding his cock deep. The pain and delight blended until she could no longer tell where one ended and the other began, all of it driving her climax to searing heights. Finally he stiffened in climax, spine arching to impale her to the balls, cock jerking as he drank and drank and drank.

Dazed from her pounding climax, panting in heaves, she listened to his rippling swallows as his brawny arms held her helpless and his cock slowly softened in her depths. Eyes drifting closed, Gwen let herself float as her Magus husband fed.

The light was odd when Arthur woke, so intense and golden, he thought it must be morning. But when he looked toward the balustrade window, he found it still shuttered.

Then the wet heat around his cock registered, and he realized he lay beneath Gwen, buried to the balls in her. Next he became aware of a metallic tang filling his mouth. Blood. Though the meaty copper taste had always revolted him before, now it struck him as deliciously erotic, like distilled sex.

His eyes widened. *I drank her blood!*

Fear sheeted through him as he realized her skin felt too cool, almost as if . . . "Gwen!"

For one horrific moment, he thought she was dead. Then he felt her slender chest rising and falling under his frantic hands. He could actually hear her heart beating, though it sounded a bit fast and far too loud. Arthur slumped in relief. "Guinevere, my lady? What happened? Did I . . . ?"

She didn't answer. God, had he hurt her?

Lifting her, he rolled her over until he could rise on one elbow and scan her face frantically. Her pretty body shone with sweat, and her chest arched, thrusting her full breasts upward. That, he realized, was because her wrists were bound at the small of her back. He snapped the cord like gossamer thread, barely noticing how easy it was. *I tied her up? Why the hell did I . . .*

Arthur's eyes locked on the two neat puncture wounds on her throat. *I bit her,* he realized anew, tasting the blood in his mouth with sick horror. *I tied her up and bit her and drank her blood. And now she's unconscious. She needs the healer.*

"Morgana!" Naked, he rolled off the bed and headed for the door. Feeling a draft, he swore and stopped barely long enough to jerk on breeches as he roared, "Morgana!"

The door opened in a blinding explosion of light. "My king?" Lancelot's familiar voice asked. "What do you . . ."

"Get Morgana!" Arthur snapped, and turned to grab the coverlet and flip it across his wife's nudity. She wouldn't want his knights to see her like that. "She's unconscious."

Voices murmured, followed by the slap of racing feet. Lance stepped inside. "Bors has gone to fetch her. What's the matter with the queen?" Forgetting his habitual deference, the champion demanded, "Arthur, what the hell did you do?"

"I don't know!" he snapped back. "The last thing I remember was drinking from Merlin's damned cup. When I woke, she was unconscious . . ."

"There's blood on your mouth," Lancelot told him in an icy voice.

"Of course there's blood on his mouth." Nimue strode in, Merlin at her heels. Brisk and calm, she bent over Gwen and pressed two fingers to the Queen's throat. "He's a Magus, and he just woke from his transition. He had to feed. And no, Arthur, you didn't hurt her."

"Fuck that, heal her!" he growled, just shy of frantic. "Heal my queen now!"

"Patience, sire." She closed her eyes. Golden sparks ignited around her fingers to dance the length of Gwen's body.

Under normal circumstances, Arthur might have felt a chill at the supernatural display. Now he didn't care what the witch did, so long as she healed Guinevere doing it.

G wen bent low over the gelding's neck, tearing down the rutted path at a pace far too swift for safety, especially considering how little light the full moon provided as it sailed behind the scudding clouds.

Yet as fast as she rode, it seemed she made no progress at all.

Arthur was in danger. If she didn't get to him, he was dead. Him, and all his knights with him.

Despair digging its claws in her heart, the queen slashed her quirt hard down across the horse's flanks. The gelding stretched out, hooves drumming on the packed earth.

A white figure appeared in her path, pale as a ghost as it melted out of the mist. Gwen raised the reins, meaning to guide her mare around the apparition.

"Guinevere, wake up!" Nimue said, her voice as plain as if she spoke directly in Gwen's ear. "Your husband needs you."

"But I'm late! I must get there or he'll die!"

"Your husband is fine, my queen. This is but a dream." She gestured. "And he fears for you. You must awake!"

With a wail of despair, Gwen felt herself being jerked from her laboring mount . . .

Gwen's eyes flew wide. To her vast relief, she saw Arthur bending over her, concern in his dark eyes. "Gwen? Gwen!"

"You see? There she is," Nimue said in a tone of elaborate patience. "Safe and well, as I told you she would be."

With a muffled gasp, Guinevere threw herself into his beloved arms. "Arthur! I had the most horrible dream. I was trying to get to you, but no matter how fast I rode, I knew I'd be too late . . ." Tears pricked her eyes.

As if in echo of her own fear, Arthur's arms encircled her so hard her ribs creaked. "Jesu, Guinevere, what happened? Did I hurt you?"

She tried to answer, only to discover she couldn't draw breath. *He's about to break my ribs!*

"Let her go, Arthur," Merlin snapped. "You're hurting her."

The arms around her vanished so fast, Gwen fell backward on the bed with a gasp of relief.

"God, Gwen, I'm sorry!" Somehow he was all the way across the room, as if he'd moved with inhuman speed. His handsome face was pale, his eyes wide and black with anguish. "I didn't mean . . ."

With an effort, she gave him a tight smile and made an effort to manage speech. "I'm fine . . . Arthur." She had to pant a few breaths before she could go on. "You didn't . . . hurt me."

"You are much stronger now than you were before," Merlin told him. "You must take care. I would suggest practicing with raw eggs until you learn better control." His too-young lips twitched in amusement. "Though it may be a bit messy at first."

Arthur, however, was not in the mood for humor. He rounded on the wizard with eyes blazing in a white face. "Why didn't you warn me? If I had known I might kill my own wife, I would never have so much as sipped from that accursed cup!"

Alarmed, Gwen scrambled off the bed and started toward him. "Arthur, you didn't hurt me!" Belatedly remembering her nudity, she checked in midstep. She relaxed when she saw she wore a white silk tunic, though not one she recognized.

"I dressed you," Nimue told her with a faint smile. "Magic is a most convenient skill."

"Then use it to undo this," Arthur snapped. "I have no desire for power that could exact such a price from my queen."

"It's a little late for that, sire. That bit of magic cannot be undone without separating your head from your shoulders," Merlin told him coolly. "Luckily, if you can but muster a little control, your queen will be in no danger from either your hunger or your strength. I suggest you apply that formidable will to the task of self-discipline."

A hot flush spread over Arthur's angular cheekbones. Gwen winced and braced for an explosion of royal Pendragon rage.

Instead he visibly reached for the self-control Merlin had just mentioned. "I will, as you say, apply myself to mastering these new abilities."

"I have no doubt of it." Merlin gave him a very formal nod and swept out.

Arthur turned to her, his gaze searching. "My love, did I hurt you?" He gestured. "I don't mean just now. Before."

She realized he meant before he regained awareness. "No, my king. You didn't hurt me." Evidently reassured by her smile, he slumped in relief, then turned to his knights and gestured for them to follow. As Lance closed the door in their wake, Gwen heard her husband ask, "All right, what passed while I slept?"

As male voices murmured reports, Gwen became aware of Nimue's considering gaze. "So, my queen, mortal or not, you seem to have survived your king's passion—despite his fears to the contrary."

"My husband is highly protective."

"Possibly a bit too much so." The witch shrugged. "But that's a problem for another day. The more immediate challenge is proving yourself worthy of powers of your own—if you are still willing."

"I'm willing." That was putting it mildly. Gwen had no desire to remain a wife who looked more like her husband's mother.

"Then, if you are ready . . ."

She blinked. "You mean . . . now?"

Nimue lifted a brow. "Unless you'd rather give Arthur a chance to 'protect' you from me?"

"Good point." She lifted her chin. "I'm ready, then."

The witch gestured to the chairs before the fireplace. "If you would sit with me . . ."

As her heart began to pound in long, fierce beats, Gwen sat down beside her. "How do we start?"

"Like so." The witch touched cool, slender fingertips to Gwen's forehead . . .

*S*he might as well have been in hell.

 Gwen stood on a battlefield surrounded by bloody chaos. All around her, men fought like animals, with swords and spears and axes, hacking and stabbing at one another with a frenzy born of desperate terror. Blood and chunks of meat flew, accompanied by a deafening cacophony: shouts of rage, howls of pain, high-pitched equine squeals. Horses reared and kicked as their riders fought to keep their saddles against clawing enemy hands. A few of the fighters wore the red and gold of Arthur's troops, but in nothing like the numbers she would have expected. Even to her inexperienced eye, they appeared badly outnumbered.

 Frozen like a rabbit by bone-deep, instinctive fear, Gwen stared out over the undulating mass of bodies. Arthur was out there somewhere. She could feel him across the width of the battlefield. And she knew every instant that ticked by carried him that much closer to death.

 Only she could save him.

 Ridiculous, whispered a life spent surrounded by warriors. I'm only a woman. Any man on the field could beat me into the ground.

 No, you can save him, breathed a seductive whisper that sounded like

Nimue. I can give you the power. All you have to do is open yourself to me.

Any priest Gwen knew would have told her that to heed that whisper was to risk her immortal soul. She didn't give a damn. Angel, witch, or devil out of hell, if Nimue could help her save her husband, she'd surrender her soul without a second thought.

"Yes!" Gwen could scarcely hear her own shout over the screams of death and combat. "Do it! Whatever I have, it's yours!"

Then ready yourself, Guinevere Pendragon. It comes.

Across the battlefield, a golden ball of light appeared, streaking toward her, trailing sparks like a comet. Her instinct was to leap aside, but she locked her knees and braced.

The comet of power grew as it arrowed toward her across the heaving battlefield, until it filled her vision with searing afterimages. Her heart thudded in her ears, terror spurring it faster and faster with each breath. Instinct shrieked that the comet would incinerate her like parchment tossed into a fire.

Arthur, she thought, forcing herself to hold her ground. *Arthur, Arthur, Arthur.* The mental chant steadied her, strengthened her. She'd ignore her terror as she'd seen Arthur ignore his own whenever duty demanded it. *Arthur, Arthur, Arthur* . . .

The ball of light filled her vision. She squeezed her tearing eyes shut and screamed, "ARTHUR!"

The power hit.

SIX

Gwen's eyes flew wide at the searing heat and light. Her veins glowed beneath her skin in delicate branching pathways like streams of burning oil. She opened her mouth to scream, but could produce only a rattling wheeze.

Then the pain grew, unbelievably, still worse. Every muscle in her body knotted and jerked as her failing legs dumped her face-first in the battlefield mud. God help me if a horse tramples me.

It was her last coherent thought as the firestorm of pain raged through her. An instant later—or possibly an eternity, she couldn't tell which—the pain was simply gone. Vanished, like a saint's miracle.

She lay in mud that smelled of shit, blood, and worse. The stench alone drove her, reeling, to her feet.

Blinking, dazed, she looked down at what had been one of her favorite gowns, now soaked through and plastered with that stinking mud. Gwen lifted an upper lip in disgust and longed for another gown, one clean and white and smelling of rose-scented soap . . .

Gold sparks spiraled down her body, igniting the filthy gown, which flared blinding bright around her. When the light faded again, she wore cool, clean white silk that smelled of roses.

Gwen stared down at herself in awed astonishment. She'd conjured a new gown with an offhand thought. It wasn't possible . . .

Except it was.

Power. Gwen could feel it now, a boiling cauldron of energy just barely leashed, ready to leap to her bidding. Somehow she knew all she had to do was reach out, and it would be there, eager to serve however she wished.

Power enough to find Arthur. Power enough to save him. Gwen no longer had to wait for some knight to lend her his strength; she could do what she needed herself. She was not helpless.

Not anymore.

"Find him," Gwen breathed, reaching out one hand as she'd seen Nimue do. Golden sparks streamed from her fingertips, pouring across the battlefield, seeking the one man in all these thousands she wanted more than her next breath. Until . . .

"There."

The hill stood across the width of the heaving, bloodthirsty, panicked mob of soldiers. Arthur fought atop it, surrounded by Mordred and a pack of his traitors, who harried the king the way dogs harry an enraged bear. Yet her husband held his own, forcing his attackers back with a sword that flashed and licked like a snake's tongue. His shield swung in great arcs, reverberating in brazen clangs as he deflected swords, spears, and axes with a speed that seemed impossible, his feet so sure and quick in the treacherous mud, he looked more dancer than swordsman.

It should have been impossible to make out so much detail over a distance so great, but that wild, golden power enhanced her senses beyond any human limit.

Magic. Magic she knew she could set loose against Arthur's enemies like a cat among mice, giving them the death they so richly deserved.

Do it. Let it go. Let it slay them. They're traitors against their rightful king. They would murder him. Arthur, who'd bled, fought, and almost died for them in thirty-two battles against Saxons and Picts and his own damned people to buy a little peace for Britain.

She thought of the hip injury that had tormented him for so long.

Remembered all the other wounds, physical and mental, including that haunted darkness she sometimes saw in his velvet eyes.

Slay them all, her own darkness breathed. *Slay them slay them slay them slay them slay them . . .*

She could do it. She could send that raging magic to cleanse the battlefield of life. She could take revenge on these fucking traitors.

But what of our men? Her gaze sought those in Pendragon red and gold, outnumbered and desperate.

They took him from me, too. Their unceasing demands stole him away. Let them die with the rest.

Slay them all. Let the magic kill every bastard one of them. Let it burn the field barren and salt the ground so nothing ever grows again.

For a moment, she hung suspended, balanced on the razor edge of bloodlust . . .

No! Convulsively, Gwen straightened. Arthur would not want this. I do not want this. With an effort, she clamped her will over the raging power so it couldn't escape, couldn't kill.

But that still left her the width of the battlefield from her husband. She had to use the power she'd been given, but carefully, ignoring the seductive, evil whispers in her head.

Gwen's hands shook as she raised them. Hesitated. *Not fire. She didn't need fire. Nor earth, nor water. She didn't want to burn, bury, or drown them. She wanted to push them. Air. I want air. The Romans' fourth element.*

Gwen called the power. It leaped to her will, joyful as a puppy set free on a cold winter's day, all eager energy. Somewhere between that golden reservoir and her fingertips, the magic became wind.

A raging blast slammed into the fighters like a giant's hand, flinging bodies into the air. Terrified screams rang out from those the storm seized and bore off like autumn leaves. More screams sounded as they hit, from both the victims and those they landed on.

Gwen winced. *Too much force.*

But the need to reach Arthur still pricked her like a knight's spurs, so she tried again. This time she went slowly, building a breeze barely strong enough to ruffle a man's hair into a gust that made horses dance in unease. Ears laid flat, they stared at her as if knowing she'd summoned the wind that frightened them.

But it wasn't enough. Gwen needed to make the men move, dammit. She needed them out of her way. The wind picked up strength at her thought, becoming a battering ram that sent men stumbling.

Yes, that's it! That's the right strength.

So with the wind blasting before her, Gwen stepped onto the field. When the thick mud sucked at her sandals, almost pulling them from her feet, she spared a thought to hardening it into a narrow path to Arthur, still battling Mordred in the moon's thin light. *So far away. I need to go faster.*

Urgency gnawed at her, its teeth sharpened by the conviction this was taking too damned long. *If she'd known where he was from the start, she could have . . .*

On the breast of the hill, Arthur swung his great sword at Mordred's head. The traitor flung up his shield. The blade hit with all Arthur's Magus strength behind it . . .

And the sword shattered.

Chunks of steel caught the moonlight as they spun in all directions, leaving Arthur staring in horror at a broken blade barely an inch long.

With a howl of delight, the traitors fell on him, slamming him to the ground. Mordred raised his own sword above the king's head as Arthur fought to free himself.

The blade flashed down . . .

No!" The shrieked protest ringing in her ears, Gwen bolted to her feet, her heart hammering as she stared around wildly. She was in her chamber, Nimue watching her calmly from one of the hearth chairs. Where was the battlefield? More importantly, where was her husband?

"Gwen?" Arthur shouted from the balustrade, accompanied by the sound of running feet.

He's all right. All the strength left Gwen's legs, and she sat down in her chair with a thump.

What just happened? Had it been a dream? But she'd never had a dream so real. The reek of horse shit lingered in her nostrils, though there was no sign of it on her gown or sandals.

"You did well," Nimue told her.

"What?" Gwen stared at her, dazed. "What did I do?"

Arthur burst in, several knights at his heels. "Gwen!" He started to drag her into his arms, only to pause as if afraid he'd crush her. Instead he contented himself with a swift glance the length of her body. "Why did you scream?"

"Sometimes my test can be a bit . . . intense," Nimue observed. "But she acquitted herself well."

Merlin had entered behind Arthur and his knights. "That *is* good news indeed. It simplifies things considerably." Still, he gave Nimue a searching look. "Are you sure?"

"Oh, aye. She . . ." Nimue began.

"Wait," Arthur interrupted, his gaze astonished. "We were scarce outside ten minutes. You tested her in that brief time? And she passed? How?"

He didn't have to sound so bloody suspicious—as if he resented that his own test had involved blades and a brush with death, while hers had scarcely mussed her hair.

Gwen glowered. She'd thought it was real, dammit. She opened her mouth, but Nimue was already putting Arthur in his place. "Time in the realm of the mind is fleet, my king. In those ten minutes, she confronted her worst fear: fighting to save you from your own rebellious subjects. She saw you die. That's why she cried out."

"Wait," Kay interrupted. "Arthur fell, yet you say she passed your test?"

"The test was to determine how she would use vast power in the face of considerable temptation to misuse it," Merlin explained.

"She could have exterminated your friends as well as your enemies," Nimue added. "She could have struck Mordred dead with a lightning bolt from the heavens. She didn't, even when it appeared you were going to die. Which means that if given such power in reality, we can be reasonably sure she won't become a greater threat than whatever she fights. This is not a minor concern. Some are driven mad by gaining magic. They must be put down, much like a frothing dog whose bite kills all he attacks."

Arthur's eyes narrowed with offended temper. "My wife is no dog, witch."

"No, she has a point," Gwen told him thoughtfully. "The power— I have never felt anything like it. It was like drinking lightning, intoxicating, but terrifying, too. The temptation to kill, even our own people . . . I almost lost control." She looked at Nimue. "And you mean to give real magic to me? Are you sure? What if I . . . ?"

The witch smiled. "You will do fine, my dear. I urged your mind to show you the worst of your fears as reality. Another woman might have seen Mordred about to carry out his vicious threats against you, but your concern was for Arthur and his people. Over the years, I've found I learn as much from a female's fears as from the way she faces them. I was pleased with both in your case."

Merlin dropped to one knee before her, his long fingers curled around the Grail. "Would you drink, then, my queen?"

"Gwen . . ." Arthur began, his tone urgent.

She didn't dare let him come up with any clever reasons why this was a bad idea. Gwen took the cup, ignoring the glowing froth riding its surface, and drank the whole thing down like a child taking vile medicine.

At first it was a sweet, fizzing mouthful. She smiled at the sensation of all those countless bubbles simultaneously popping.

An instant later, her throat went white-hot from tongue to belly. A spasm of coughing seized her, each reflexive hack sending another fiery blast through her body. It felt like whatever was in that potion was eating its way through the walls of her stomach and painting her veins with fire.

Dimly, she sensed Arthur's big hands lifting her from her seat, intensely careful as he cradled her. Comforted—*He's safe. His death was only an illusion*—she let herself spin away into the dark.

W hen night fell again, Gwen still slept.
     Arthur balanced a grape between his teeth, concentrating on keeping his fangs from puncturing its thin green skin.

He failed. A blink later, tart juice coated his tongue. His grimace tightened his jaws, driving the fang completely through the grape with a squish.

Fuck. He spat the fruit into his hand and tossed it back into the bowl he'd taken it from. He'd learned he could no longer stomach more than three or four grapes before his body expelled them. Juice, wine, those he could tolerate. Food was problematic. All he wanted was blood.

Preferably Gwen's.

The trick was to ensure he didn't hurt her in the process of drinking it. Grimly, he popped another grape into his mouth and concentrated on not damaging this one.

He knew he could do it; after all, he'd gotten the hang of eggs. True, twenty of them had been crushed in the process, earning Arthur the silent displeasure of Camelot's cook.

The grapes were even more important. Unless he could be sure he wouldn't pierce delicate flesh with his fangs, he didn't dare go anywhere near Gwen.

But what really terrified him was the thought of draining her white again. He knew she'd be stronger thanks to her transformation, but when he remembered the pallor of her skin, the limp body, the closed eyes . . . Arthur shuddered. How could he have treated the woman he loved as food? Not even as cunt, but food? The thought horrified him.

And yet he had to admit it hadn't been the first time his need for her had taken on a very dark cast. When Gwen had urged him to be

rougher, more demanding in his lovemaking, she'd stoked a deeper
urge in him to dominate and control her. He'd restrained that urge,
as he expected any civilized male would. But in the wake of his transformation, it seemed to have strengthened again. Now it felt almost
as powerful as the need for her blood.

His gaze lingered on her face. She looked only slightly older than
she'd appeared the day he'd first seen her seventeen years ago. Her
hair had blazed in the morning sun, her merry laughter ringing as she
pelted one of her sisters with crabapples. The sister—he thought it
was Branwyn—had winged one back. Gwen snatched it out of the air
and bit into it with small white teeth. There'd been such sensuality in
the gesture, he'd sprung a cock-stand on the spot. Feeling eyes on him,
Arthur had whirled, ready to snarl, only to find Gwen's father watching him, a faint smile on his seamed face.

Leodegraunce had had his measure from that moment. Uther had
nothing on that old man in sheer cunning. Gwen's father made Arthur
pay well for what he wanted, seeing to it Gwen got dower lands and
the means to keep them in their marriage contract.

The king hadn't begrudged her one denarius. He hadn't wanted
that laughing girl left impoverished by the vagaries of a queen's fate.
He'd made damned sure she would never suffer for his craving for her.

Until last night anyway. Leodegraunce would have had his head.

Arthur stole a guilty glance at his wife. She lay dressed in a white
gown that made her look like a virgin, a light coverlet folded over her
sweet breasts.

Sometime in the past day, the faint crow's-feet carved into her face
by her years as queen had vanished, so she looked no older than twenty.
He frowned, discovering he missed those delicate lines. They'd recorded
the battles, the losses, the fear and the laughter, the steely will he hadn't
noticed as a nineteen-year-old idiot. Those faint lines had made Gwen
human, rather than the lovely doll he'd imagined her then. He'd had
no idea how lucky he was to get a steel-willed beauty instead. He'd have
broken the doll in a year.

And she made him more than he'd ever been.

Gwen had believed in him, had given him the courage to meet and defeat men stronger and more ruthless than he could ever hope to be.

She often accused him of being overprotective, and he supposed she had a point. Yet the fact was, he protected himself and his kingdom as much as he did her by making sure she was safe.

Gwen saw him as a great king. A hero. He'd had no choice except to become exactly that. For *her*. Not for Britain, not for Uther's soulless memory. For Guinevere Pendragon, queen of his heart.

Jesu, that last thought sounded so sickeningly sweet, like honey candy. And yet that was exactly what she was.

He'd nearly killed her, for he'd been so blinded by hunger and unnatural need, he hadn't even recognized his own wife. He didn't dare let it happen again.

Even at this distance he could smell her, that lovely erotic musk that made him crave sex and blood and woman.

His fangs pricked his lower lip, and he grimaced at the sour flavor of his own blood. It tasted nothing like the sensual richness he could smell wafting from Gwen. It made him want to take her, hold her down and fuck her . . . Which was why he had to get the hell away from her before his self-control shattered. Arthur had come in here to watch her sleep with his bowl of grapes in order to build his willpower so he wouldn't hurt her when she was awake and flirting.

And she would flirt, his fearless Gwen. She'd try to seduce him— not that she'd ever had to try all that hard in the first place. But this time, he could not afford to let her tempt him into bed. Not with these unnatural fangs pricking his lips. Not with his cock like a blade in his breeches.

If it were only sex he craved, he'd indulge her joyfully. She'd wrestle him with her maddeningly luscious body, and he'd flatten her beneath his weight and plunge to the balls as his hungry body demanded.

But that was less than half of what Arthur craved. He also wanted to sink his fangs into the delicate throbbing vein of her throat, taste the blood running bright and luscious just beneath her skin. Her sweet, sweet skin.

What kind of beast was he? How could he think of her in such terms? She was his love, his queen, his heart—the very best of what made him a king.

What she was *not* was food.

"You will not hurt her, my king." Merlin's surprisingly deep voice sounded oddly gentle as he spoke from the chamber doorway. Arthur had locked that door, dammit. "Even if she were no more than one of the ladies of your court, you would not take more than you need. You will certainly not put your wife in danger."

The king didn't dare look at him. He flexed his hand around the hilt of his sword and fought the bloody impulse to draw it. "Get out of my sight if you value your head."

Merlin snorted as he moved into the chamber, an absent wave of his hand closing the door. "I'm almost tempted to let you try. You could use a little humility."

"Get. You. Gone."

"No." Merlin looked at him with those black star-flecked eyes. "Your woman will need your body when she wakes, just as you needed hers. Don't deprive her out of fear."

Arthur's lips peeled off his fangs. "My wife's needs are none of your affair, wizard."

"They are if your fears destroy you, her, and your people." Merlin studied him as if deciding on a new tack. "You may wish to consider a Truebond—a kind of magical link between you. Nimue and I have such a link, and it allows each of us to sense what the other feels and thinks. You'd know if you were drinking too much of her blood, and you'd be able to stop in time."

Arthur looked at him, intrigued out of his rage. "How would we do that?"

"She'd use magic to bind your minds. You'd find it quite useful in everything from ruling to combat. You could consult her without having to speak aloud, or be able to ask her to work spells for you on the battlefield." He paused. "There is, however, one very significant drawback."

"I'm not surprised. I'm not sure I want my wife knowing my every stray thought."

Merlin smiled. "Neither would I. Fortunately, you quickly learn not to project everything you think, any more than you always speak at the top of your lungs. She won't be any more eager to have you know her every thought, either."

Arthur frowned. "Then if not that . . ."

"The real problem is that if something kills one of you, the pain of sharing that death would kill the other."

Arthur stared at him, appalled. "Merlin, I'm a warrior. The probability that I will die in combat . . ."

"You're also a Magus. Killing you is now far more difficult, especially since you can heal virtually any injury short of decapitation or cutting out your heart, simply by shifting to wolf form . . ."

Arthur blinked. "We can do that? You didn't mention this."

Merlin shrugged. "If you but concentrate, picture a wolf in your thoughts, and will yourself to transform . . ."

Before the wizard could finish, the king closed his eyes and thought of the wolves he'd seen over the years, imagining himself changing. Heat exploded over his skin, a sense of bones and muscles twisting, reshaping themselves . . .

When he opened his eyes again, he thought for a moment he'd fallen to the floor, but when he glanced down, he saw a pair of narrow wolf forelegs where his arms should be. A high-pitched canine sound of alarm made his ears twitch, and he looked up.

Merlin gazed down at him, a smile curling his lips. "Very good, sire. Now reverse the process, and you can turn back."

He obeyed. Once he was human again, the wizard continued, "Even if you were hurt so badly you didn't have time to shift, Gwen would sense it and heal your injuries before they posed any danger to her."

Arthur frowned as his instincts growled in rebellion. "Battlefields are no place for women. Particularly not my wife."

Merlin stared at him, his expression first stunned, then appalled, then disgusted. "You're such a brilliant man, I sometimes forget you're also the product of a primitive culture."

Arthur stared back, puzzled by his reaction to an obvious truth. "How is it primitive to wish to spare my wife the blood and terror of war?"

"It's not primitive at all, given females with but a fraction of male strength. But the queen is now stronger than most men . . ."

"What? You didn't mention that." It was comforting to know she could defend herself against attackers, once he taught her how.

Merlin lifted a brow. "I didn't mention it because magic is a far greater advantage than muscle. As you may discover the hard way, if you insist on treating your wife as less than she is."

Stung, Arthur glowered at him. "I never treat Gwen as less than she is."

"I hope that's the case, not just for the sake of your marriage but for your entire species. As it is, I fear you're in for a very unpleasant education."

"You let me worry about that."

"Nothing would please me more. But whatever you decide about the Truebond, I must stress the importance of meeting your wife's needs when she wakes. Don't be fool enough to leave her alone out of some stupid impulse to protect her. The Grail's spell affects not just you, but all your descendants as well, and it's incredibly powerful. It therefore intensifies the body's need for sex, for reproduction. That will be as true for her as it was for you. Don't refuse what she must give you. She is no longer human, Pendragon. If you try to treat her as though she is . . ." His voice dropped to a lethal whisper. ". . . you will rue it. Of that I assure you."

Then the wizard was quite simply gone. Only a few golden sparks remained, floating lazily above his seat.

Arthur turned his gaze to his sleeping wife again. She'd stirred while Merlin had distracted him; the coverlet had fallen to her waist. He could see the elegant rise of her breasts, full and sweet, capped by delicate pink nipples that were clearly visible beneath the gown's diaphanous silk.

God, he wanted to taste those nipples. He wouldn't bite. He only wanted to lick that tempting flesh, discover if it tasted anything like the scent that tormented him from across the room.

It smelled like Gwen. But . . . not. As if Merlin was right, and whatever that potion had done had changed her into something no longer human.

Blinking, he realized he stood over her. A moment ago he'd been sitting all the way across the room. He had no memory of crossing the distance.

It was obvious why he had. The scent of her flooded his nose until he could almost taste her. The lavender from her soap, achingly familiar, blended with the light musk he'd always associated with Gwen. Then there were the new notes in her scent: the copper tang of the blood running beneath her skin, mixed with something else. Something not Gwen that taunted him like sex distilled. It made his fangs ache almost as much as the cock-stand bucking in his britches.

Sweet mother Mary, he had to get away from her. Now. Before he woke to find her truly dead, not simply drained to pallor.

He should go find Merlin and kill the little fuck. Arthur spun on his heel, meaning to seek out his armor, his shield, and his blades . . .

"Arthur?" Gwen's lovely voice sounded throaty.

From sleep, not seduction, he told himself. *Just sleep.* He headed for the door, desperate to escape before his fangs and his dick drove him to something he could never forgive himself for.

"Arthur, I dreamed Mordred killed you."

Devils take him, there were tears in Gwen's voice. Turning back, he spread his arms wide and forced a smile. "I'm well, as you can see. I kicked that bastard's arse two days back."

She frowned at him, troubled and lovely. Saint Sebastian's blood, he'd forgotten how very beautiful she'd been before worry and royalty had aged her. "I saw a battle on a hill. Thousands of men fought. And most of them weren't ours. They followed Mordred, Arthur."

A chill stole over him, but he made himself scoff. "That oath-breaker? Not likely."

"Better an oath-breaker than a blood-drinker."

He stiffened. "Is that what you think me?"

"You know better. In any case, the problem is not what I think, it's what do our people believe? I'm a witch now. The Bible itself says I should not be allowed to live."

"Some priest jealous of your influence might interpret it thus." He bared his teeth, fangs and all. "He'd best not say it in my hearing. I speak Latin as well as any jumped-up peasant in a miter."

"Arthur, you do almost *everything* better than anyone." She gazed at him, her eyes huge in the dim lamplight. Vulnerable and seductive all at once. "Come here, my king. I need you." The way she said "need" made it damned clear what she meant. His cock, which had softened at the talk of priests, hardened like forged steel.

And the scent of her—musk, and heat, and that maddening copper tang. *Gwen. Saints and devils, Gwen . . .*

No. Despite her pleas, despite Merlin's warnings, he knew he didn't dare give in to his clawing sexual hunger. What if he started drinking her blood and couldn't stop? "Gwen, I can't. Percival, Marrok, and Cador rode in while you were sleeping. I sent them off to accompany Mordred to the Channel, to make sure he left the country . . ."

"Yes, I remember." She frowned. "Was there a problem?"

"You might say that," Arthur said grimly. "They were ambushed by a troop of Varn's rebels barely five miles from the Channel. They were so heavily outnumbered, they barely escaped with their lives. Mordred fled with the rebels."

Gwen stared at him, appalled. "Arthur, we have to recapture him. You can't just let him run loose; saints know what he'll do."

"Exactly. I've sent several contingents after him, but nobody's managed to bring him in yet. I'm going to join the search. We've got to find him before he starts gathering more followers for Varn, or that dream of yours could well come true." And dammit, his new fangs made him lisp like a four-year-old.

Her lids dipped over those remarkable eyes. "Come here, Arthur."

He didn't dare. He knew damned well he couldn't make love to her without drinking from that sweet throat. "I can't, Gwen. I almost drained you the last time."

"I was human the last time." The way she said it, like sin and sex given voice. She rose from the bed, as gracefully seductive as Salome.

Get out boy, or you're lost. And she will be, too. "Gwen, I can't let Mordred escape while I dally between your lovely thighs, no matter how I wish to."

Forget the armor. He'd take Gawain, Galahad, and their fastest horses, then send the boy back for his hauberk. He reached for the door, meaning to jerk it open.

"Mordred broke your sword. In my dream, I mean." She stopped there, her heated gaze going lost. "There were dozens of them. The weight of their bodies bore you back into the mud, and Mordred took your head."

"It was only a dream, Gwen." He forced another smile. "You dream of my death before every major battle. I'd worry more if you *didn't* dream I died."

"This was no wife's nightmare." She slumped, sounding defeated and weary, as if she did not expect him to believe her. "This was a witch's vision."

"Mordred is not going to kill me. I'm a Magus now. I could slay

twenty arrogant little shits just like him without breaking a sweat."
And he had to get out of here before he lost what passed for his mind.

"Arthur, please." Jerking her gown off over her head, she threw it
to the floor like a rag. "I *need* you."

SEVEN

Gwen stared at Arthur, impossibly lovely breasts heaving, her bright hair caressing bare, silken shoulders. Her eyes looked gemstone-brilliant, lips parted and pink. Stiff nipples blushed a shade darker than her mouth, and the blond triangle of her maiden hair looked damp from her need.

God's teeth, she was wet.

Every breath Arthur took seemed to wrap the raw temptation of her scent around his cock. He wanted to swirl his tongue through her thick cream, drink it down like honey mead. He wanted to pump his fingers in her tight, tight sex.

And her arse. Not just with his fingers, either. They'd joked about anal sex for years, taking turns teasing one another with the idea of his sodomizing her. But now the thought of penetrating her there made Arthur hard as a sword blade. What's more, judging by the references she'd made to it, she evidently loved the idea just as much.

Hot as she was, she'd spread her cheeks for him, let him oil her tender, virgin channel and drive his cock in to the balls. Fuck her slowly, carefully, as that tiny opening stretched wide around his ravenous shaft. He'd tease her clit and her nipples to build her hunger, enhancing the pleasure-pain of his possession. While he pumped and pumped until he came in roaring gouts . . .

His hands shook.

Gwen moved toward him slowly, the way a woman would approach a half-wild stallion she feared might bolt. "Saints, I'm hot." She breathed the words so softly, he doubted he could have heard had he not been what he was now. "I have never been so hot for you, Arthur." Her smile flashed. "And you've made me insane with yearning so many times." The smile vanished. "But not like this. I am fair mad for you, my love. Don't leave me aching."

The quiver ran from his head to his heels, shaking him like a fever. "I'd kill you, Gwen."

"Arthur, you didn't kill me when you woke unable to speak in more than growls that terrified your own knights." She laid one delicate hand over his desperately pounding heart. "The only word you could speak to me was 'mine.' And you were right. I am yours, and no other's. I'm in no danger from you, my heart. No matter how you growl and flash your fangs, you will do me no harm."

He wanted to grab her, lift her high, and bury those fangs in the velvety column of her throat. Wanted to fuck her hard while he drank, first in her virginal arse and then in her cream-slick pussy. He burned to take her in every way he knew, then invent a few more and have her in those.

Arthur fought himself with all the strength of will more than two decades as king had taught him. It was far too near a thing. "Get away from me, Gwen."

"Don't leave me, Arthur." Despair filled his wife's sapphire eyes. "*I saw him kill you.*"

"Mordred couldn't even beat me when I was nothing more than human," he told her roughly. "He doesn't have a prayer against me now."

"He will." Gwen's voice shook with the force of her fear. "I know what I saw."

"You had a nightmare."

"I *lived* it, damn your arrogant male stupidity!" Her eyes blazed with fury now.

Arthur stared down at her, anger drowning his prowling need. "You only dreamed. That's all. I'll bring the bastard's head back and prove it to you."

"Arthur!"

He slammed out of the room before she could stop him with her exquisite nudity and intoxicating scent. Using the time to let his cock-stand subside, he stalked along the balustrade to the rooms of the unmarried knights. A shout brought Galahad and Gawain from their respective chambers.

"Yes, sire?" Galahad asked. His voice and face were so changed, Arthur had to look twice to be sure who it was. Unlike the rest of them, the Grail had left Lancelot's son looking older than his eighteen years. Which made sense, Arthur supposed. If Galahad had ended up that much younger, he'd be in swaddling clothes.

"Pack your gear, gentlemen," Arthur told the pair. "We're going after Mordred. Galahad, get my saddlebags and armor. Gawain and I will ready the horses."

Normally Arthur's squire would have packed for him, but he didn't trust the lad to keep his hands off Gwen in her current mood.

Gwen, pale and perfect, dressed in nothing but blond curls glowing gold in the soft lamplight . . . She'd never cuckold him, not his Gwen, just as Galahad would never lift a greedy hand against his queen.

Not even when she smelled so intriguingly like sex and blood and sin.

Gwen stared at the closed door and shook. She thought of dragging Arthur back into the room with chains of magic, binding him so she could fuck that beefy cock until her desperate need was sated. Until his massive body lay helpless on the white sheets.

So helpless he actually listened to her about her visions about Mordred instead of dismissing them out of hand.

He was her king. He held her heart. Yet at the moment, it was all she could do not to box his regal ears.

And he'd stormed out without his hauberk, helm, or shield. Ass. Naked, she stomped around their quarters, gathering his clothes and packing them into his saddlebags.

Only to stop dead with a frown, remembering Nimue's warning about the danger of sunlight. An idea flashed into her mind—a solution to the problem with the added benefit of giving her a way to rechannel her vivid lust. *Assuming I can actually do it, of course.* She hesitated, remembering the way she'd used her magic in that test of Nimue's. If it works the same way . . . Picturing what she wanted, she began to conjure, channeling the desperate need she felt into magic . . .

Sure enough, a moment later a large leather bag lay on the floor. Picking up Arthur's sword, the queen thrust the big weapon at the bag. Its point sank into the leather as if slicing into mutton. Curling a lip in disgust, she cast a spell on the bag she'd created.

Two attempts later, the leather blocked her hardest thrust.

Taking a deep breath, Gwen gathered her magic and gestured. A dozen cylindrical bags just like it appeared in a pile on the floor. Lifting one, she found it felt as soft and supple as anything a skilled tanner could have produced, yet her magic had made the bags impenetrable even to the sharpest blades.

Once Arthur and his knights laced themselves into the bags for the day, they'd be as safe from both sun and human enemies as if they slept between the foot-thick walls of Camelot. Yet the empty bags could be rolled up until they took up less room than a bedroll.

Magic, damn Arthur's stubbornness, could be useful.

After tying the bags into neat bundles, Gwen went to work packing the rest of the king's gear. Removing the hauberk, shield, and helm from the carved chest at the foot of the bed, she laid a spell of protection on them and packed them into his saddlebags.

As she dropped them on the bed to wait for his squire, she realized Merlin's spell had made her stronger. Much stronger. Prior to her transformation, Gwen would have been hard-pressed to even lift his mail. Now it seemed to weigh no more than a silk shift.

And that scent. Jesu, Mary, and all the saints, that hot male Arthur scent seemed to stroke her right between her nether lips, sending teasing, insubstantial fingers to brush her stone-hard clit.

The maddening frustration of it sparked her temper like steel to flint. Why had he refused her? He had never refused her, not in all the years of their marriage. Not in the midst of diplomacy with some stubborn rebel lord, not even still smelling of smoke, blood, and combat. Arthur had ever been ready to meet her passion with his own. Especially since his blazed even hotter.

Yet tonight, he'd turned away. Had shown all the signs of a man who wanted to get as far from his randy wife as fast as his horse could take him.

Perhaps he does need to find Mordred, but right now? Right at the moment I need him most?

Hungry claws of need raked her nipples, clit, and every inch between. Blood of the saints, she wanted to fuck her husband. She'd craved his touch many times, often fantasized about making love to him whenever war and duty separated them. Every time she'd grown especially needy, Gwen usually found an excuse to ride wherever he was for an amorous little visit. He'd always welcomed her with slow kisses and slower thrusts that drove her to the apex of pleasure.

Now she remembered all those hot trysts and felt heat flash over her desperately needy body. She wanted to throw herself down on the bed, fling her legs wide, and masturbate to a blistering climax. It wouldn't take longer than three or four frantic minutes.

But what she needed was Arthur.

Hefting the saddlebags in either hand, Gwen dropped them by the fireplace. Arthur's squire would no doubt show up looking for them any moment now.

Heat streamed from one bare nipple. She looked down to find her hand absently stroking and tugging the aching peak. With an effort, Gwen pulled her fingers away, though she wasn't sure why she bothered. Why not pleasure herself when her husband had left her aching?

To hell with it. Five minutes should be more than enough time to climax. Then at least she'd be able to sleep.

Likely only to dream of Arthur's death at the hands of that wretched boy. Again. How many times had it been now? She'd lost count.

Gwen cursed as she rarely did, vicious, rolling invective learned from years among warriors. Sliding a hand between her aching thighs, she plunged two fingers deep. Wet. She was so very wet. Dropping onto the bed, she began to pump furiously, her free hand twisting her nipple almost viciously.

Two minutes later, Gwen trembled on the verge of coming, when knuckles rapped the door. "My queen?" a deep male's voice called. "The king sent me to pack his equipment. We ride out as soon as I have the pack horses readied."

The orgasm vanished like candle smoke in a draft. Gwen wasn't sure whether to curse or cry amid her body's frustrated howls.

Another short rap. "My queen?"

Tell Arthur to muster the balls to come for his own bloody gear. Instead she sighed and rolled out of bed, dressing herself with a quick conjuration. Decent again, she opened the door.

The man who stood on the other side was big, broad, and powerfully built, with long dark hair and vividly green eyes.

And she'd never seen him in her life.

Considering Gwen knew every man in Arthur's service, that was not good at all. *Mordred has sent an assassin!*

Before she could either fry him with a spell or slam the door in his face and scream for Arthur, the man's eyes widened. "My queen, it's me—it's Galahad!"

Gwen gave him a confused blink. "What?" Now that she looked at him, he bore enough resemblance to Lancelot to be the champion's brother. He was definitely no longer a youth, being taller by inches and at least two or three stone heavier than he'd been the day before. "The Grail made Arthur younger." She stepped back to let him enter. "How did you end up aging?"

He shrugged those massive shoulders. "Merlin told me the spell determines what your ideal age is for peak strength and speed, and remakes you accordingly." Giving her a smile, the big man stepped inside. "If you're older than that, you get younger. If you're younger, you age. And you apparently gain the muscle to match in either case." His smile grew into a grin, and Gwen suddenly saw the eighteen-year-old he was. "The girls do seem to like it."

She laughed. "Best watch your step, lad, or you'll find yourself married to one of your flirtations before you can blink. As to Arthur's gear . . ." She gestured toward the pile on the bed. ". . . It's ready to go."

"Oh, thank you, my queen." Galahad sounded surprised. Arthur had likely warned him her temper was so foul, he'd have to pack while she pitched crockery at his head.

"By the way, I conjured bags you can sleep in during the day. Take the ones you need, and I'll give the rest to whomever else Merlin chooses."

Galahad's eyes widened as he stared at the pile by the hearth. "You made those, my queen? With magic?"

"Yes. Not only will they protect you from sunlight, but they'll block sword strokes better than armor as well." At his questioning glance, she explained, "I tested them with Arthur's blade myself."

"Thank you, my queen. They should be quite helpful." Giving her a grateful smile, he grabbed three of the bags, then collected the packed saddlebags from the bed.

Gwen watched him, her attention reluctantly caught. Galahad wore riding leathers that looked vaguely familiar; she suspected they belonged to his father. Probably nothing the boy owned fit anymore. As he bent to pick up the bags, muscle leaped and worked in his powerful upper arms. His shoulders looked impossibly wide, especially compared to his narrow, muscular flanks.

Lust torched her like a flame running from her juicing pussy to her stone-hard nipples. She gasped before she could swallow the sound.

Galahad turned, the heavy saddlebags dangling negligently from his big hands. His gaze met hers.

They both froze.

The knight inhaled sharply at whatever he saw in her face. His green eyes widened as the muscle she'd been ogling went rigid across his shoulders and down his arms. His nostrils flared as if he scented her.

He likely had, being a Magus now.

An image flashed through her brain—Galahad's newly brawny arms around her, his mouth on her throat, suckling . . .

Mortified, guilty heat flooded Gwen's face.

As if he'd somehow shared that incendiary mental image, Galahad jerked his eyes from her, blushing like a maiden. Without another word, he exited the chamber with leggy, hasty strides, both hands full of bags.

Shame hit Gwen in an acid bath of guilt and mortification. True, it hadn't been the first time she'd noticed one of Arthur's knights. They were all big and very male, and she was only human.

But to feel such a thing for Galahad, of all people . . . No matter what he looked like now, he was still a boy beneath it. One who'd almost died saving Arthur's life, to boot; he'd leaped between his king and an assassin's arrow and had damned near bled to death for his trouble. It had been all Morgana could do to save him. When he'd survived, Arthur had knighted him and made him the twelfth member of the Round Table.

Which was why lusting for him was so very wrong. If it had been Lancelot or Gawain, that would have been bad enough, but Galahad? He was probably still a virgin, for Mary's sweet sake.

After she went to confession in the morning, Father Jacob wouldn't be able to meet Gwen's eyes for a month. She'd still be on her knees in the chapel when Arthur got back.

If he gets back.

If Galahad tells Arthur . . . Grinding her teeth, Gwen splashed her face with lukewarm water from the pitcher her maid left for her every night. She found the roughest rag in the clothes chest and used it to scrub her randy sex until the last vestige of lust was gone.

She didn't dare touch her nipples.

The scraping cloth did the trick, dousing her desire like a lit candle left on a windowsill at the height of a thunderstorm.

The death of that embarrassing need left her brain able to function again. Galahad wouldn't tell Arthur, because that would never occur to him. Instead, he'd slink around the fortress for the next month, mentally scourging himself for his sin.

And it was all Gwen's fault. Arthur had never lifted a hand to her in all their years of marriage, but he'd paddle her arse bright red for weighing Galahad's boyish soul with such guilt.

The thought triggered a memory of the night Arthur woke, when he'd simply overpowered her in that deliciously erotic way. All the need she'd felt, the inarticulate desire that he'd show that part of him—the instinct to dominate he'd always controlled so carefully. It was as if his lust for her blood fed that sensual darkness she'd always sensed in him—along with her own hunger for his domination. A hunger so intense that even as guilt tormented her about her reaction to Galahad, she found something wickedly exciting about the idea of Arthur giving her that paddling . . .

Why the hell had he left her like this—so desperate with need that even a boy tempted her? She had all but begged him not to abandon her. *And that matters not at all. If I sin, the fault is mine.*

Flinging a cloak around her shoulders, Gwen stalked from the chamber. She'd spend the rest of the night prostrate before the altar in Camelot's chapel. A few hours shivering on chilly stone would cool her lust and remind her of her marriage vows. She'd pray to the Blessed Virgin for strength to battle both her body and her nightmares of her husband's death.

The balustrade was dark and cool enough to drain the lingering heat from her cheeks. It was late, and the fortress was still, dark, and quiet as it so rarely was. All the servants were likely abed. As for Arthur and his new Magus knights, they were no doubt already off on Mordred's trail.

Remembering her vision, Gwen frowned. Had it been no more than a nightmare, as Arthur insisted? After all, the enemy forces' sheer numbers in the dream suggested a full-fledged rebellion. Either the battle she'd seen was months away, or it wasn't precognitive at all. *Saints, I hope not.* But no. Her heart sank as the certainty rang in her like the tolling of cathedral bells: she had seen the future, and unless she somehow got Arthur to believe her, he was a dead man.

Her shoulders slumped, and she slowed her furious strides toward the chapel. *What does a moment's lust matter compared to Arthur's death? Even if I did bed one of his knights, it would at least get his attention . . .*

Oh aye, I'd have his full attention—while he killed me and whatever poor bastard I'd committed adultery with.

Besides, the bitter truth was that she'd never wanted anyone but Arthur. Not since she'd watched him ride into her father's fortress at the head of his army, a young god with a body scarred and hard from five years of war, his dark gaze gleaming with fierce intelligence.

It was only when he looked at her that he'd appeared anything like nineteen. Tough as he was, he'd seemed dazzled, as if Gwen were far more beautiful than she'd known herself to be.

There were times even now when he looked at her just that way. As if her beauty was still fresh instead of worn by almost two decades of war, contentious peace, miscarried babies, and a stepson turned viper.

Gwen thought of Arthur's laughter, of his deep voice barking commands, of the hot temper that secretly aroused her even when it was directed at her. Sometimes the sex was at its most perversely delicious when Arthur was in one of his rages. How could any other man compete with that, even a Knight of the Round Table?

She loved Arthur. Man, king, or Magus, it didn't matter. He held her heart and always would, even if her body did give another man its fleeting attention.

Mordred was not going to kill him, vision be damned. If Gwen had to take up armor, shield, and sword herself, she'd see her husband safe.

A groan rang along the balustrade, followed by the slam of a heavy body hitting wood and a woman's cry of fear. The queen went still, listening. Another boom and rattle, another cry, definitely female.

It came from the bachelor wing, where the knights had their chambers. Gwen broke into a run toward the sound.

A red-haired girl sped along the passageway toward her, her lamp swinging in dizzy, panicked arcs. Her eyes looked huge in a paper-white face.

"Yveri." Gwen caught the servant's shoulder before she could fly past. The girl winced at her strength and teetered to a stop. "What happened? I heard someone cry out. Are you hurt?"

"No, my queen." A trace of shame darted through Yveri's blue eyes, followed by a kind of sullen defiance. "Not yet anyway. Though I would be, right enough, if I stayed in there with him."

"Who?"

Again that mix of fear and resentment. "Lord Lancelot, that's who. They told me he'd need blood when he woke. I thought t'would be no more than a nip, p'haps a bit of bouncin' on the sheets—begging your pardon, my queen." She bobbed a quick, apologetic curtsy. "They didn't tell me he'd be a bloody ruttin' beast with teeth like a boar hound. I'll serve you willingly, but I'll not die in sin with some hell-spawned devil."

Sympathy fleeing at the venom in the servant's tone, Gwen gave her an icy glower. "You forget yourself, girl. Lord Lancelot is a Knight of the Round Table who has saved my life more times than I can count."

"Yes, well, now that wizard and his cursed cup have made a beast of him."

The queen's temper exploded into a fine Pendragon rage that would have done her husband proud. "He is no beast! Get your things and get you from Camelot. And if I hear of you spreading such malice, I'll have you whipped."

The servant sneered. "Suits me. I'd not stain my soul in this den o' sin any longer."

She flounced away just in time. Gwen had never struck a servant in her life, but she was sorely tempted to fetch Yveri a slap that would make the girl's ears ring for a week.

As for Lancelot . . . Another thud shook the door of his chambers until it rattled in its frame. Fortunately, the door was bolted, the key still protruding from its lock.

They were lucky Lance hadn't already broken it down. Another blow or two like that one, and it would fly right off its hinges.

But I can stop it, a seductive voice whispered in Gwen's mind. *I can use magic to bind him, then feed him enough of my blood to bring him back to himself.*

She could feel the power like a bonfire burning, just waiting to leap to her will. It was intoxicating, as if she could do anything. As if she could contain any man's strength, even that of a Knight of the Round Table.

Even a Magus's.

Still, it might be wise to practice the use of that magic on Lancelot; her husband had a way of turning the tables on his opponents. Though Gwen had never considered herself Arthur's "opponent"; husband or not, he was still her king.

Which didn't mean he was always right. An image flashed through her head: Mordred, sword lifted over Arthur and his broken blade . . .

She'd do whatever it took to keep that vision from coming true, even if she had to make Arthur listen. If she could use her power to force his champion to submit, that would certainly be a good start.

Gwen moved to the door and leaned to speak through it. "Lord Lancelot? It's Guinevere. I'm coming in." Her heart began to thunder, but she squared her shoulders, threw out a hand, and sent a stream of power at the door.

It flew open and hit the wall with a reverberating boom that made Gwen jump. Recovering quickly—she'd found appearing confident a vital weapon when dealing with arrogant men—Gwen strode into the chamber and gestured the door closed. This time it obeyed far more quietly.

She gave it a satisfied smile, and turned . . .

To find Lance looming before her, stark naked, fangs long and white in his smile. A smile that looked more than a little evil.

So did his erection, which was every bit as impressive as Arthur's.

He didn't even look like the man she knew. Not only had the strands of gray vanished from his hair, but his face also looked sharper, more animal. And it wasn't just the fangs she could see in his hungry, too-male smile.

He reached for her . . .

"Lord Lancelot, you forget yourself!" Gwen snapped with such ice in her voice, it brought him up short, his feral expression dissolving into confusion. Seizing the opportunity, she sent a ribbon of magic out to wrap around his powerful arms, lashing them tight to his sides.

Saints and devils, the man was huge. He was taller than Arthur by two inches or more, though she'd rarely noticed, given the king's way of taking over any space he occupied.

Cheeks blazing at Lance's intimidating nudity, Gwen struggled to keep her gaze from dropping below his waist. Unfortunately, that left her nowhere to look but his furious eyes as he snarled and fought her power. Unlike Arthur, he didn't appear to know her at all.

And God's teeth, he was strong. His big body surged against his magical restraints, on the verge of breaking free. *I should have conjured chains.*

Too late now. If she diverted her attention to creating something more substantial, he'd escape for sure. As it was, he fought her like a trapped wolf. With the way his arms were pinned, that made the thrust of his cock even more menacing.

Staring at him in fascination, Gwen realized he wasn't built precisely like Arthur. His greater height made him appear leaner, though the muscle of his big body was just as thick and beautifully sculpted, from massive shoulders to brawny thighs to big bare feet. Her gaze lingered on the straining V of his torso as he fought his magical bonds, only to drift back down to that forbidden erection. Was he bigger than Arthur there, too?

Traitorous thought.

No, she decided a moment later. He was just very aroused and very, very angry. Not to mention hungry, judging from the length of his fangs. Gwen had intended to give him her wrist, but in his current mood, she was afraid he'd bite her hand off.

And wouldn't that be tough to explain to Arthur?

This had been a colossal mistake—one of her worst ever, in fact. She needed to get out of here, lock the door again, and find some witch who wasn't married to Arthur Pendragon to feed his best friend.

Instead she hesitated, her gaze helplessly tracing all that long, brawny muscularity one more time. Her own frustrated body clamored. *Surely it won't hurt anything just to touch him? Maybe it would even calm him down. Arthur would understand.*

Like hell.

Before she could flee the room, Lance's back arched as he grunted in agony, and slumped in his bonds.

Gwen gaped at his limp, motionless form. *Oh God, did I hurt him?* Had she used more force than she'd thought and crushed his bound arms? Had she mistaken cries of pain for lust?

Horror sent her jolting forward. Lance had always been her most loyal supporter, second only to Arthur himself. If she'd hurt him . . . Worried, frantic, she lowered him to the floor and dissolved his magical bonds . . .

And thought, *I'm an idiot*, about half a second too late.

EIGHT

Lancelot tore free of her magic and pounced on Gwen like a wolf on a lamb. His arms clamped around her as the room wheeled dizzily before her back hit the knight's narrow bed.

Frantic, she reached for her magic, meaning to blast him across the room, Arthur's best friend or not.

Long fingers curled around her jaw without exerting pressure, though the threat was definitely there. His eyes blazed red down at her. "Don't." If a lion had been capable of speech, it would have sounded just like that. He leaned lower until his eyes were barely three burning inches from her own. "Mine."

"No," she corrected frantically. "Arthur's. King Arthur's." *Who will kill us both—if I live.*

Rage blazed up into his savage gaze. "Mine now."

Gwen's heart sank. She could tell from the animal gleam in Lancelot's eyes that not only did he not recognize her, he had no idea who Arthur was, either.

Again, she considered blasting him. Or at least, blowing him across the room. But that big hand still gripped her jaw, and she knew if he chose, he could crush it, perhaps even break her neck.

"Don't hurt me." The words emerged without her conscious intent, followed instantly by a hot wave of shame. She'd never begged anyone for anything. Well, except for Arthur, and her pleas then could be summarized by the word "more."

"Won't. Hurt." He paused, looking frustrated, then managed, "If you don't fight."

I'm the least of your worries, Gwen thought. *Arthur is going to kill us both.*

Lancelot shoved his face against her throat. He inhaled hard, deeply, like a starving man in the kitchen on feast day. With a low growl, he closed his mouth over her carotid. His lips felt like warm velvet on her skin, brushing over the pulsing vein. He purred in pleasure and bit. Gwen cried out at the sharp pain, but as he drank, the sensation changed, going hot, arousing, as if he were suckling her nipples instead. Simultaneously, he began caressing her breasts, milking both tight tips with twisting tugs. Gwen panted, eyes closing, as the desire that had been simmering in her blood since she'd awoken from the Grail sleep burst into full boil. Wrong, she thought. *This is wrong!*

And yet she couldn't seem to do anything about it. The need she felt made it impossible to concentrate enough to summon her magic.

Lancelot rumbled in satisfaction and reached down to pull up her skirt and palm her sex, stroking her there as if she were a cat. Her hips rolled. Even as she struggled to control her growing desire, her body readied itself, thighs loosening, sex swelling and flooding with thick cream. The hunger was so intense, so stark, that she felt as if she were skidding out of control, with no way to keep herself from plunging over the edge.

Still feeding, the knight slid one finger into her sex. Stroking deep, he purred against her skin at her slick heat. Carefully, he withdrew his fangs so he could lift his head and stare down into her face, triumph in his amber eyes.

Lance didn't look at her as he always had, with that respectful courtier's distance, that loyal knight's attention. He looked at her as if she was something delicious, and he was starving.

No, more than that. As if she were prey, and he, the ravenous wolf who'd caught her—and now was playing with her before his feast.

And why in the name of all the saints do I find that thought arousing? Gwen stared up at him, feeling wet inner muscles burn and flex shamefully.

Lance's fingers curled around her jaw even as his free hand probed her swollen sex. "Mmmmm. Yesssss. Ready . . ."

"Stop!" she gasped.

"No." His eyes narrowing in the dim light of the room's single oil lamp, he rolled on top of her. "Ready to be fucked." He rolled his hips, pressing that heavy erection against her belly. It felt so damned tempting. He'd fill her so full, finally satisfy the need that had been clawing at her since she'd opened her eyes earlier tonight. Since Arthur had denied her, had rejected her to go chasing after Mordred.

I've got to stop him. But she couldn't think how, couldn't seem to muster the will for magic, not with her blood boiling like a dragon's breath with frustrated need.

The lamp behind him painted golden highlights on his dark hair and broad shoulders, the brawny arms that rippled as he stroked her sensitive flesh. *Beautiful,* she thought, dazed. *He's so beautiful . . . But he's not my husband. He's not . . .* She closed her eyes, trying to fight the ripping hunger even as Lancelot worked to build it with his big hands and clever mouth. *I can't. I can't, I . . .*

But it felt so *good.* The warm hands that tugged her hard and aching nipples, the thick cock pressing against her belly . . . All those delicious sensations strengthened her need, driving it higher and higher. When she opened her eyes again, looked up at the silhouetted figure looming over her, guilt and Grail-born desire made it seem she looked into the face of a different dark-haired man. Made her think she recognized the touch of those skillful hands, the stroke of his soft lips, the arousing rake of his teeth, and the suckling swirl of his tongue.

The entire rigid length of Arthur's cock slid inside her in one delicious stroke. The heat in her exploded into a roaring conflagration as he began to thrust. He ground in hard, filling her so completely, there was room for nothing else but pleasure. Not thought. Not conscience. Just deep, rolling pulses building toward ecstasy. Her mind went white. Mindless, lost, she hooked her calves over her lover's arse, spreading herself wider. His heavy body rocked hers, each stroke a knifing pleasure.

Gwen writhed, feeling a climax gathering, her sex swelling tight around the thick length. "Arthur," she moaned in shuddering delight. "Jesu, Arthur!"

He broke rhythm, hesitating in the midst of a stroke, as if reacting to the sound of a name that wasn't his . . .

This isn't Arthur.

Cold horror snuffed Gwen's building climax. Her mind registered that Lancelot's teeth were no longer locked in her throat, and he no longer gripped her jaw. He'd ceased holding her down, instead bracing his hands on either side of her shoulders as his hips pumped. His fangs gleaned in the lamplight as he growled again.

This was her chance.

Magic blasted out of Gwen in a furious wave of gold that picked him up and swept him off her body, carried him across the room, and slammed him into the wall with a thud.

Stunned, he went limp.

Her outstretched fingers curled into a fist. Chains wrapped around him, solid steel links this time, coiling tight around arms and legs until he couldn't even twitch.

Pulling down her skirts, Gwen rolled off the bed and stalked over to him. Lance shook his head like a man who had suffered a hard blow to the skull. Which he likely had, given the way she'd flung him against the wall.

Registering that he was no longer riding Gwen like a tavern wench, he snarled in frustrated rage. "Let go!"

"Silence," she snapped. "Or I'll walk out of here, seal that door, and leave you to starve." At the moment, she was furious enough to do it.

Surprisingly he subsided, his lips closing over those threatening fangs. Something more human, more aware, flashed in his eyes.

Good.

"Now, listen," Gwen snarled. "You and I have just thoroughly wrecked our lives, but it's not your fault. I'm the one who is at least nominally sane here, so I'm the one who must save us." Though it wasn't at all clear they could be saved.

She studied him. At least that distracting cock-stand had subsided. "Tell me you didn't come."

He blinked, obviously having no idea what she meant, much less the implications of fathering a bastard on the wife of Arthur Pendragon.

Quit panicking, Gwen. Solve this problem one step at a time. Oddly, the advice sounded like Arthur's voice. Probably because he'd uttered it during various other crises. Not that anything had ever been this incredibly, mortally bad . . .

"Well, the first problem is that you're still not you," Gwen told Lance, "which means you need blood. And since the last thing we need is a witness, I can't call in some other woman to give it to you."

He growled and bucked, rattling the chains alarmingly.

"Stop that!"

Surprisingly, he obeyed.

"Yes, you'd better look wary," Gwen snapped. "I could conjure a sword as easily as those chains. I could end you, Sir Knight."

Unfortunately, this mess was more her fault than his. She was the great fool who'd walked in that door. *Thus hurtling both of us into adultery and treason.* Drawing her belt knife, Gwen pressed the blade to her left wrist.

"No. Do not!" He began to struggle again, his expression alarmed.

Well, he grasped that concept at least.

"I'm not going to kill myself, Lance." *Not that the thought doesn't have merit. What's one more mortal sin, if it means I wouldn't have to face Arthur?* Ignoring that lethal temptation, she glared the king's champion into stillness. "I'm going to give you my wrist, but if you hurt me, I swear I'm going to stick this blade between your ribs."

She made the cut in one stinging swipe. Red blood welled as she stepped quickly up to Lancelot and pressed her bleeding wrist to his lips, resting the point of the knife over his heart as she did so. "Now drink—but if you move anything except your mouth, you will not enjoy the consequences."

Lance hesitated, glowering at her, before his mouth finally closed over the cut. He began to swallow, and his gaze went hot again with sensual bliss.

Something deep within her coiled and heated again. Gwen thrust the rising desire down again. She had more important problems, like keeping Arthur from killing his dearest friend.

And making sure that friend came back to himself.

Grimly, Gwen fought to ignore both the champion's feral gaze and the erotic, pulling sting of his mouth at her wrist. The effort grew much easier when she imagined her husband's reaction.

There was no doubt in her mind that Arthur loved her—and Lance, too, for that matter. But they'd also put the king in a completely untenable position. Cuckolding any man was the ultimate humiliation, but to cuckold the High King of Britain? How could he rule with the whole world snickering at him? He'd have to kill Gwen and Lance even if he weren't insanely furious. A dead queen and champion weren't the sort of thing anyone snickered at.

Shocked silence—and more than a little fear—was an infinitely preferable reaction from the standpoint of discouraging potential rebellion. Especially if Arthur and his men failed to find Mordred.

God's teeth, look at the weapon I've just handed the little bastard. And think of what he could do with it.

It was enough to make her want to plunge the knife into Lance's ribs herself—and then into her own.

An idea with a certain merit. The thought blew into her brain like a cold wind. *It spares Arthur the ugly necessity of executing us.*

He'd think Gwen had killed Lance for raping her . . . And that would not do. The knight may have tricked her and taken advantage of her body's helpless lust, but it hadn't been rape. She wasn't even sure it had been Lance who'd done the tricking.

Her attention drifted to the way his mouth drew on her wrist, the gentle suction. The movement of his lips felt like the stroke of silk over her skin, so incredibly erotic . . .

But he's not Arthur.

With a gasp, she jerked her arm away. Lance snarled at her, his handsome face going as fierce as a frustrated wolf's.

"Sir Lancelot!" Gwen snapped.

His icy glare didn't waver.

His mind has not yet returned. Which meant she couldn't stop, or this whole hideous incident would be futile. So would letting him drink from her if it meant that Arthur executed him the moment the king returned to Camelot.

She had to come up with an explanation that shifted the blame entirely to her own shoulders.

What's more, *Lancelot* had to believe it—and be furious enough not to later lie and take the blame for everything, if only to spare his friend the pain of Gwen's betrayal.

For there *would* be pain, and it *was* a betrayal.

She winced, imagining Arthur's reaction. He'd be devastated, not to mention utterly enraged. *Maybe it would be better to tell him the truth.* Neither of them had intentionally betrayed him . . .

"So it was an accident?" Gwen could almost hear Arthur's sarcastic drawl. *"Did you trip and fall on his dick?"*

Except he'd probably sound far more murderous. Gwen was his

queen; her betrayal was undeniably the worst. Yet Lancelot obviously hadn't been taken against his will, or sex wouldn't have been possible.

Perhaps she could use a spell to make Lance forget any of it had ever happened. Then she could just keep her own mouth shut.

Gwen stared at her captive. He glared back, hungry and resentful in his magical chains. "Lancelot," she breathed, and sent a gentle tendril of magic questing out to curl around his head.

He snarled and started fighting, his fury a red-hot barrier that sent pain screaming through her brain. She kept trying anyway.

Hungry. He's so very hungry. So very desperate.

Gwen blinked and found that without even knowing it, she'd stepped against his chained body and pressed her bloody wrist to his mouth again. The painful need abated, his rage fading as he began sucking in furious pulls, as if he feared she'd take her wrist away again.

It feels so . . . good. Her nipples hardened as hot cream flooded her sex. Her arousal began to build again.

What would it be like if Arthur took her wrist like this, fucking her while he drank?

It had felt so shamefully delicious when Lance did it in the fleeting moments before she'd realized the black sin they were committing . . .

I will not think about that. It's bad enough as it is.

Could she alter Lance's memories of what had happened? According to Nimue, it was possible to touch another's mind in this Truebond she'd mentioned. If Gwen could touch Lancelot's thoughts the same way, could she make him recall something different?

And is doing so an utter betrayal of both men?

Probably.

Unfortunately, Gwen had no choice. She had to come up with an explanation Arthur would believe that did not leave Lancelot culpable. Perhaps she could use her powers to *make* Arthur believe. But that would definitely be a betrayal of her husband. Indeed, it was outright treason.

As Lance drank, she worried at the problem, until finally her mind began to float. It was only when dark spots started dancing before her eyes that she realized she was about to faint. A moment later she felt the jolting impact of her knees hitting the stone floor, the fall pulling her wrist from Lancelot's mouth.

The black spots expanded until her vision went completely dark.

A voice emerged from a buzzing gray fog: "... Queen Guinevere? Guinevere?" The voice's tone slid from urgency to outright panic. "Gwen!"

"Lance?" Her voice rasped. She swallowed and licked her dry lips. "Lancelot?"

"Did I hurt you?" He sounded almost ... frightened? "What happened? Why am I chained and naked? Your majesty, did I ..." He broke off. "Did I hurt you?" *Did I rape you?* He didn't quite say the words, but she could hear the panicky question in his voice.

"No," Gwen managed, the reply automatic even though she was barely conscious. Lancelot wasn't capable of such a betrayal.

"Then why am I chained? I remember ..." He broke off, true horror dawning on his face.

Oh, sweet Jesu ... She started to roll to her feet, only to find herself grabbing at his thigh as those dancing black spots returned, threatening to drown her again.

"I did hurt you, didn't I? That's why I'm chained." His voice might as well be coming from the mouth of the dead man, so lifeless did it sound. "I *raped* you."

"No!" Gwen dug her nails into his bare thighs, even as she absorbed the fact that he was still chained. Apparently the magic had persisted even when she lost consciousness. "You did nothing against my will. I wanted ..." She broke off, unable to say she'd *wanted* to betray her husband and her king.

Now the helpless confusion on Lance's face mirrored hers. "But why did I ... ? Why did you ... ?"

Panic clawed at her. She had to explain this in some way that wouldn't leave both Lancelot and Arthur seeing him as the worst sort of betrayer.

Because even if Arthur decided to spare his old friend, Lance would never forgive himself. Guilt would eat at him until it destroyed Arthur's champion more thoroughly than any sword thrust.

The way it's already destroying me. She had to salvage something out of this unmitigated disaster. Lance had not been in his right mind when he took her. She had been. If she hadn't walked into his chambers, arrogant in the belief she could control him, none of this would be happening.

Gwen was responsible. If anyone had to die, it should be her. Besides, her death would ultimately silence the gossips in a way Lance's would not. As long as she was alive, there would be rumors she was cuckolding the king again, even if she was as blameless as the Blessed Virgin. That was simply the way gossip worked. You could never truly silence wagging tongues, no matter what you did.

Besides, the simple truth was, Gwen *had* betrayed Arthur. She'd had sex with another man. She'd committed adultery. There was a reason they called it a mortal sin.

"Queen Guinevere, you must call Sir Kay," Lancelot told her in that dead man's voice. "You put yourself in danger by being alone with me, if not physically, then from the gossips. You *must* call Kay."

Gwen thought of what Nimue had told her about the Truebond. It was too bad she didn't have that perfect psychic connection with Arthur right now. If he'd known the way she'd felt . . .

"Sir Kay!" Lancelot's bellow made her jump. "Sir Kay, the queen needs you!"

Panic clawing at her, Gwen grabbed for her magic and sent it streaming toward his head—right between his thick dark brows. Lance gasped, eyes widening.

Praying she wasn't using too much force, Gwen concentrated on what she wanted him to believe—the story she'd just concocted. She only hoped it would be convincing enough to save Lancelot.

There was no hope for Gwen herself. Arthur would kill her, and it was no more than she . . .

"What have you done, *you bloody bitch?*" The vicious male snarl made her jump. Startled, Gwen looked up into Lancelot's face to find his handsome features twisted with rage and contempt. "*Why did you do this to me?*"

For a moment she couldn't speak a single word.

"Why the hell did you force me to sleep with you?" His lips curled off his fangs in an animal snarl of fury. "What made you think you could *make* Arthur form this . . . Truebond with you, you faithless little . . ."

Something struck the door so hard, it hit the wall with a thunderous boom. "What the *hell*," Kay snarled as he filled the doorway, "is going on in here?"

I t was uncomfortably close to dawn when Arthur rode through Camelot's massive timber gates, Galahad and Gawain in his wake.

Exhaustion dragged at the king until all he wanted was his bed and Gwen, not necessarily in that order.

Jesu, he craved her. Thirst had nagged him for the three days he'd been gone, making him imagine the long column of Gwen's white throat, the feel of silken skin yielding to his fangs, the intoxicating taste of her blood flowing over his tongue.

He'd tried to ignore that fantasy, to block it from his thoughts, but his body refused to cooperate. The thought of her kept creeping back, over and over, every time he'd been distracted.

And he'd been distracted a great deal. They had ranged all over the surrounding area, but Mordred might as well have been a ghost for all the signs they'd seen of him.

That was when Gawain began arguing they needed to return, pointing out that this was not normally the kind of problem a king wasted his time on. And he was right. Arthur had many more urgent concerns. Tracking Mordred down was important, but the search would be better conducted by a detachment or two of royal troops.

Of course, finding Mordred had never been Arthur's primary objective. He'd really wanted to buy time to think, to find the necessary self-control to avoid hurting Gwen.

After three fruitless nights, worry had begun to nag at him. How was Gwen managing her transformation from woman to witch? *I'm fair mad for you, my love. Don't leave me."* She'd sounded so desperate.

Then there was Merlin's warning. *"She is no longer human, Pendragon. If you try to treat her as though she is, you will rue it."*

Now Arthur tried to remember how he'd felt when he'd awoken a Magus. To his frustration he could recall little beyond a gnawing ache, a thirst so intense that speech, even simple thought, had been beyond him.

Gwen had saved him from that.

She'd given herself to him without any hesitation at all. Indeed, his first clear memory was the feel of her slender body, the taste of her blood in his mouth. He couldn't even remember if he'd known it was Gwen.

And she'd been only human then.

When it had been her turn to change, she'd begged him for only a fraction of the trust she'd given him. He'd refused her. All she'd wanted was his body, and he turned away.

You will rue it.

He'd ignored that warning, ignored Gwen's pleas. Now he was haunted by the fear that he'd been a fool.

Arthur still wasn't sure he trusted himself with her, but he knew he had no choice except to try. His only other option was to drink from another woman, but that seemed too much like adultery. Especially given that his need for blood and his need for sex seemed harnessed like a chariot team.

Reaching the stables, Arthur dismounted and handed his gelding off to a stable boy, who led the big black horse away for grooming and a meal.

As Galahad and Gawain dismounted, Arthur started toward the main building, intent on repairing whatever damage he'd done to his marriage.

Sir Kay strode toward him. One look at the big blond's grim face made his every muscle tense. His foster brother only wore that particular expression when they faced disaster.

"God's teeth, what's wrong now?" Arthur braced, expecting to learn that Mordred and the rebels had seized one of his allies' holdings. That or worse.

Kay hesitated a little too long, then said as if to buy time, "All the Knights of the Round Table passed their tests—including me. Everyone's completed the transformation."

"Good." Arthur lifted a brow. "But somehow I doubt that's what made you look like we're arse-deep in dragon shit."

"No, but I'd rather not go into it out here." Kay's voice dropped. "This is not a conversation you want overheard."

Gwen sat in the dark. Not that anyone had refused her a lamp—she just hadn't cared enough to light it. And she could have.

A flick of her hand made fire appear and dance along her fingertips, flame leaping from index finger to middle finger to ring finger, where it lapped coolly at the huge sapphire Arthur had given her when they wed. The flame winked out, leaving her in darkness once again. *He could burn me, I suppose.*

No, probably not. Arthur had never had a taste for vicious cruelty in his revenge, even when warranted.

Gwen remembered the appalled horror on Kay's face when she told him, an expression that quickly turned to incandescent rage.

For a moment, she'd thought he'd kill her and save Arthur the trouble. He was tempted. She could see it in his hazel eyes.

She'd found herself hoping he'd do it.

Then a flare of animal hunger replaced the rage as his eyes went fixed in lust. She'd tensed . . .

Kay had turned away and sent her to her chambers, where she'd been under guard ever since. *Human* guards. This was not the job for Arthur's Magus knights.

One corner of Gwen's lips curled, but it definitely was not a smile.

The door opened, admitting a spill of balustrade torchlight and the cool waft of night air. The door closed again, leaving them in darkness.

She tensed but did not look up, instead flicking her fingers to call the fire again.

"Gwen, you'll burn yourself." Arthur sounded alarmed rather than angry, as if he automatically feared for her, forgetting what she'd done to them. No, to *him*. There was no "them" anymore. She'd seen to that.

"I'm in no danger—from this, at least. The flames burn without heat." The fire went out. She gestured again, making them lick and dance. Index finger, middle finger, ring finger . . . The sapphire seemed to explode into blue flame, as if the stone had become a torch. "I'm a witch now, remember? Not human anymore. Like you."

"Kay says you slept with Lancelot." He said the words baldly, with no emotion at all.

He was too damn calm. Why wasn't he angry? She'd expected rage. "What does Lance say?" Index finger, middle finger, ring. The sapphire flared bright.

"He says he raped you."

Damn you, Lancelot du Lac! Gwen's gaze snapped to her husband's face. Why wasn't he angry? "He didn't. If anything, it was the other way around."

Arthur's cool gaze probed hers. Bloody hell, he was *investigating* this. Trying to determine what had actually happened, as he had before when some delicate mess landed in the royal lap. "I fail to see how you could have forced a knight who outweighs you by seven stone.

And somehow I doubt the unwillingness of a man stiff enough to do the job."

"I'm a witch, Arthur," Gwen said. "I chained him like a stallion at stud, and I mounted him. He'd just awoken from the sleep of the Grail, and he didn't even know who I was. I fed him from my wrist, and then I fucked him."

She braced for the explosion.

NINE

Instead of flying into a fury, Arthur frowned at Gwen, his expression searching. "Why?"

"I wanted him. You weren't here. He was naked and handsome enough to tempt a nun to sin. So I took him." Why didn't he rage at her? Why didn't he draw the blade that hung at his hip and *end* this agony?

Still no fury, though there was pain in those dark eyes now. Pain and confusion. "He denied you'd been carrying on some . . . love affair."

"Because we weren't."

"Well, *that* was pure truth, at least."

She frowned. "What do you mean?"

"Thanks to the Grail, I can smell a lie now. I know, because people have been lying to me for days, saying they haven't seen Mordred. Apparently he's been making the rounds. Recruiting."

Gwen cursed softly. "And men have answered his call." She thought of the dream that woke her again and again these past three days. "There'll be so many of them at the battle . . ."

"What battle?"

"When he breaks your sword and kills you, Arthur. The one I've been warning you about for days. Why won't you listen?"

"Did you fuck Lancelot?"

She showed mercy to neither of them. "Yes."

"To force me into a Truebond?"

That was what she'd made Lance believe, but if Arthur could smell lies . . . "No." She swallowed, guilt, anguish, and fear a roiling stew in her heart. "I lost control. I just meant to feed him from my wrist, but the need I felt . . . I had him bound in my magic, but he broke free. He didn't even know who I was, Arthur. It wasn't his fault."

He stared at her, numb shock in his dark eyes. "You did it. You actually betrayed me." He looked so young now. Stripped of the crow's-feet and battle scars, the pain showed that much clearer.

No matter what she'd said, Gwen hadn't expected to see such devastation on her husband's face, as if his world had ended. As if she'd cut the heart out of his chest and served it to him with carrots and spring greens. "Arthur . . ."

Now came the rage. "The servants already whisper of this. They don't know I can hear them." A muscle jerked in his broad, sculpted jaw. "They say you used black witch magic to take my best friend, to bind him with chains and rape him. They heard him rage about it to Kay when he caught the two of you. Apparently, Lance's fine deep voice carries quite well when he's in a killing fury." Something vicious slid into his eyes, cruel and predatory.

For the first time in her life, Gwen found herself afraid of Arthur Pendragon. Swallowing, she gazed up into furious black eyes and struggled not to cringe. "I didn't intend . . ."

"Didn't you? It's been three days, Gwen," he spat. "By now the rumors are halfway to Dover. I wouldn't be surprised if Mordred's spies have already delivered the news. He's likely using it as a recruiting tool by now. Hell, the bards are probably composing songs!"

The hiss as Arthur drew his sword chilled Gwen's blood. She tried

to remind herself this was what she'd wanted: a quick death to silence
the whispers and avoid weakening him any further.

There would be consequences, of course. Likely the Pope would
threaten to excommunicate him again. But then, Arthur often joked
he was threatened with excommunication every time he skipped morning Mass.

The point of the great blade hovered inches from her chin. Gwen
watched it with a kind of hypnotized fascination.

"How am I to rule with my crown balanced on a cuckold's horns?"
Arthur asked in a deadly velvet whisper. "Who follows a king who is
the butt of jokes? In years to come, who will remember how I stitched
a dozen warring kingdoms into Britain? They'll know me only as the
fool betrayed by his wife and his champion. And your one night of lust
will become a doomed, immortal romance."

The sword came to rest on her throat. She closed her eyes and
waited for the cold bite of his swing.

"You think I'll actually do it." He sounded surprised. Almost wounded.

But when she opened her eyes to study him, whatever he was feeling hid behind a warped smile. "Though I'll admit, it would certainly
quiet the rumors. No trial, no pretense of Solomon's wisdom. Just a
bloody end to seventeen years of love, *God curse you, Gwen! Why the
fuck did you do this to me?*"

The sword clattered into the corner, making her jump. As she
stared after the weapon, he snatched her into his arms.

Instinctively, Gwen planted her palms against Arthur's chest in a
futile effort to keep those furious eyes at a safer distance. He bared his
teeth at her—and Mary help her, she'd seen duller fangs on a winter-
starved wolf.

"I know that's not the best you can do, darling." The menacing purr
in those words made the hair rise on her vulnerable neck. "Where are
the magical chains, Gwen? You'd better start conjuring, love—because
it's been days since I've drunk from that pretty white throat. And I'm
hungry."

*   *   *

Gwen's blue eyes looked huge with terror, and her arms shook as she tried to hold him off. The fact that she now looked so bloody young made Arthur feel even more like one of those men he despised: the kind who abused women.

Under the circumstances, her vulnerability only added a nasty edge to his fury.

Still trying to draw rein on his temper, Arthur threw himself down on their bed, grabbed her by one wrist, and dragged her across his lap.

His hand smacked down across her rump. With a startled screech, she bucked. He stopped, hand raised. "Did I hurt you?"

"Why—are you going to try again if you didn't?" She tried to jerk off his lap, but he planted a hand in the small of her back and held her there.

Just last night, Arthur had broken the arm of a soldier who'd made the critical mistake of drawing on him. Not that the bastard didn't deserve a broken arm for attacking his king, but Arthur hadn't intended to do it.

If he'd inflicted such damage on a grown man, he was lucky he hadn't broken Gwen's pelvis just now.

The mere thought sickened him—and infuriated him all over again. Grabbing a fistful of her skirt, he jerked it to her waist, meaning only to give her a well-deserved spanking while making sure he didn't lose control again.

Instead he froze, balanced on a blade's edge above a burning abyss.

Gwen's arse looked pale, firm, and beautiful.

Staring down at its ripe curves, Arthur felt his mouth flood with saliva. He couldn't remember feeling such lust in his entire life. His cock stretched to its full length, aching like a sore tooth.

But he also knew he was far too close to some bloody act of madness. *I have to get the hell away from her before I do something I can never set right.*

But she looked so lush, so utterly helpless splayed over his lap, the thought vanished like a leaf in a windstorm. His palm slapped down on that impossibly tempting arse in an immensely satisfying, highly erotic swat. Somehow he pulled the blow at the last second.

Gwen jerked, visibly biting back a yelp as she glared over her shoulder at him with outraged blue eyes. "Arthur, what the hell are you doing? Stop!"

"No." He admired the pink handprint he'd left on that pale, lovely backside. Somehow it soothed his fury. Slowly, he began to spank her with carefully controlled slaps, watching the white flesh take on a fiery glow. By the third stroke she was yelping. By the sixth, a scent rose that made him smile like a demon.

Despite everything, Gwen was growing aroused, even as she kicked and cursed. "Dammit, Arthur, this isn't the kind of problem that you can solve with a spanking and a poke up the arse."

"How do you know? I've never tried it." He'd never laid a violent hand on her in his life. "As for the poke in the arse . . ." SWAT. She jerked, rocking deliciously across his thickening cock. It felt like a tree trunk. "Thank you for the suggestion. I do believe I will." SWAT.

Hard and hungry, Arthur went on spanking his wife with measured strokes, enjoying the jiggle and flex of that sweet, tempting little arse. Drinking in the scent of Gwen's heat, until he clung to self-control by ragged fingernails.

Arthur's cock pressed against Gwen's belly, a long, hard testament to his feral lust.

For days, she'd been imagining this confrontation. Perhaps a swift arrest by his knights, followed by a quick trial, the inevitable verdict, and the headsman's axe.

Or he might skip all that and just kill her on the spot, the way he'd come so close to slaying Mordred.

Not once had Gwen imagined he'd resort to this kind of seductive revenge. Probably because he'd never even threatened to spank her before, as if there was no connection between his wife and physical aggression in his mind. Not even as part of sexual play.

Maybe we should've tried it, Gwen thought numbly. *It's surprisingly erotic.*

Was he trying to forgive her? Or would he just fuck her, then order her arrest? No, that would take a degree of emotional frigidity Arthur simply wasn't capable of. Yes, he could be as ruthless as any other king when he needed to be, but when it came to his family . . . *He couldn't even kill Mordred, who richly deserved it. How could I imagine he'd slay me?*

Arthur's big palm cracked down on her arse yet again, startling her into another bucking yelp. Gwen braced herself, but instead of doling out another slap, he paused.

"That's a lovely shade of pink." The king's deep voice sounded rough with desire. His fingertips traced the burning contours of her rump in a honeyed caress. She drew in a shaking breath as his hand slipped down between her legs, fingers stroking the plump, creamy lips of her sex before delving between them. "You're very wet. If I didn't know better, I'd think you found your spanking . . . arousing."

"It's pretty obvious *you* do," Gwen shot back. She was proud her voice didn't shake.

"Now that you mention it, yes. It is arousing, warming up this pretty arse for the fucking I'm about to give it." Arthur brought his hand down in another SWAT. The stinging pain made her jerk on his lap.

Again he paused to caress her sex, delving in slow, erotic strokes that went deeper and deeper with every entry. Gwen squirmed, helpless, so hot she burned.

He laughed softly and drew his slick finger from her sex, then brushed her anus. Slowly, deliberately, he pressed, sliding the finger deep. Gwen bit back a moan at the wicked pleasure.

How would it feel when it was his cock stroking deep and hard, stretching her virgin anus with relentless strokes?

"I do believe you're ready. God knows I am." Arthur lifted her off his lap and dumped her on the bed as though she weighed no more than a cat. She watched warily as he strode into her dressing chamber. He was back a moment later with a familiar glass bottle: the lavender oil she used to scent her bath.

Judging by the stark hunger in his eyes, he planned a very different use for it now. Gwen swallowed as her pounding heart began an outright gallop.

Arthur lifted the little bottle and rotated his wrist, swirling the oil suggestively. "If you're going to say no, now would be the time."

Her mouth felt dry as a cured hide in the sun. "I'm not saying no."

Her husband grinned darkly, flashing fangs. "I didn't think you would."

He put the oil down on the chest at the foot of the bed and began to undress. Impatient hands jerked at the knot of his sword belt and whipped it from around his waist before tossing it aside. The scabbarded blade thudded to the floor. Arthur's chain mail hauberk was next, ringing as he dragged it over his head, then the heavy padded tunic he wore under it, both tossed carelessly over the chest. His bare torso looked as broad as a wall, muscle flexing and rolling as he toed off his boots, unlaced his britches, and stripped them down brawny horseman's thighs.

Straightening, Arthur stared at her, angry need in his black eyes, gloriously naked, his cock jutting in blatant demand. "Are you going to strip, or do I get to rip that pretty tunic off?"

Licking dry lips, Gwen rose from the bed on shaking legs and pulled her gown over her head, tossing it on the chest. It draped across his armor, thin silk veiling gleaming chain. Squaring her shoulders, she forced herself to stand naked before his lust and anger.

He swept her with a stare that made her feel like a slave on the auction block. "Very nice. I particularly like the new perk to those tits."

He bent and picked up the belt. It felt warm from his body, smelling of steel and sweat and man.

"I realize you could wave your fingers and make this disappear," he drawled. "But I would strongly advise against it."

"I'm not going to fight you, Arthur."

He shot her a glittering, hostile look. "I haven't even started yet. You may not find martyrdom all that appealing."

As she met his gaze, a chill slid over her. If she thought he'd spent his rage in that spanking, she was wrong. Those black eyes simmered with a stew of lust and pain and a trace of bewilderment, silently echoing his earlier demand: *Why the fuck did you do this to me?*

She'd always hated it when Arthur was in pain, though she'd never been the one who hurt him before. Not like this. Her instinct was to reach out to him, to apologize. But he wasn't ready to hear it. Not yet.

She was going to have to pay first.

"On your knees." He gave the order in the frigid tone he usually reserved for someone he was contemplating killing.

Gwen obeyed, sinking to the floor. He still held her bound wrists, so kneeling raised them over her head. Angling her arms back, he forced her spine to arch, thrusting out her breasts. Staring at their hard rosy crests, he licked his lips. She glimpsed the tip of a fang.

His cock was so hard, it angled slightly upward, an elegant curve of hard flesh. "I've always loved your tits," he told her, still in that distant voice. "I'm tempted to bite one of those pretty pink nipples. Drink from you while you squirm."

Gwen's first reaction was to recoil. *Mary, that would hurt!*

But then another image flashed through her mind: Arthur's dark head bent over her breast, the sting of his fangs blending with the pleasure of his mouth working her nipple, tongue swirling in time to his long pulls. Desire flooded her, stark and hot, heavy as honey.

He transferred her wrists to his left hand and used his right to aim his cock at her mouth. "Suck me. Now."

Gwen hesitated. She wasn't sure she liked this game he was playing. If it was a game, and not a cold prequel to something she wouldn't like at all.

"I'm getting impatient." That intimate growl made wet heat bloom between her thighs. She leaned forward, arching her body even more, and engulfed the silken head of his cock. It tasted of arousal and salt and Arthur, and she damned near moaned at the taste, so lush and familiar even in the midst of this heartbreaking nightmare. A thought flashed through her mind: *Whatever he does to me, I'm going to make him remember this.* She angled her head to take him deeper down her working throat.

"You're not usually this submissive," he said in a sensual growl. "I think I like it."

Gwen ignored him, intent on his cock, sliding it as deep into her throat as she could, then pulling back slowly. An awkward process with her bound hands held over her head, yet somehow the discomfort of the pose made her more aware of him. Looming over her, with his big bare feet braced apart, his gaze predatory as he savored the sight of her lips wrapped around his cock.

Gwen could feel her pussy growing slicker with every sucking pull, every lick and erotic nibble. She wasn't really helpless, not with her magic, but she felt that way. And Jesu, it was arousing.

His free hand lifted, and she instinctively shied. Arthur hesitated, then curled his hand around his balls to caress himself. "You're not done." He sounded cold and distant again, deep in his King-Arthur-is-pissed mode. "I want my dick deeper than that."

Gwen thought about telling him what to do with his dick, but need growled louder than her pride. She drew off him to the fat plum head, then engulfed him again with a swirling lick.

"Deeper." He rolled his hips. "Pretend I'm Lancelot."

She gave serious thought to biting him for that, but instead sucked harder, rising on her knees, the better to angle her head down over the thick shaft.

There was pain buried beneath all that royal ice, and she'd never been able to resist Arthur in pain.

They both needed to escape what she'd done, if only for a moment. And she wanted—no, desperately needed—to forget just how bad the situation was.

Arthur's cock made a delicious distraction.

Watching Gwen suck him off while he held her bound wrists was so darkly erotic, Arthur knew he wasn't going to last long. "Deeper, Gwen," he growled. "I want to hear you gag."

She gave no indication she'd heard him. Instead she drew away entirely to swirl her tongue over the head of his cock, licking him with single-minded attention, as if he were covered in honey and she were trying to clean it off. And the sight of her—that beautiful face, blue eyes intent on his bobbing erection, licking, sucking, then taking him to the root, her full lips so soft, her throat so snug. Drowning him in sensation.

She didn't gag.

It was hard to play the bastard with Gwen's tongue dancing along his shaft. She seemed to know every single place his cock was most sensitive—the rim of the mushroom head, the vein that ran along its underside, the fold of skin along the bottom of the shaft.

And there was something dark and primitive in him that loved the sight of her bound on her knees with his shaft in her mouth. Hot arousal pumped through him as he looked down at her, watching her pretty pink lips stretched around his width as she worked him deeper and deeper still, until her nose was buried in his pubic hair. He rolled his hips, driven by that darkness in him, the need to take her roughly, make her submit. A hunger given even more power by her sensual response to his dominance.

Another ruthless thrust into that soft, clinging mouth. She sucked, pulling hard, once, twice, and . . .

Heat pulsed in his balls and poured up the shaft in a pumping rush. Arthur's head rocked at the stark, white-hot pleasure. Its blazing intensity drove every other thought out of his skull. "Swallow it, Gwen," he gritted through his fangs. "Drink it down. Every drop."

As he watched, his wife did just that, her lovely blue eyes rolling up to watch his face. At last she drew off his sated cock.

She fucked Lancelot. The thought pierced him like a stiletto in the dark, a cold, slicing pain.

Arthur's lips curled into a smile. He suspected it looked vicious. "You do realize I had you suck me off so I'll last longer when I fuck your arse?" He pulled up on her wrists, lifting her to her feet with his Magus strength. "I'm going to take my time, really grind it in." The king lifted a brow, recognizing what an utter prick he was being. "I assume Lancelot didn't beat me to it . . . ?"

"Damn you, Arthur!" Gwen spat, finally goaded into speech. Just as he'd intended. "I didn't mean to do this to you—to us. I was just trying to . . ." She broke off.

"To what? What were you trying to do? What happened, dammit?" He had to know. Ached, burned to know.

Her pretty face closed down in a stubborn expression he'd come to know all too well. Gwen had made up her mind. He wasn't going to get a word out of her. And he knew why.

She was protecting her lover.

Rage bolted through him, a bloody, jealous demon that curled his lips into a fanged snarl. "You should be worrying less about du Lac and more about yourself."

He caught her around the waist, swung her toward the bed, and took her down with him.

They landed on the thick, feather-filled mattress, him on top, though he made sure his knees and elbows took most of his weight. Catching her bound wrists with one hand, he pinned them to the bed above her head. "You need to think about what I could do to you." He was acutely aware of her soft breasts pressing against his chest.

Her nipples were hard.

He remembered the threat he'd made earlier—to bite one of those little peaks and drink. He hadn't meant it, had no intention of inflicting such pain on that tender, sensitive flesh.

But he wasn't above making her think he would. His wife needed to take him a hell of a lot more seriously—needed to grasp just how much danger she was in.

Kay had urged him to kill her.

Arthur loomed over Gwen, his big body pressing hers into the mattress. She should've been terrified. Instead she felt aroused. Hot. Wet and needy.

He braced on one arm, the other hand still holding her wrists, and studied her breasts with silken menace. "You don't seem to realize what I could do to you." Slowly, his head lowered toward one of those stiff little peaks.

Gwen's heart banged like a rabbit's as her mouth went dry.

"I've always loved the taste of your nipples." He gave her a lick that sent hot pleasure bolting through her. She managed not to whimper. "Now I'm wondering what it would be like to use these new fangs on them."

Arthur looked up at her, his parted lips revealing sharp tips barely an inch from her left nipple. "I'm tempted, Gwen. I'm very, very tempted. But it would hurt, wouldn't it? You, I mean." He laughed, dark and seductive. "*I'd* love it."

She swallowed a whimper. She didn't want to give him the satisfaction.

The king bent his head over that tight, erect peak. His warm, soft lips brushed the tip as he whispered, "My fangs are sharp, Gwen. It wouldn't hurt. Much. Probably." Turning his head back and forth, he flicked the peak with first one fang, then the other. "I could try it and see." His black eyes flicked up to hers. "Shall I?"

Excitement jolted through her. She felt her lips curve in a taunting smile. "You wouldn't. You've never hurt a woman in your life."

His heated gaze went cold. "Don't tempt me."

Arthur closed his mouth around her nipple.

Gwen jolted, but he didn't bite. Instead he began to suck, his tongue swirling over and around the little point. Waves of sweet delight began to roll through her, until she had to fight the need to squirm.

She ached to touch him, ached to run her fingers along the hard muscle of broad shoulders and powerful arms, to tangle her hands in the thick black silk of his hair. But he still held her bound wrists pinned.

"Arthur," she gasped, "untie me. I want to . . ."

He lifted his head and shot her a molten glare. "No."

Arthur lowered his head again, but this time, he paused and ran the tips of his fangs along the curve of her breast, framing her nipple between them. It wasn't a bite, though he almost broke the skin. It was a message, Gwen realized: *you're helpless, and I can do whatever I want to you.*

If any other man had done such a thing to her, Gwen would have force-fed him a magical fireball. But this was Arthur—the man she'd loved for seventeen years.

She'd always known he had an edge, a capacity for both steely menace and the ability to carry out his threats. She'd seen him reduce battle-hardened warriors to stammering terror with one icy glare.

But that edge had never been turned toward her. Arthur had always treated her with a lover's careful deference. Having him suddenly stretch her out beneath him and turn that ferocity on her somehow struck her as darkly erotic.

And she had no idea why.

By all rights this should terrify her, especially considering the situation. If he killed her for cuckolding him, nobody would even question it. He was, after all, High King; he answered to no one, with the possible exception of the Pope and God.

Yet Gwen felt no fear of him. Certainly not the way any intelligent woman should fear a man with total power. Instead, her perverse body heated with creamy arousal with every swirling lick, every scrape of his fangs.

Arthur went still. His head lifted as his perceptive gaze locked on hers. "Do you want me to bite you, Gwen?"

"Does it really matter to you what I want?"

"Not really." He raked his fangs across her breast again, this time pricking her aching nipples in the process. "But you're welcome to pretend it does."

"Then why don't you pretend whatever gets you hard." Which was definitely not the kind of thing you said to the husband you'd just cuckolded.

He smiled, the expression so charming, she almost missed the lethal rage in the depths of his eyes. "I do believe I will."

And he bit her.

Arthur had been right. His fangs were so sharp, she barely felt the sting as they sank into her breast on either side of her nipple. Just as the pain detonated in a needle-sharp burst, he began to suck. His tongue flicked and stroked, teasing starbursts of pleasure from the peak even as her breast throbbed.

This time she was unable to suppress her moans, her need to squirm.

He ignored her helpless struggles, intent on her blood. His free hand wandered down her body to stroke between her legs. Her hips rolled, urging him on.

But instead of seeking out her creamy pussy or desperate clit, he drove a finger up her arse. She froze, sucking in a breath.

Arthur went right on drinking, still playing his tongue across her nipple, each lazy lap sending smoky tendrils of pleasure through her in time to his swallows. Simultaneously, as if to remind her of his anal threats, his finger stroked in and out of her rump. The sensation felt as alien as the fangs in her breast, yet it was undeniably erotic. So arousing her hips began to rock again, fucking her own ass on that impaling finger.

Abruptly he drew his hand away and lifted his head. Gwen moaned helplessly as his fangs slid from her breast, leaving behind a pair of thin scarlet rivulets. He paused to lick them.

Feeling dazed, she watched him rise, tongue sliding over his lips to catch a last scarlet drop. "Well, that was tasty," he told her as he walked over to wash his hands in the bedside basin. "Doing what I want and pretending you gave me permission has a great deal to recommend it." His grin was downright nasty. "In fact, let's pretend you told me I could fuck you up that tight little arse." He strolled over to the chest and picked up the bottle of lavender oil.

"Arthur . . ."

"If you say one more word," he told her pleasantly, "I'll gag you. I think you need to remember who rules here. And it's damned well not you." Deliberately he poured the oil onto the palm of his hand and started stroking his cock, his gaze still locked on her, hooded and feral.

Gwen stared back, her mouth so dry, she doubted she could speak even if he hadn't forbidden it.

She had long since lost track of how many times she'd made love to Arthur, but somehow his cock had never looked so very . . . threatening. She had made love to him only a few days before—his cock couldn't have grown since then, for God's sake. Except she could've sworn it had, its heavy shaft curving over fat, furry balls. *Thick, oh my God, he's thick. This is going to hurt.*

She wanted it anyway. Whether for its own wicked sake, or because she hoped it would soften his rage, she didn't know.

When he was finally satisfied he had his cock sufficiently slick, he stepped toward her. The long shaft swung with the motion, and she stared at it, helplessly fascinated.

Arthur laughed, the sound more than a little sinister. "I find the look of terror on your face perversely satisfying." His grin broadened. "But I'll wager I'll find actually fucking your tight little hole even more delicious."

He grabbed her by one hip and flipped her over onto her stomach, then pulled her onto her hands and knees. His hand landed on her neck, collaring it in long fingers and forcing her head back down. "Arse in the air, darling. That's better. Now, brace yourself." His voice dropped to a growl. "This will hurt."

TEN

Gwen felt the smooth heat of Arthur's cock press against her anal opening.

"Don't tense, push," he told her, his voice all dark velvet seduction. "It'll hurt less."

She laughed. It sounded strained even to her. "I'm not even going to ask how you know so much about . . . Wait, how do you know so much about this?"

"A man hears things."

"Mary, from *whom?*"

But he was already sinking inside, despite the instinctive resistance of her anal muscles. Her flesh strained and stung as he forced his cock deeper by slow inches, stuffing her mercilessly. Gwen's eyes watered at the hot, edgy pain.

He felt huge, thick. Overwhelming. Yet something about the massive impalement struck her as incredibly erotic, especially bound as she was, his big hand wrapped around the back of her neck, pinning her for his use.

"I think I like this," he rumbled, when his balls finally rested against her bottom. "You have a very tight arse. Does it hurt?"

"Do you care?"

"Not especially." He began to withdraw.

In contrast to his entry, the exit stroke felt delicious. And he knew it, too, because he pulled out slowly, spinning the pleasure into a long, golden thread of delight. He drew all the way out, his cock leaving her like a cork from a bottle. "I think you need more lubricant," he told her, a note of dark anticipation in his voice. "I'm going to want to fuck you deep and fast, and I want a slick ride."

"You just like cramming that club of yours up my backside."

He laughed. "You do know me well."

"I thought I did."

His voice chilled. "Yes, I suppose we both found ourselves unpleasantly surprised this night."

She winced. *Keep your foolish tongue behind your teeth, Gwen.*

Strong fingers clamped down on her cheeks, prying her open. She heard the pop of the cork leaving the oil bottle, then felt the cool trickle of oil into her opening. Again, she suffered through the nerve-wracking wait as he coated himself with the lubricant. Her breath came faster until she was all but panting.

Arthur entered her arse even more slowly this time, purring in pleasure as he impaled her. So slowly, so deliberately, she knew he was making sure she felt every massive inch of his invasion. "If you fight it, it will hurt more."

"Which is exactly . . ." She stopped to pant as he worked in another burning inch. ". . . How you want it."

"Do you deserve anything less?"

His voice held such silken menace, she shivered. "No."

Damn her, she didn't have to sound so bloody lost.

Any other woman would have played to his ego and lust, Arthur thought, exaggerating her submissiveness to blunt his rage. Gwen defied him, though she must know she was saying exactly the wrong thing at exactly the wrong time.

Yet just when he was about to lose control completely, fuck her as

mercilessly as his lust and fury demanded, that faint note of broken
pain in her voice reminded Arthur this was his Gwen. His wife.

His love.

The stark agony in that thought made him want to howl like a
wounded wolf.

Luckily her arse felt delicious, so exquisitely tight, the pleasure
made a fine distraction from the brutal pain in his chest. And why
not? Why not ream her so hard he forgot everything else? If he hurt
her only a fraction as much as she'd hurt him, so much the better.

Still, Arthur fought the clawing hunger until he could thrust
smoothly, carefully. Sliding slowly up her delightfully snug passage
until he was in to the root.

There he paused, admiring the sight of the pale, perfect curves of
Gwen's arse, with its silken flesh and shadowed cleft, impaled on his
massive erection.

She made a soft, anxious sound, tinged with pain. That whimper
had the effect of soothing his prowling anger. He smiled, and suspected
there was more than a little savagery in the expression as he began to
pull out. She caught her breath. This time he detected a note of pleasure in her whimper, a reluctant enjoyment. He reached the head and
pushed deep again, as slowly as he could stand.

Again he pulled out, a delicious glide through Gwen's tight, slick
depths. "God, you feel so good," he gritted through his teeth. "Tighter
than a strong man's fist." He forced his cock deep again. "Utterly
perfect."

"You . . . you feel so damned . . ." She broke off. "Hurts, but it . . .
feels good."

"Then let's see how long I can make it last."

Clawing for control, he fucked her, one hand locked around her
neck, keeping her pinned and helpless while he plundered her rectum.
Her pulse leaped against his fingertips. His fangs ached with the need
to bite into that soft, soft skin. The thought of possessing her so utterly
she would never again forget whom she belonged to—God, it tempted

him. He wanted to feel her pulse leaping against his lips as he fucked her, drinking her blood.

It scared the hell out of him.

The craving for blood—*Gwen's* blood—was so alien, yet it seemed to reverberate in his bones. A black, aching need he couldn't resist. Couldn't deny. A hunger that had throbbed in the background of his mind since he'd last had her, too many days ago.

He'd fought it, feared it, refused its demands. Yet when he'd learned what she'd done, his anger had intensified his thirst until it slid right out of his control. Somehow he'd managed to turn it into lust, like a man dragging on the reins of a runaway horse. Forcing it to find expression in his plunging cock and Gwen's tight arse.

Arthur needed blood. He could feel himself growing weaker. The hunger roared so loud in him now that it was hard to think. *A taste.* The words seemed to pound in his heartbeat in time to the thrusts of his cock. *Just a taste.*

God, her arse felt so tight, so slick. And her pulse beat against his fingertips.

A taste a taste a taste . . .

The next thing he knew, he'd released her throat, slid a hand under her right arm and across her chest to lift her upper body as he sat back on his heels. Dragging her up onto her knees, he rolled his hips and speared his cock into her arse. She cried out, her voice high with blended pain and pleasure. Her head fell back to rest on his shoulder. He turned his head to the pulsing artery just under her silken skin. He could hear its seductive thump, feel its heat. Almost taste it.

God's balls, his mouth was dry.

Arthur tried to stop, tried to fight the clawing need, but he knew he was damned to lose like a soul being dragged into hell.

A desperate idea flashed into his mind. "Use your magic to link with me," he growled just above his wife's taut skin. "Now."

Gwen jolted, her arse tightening deliciously around his cock. The sensation poured oil over the flame of his hunger, making it leap. "Arthur, no—if I died, you . . ."

"Do the magic, witch," he snapped, fighting to hold himself back in spite of the impossibly arousing temptation of her sweet pulse. "Truebond us. Your husband—your *king*—orders it."

"Arthur . . ."

"Now!" His fingers tightened around her throat. His fangs ached savagely, their points brushing the banging vein as he spoke. "Do it."

With a despairing cry, she lifted her bound wrists. The belt around them vanished in an explosion of sparks as she flung her arms apart. Golden light poured from her fingers, raining sparks over their shoulders. A bright braided cord flashed into being, snaking from her head to his. He felt something warm flood his consciousness, something kind and tender and . . . Gwen.

"Arthur. God, Arthur, forgive me. I can't bear your anger. Please God, let him forgive me. I will die without him. I know I don't deserve it after what I've done . . ."

Guilt and despair hammered him in an agonizing flood that made him cry out.

"God, Arthur . . ."

I'm feeling her pain. This was Gwen's guilt, Gwen's despair. Emotions so strong, they drowned even his burning anger. Tears pricked his lids in the kind of unmanly display his father had always beaten him for.

Time to give both of them something else to think about.

He bit her.

Blood flooded his desert-dry mouth, triggering an explosion of lust that stiffened the cock that had damned near gone limp from her suffering. In five hot heartbeats, his shaft was hard as a sword blade again. He thrust upward . . .

And the sensation of a huge cock ramming up his arse almost made him choke on the blood. He froze in pain. *Christ!*

Amusement rippled through him like quicksilver. A distinctly feminine amusement. *"Not quite as much fun being on this end of the dick, is it?"*

He started to pull out, only to freeze again at the sudden hot pleasure.

"Then again . . . Oh, Arthur, that's lovely. Do it again."

Slowly, warily, he began to withdraw. She was right. The pleasure of her tight anal grip, the way it milked his cock . . . He thrust deep in sheer reflex and sucked in a breath at the thorny pleasure.

"Sweet and brutal," she thought. *"Like you."*

"Whereas you are just sweet." He swallowed another mouthful of that deliciously intoxicating blood. And began to thrust again, far more carefully. Afraid he'd hurt her, tear her, big as he was. If he'd realized sooner how it had felt . . .

"You'd have fucked me like this anyway. You're so angry, Arthur. So hurt."

He growled against her throat as his prodded rage roused like a dragon in its cave. *"Shut up. For God's sake, shut up. Please."*

Pain and guilt cut through her so sharply, it hurt him far worse than the sensation of his cock in his own arse. *"I never realized I was quite this well-endowed . . ."*

"I've certainly never complained." Despite the arch humor in the thought, her suffering made the link between them vibrate like a plucked lute string. *"I never meant to . . ."*

He didn't want to hear it. Punishing both of them now, he started fucking her hard. Despite the pain, pleasure began to lash them, waves of it as he drank from her in deep, hot swallows.

Merlin was right. The Truebond kept him aware of her, kept him from losing control.

Orgasm hit them in a great burning wave, so intense it was impossible to tell who'd come first, since that climax triggered the other almost simultaneously. The power of their shared orgasm was greater than any delight he'd ever known, blazing hotter and brighter until they burned, Gwen screaming, his own cry muffled by her throat as he shot and shot and shot into the tight, slick depth of her arse.

They woke together. Gwen lay curled in the shelter of Arthur's big body. His softened cock had slipped from her arse, just as his fangs no longer pierced her throat. Yet their minds remained joined.

"Why? Why did you do this to us, Gwen?"

The answer flashed through her consciousness like the blinding illumination of a lightning bolt, so fast and intense he could make no sense of it.

"What? I didn't catch that. Remember. Show me what happened."

Fear shot through her—not for herself but for . . .

"I won't kill him. How can I fault him when I did the same? I came back with no recognition of you, either."

Arthur remembered that much. Or at least, he thought he did. Misty, vague recollections of a beautiful blonde, soft pale breasts, the tight grip of cream-slick flesh . . .

So Gwen showed him that night with Lancelot. Showed him the way she'd paced the corridor in pain and despair at her conviction that Mordred would kill Arthur. Showed him the moment she'd seen the maid flee Lancelot's room, and decided to feed him herself. Even showed him the moment she lost control of her own desire in the face of Lance's handsome nudity—and how he'd tricked her by feigning injury.

"Dammit, he did force you! I'll kill him!"

"No! Yes, he took advantage of my distraction. But you know as well as I do he would never have done such a thing to any woman if he'd been aware of himself. He certainly never would have done it to me."

Despite his anger, Arthur knew she had a point. And that made him angry all over again. *"So why does he believe you somehow forced him as part of some stupid scheme to drive me into a Truebond?"*

"Because I panicked." She showed him the spell she'd cast, and the reason she'd cast it.

"Dammit, Gwen! Did you truly think me such a jealous, stupid fool, I'd murder my best friend without listening to you?"

"Well, you did just threaten to kill him."

"I also listened to you tell me why I shouldn't."

"The politics . . ."

"Fuck the politics. The politics wouldn't be a problem if you hadn't made the situation so much worse by trying to cover it up."

"Yes," she admitted, "I've wished a thousand times since then I'd kept my mouth shut, my spells to myself, and simply sneaked out the door. No one would have had to know anything, including Lance. He probably wouldn't even have remembered I was there."

"Too bad he drank you unconscious instead. God's hairy balls, I'm going to kick his arse!"

"Arthur . . ."

"Gwen, Lance and his bloody pride have plunged us all lip-deep in dragon shit. He just had to yell for Kay and rant until the whole damn fortress heard him. He knows better than that."

"He would never have done it if not for my stupid spell." She sighed, stirring her fingers through Arthur's thick, curly chest hair. "But I truly believed he wouldn't have been able to deal with what he'd have seen as a betrayal of you. It would've destroyed him sooner or later. I had to make sure he didn't remember anything at all, that he thought it was my fault."

"And as usual, you were too bloody efficient. Little martyr." Arthur sighed. "Well, we're just going to have to deal with the aftermath."

"God help us."

At least his lethal rage had been replaced by weariness—though damned if he knew what they were going to do about the situation.

With the exception of Lancelot—who was cooling his heels elsewhere—the Knights of the Round Table stood on the balustrade, tension obvious in the way every man held himself.

Kay sensed Arthur and Gwen's approach first and turned. Arthur saw relief flash across his foster brother's face when he saw Gwen. As if despite everything she'd done, he didn't want her dead any more than Arthur did. A moment later Kay frowned, taking in the protective way Arthur circled her slim back with his arm, plainly seeing the political ramifications of the king's sparing his adulterous queen.

Then the other knights turned and spotted them, and the same relief flashed across every man's face. Arthur wasn't surprised; Gwen had always been popular with his men, for she'd treated them with a kind of warm respect for their heroism and sacrifice, yet she never fawned over them. What did surprise him was their obvious expectation that he'd slay her out of hand. Did they think so little of his self-control, his basic chivalry? Arthur stopped and stared at them. "You expected me to kill my queen."

"You were pretty angry, sire," Gawain said, with his usual blunt honesty.

It took a moment for Arthur's outrage to cool enough for him to see their point. "True enough," he admitted. "And I have my father's temper. But I am satisfied my queen committed no treason."

Anger flashed across their faces. Gwen mentally shrank back even as she lifted her chin and pasted an expression of royal hauteur on her face.

"Then Lancelot did force her?" Tristan demanded.

"No!" Startled, Gwen stared at them, realizing belatedly they were angry for her, not at her. "He didn't know who I was. He didn't even know who *he* was."

Kay's frown deepened. "So he did use force, then?"

"My wife said he did not," Arthur growled, icy menace in his voice. "Suffice it to say I know exactly what happened. We are True-bonded."

"Arthur . . ." Kay began in an involuntary protest that died the moment his king looked at him. The seneschal could get away with a great deal, but he also knew where the boundaries were. He knew to the inch how far he could push.

Arthur had been pushed entirely too far as it was.

Lancelot was locked in one of the cells for rebel prisoners in the barracks. Gwen hadn't been happy to learn Kay had put him there, but Arthur had only shrugged. "He had to be locked up somewhere until I made a decision, and it kept the other knights from beating his arse. From what I understand, he wouldn't have put up much of a fight."

He had the guards open the cell and ordered them to withdraw. Judging from their expressions, the two men didn't think that was a good idea, but Arthur gave them a look that sent them out anyway.

Gwen walked in on her husband's arm to find Lancelot on his knees, his dark head bent. There was nothing in the pose that suggested fear, or anything except calm acceptance. Knowing Lance, that calm wouldn't break even if Arthur drew his sword and prepared to behead him on the spot.

The king sighed. "Speak, du Lac."

"I do not ask for forgiveness, my king. The crime I committed against you and the realm is unforgivable. The fault lies entirely with me—I forced the queen . . ."

"Am I my father?" Arthur snapped.

For a fraction of a heartbeat, Lancelot's gaze lifted and met his before flying back to the stone floor. "No, sire."

"Am I a violent, jealous fool, incapable of recognizing that the greatest of my knights committed no crime?"

"No, sire, but I've . . ."

"Am I so lost to human compassion I can't understand a moment of weakness I knew myself but three days before?"

"Of course not, but . . ."

"Am I so bloody stupid I would deprive myself of my greatest knight going into a civil war that may destroy my kingdom?"

"You have ten other knights who more than match my skills."

"Am I in the habit of flattering you, Lord Lancelot?"

"No, sire."

"Then quit fucking questioning my judgment!" His lip curled. "It grows tiresome."

Another man—including many of those who occupied the Round Table—would have flinched in the face of Arthur's royal fury. Lancelot simply knelt there, as erect as a sword blade.

"Talk to him, Gwen. Make him see reason, or cast a spell on him, I care not. Just do something before I lose my mind and knock his teeth down his throat."

Unfortunately, she knew talking to Lancelot was an exercise in futility, given the spell she'd cast on his memory. She had to break that spell before he'd be willing to listen to reason. But when she reached for his face to begin the counterspell, he jerked away. His gaze met hers with such pain, betrayal, and fury, the emotional impact felt like a blow from his fist.

"She does not deserve your rage, du Lac," Arthur ground out. "She only tried to save your ungrateful life. Gwen . . ."

But when she tried once again to cast the spell to reverse her magic, she slammed right into a mental wall, a psychic fortress around his consciousness built of rage, guilt.

And most of all a sense that she'd betrayed him as much as Arthur by using him to force the Truebond her spell insisted she'd wanted.

As her heart sank, she realized Lancelot's mind was locked beyond the reach of hers, in a mental fortress more impregnable than Camelot's stone walls. One thought sliced through his furious mistrust: *I loved you. All these years, I loved you, and you did this to me.*

Gwen stared at him, feeling sick. He didn't drop his eyes. Desperately she fought to penetrate his mental barriers, but she couldn't get through.

Finally Arthur had enough. "Get out of here, du Lac, before I forget our years of friendship."

Lance rose without a word and stalked out. The cell door closed behind him with such exquisite control, it barely made a sound.

The king sighed. "*Maybe Merlin can undo the spell. Lance is not going to let you in. Period.*"

Gwen looked up at her husband, bewildered. "*I had no idea he felt that way.*"

"*I did. I've known for years. There were times when he looked at you, and his face lit with the same kind of love I feel. I also knew he'd never act on how he felt, which was why I was so pissed off when it seemed I'd been wrong.*"

"*But you weren't.*"

"*No. But he's crazy if he thinks it's that easy to fall out of love with you. God knows I couldn't do it.*"

The following night, the Knights of the Round Table gathered to train. Arthur had led his men in training sessions on a daily basis for years, but this one was very different from the ones that had come before. They were Magi now, and they had to learn how to combine their formidable sword skills with their new supernatural strength.

"Having power does no good without the knowledge of how to use it," Merlin told them as they stood or crouched, listening. "It becomes too easy to overshoot your target, to try to leap over a blade only to come down on top of someone else's instead. There are also your other magical talents, like shape-shifting into wolf form. Used strategically, these abilities can make all the difference in battle—but only if you know how to use them."

He called Marrok over to demonstrate. The big knight was more than a foot taller than the wizard, and likely outweighed him by nine stone or better. He should have been able to break the boyish sorcerer like a rotten twig.

Instead, Merlin attacked in a furious blur, his sword licking out with such speed, Marrok was obviously hard-pressed even to see where it was, much less block it with his shield. The big knight was forced into a retreat, crouching behind his shield as Merlin's attacks dented it with their raw power.

Until Marrok's dark eyes narrowed with an expression his fellow knights knew well. He was beginning to lose his temper—and that meant trouble for whomever he faced. His rages in combat, combined with his size and strength, made him a man to be feared.

He attacked, barreling toward Merlin, who leaped back, simultaneously driving his shield into Marrok's sword so hard, the weapon snapped, its pieces cartwheeling into the moonlight. Before the big knight could retreat, the wizard had his blade pressed against Marrok's throat.

"As you are now, few men could defeat you—unless you defeat yourself through clumsiness or miscalculation," Merlin said softly, not taking his eyes off Marrok.

When the big knight backed up, his empty sword hand lifted in surrender, the wizard turned toward the watching warriors. "Pair off. I would suggest beginning your practice with hand-to-hand, until you have a better sense of what you're doing."

Up on the balustrade, Gwen watched with the eleven other ladies who'd received Merlin's Gift. She knew all of them well. Morgana, of course. Elaine, Fenice, Iblis, Lynet, Tyra, Yserone, Vivien, Prydwyn, Lunet, and Diera.

"Mmmmm," Diera purred as the men faced off hand to hand. "That looks like thirsty work. I don't know about you ladies, but I'm looking forward to helping someone either celebrate his victory or lick his wounds."

"More like lick your wounds," Iblis shot back, snapping her teeth in a mimed bite.

"I'd like to lick Tristan's wounds," Vivien murmured wickedly.

"Tristan's married, Viv," Diera reminded her.

"Barely," Vivien retorted. "Isolde failed her challenge, and she's pissed that Tristan didn't—and accepted the Grail anyway. She's left him. Left Camelot, come to that. They say she's gone home to her parents' holding." The Maja sighed, her sad tone in contrast to the heat in her eyes. "Poor Tristan. All alone and *hungry*. Whoever shall he eat?"

"Viv, you are such a slut." Iblis shook her head.

"Oh, come on, just look at him. So blond and big and good with his blade . . ." A roll of her hips said the weapon she spoke of was not the one in his scabbard.

As her women traded gossip and good-natured raillery, Gwen straightened, her gaze on her husband.

Arthur strode across the courtyard, headed right for Lancelot, his eyes narrow. The twisted grin on his face suggested he was looking forward to burning off some of the frustrated rage Gwen knew he'd felt since she'd landed them in this mess.

"Looks like the king is in a mood," Fenice observed. "This should be good."

Gwen knew what she meant. The Knights of the Round Table— including Arthur—were as prone toward getting angry at each other as anyone else. They'd always used the combat practices as an opportunity to burn off any resentment and anger they felt so it didn't grow into a problem.

Of course, as king, Arthur could have used his authority to punish his men in other ways—and did on occasion, at least with lapses of discipline he considered more serious. But his current problem with Lance was personal, and he obviously wanted to solve it in a more personal way: by giving his champion that threatened arse-kicking.

Judging by the set of Lance's broad shoulders as he watched his king's advance, the knight was in the mood to give him a fight. Normally, of course, the champion wouldn't even consider offering resistance to anything Arthur cared to do to him. However, when it came to practice combat, the king had given his men standing orders not to hold back when they fought him. *I can assure you, neither the Saxons nor Varn and his rebels will hesitate to slit my throat—if they can.*

So now Lancelot took him at his word. With a bellow of rage, the champion bounded into the air to come down on the king like an avalanche.

Everyone—knights, ladies, Gwen, even Merlin—froze in shock.

But Arthur had never been anyone's idea of easy prey, even before his transformation. Now . . .

He kicked his champion squarely in the belly. Lance went flying, hit the ground rolling, and bounced to his feet to launch another attack. The two men collided with a meaty thud and a chorus of snarled curses that sounded more animal than human. Blocking, punching, kicking, they traded brutal blows.

"Sweet mother goddess," Morgana breathed at Gwen's shoulder, "I wouldn't have expected Lance to put up that much of a fight after he . . ." She broke off, as if belatedly remembering who she was talking to.

"Lancelot blames me," Gwen told her softly. "But since he can't punish me, he's taking it out on Arthur."

"Is he insane?" Tyra demanded. "He's lucky the king didn't kill him."

"I'm not sure Lance sees that as 'lucky.'" Feeling the eyes of her women locked on her in speculation, Gwen pointedly ignored them. Still, her cheeks grew hot.

Morgana's hand fell on her shoulder in a comforting squeeze. Bless her. There was a reason she was Gwen's dearest friend, Arthur's old lover or not.

Yet within minutes, Gwen had forgotten her discomfort in her fascination with the fight. It was hardly the first time she'd seen the two men go at it, even with one of them enraged about something.

This was different. Not least because she had the uncomfortable feeling neither of them was fully in control. They fought with such blurring speed and brutal force, it wasn't long before arcs of blood flew. There was an animal savagery to their attacks that was as fascinating as it was horrifying. More than once, Gwen nearly begged Merlin to put a stop to it.

She'd lifted one hand to cast a spell of her own when Morgana caught her wrist. "Don't, Gwen. You'll only make it worse," her friend said so softly, she doubted anyone else could hear. "If you let them work through it, maybe they can save their friendship."

Knowing she was right, Gwen let her hand fall and the magic bleed away. Then, driven by sheer dark fascination, she reached for the Truebond.

It was like being swept up in a raging ocean storm. Fury burned in Arthur, an incandescent need to make the knight pay. Not only for taking Gwen, but for hurting her, forcing her to embrace her own destruction in an effort to save Lance's life. For putting Arthur himself in the position of damn near killing the woman he loved. And for having the goddamned arrogance to blame her for all of it.

He wanted Lance's head. He wouldn't take it, but he wanted it. Wanted to make Lance suffer as he'd suffered, as Gwen herself was still suffering.

"Arthur, it's not his fault!"

"I don't give a shit. He's lucky I don't fuck him up the arse. And I may do it yet."

Then Arthur threw her out of his head.

She actually staggered and would have fallen, if Morgana hadn't caught her arm and held her up until she managed to get her feet under herself again.

"Are you all right?" the healer asked softly.

"Fine," Gwen murmured, though she was shaken—and more than a little frightened.

Down in the courtyard, Arthur and Lance circled, crouched, watching each other with a black hostility that made her cringe.

Then Arthur turned into a wolf.

One minute he was a man. The next, a magic boiled around him, knocking him to all fours as his powerful body twisted, vanishing into a swarm of sparks. The sparks coalesced into a glowing, four-legged shape. When the glittering cloud vanished a heartbeat later, a muscular beast the size of a pony had taken his place. The wolf's thick fur was the same shining black as Arthur's hair. A couple of Gwen's ladies screamed in shock and horror as he leaped for Lance's throat.

"No, Arthur!" Gwen yelled.

Morgana grabbed her forearm and dug in her nails. "Hush," she hissed. "Don't give the gossips more ammunition."

Gwen scarcely heard her. With a startled shout, Lance had gone down beneath Arthur's vicious attack.

Magic flared, and suddenly there were two wolves, rolling and snarling and ripping at one another. Blood flew until even the Knights of the Round Table stepped back from their lethal violence.

Belatedly, Gwen realized Arthur might be in just as much danger from Lance as the other way around. She forgot her worry for her friend in fear for her husband. "Damn you, Lance, back the hell away!"

"That's more like it," Morgana muttered. Gwen ignored her.

The black wolf's jaws locked onto his opponent's brown-furred throat. Lance snarled, twisting, clawing, trying to rip free, but he couldn't break Arthur's hold. Gradually his struggles weakened, until he stopped moving at all. Alarmed, Gwen reached out with her magical senses and realized he still lived; Arthur had simply choked him unconscious.

The black beast released him. Gold sparks wove across the furry brown body, and Lancelot was human again, sprawled unconscious on his back. His throat was now undamaged, but he was obviously still out cold.

Gwen blew out a breath and slumped in relief.

Only to tense again when the black wolf turned and looked up at her with feral eyes. Arthur flashed to human form in an explosion of gold. Taking three running steps, he leaped fifteen feet straight up to the balustrade as Gwen's ladies scattered. Snatching her into his arms, the king strode toward their chambers.

Behind them, Diera said, "Lucky bitch."

"Diera!"

"As if you weren't thinking the same thing, Tyra, you little prig."

Arthur laughed wickedly and kicked the door closed.

ELEVEN

"Y ou and I are going to have a little talk about this habit you've acquired of trying to protect du Lac from me," Arthur told Gwen. "Especially since the one who really needs protection is you." Putting her down, he stripped off her belt, overskirt, and tunic, tossing them carelessly aside. Lifting her again, he pinned her against the wall and grinned down into her eyes. "Speaking of which, I think I figured out how to fuck you up your arse without fucking me up mine." His smile was distinctly menacing. His nostrils flared as if scenting her, and his brows lifted. "Why, Guinevere Pendragon—I think you like it when I threaten you."

She swallowed, feeling her nipples tighten with arousal. "So do you."

He laughed, the sound a bit nasty. "Oh, no, darling—I like *carrying out* the threats."

"You've always been a bit of a bastard."

"And you'd do well not to forget it." His eyes narrowed. "And even better to stop defending du Lac." Wrapping a fist in her hair, he dragged her head back and raked the points of his fangs along the pulse in her throat. "Shall I bite your throat—or one of those sweet little nipples?"

She swallowed. "Brute."

"We've already established you like my brutality." His mouth closed over a nipple for one of those delicious, tongue-swirling sucks he did so well, his big hands supporting her as if she weighed no more than one of her gowns. She locked her ankles around his waist and her arms around his neck, letting herself savor his delicious attentions.

It felt so good to have him make love to her again instead of fucking her out of vengeance and pain.

"Don't be so quick to assume I've finished punishing you," Arthur rumbled, his dark eyes flashing up to meet hers. "I may have made my point to du Lac in front of the whole court, but you will not escape so easily."

She stared at him, her heart sinking. After the Truebond, she'd hoped the damage to their marriage had been mended. "I thought you understood." Her voice sounded thin and hoarse to her own ears.

"Oh, I understand, but I don't like it. And, no, you are most definitely not forgiven." His mouth crashed down on hers in a devouring kiss. His tongue plunged into her mouth, and he caught her lower lip in his teeth hard enough to prick it with the points of his fangs. His hips rolled between her thighs, letting her feel the thick ridge of his cock against her belly.

But in that moment, all she felt was pain. She kissed him back, tasting salt as one of her own tears rolled into the corner of her mouth. "Oh, Arthur, God, Arthur . . ."

"What did you expect? You're the other half of my very soul, and you ripped out my heart by the roots."

Bracing her back against the wall, he caught one of her wrists and peeled her arm from around his neck, then pinned it behind her, supporting her back with that arm. Automatically, she tried to pull free, but it felt like his grip had turned to solid steel. For a moment, she stared, stricken, into his face as a muscle worked in his strong jaw. Then he spun them away from the wall.

And let her drop.

She yelped as her upper torso fell backward, only to snap to a stop, supported by her legs wrapped around his waist and the big male hand gripping her wrist behind her back. She dangled there, her upper body arched painfully, her right hand planted on the floor, keeping her head from rapping against it. Helpless, caught. Utterly at his mercy.

With her heart pounding ferociously in her ears, it took Gwen a moment to realize he had a better hold on her than she'd thought. One arm wrapped around her hips while the other held her arm, supporting her back in the process. "Damn you, Arthur!" She twisted her head back to eye the floor. It was definitely too close to her head. "What are you *doing?*"

"Put your knees over my shoulders." His voice was a velvet rumble, but his hard gaze made his words an order.

"Why?"

"Why do you think?" That fine jaw muscle ticked again. "Gwen, I'll not drop you no matter how angry I am."

She stared at his handsome, implacable face. That cold black gaze said one thing, but the thick cock rubbing against her crotch said something else again. "I don't believe I like this game of yours, Arthur."

"That *is* too bad. Am I in the habit of giving an order twice?"

She was coming to hate that silken tone—the one he'd always reserved for those who'd earned his displeasure. He'd never used it on her. Until now. "Why are you doing this?" She wasn't talking about the position she was in.

"Because I want to. Because you like it. Because you hurt me. Pick. One." His voice iced. "Now, Gwen."

Uncoiling each leg from around his waist, she maneuvered them, one at a time, to hook over his shoulders. Still supporting her back with the grip on her wrist, he shifted the hand holding her. He shifted his grip from one hip to one of her arms until he could support her back. She grunted as the move twisted her arms higher against her spine.

"Gwen." Just the one word, but it all but glittered with metallic threat.

Gwen tightened the grip of her legs, then lifted her bracing hand to position it with the hand he still held. His warm fingers opened and manacled that wrist, too.

Now she had no way to catch herself, at least not physically. Of course, she could conjure an entire featherbed if she chose, but that did nothing for her acute sense of vulnerability.

Arthur purred as if sensing her discomfort. His lips curving into a hot smile, he transferred his attention to her pussy. Her maiden hair almost touched his lips. His lids veiled his dark eyes as he opened his mouth and gave her a long, teasing lick.

Sensation bolted through her, a hot flood of it raging through her body. He licked her thoroughly, pausing often as if to savor her, the tip of his tongue sliding between her labia, drawing lines of fire. It seemed each stroke made her entire body reverberate like a cathedral bell. Up. Down. Slow, lazy circles alternating with quick, lashing strokes over her clit that made her buck.

She was acutely conscious of his supporting arm cradling her back, both her wrists in the grip of his free hand. It was not a pose a mortal man could have held, but Arthur was not a mortal man. The discomfort should have made arousal more difficult with the worry he might drop her. Instead that tension only added to her heat.

Helpless. She was helpless. And she liked it that way.

So did he. She could see it in his glittering eyes, in the flash of his fanged smile between licks. In the possessive way his gaze lingered on her nipples and the pink sex inches from his mouth.

"You taste like sin," he murmured. "All musk and juice. Begging for cock." That grin again, broad enough to reveal fangs. "I see no reason not to oblige you."

He carried her to the bed and lowered her to the cool sheets. Straightening, Arthur paused and looked down at her, his gaze lingering on peaked nipples and the sex now wet from his mouth.

She stared back, taking in the breadth of his shoulders and the jut of his cock, its ruddy curved shaft and heavy balls. He looked like a handsome demon, come to drive her insane.

"I think you need something to remind you of your place." He looked around the room until his gaze fell on the pile of protective sleep sacks she'd created days before. He grinned. "Ah, those will do." Sauntering over, he bent over the sacks and busied himself. When he rose a moment later, he held a number of long leather laces in his hands.

Arthur tied her up like a lamb on fair day, bending her legs so he could loop the leather in a figure eight that bound her right calf to her right thigh. After tying her right wrist to that ankle, he repeated the process with her left leg. When he was done, she was curled in a tight ball.

"Just the way I like you: ready to be fucked." Spreading her bound legs, he studied her helplessly creaming cunt. "The question is, with what?"

He moved away again. When he came back a moment later, he held two knives. One was a slim dagger, but the other was a heavy hunting knife. When he started coating its thick deerhorn hilt with lavender oil, she knew where he intended to put it.

One by one, Arthur drew the blades from their scabbards. Gwen stiffened, not sure she liked where this was going.

"You look a bit nervous." Giving her that demonic grin, he slid the hilt of the dagger into her pussy. Then, gripping the hunting knife by its bare blade, he pushed its handle slowly, so slowly, into her anus. The hot stretch made her hiss.

God, it felt incredible—the textured hilts of the knives probing in slow, hot thrusts, satisfying the hot need that had been rising since he'd pinned her against the wall. The sensation only intensified when he twisted the one in her arse, pumping hard.

"Pretend it's me and Lance," he told her, and curled a lip. "I, of course, am the one up your arse."

"He wouldn't touch me if you gave him a royal command."

"Don't fool yourself, darling—he'd jump at the chance. He may have had you, but he doesn't remember it. I'd wager the royal treasury that's driving him insane." Slowly, Arthur slid the hilt of the dagger in and out as he buggered her with the hunting knife's handle. In with one, out with the other, the taunting strokes deep as he brushed her clit with his thumb. "He'd kill to sink into this pretty pink pussy. Oh, he might tell himself he's punishing you, but a man will tell himself any lie to touch his dream."

God, he was driving her insane. Those hilts grinding in and out in opposite strokes, stretching and tormenting her arse and pussy, pain and pleasure blending in an erotic stew that maddened her until her hips rolled helplessly. "Arthur, you wretch. . . ."

"You like that, don't you?" Fangs flashed. "God knows I do." A lock of hair fell over his eyes, and he lifted one hand to brush it back, leaving a smear of red across his temple.

"Arthur, you're bleeding!" Despite her bonds, Gwen tightened her stomach muscles until she could look at his hands. Both of them bore bleeding slashes where he gripped the bare knife blades. "What are you doing? Stop that!"

"No." He went right on thrusting the two knives, teasing her pussy and arse.

Gwen was no longer in the mood to be teased. "Dammit, Arthur! What is this, some new way of punishing me?"

"Perhaps you're not the one I'm punishing."

"Stop it!" Horrified, she watched the blood drip between his fingers to plop softly on the stone floor in a quiet rain. "Saints, Arthur . . ."

"Merlin warned me not to leave you after your transformation, that I would rue it if I did. Like a fool, I didn't listen—and left you and my best friend at the mercy of that damned Gift of his."

"I don't care! Let me heal you, husband. Please!"

"I can heal myself." He pulled both knife hilts out of her and tossed the weapons aside with a clatter of steel on stone. "All I have to do is turn into a wolf."

Sparks exploded in a silent detonation, and there was a black wolf standing there on his hind legs, massive head between her thighs. He gaped his jaws at her in a lupine grin, tongue lolling. He looked even bigger up close than he had down in the courtyard, fighting Lance.

"Ummm." Eyes widening, Gwen stared at him. *This is headed in no good direction.*

She wasn't at all surprised when he lowered his head and gave her cunt a long lick with that wet wolf tongue. "Stop that! You sin, Arthur!"

His eyes rolled up to look at her, but he went right on licking, his thin, agile tongue curling over sensitive flesh as she squirmed helplessly. Gwen could feel his unrepentant amusement through the Truebond despite the mental barriers he'd erected.

His tongue felt very wet, and his hot breath gusted over her with every lick.

Gwen squirmed in a combination of arousal and intense discomfort. Glaring at his big black-furred head, she growled, "I should feed you a fireball."

He looked at her and growled in warning, a harsh whipsawing sound. When he jumped up on the bed, the mattress sank under his considerable weight. Hot black eyes locked on her face as he stepped between her bound legs and paced up over her curled body. Coarse sable fur brushed over her knees, and the tip of his tail teased her thighs. He was so big, he barely had to spread his paws as he straddled her.

Looking down at her with feral dark eyes, Arthur curled his upper lip, revealing an impressive collection of very sharp teeth. His hot breath smelled of mead as he loomed over her, and she shivered in reaction. There was a threat in his gaze she was glad she didn't understand.

With another explosion of gold sparks, he became human again.

Displaying healed hands as he knelt astride her, Arthur lifted a dark brow. "You're not the only one who can do magic."

"Lovely. You do realize I don't bed things that have more legs than I do?"

He smiled, all teeth. "You're assuming I'd give you a choice."

"Oh, I have a choice. I could work a spell to make myself a wolf-skin rug."

"I'm terrified."

"You should be. I'm not joking."

"And I don't take well to threats." He knelt, straddling her head, and cupped the back of her neck. "Unlike you. Get ready to suck, Gwen. Or I'll bend you over my knee again." Taking his cock in one hand, he presented it to her lips, caught her jaw, and pressed his thumb into the hinge to keep it open as he thrust his cock inside.

She was tempted to bite him, but an idea made her instead suck hard on the smooth shaft and its velvety mushroom head.

For a few minutes Gwen let herself savor the textures and tastes of Arthur Pendragon's cock. Fellatio made a lovely distraction as she threw up her own mental barrier in the Truebond, and plotted.

"That's better," he purred, rolling his hips to fuck her mouth. "You need to remember who rules here."

"And you need to remember I'm a queen, not a slave."

"You're whatever I say you are. Deeper, Gwen. That's it, right to the balls."

His eyes shuttered in delight, he thrust his cock deep in her mouth, driving faster and faster as his climax approached. She sucked harder, judging her moment, letting him get closer to the edge. He drew in a breath to roar . . .

And she jerked her head off his cock and destroyed her bonds with an explosion of magic. A sweeping gesture flattened him on the bed with his legs chained wide apart. More chains circled his chest, binding his arms tight to his torso, wrists behind his back.

Arthur's eyes widened with astonishment that turned quickly to flaming rage. He began to buck and thrash. "Dammit, Gwen! What the hell do you think you're doing?"

"Teaching you a badly needed lesson." She paused to admire the sight of his big body straining against the steel links, chest arching with effort.

He showed her gritted fangs. "I'm going to teach you a badly needed lesson you're not going to like at all." Cords stood out starkly on either side of his flushed throat, and his eyes glittered with angry heat.

If she hadn't been so furious, that tone would have made her quail. "Silence." An imperious gesture tightened his bonds and added a thinner chain to encircle his balls and the base of his cock.

He snarled. "The ice under your feet grows thin as parchment, wife."

"I could say the same to you." The thin chain tightened so sharply his teeth clicked together.

When he glared at her but wisely said nothing more, she nodded in satisfaction and flung one leg across his narrow hips. Reaching between her legs, she caught his thick cock and angled it upward before sinking down, engulfing it one delicious inch at a time. "Ahhhh," she purred, and gave him a deliberately taunting smile. "That's better."

Chained like a breeding bull, Arthur fought to maintain the glare as his wife's strong thighs flexed, lifting her off his cock. The sweet, sliding grip almost tore a groan from his throat, but somehow he managed to suppress it. He couldn't believe she'd had the gall to do this to him.

He also couldn't believe how arousing it was. Despite his Magus strength, Gwen had managed to conjure chains he couldn't break. Bound, helpless, all he could do was lie there in this bloody uncomfortable position, and watch Gwen's beautiful tits bounce as she fucked him. Her lovely blue eyes were bright over flushed cheeks and full, parted lips. Her body looked slim and tight and pale. Long pink nipples graced those delightful breasts, and he stared at them hungrily.

"Your cock," she gasped, "it feels a yard long . . ."

"And you feel so slick and tight." Despite the shackles that held his legs spread wide, Arthur rolled his hips to meet her thrusts.

The clamping grip of Gwen's sex felt tighter than he'd ever felt it, perhaps because of her transformation. Each sliding stroke gripped him with the perfect slick friction, dragging him closer and closer to coming.

Gwen leaned back and grabbed her ankles, plunging up and down on his cock. Arthur drew in a hard breath, admiring the pale, graceful arch of her body and the sight of her creamy red labia wrapped around his cock as she slid up and down.

She moaned as her beautiful eyes slid closed. "Arthur." She bit her lip. "Oh, sweet Lord . . ."

One of her hands found a bouncing breast, caught a deliciously erect nipple, and began to twist. The other hand slid between her legs, where her fingers went to work on her clit.

In seconds, deep pulses began in her slick depths, massaging his shaft. Gwen arched with a cry that spiraled up to a piercing note as she writhed, coming. Her twisting grip added the last push to shoot him into orgasm. He roared, driving his hips up to impale her even deeper.

The blast of pleasure shredded his mental shields. Her orgasm stormed into his, spurring his climax higher, which in turn intensified hers still more. Around and around, higher and higher as he emptied himself, bellowing in time to her helpless screams.

Gwen collapsed over him, winded from sheer pleasure more than exertion. As sweet as that had been, however, she knew it hadn't accomplished anything. Somehow she had to make him see reason. Even if she had to play a little hard to do it.

But he wasn't going to like it. Not at all.

With a mental wince, she swung off him and rose to her feet. A gesture conjured gown and overskirt, returning her tumbled hair to a proper regal coif. *That's better.* She pasted a haughty expression on her face with an ease born of seventeen years as queen. "You've been showing me what you can do with your magic," Gwen told him coolly. "Perhaps you need to see what I can do with mine." A flick of her fingers, and a fireball appeared between Arthur's spread legs, boiling with such heat, he instantly broke into a sweat.

The king froze, staring at it with lifted brows. "That's quite a trick." His tone was so elaborately cool, she knew she'd managed to unnerve him. Which was encouraging, given how hard that was to do.

"Nimue took my ladies and me out into the hills while you and your Magi slept this morning. We spent hours shooting magical blasts into a mound of earth created for that purpose." Gwen gazed at the fireball with grim pride. "Just imagine something like that on the battlefield. Mordred and his traitors would run screaming."

"He might," Arthur drawled. "If he thought you could actually use it on anyone."

"Oh, I could use it on him."

"It's easy to talk about all the men you could kill, darling. Just walk into any tavern, and you'll find a dozen drunks happy to tell you about the rivers of blood they could spill." His gaze turned grim and distant. "But look into your victim's eyes stone-sober, and actually driving the blade home is a different matter."

"I'd kill a hundred Mordreds to save you."

Arthur snorted. "I know you, Gwen. You could no more watch that boy burn than you could fly."

She gave him a cheeky grin. "Actually, I'm pretty sure I could fly."

It seemed he wasn't in the mood for her humor. "Do you know how many men I've killed?"

She opened her mouth, about to spout something cheeky, only to close it again. He was not in the mood. "No."

"Nor do I. Yet Mordred still lives, because I couldn't kill him. I knew you and I and Britain might well pay the price, but I still couldn't end him. I lifted my sword, but all I could see was an eleven-year-old's gap-toothed smile." He jerked his chin at the fireball hovering between his knees. "You can burn me with that if you want, but I will not put you in the position of being forced to kill Mordred with your magic. Not because you don't have the courage to do it, but because you wouldn't be able to live with the memory afterward."

"Better to live with his death than yours." She gestured, and the fireball disappeared, leaving behind the smell of singed sheets.

He sighed. "Gwen, the screams of a stranger can haunt a man until he thinks he'll never sleep again. I won't have you listening to Mordred's ghostly howls."

She eyed him before saying, almost gently, "It's not your choice, Arthur."

He stared at her, his expression grim. "It is so long as I'm High King." One dark brow lifted. "Unless you plan to change that?"

Dammit, it was like arguing with the ocean tides: all one got was wet. "No, Arthur. I have no desire to change that."

"I won't have you or your ladies on the battlefield. Women risk their lives to bring life into the world; men risk theirs to take it. I don't want you to wake every night screaming from nightmares of dying men, of standing hip-deep in blood and shit. I want to come home to you knowing your heart and body are whole."

"And I want you to come home instead of dying under Mordred's blade."

He looked at her, his gaze level with that cool, unmovable determination she knew so well. "I'm going to come home, Gwen. My bastard doesn't have a prayer."

She sighed and gestured. The manacles dissolved into sparks, which floated silently away. "Don't let those new abilities of yours make you overconfident, Arthur. We both know what happens to an overconfident man on the battlefield."

* * *

The months of summer dragged by, heavy, hot, and sticky. And worse, bloody.

Mordred had recruited a large number of followers with the help of ambitious nobles who saw the situation as an opportunity to further their own political interests. Most of them were the same people Arthur had defeated in combat a decade before, so they knew they were unlikely to see big rewards from supporting the king. His son, on the other hand, had promised to reward them handsomely for their support.

Adding tinder to the fire, Mordred and his rebels were spreading the most appalling rumors that superstitious peasants were only too happy to believe. It was said Arthur drank the blood of infants, while Gwen and her ladies had unholy relations with demons they then sent off to kill peasants and nobles alike.

People had indeed died, but they'd been the victims of Mordred's vicious raids. Unfortunately, he left no one alive to tell who the real villain was.

Arthur had done his best to combat the rumors while searching for his son and the rebels. The few times he and his forces had succeeded in finding them, the king had won the resulting battle.

The problem was, those victories were getting more difficult with every passing day. Arthur's army was bleeding men in a constant flood of desertions. Apparently, the fact that the king now had to do all his fighting at night did not endear him to his men, even those who'd served in the royal army for decades.

Arthur had tried everything he could think of to stanch the losses among the ranks, but nothing worked—not pay increases, promises of farmland, or even fiefdoms seized from rebellious nobles. He was forced to finally order the execution of anyone caught deserting. Hangings became a nightly ritual—which did not exactly endear Arthur to the survivors.

But the desertions slowed to a trickle.

Meanwhile, Guinevere and her ladies went on practicing magical combat under Nimue's tutelage. As the days passed in sweaty mock warfare, the twelve learned how to throw fireballs at one another and erect magical shields to protect themselves.

Arthur, however, didn't care. He was adamant that the ladies were going to stay off the battlefield, particularly Gwen. It didn't seem to matter how often the new witches demonstrated their abilities; the king remained unimpressed. Or at least unwilling to admit to it if he was.

Gwen had no way of knowing what the stubborn wretch actually felt. He'd gotten so good at shielding his mind, she sometimes felt they had no Truebond at all.

It was terrifying.

Every time he went out to hunt Mordred, she was afraid he wouldn't return. That he'd manage to get himself killed, and the first she would know about it was when she dropped dead from the Truebond.

When she mentioned this worry, Arthur only snorted. "Mordred will be in hell before he knows what hit him."

This despite the fact that the king himself had often said overconfidence was as lethal in battle as blind panic.

Gwen suspected he didn't believe defeating the rebels would be that easy. Unfortunately, he had no intention of admitting as much.

As it was, every nightmare she had—and she had a lot of them— resulted in a row over his refusal to allow Gwen and her ladies to play a part in any battle whatsoever.

Between that and the desertions, Arthur grew more and more distant, as if determined to hide any worry he felt. As a result, the tension between the king and queen grew so intense, it made even the Knights of the Round Table uncomfortable.

It soon reached the point where they made love only when hunger literally drove Arthur to it.

For her part, Gwen was miserable. She was losing the man she loved. Worse, she had the horrible feeling that soon that loss would become permanent.

And Mordred the Bastard would be High King of Britain.

TWELVE

M erlin and Nimue had disappeared again.

The witch had explained they needed to find more champions of humanity in other lands, people who would eventually serve as Arthur's agents. Yet to Gwen it felt as if the magical pair were abandoning them when they most needed the help.

At least the witch had left her a way to get in contact, if absolutely necessary.

In the meantime, Gwen was on her own. She had to get through to Arthur, whether he was blocking the Truebond or not. She'd taken to demonstrating her magical skills at every opportunity, even with something as mundane as mealtime.

They'd been gathering in the Round Table chamber for meals since Gwen first became queen. Though the Magi no longer ate, Arthur decided the practice was still useful because it gave him a chance to observe how the witches dealt with his knights.

Which generally boiled down to a great deal of flirting.

Initially, the idea of conjuring food came about because so many of the household servants had fled Camelot. Gwen and her ladies could easily have cooked their meals by hand, but the queen thought using

magic while everyone watched was actually a better way of making
Arthur realize what magic could do—or more to the point, what
Gwen and her ladies could do with it. Yet so far nothing seemed to
have made an impression on him; he always looked faintly bored. It
made Gwen feel like that particularly clumsy juggler who had tried to
entertain the court one day last winter.

It was intensely frustrating. There were times she could have cheer-
fully beaten his thick head in.

So much for the Truebond.

One particular night in late August, the ladies passed their conjured dishes back and forth while the men discussed how best to deal
with Mordred's machinations.

Gawain, who'd been watching Morgana like a hungry fox eyeing a
chicken, suddenly glanced around and frowned. "Where's Tristan?"
The two were best friends; where one was, the other was usually somewhere nearby.

Lancelot shrugged. "Trying to mend his marriage, most likely."

Gawain blinked. "How does he mean to do that? He hasn't even
spoken to Isolde in weeks."

"She seems to have had a change of heart. I saw them on the stairs
today, and she was laughing and talking to him. He looked more than
a bit puzzled."

No wonder. Gwen grimaced. Isolde was Tristan's wife of twenty
years, but she'd failed Nimue's test. To Isolde's fury, Tristan had
accepted the Grail anyway, even knowing she would remain mortal.
As one of Arthur's greatest knights, he evidently hadn't wanted to
deprive the kingdom of his skills at a time when everything seemed
well on its way to going to hell.

Gwen spoke up. "So they've reconciled?" At least somebody had.

Lancelot gave her a narrow, icy glance that said very clearly how
deeply furious he still was. "So it appears."

"I hope they can mend their marriage." Gwen absently used her
fork to push her food around on her plate.

Arthur leaned down to whisper, "You need to eat, Gwen. It does no one any good if you starve yourself."

Gwen shot him a cool glance and replied so softly a human couldn't have heard her. "Yes, I'd imagine the blood of a starving woman doesn't taste nearly as good."

He gave her a long, cool look. *"We are not going to do this here. Save your ire for our chambers, my queen."*

Gwen knew he was right. Fighting in front of the knights and ladies of what was left of their court was *definitely* not a good idea. She sealed her lips and went back to pushing food around her plate.

Across the width of the table, Gawain looked up and gasped, then leaped up to stride around the table. Gwen glanced around in alarm.

Tristan leaned in the doorway, naked and covered in blood. One shaking, gory fist held a knife that dripped scarlet on the stone floor.

As the others exclaimed and jumped to their feet, Gawain reached him, hooked an arm around his waist, and lowered him carefully to the floor.

Morgana beat Gwen and Arthur to the pair. When the other knights and ladies tried to gather around, the healer looked up and snapped, "Give me room to work!"

Instinctively responding to her tone, everyone but Arthur and Gwen fell back. "Tristan, shift to wolf form," the king ordered, his tone urgent. "Let your magic heal you."

Tristan's only response was a low, barely conscious groan.

"I don't think he can shift, sire," Morgana told him, examining the knight in worry. "He's too badly hurt. His attacker's knife missed his heart, but only just."

"Isolde . . . Isolde . . ." Tristan murmured, his eyes fluttering closed, only to open again. "God, Isolde . . ."

"Is your wife in danger?" When Tristan only moaned, Arthur glanced up and caught Lancelot's gaze. "Make sure Tristan's attacker didn't get his wife."

But before Lance could make it to the door, Tristan spoke. "No point. Dead . . . Isolde's dead." He started to cough. Blood sprayed across the stone floor.

Morgana drew her belt knife, slashed it across her wrist, and presented the bleeding cut to the blond knight's mouth. For a moment it appeared Tristan was too disoriented to take the blood she was offering. Then his nostrils flared, and he latched on to the cut. The healer winced at his desperate sucking. Normally, feeding the men was deliciously erotic, but foreplay did have its place; at the moment, Tristan was apparently too badly hurt to realize he was hurting her.

Arthur looked around at Lance again. "Find me the one who did this. Galahad, go with him."

"Aye, sire." The two knights strode out.

Though obviously impatient, Arthur waited until Tristan released Morgana's wrist and raised his head. "Did you see the assassin? How many of them were there? Where did they go?"

"No assassin." Tristan met the king's gaze, his mouth tight with pain. "*I* killed her."

Everyone froze.

"*What?*" Arthur demanded, as the knights and ladies stirred and murmured in shock.

Gwen shared his astonishment. It was almost impossible to imagine Tristan laying hands on any woman in violence, especially his wife.

The king stared at him in astonishment and growing rage. "Why would you do such a thing?"

"She . . . She stabbed . . . me . . . first." Tristan panted, his handsome face contorted in pain. "Tried to kill me. Missed."

"I don't understand. *Why*, Tristan? What happened?"

"Sire, a moment." Morgana looked down at the knight. "Do you feel well enough now to shift?"

He nodded. "Your blood helped, my . . . my lady."

Magic fountained around him. When it was gone, a huge wolf lay on the floor where Tristan had been. There was no sign of blood on his shining honey-gold fur. He looked up at them with Tristan's blue eyes and made a sound as if attempting to speak. All that emerged was a low, lupine whine that became a growl of irritation. The knight transformed yet again. Though his skin was as bloody as it had been when he staggered into the room, it was obvious his injuries had healed.

Tristan groaned in relief. "God's teeth, that's better. Isolde was better with a blade than I thought." He looked down, seeming to register at last that he was naked.

Even as he colored in embarrassment, Gwen gestured, conjuring a tunic over his nudity. "Thank you, my queen." He scrambled to his feet before helping Morgana to her feet with automatic courtesy.

"I'm glad to see you back with us," Arthur said. "Now what the *hell* happened?"

"Isolde approached me in town. She'd been treating me like a leper for weeks, so I was surprised when she said she wanted to be . . ." His eyes flickered. ". . . Alone. We went to our chambers, and she confessed she's the one who's been spying for Mordred." His big hands curled into fists. "She claimed she'd only done it because she was so hurt and angry that I'd accepted the Grail."

Arthur growled a low curse.

"I was all set to drag her before you, when she told me she knew what Mordred's plans were. She said she'd spy for us if only I would forgive her." He curled a lip in self-disgust, his gaze tortured. "She *begged* me, sire, vowed that she'd realized how wrong she'd been. She swore by Christ's wounds she wanted to make amends for what she'd done, if only I'd make love to her."

Arthur lifted dark brows. "And you believed her?"

Tristan raked a harried hand through his hair. "She was my wife, sire. I loved her once."

With an effort, Arthur managed to avoid a telling glance at Gwen. There were any number of things he could have said to his knight then, but the king kept his silence; it was obvious Tristan well knew how thoroughly he'd erred. "Go on."

The knight's bark of laughter sounded edged in acid. "She waited until I was distracted to jerk the knife from beneath the pillow and drive it into my chest. Evidently she didn't know that wouldn't do the job." A muscle worked in his cheek. "So I pulled the dagger and used it on her—and *I* damned well know what I'm doing."

Now everyone in the room winced in pained sympathy. Arthur laid a hand on the knight's powerful shoulder. "I'm sorry, Tris."

"Sire, I did manage to get one bit of information out of her before she died." Tristan's face twisted in such pain, Gwen decided she really didn't want to know how he'd extracted that information. "She told me Mordred plans an attack on the village of Camlann. He means to burn the town to the ground and slaughter everyone there."

This is the battle, Gwen realized. She had absolutely no grounds for that belief—except for the cold certainty sweeping up her spine. *This is what I've been dreaming about all these months.*

Arthur would die at Camlann—unless she convinced him to let her prevent it.

I t was easily the worst row they'd ever had. Gwen stopped just short of pitching crockery at his head. Arthur, for his part, informed her icily that her dreams had been only that—dreams. What's more, if she dared set foot on the battlefield, he'd throw her in gaol for a year—in the unlikely event she managed to survive the battle at all.

Then he stormed out, bellowing for his knights.

Gwen gazed mutinously after him. "If you think I'll give up that easily, you know me not at all, my love."

Mary, Joseph, and all the saints, she wished Nimue and Merlin were here. Luckily the witch had left Gwen with a way to contact them wherever they'd gone.

The queen headed into her dressing chamber. There, in the corner beyond her big bathing tub, stood the largest mirror she'd ever seen.

Fully her own height, it was so large as to be impossible to manufacture by any technology even the Romans had had.

Nimue had conjured it in but a moment.

As the witch had instructed her, Gwen stepped up to the mirror. "Nimue."

The image of a woman appeared, but it wasn't anyone Gwen had ever met. Her features were exotic, with odd-shaped brown eyes set aslant in a round, delicate face. She had a nose like a child's, though there was nothing childlike about her small, lush mouth. Her hair hung long and straight to her hips, shining black like a crow's wing. She wore flowing robes of white silk such as Gwen had never seen. She said something in a language Gwen had never heard before, then paused, and added, "Oh, Queen Guinevere! Hello."

A blink later, the exotic woman became Nimue. "Something's happened, hasn't it?" Nimue's dark gaze searched hers. "Something has gone very wrong."

"Arthur is taking his army to fight Mordred. I think—no, I know—this is the battle I've been having nightmares about." Gwen had taken care not to sound the alarm about any of Arthur's other skirmishes for this very reason: she wanted Nimue to take her seriously when she was sure the crisis had arrived.

Nimue's gaze searched hers for a long moment. Just as Gwen's nerves began to scream, the witch nodded. "Very well, I'll come. Don't fear, Gwen. We'll sort it out."

A shimmering point of light appeared in the air, growing swiftly into a wavering opening. Nimue stepped through into the bathing chamber, and the gate vanished.

"Merlin cannot leave this new batch of candidates just yet; things are at a particularly delicate point," the witch told her. "But judging by your expression, things are just as delicate here."

"I'm afraid so," Gwen said. Feeling suddenly weary, she led the way into the bedroom, where she sank into one of the hearth chairs.

Nimue sat down beside her. "Tell me what happened."

Gwen recounted the events of the past two hours, though she had to stop to blink back tears more than once. "This is the dream. I know this is the dream. This is the night Arthur dies."

The witch leaned over and took her hand in a warm, strong grip. "Arthur is not going to die. Or at least, you and I are going to do everything in our power to prevent it."

Gwen blinked away more of those shameful tears. "But what are we going to do?"

Nimue's gaze met Guinevere's, level and determined. "We're going to make Arthur a sword."

They stepped through Nimue's gate into a huge cave with quartz walls, the faceted rock glittering in the light of the witch's magic. The patter of falling water drew Gwen's attention to the other end of the cavern, where a waterfall tumbled down the stone wall into a dark pool. In its center lay a circular island of smooth dark stone, too regular to be anything but a conjuration.

"What is this place?" Awestruck, Gwen turned in a circle, gazing up at the stone ceiling three stories overhead. The very air seemed to glow with power, a sense of magic so strong, gooseflesh spilled across her skin.

"The Sidhe natives call this cave the Womb of Magic, and they've been using it for major workings for hundreds of years. The crystal acts to focus the magic of this world."

"This world?" Gwen moved over to the nearest cavern wall and hesitantly stretched out a hand to touch it. It felt warm, almost throbbing with power.

"My people call this universe—this world—the Mageverse, the realm of magic." Apparently realizing how puzzled Gwen was, she elaborated. "Magic is not native to your world, which is why we had so much difficulty giving you your abilities. When you draw on your power, the Mageverse is its source."

Purely as an experiment, Gwen gestured. The magical flames that leaped from her fingers burned brighter than she'd ever seen them blaze. What's more, they came with ease. "Magic does seem much stronger here."

Nimue nodded. "It is. When you intend a major working like this, you would be well-advised to gate here to do it, thus our trip now. This is going to be a particularly difficult bit of magic, and I need all the help I can get."

Nimue had earlier explained that the phrase "major working" referred to a powerful magical object or spell intended to last hundreds of years. That called for more than simply willing the object into being, as one did with a standard conjuration.

"The potion you drank from the Grail is a major working; that spell must be active in every descendant any of you ever have, no matter how remote," she'd said. "That's why it took at least twenty-four hours for the spell to finish transforming the first of you into Magekind. In the future, your descendants will become Majae or Magi almost immediately."

Now the witch caught Gwen's hand and drew her to her side. She gestured, spilling a glittering golden path out to the stone platform in the middle of the pool. As it solidified, Nimue strode out along the narrow bridge, Gwen at her heels. "I'm going to need your help," she explained as they walked. "I must bind the sword to Arthur. Since he's not here, you and your Truebond must serve as my conduit. Concentrate on your link with him; it will take more effort with us in the Mageverse. Maintain the connection so I can use it as the basis of a bond between him and the sword." She began to paint the stone circle with a stream of saffron light that flowed from her tapered fingertips.

"So this is going to be more than just a sword?"

The witch smiled. "Yes, Excalibur will definitely be more than 'just' a sword."

Nimue breathed a word, and the spell circle rolled upward, forming a hemisphere over their heads. Its curve shimmered with the same glowing symbols that made up the circle, revolving slowly in brilliant waves as the crystal cavern's walls reflected the unearthly glow. Gwen had no idea what the symbols meant, and she didn't dare interrupt Nimue to ask.

The witch began to chant in a low, resonant voice, energy pouring from her fingertips to form the rough outline of a sword. The insubstantial weapon began to suck magic from the globe, two funnels of golden light pouring into it at point and pommel. Magic prickled over Gwen's skin, the crawling sensation skittering over her like the claws of countless insects.

The sword gradually grew more substantial, solidifying as it drank the circle's magic. Gwen had to fight not to fidget, knowing their time was growing short. Arthur was on his way to Camlann in a desperate effort to reach the town before Mordred and his army.

Unfortunately, if the dream was to be believed, Mordred would have five men to every one of Arthur's. Gwen feared that every moment spent conjuring the sword could be the one when the king lost his life. Waiting under such circumstances was the worst torture she'd ever suffered.

Still chanting, Nimue beckoned Gwen closer. As the queen obeyed, she met the witch's gaze. Points of light filled the woman's black irises until it was like looking up into the night sky.

It unnerved the hell out of Gwen, but she stubbornly refused to let her fear overcome her.

Then Nimue's long, cool fingers touched her forehead, and it felt as if a dragon had sunk flaming claws into her soul and jerked with brutal, wrenching force. It was all Gwen could do not to scream.

Her knees buckled, but she caught herself, fighting the urge to hit Nimue with a power blast that would have knocked the witch on her backside. Instead, Gwen concentrated on maintaining the connection to Arthur, letting Nimue draw on that link as she labored on the sword.

"Gwen?" Her husband's voice reverberated through the Truebond. "What happened? You're in pain. . . ."

"Nothing." Ignoring the flow of blood trickling from her nose, she told him, *"It's nothing."*

"It doesn't feel like nothing. That hurt even me, as far away as I am."

"Don't you have a battle to fight? Keep your mind on your job before Mordred kills you."

"I asked you what you're doing." He had that implacable note in his mental voice she knew too well. *"Answer me."*

"I'm fine, dammit. I'm just working on a spell."

"A spell to do what?"

"Nothing that concerns you. Shouldn't you be killing people?"

"Shouldn't you be doing needlework?"

That was the problem with pissing Arthur off; he made you pay for it. *"Arthur, I'm fine. Go. Away!"*

With a frustrated growl, he finally retreated. Gwen heaved a mental sigh of relief. She was lucky she'd been able to lie to him at all, given the Truebond. Fortunately, Arthur's own shields had been firmly in place, barely permitting mental speech. He must have been doing something he didn't want her to see, either.

Most likely he really had been killing somebody.

That, or fighting for his life. Arthur *needed* that sword.

Gwen went back to pouring power into Nimue—and paid for it as the pain built, ripping at her consciousness until it seemed her very soul was being dragged out by the roots.

When the brutal pull finally ceased, Gwen went down like a felled doe. Lying on her back in the wide stone circle, she panted as she watched the globe's glowing symbols fade around her. Finally the circle vanished completely.

"Are you all right?" Nimue asked in a strained voice, moving into Gwen's field of view. She was breathing hard, as if she'd been running for her life. "That was . . . a rough one."

Gwen stared up at the woman, blinking in shock. Nimue appeared to have aged decades since they'd stepped into the circle. Her skin had taken on a sickly gray-green hue as it lay in deep hollows over the knife-edged contours of her face, and her dark hair hung limp with sweat.

But Nimue held the precious sword, solid now and glowing brilliantly enough to make Gwen's eyes water. The power it radiated seemed to crawl over her skin like the feet of countless insects.

"Let me have it." Gwen struggled to her feet, though it took so much effort, she suspected she looked every bit as haggard as Nimue.

Without a word—the witch might not have been capable of speech—Nimue handed over the blade.

Balancing the great weapon on her palms, Gwen studied it with awe. It was almost two hand spans longer than most swords, though it felt far lighter, as though made of something other than steel.

It was also the most beautiful weapon Gwen had ever seen. Its blade was intricately engraved with the same magical symbols as the spell globe. The pommel of its cross-guard hilt featured a brilliant yellow gem the size of a baby's fist. Two matching smaller stones were inset in its quillons. Magic radiated from all three stones, winding along the blade in a blazing golden braid. The overwhelming sense of power lifted the hair on Gwen's neck.

The brilliant glow faded a moment later, leaving the sword looking like nothing more than a sword. Gwen wasn't fooled. "It's incredible, Nimue. I have never seen such a weapon." But as she glanced up at the witch, she frowned in worry. "Are you going to be all right?"

"I will be fine. It's a good thing we did the spell here. I doubt I could have survived trying to work it on your world." Nimue rolled her head on her shoulders as if to loosen the knots that had gathered there. Closing her eyes, she seemed to concentrate, as if drawing in power. Her back straightened as her shoulders squared, but she still looked gray and drawn.

"Its name is Excalibur, which means 'cut steel,'" the witch continued, once she'd recovered enough for speech. "Which is exactly what it will do, when swung with a Magus's strength." Her lips twitched in a grim smile. "I assure you, Mordred will not break *this* weapon."

"I can certainly believe that." Gwen gave the great blade a respectful glance, then smiled at the witch. "Thank you for what you've done for us, Nimue. I know it cost you."

"Just get the sword to him, Gwen." The witch sounded so exhausted, she was slurring her words. "Save him."

Gwen frowned, remembering snatches of that horrifying dream. "But how do I get there in time?"

"Concentrate on the Truebond and focus your will on reaching him. A gate will answer your need. Like so . . ." Turning, she gestured sharply. A shimmering point appeared in the air, blooming into a gate. "I must get back to Merlin. The situation on Nippon grows dangerous."

"What if we need you?" Gwen bit her lip, remembering the wretched odds in her dream.

"You can handle it," Nimue added with a glance over her shoulder. "And if you can't, you're not who we thought you were." Then she was gone.

Well, it seemed Gwen was on her own. Except she didn't have to be, did she?

Taking a deep breath, she gripped the precious sword and pictured her own chamber. The magical point appeared in the air, expanding in the blink of an eye. With a sigh of relief, the queen stepped through into her own familiar chambers.

Familiar—and yet not. She felt the sharp decrease in magic as she passed from one world to the next. Determined to ignore the weakness, she banged the chamber door open, strode onto the balustrade, and shouted, "Ladies of the Round Table, we ride!"

For the first time in her life, Guinevere Pendragon wore armor. The chain mail hauberk should have been heavy, but thanks to the spell she'd used to conjure it, it might as well have been thin silk as its skirt swung around her thighs. In one hand she held Arthur's new sword, its length blazing with such power, it made her very bones seem to buzz.

She strode along the line of her women, acutely aware of their eyes watching her. Gwen had watched Arthur pace the courtyard as he inspected his troops in just this way. She wondered if his heart ever pounded as hers did now.

The eleven other ladies of the Round Table also wore conjured armor, though they looked uncomfortable in it. Not to mention nervous as cats surrounded by a pack of wolfhounds.

That was probably to the good. Arthur often said that only a fool felt no fear going into battle. With proper training, he said, the fear left you, until all you knew was the mechanics of battle, of using sword and shield to attack and block.

Unfortunately, Gwen wasn't sure she or her women were well trained enough in the use of combat magic. Particularly not compared to the decades of training that knights had.

But she also knew none of her ladies would let their comparatively thin instruction stop them. Despite whatever fear they felt, their resolve to save the king and his knights was palpable.

Arthur was going to be furious. He'd probably fuck her up the arse again. At least, she profoundly hoped so; that would mean he was alive to do it.

"This is not going to be easy," Gwen told them, pivoting to pace in the other direction. "But remember that the enemy is mortal—only human. We're not." She flashed them all a hard glance cribbed straight from Arthur. "Show them no mercy. I can assure you, they'll show us none. Mordred has spent months spinning tales of how evil and demonic we are." She smiled grimly. "Fortunately."

"Fortunately?" Diera asked, her tone incredulous, just as Gwen had known someone would.

"Yes." The queen bared her teeth in Leodegraunce's favorite grin of pure bloodlust. "It'll make them that much easier to panic. If we play our cards right, it won't take much to send them running home to mummy."

She didn't add that if they played their cards wrong, the bastards would rip them all apart. The ladies knew that as well as she did.

In twenty years of fighting, Arthur had never seen odds quite this bad. By his rough estimate, Mordred's forces outnumbered his by at least five to one. He had no more than three thousand men against a good fifteen thousand rebels.

They battled in the light of a full moon—Mordred and his rebels against Arthur, a handful of loyal lords, and their forces. The king had sent his knights to play bodyguard to his loyalist lords, knowing that given the odds, the humans wouldn't otherwise have a chance.

"You should've let the witches come," Lancelot shouted over the howls and curses of battling men.

"And bring my wife into this?" Arthur bellowed, as he sent his opponent's head spinning with a single powerful sword stroke. "Not bloody likely!"

Lance swept his shield around to block an enemy fighter's sword attack, then drove his own blade through the man's chain mail hauberk as if it were thin wool. "Which won't stop her from dying if you're killed. It's going to take magic to keep us all alive. Use your bloody Truebond and call her!"

Lancelot had a point, loath though the king was to admit it.

But just as he started to open the Truebond, a nearby axe-wielding foe hacked off someone's arm. As the victim shrieked, Arthur watched the limb spin, spraying blood across his face, to land at his feet. *No, dammit. She has nightmares enough. I need to protect her from this, keep her safe . . .*

The wind shifted, bringing the scent of death and blood and shit to Arthur's nose. And something else, a smell he recognized.

He whirled, to see Mordred's narrow, hate-filled gaze blazing at him over the arc of his sword swing.

Right at Arthur's neck.

* * *

Her husband had closed their Truebond down to a bare whisper, but Gwen's ferocious concentration locked on to that ghostly voice with all her strength of will.

She only hoped it would be enough to guide them in.

As Nimue had instructed her, Gwen poured magic into a point in the air, watching in sweating anxiety as it expanded into a wavering doorway.

Morgana, mounted on a bay gelding next to her own white mare, shot the queen an excited grin. "You're doing it!"

The gate wavered a moment, seeming to fight her control before it finally stabilized, revealing a landscape that was all too familiar.

Gwen's heart sank. She'd been right. It was her dream brought to life—a hellish landscape of men locked in battle to the death, killing and dying in a writhing tangle of blood and steel. Behind her, one of the watching witches breathed an appalled, low-voiced curse.

Gwen ignored her. Unless they moved quickly, Arthur was dead.

If he's not already.

THIRTEEN

Digging her heels into her mare's side, Gwen clucked to urge the horse forward. But before they passed through the gate, the beast's head flew up as if she'd struck something nose first. Rearing, she bugled and twisted aside so violently, it was all the queen could do to keep her seat. She dragged at the reins and jerked the mare's head around, determined to force her through despite her resistance.

Gwen had to get to Arthur. Excalibur blazed in the scabbard hung across her back, its buzzing magic a silent goad.

"Wait!" Morgana said urgently. "There's something wrong with the gate. It looked like your mare ran into some kind of barrier."

"We'll see," Gwen murmured grimly, and thumped her booted heels against the horse's ribs. This time, however, there was no mistaking the impact of Snowcap's nose with whatever blocked the gate. The outraged mare started to buck, but the queen gestured, settling her with a calming spell. Biting her lower lip, Gwen examined the gate in frustrated anger. "I don't understand this! I conjured a gate not an hour ago, and it worked fine. What's gone wrong?" And why now, when she could least afford delay?

But as she stared through the doorway, she saw it appear to slide aside. A man's wide-eyed, horrified face suddenly stared back at her through the opening just before the gate rolled off into the crowd like a child's ball. Nimue's gates had never had such a problem. "Why is it doing that? What's going on?" They had to get through that gate before Arthur fell, or all was lost.

"Maybe there are too many people around it," Morgana suggested. "Perhaps they're interfering with it somehow, something like stones in the path of the river."

Hands tight on Snowcap's reins, Gwen nodded thoughtfully. "That does make sense."

"What if you try it somewhere closer to the edge of the battlefield, where the crowd isn't as thick?" Diera suggested. "You'd run into less interference that way, and maybe we could get through."

"Good idea," Gwen said, even as she realized that would also put them farther away from Arthur.

Unfortunately, they weren't well blessed with alternatives.

She let the gate collapse and tried again farther from Arthur's current position. Again the gate shivered and slid, but this time she noticed that there did seem to be some kind of resistance that fought her spell.

Allowing that gate to collapse, Gwen tried a third time, forcing herself to be patient, despite the voice in the back of her head chanting *Hurry, hurry hurry hurry hurryhurryhurryHURRY!*

Arthur thrust up his shield, blocking Mordred's sword blow with a thunderous THOCK of impact. The king swung his own weapon with lethal force, but his son's shield deflected it at an angle, sending the blade glancing away. Arthur brought the blade back into line as he blocked Mordred's next attack with an inhumanly fast sweep of his shield.

"I laid the . . . snare for you, and you stepped . . . right into it!" Mordred bellowed over the din of battle as he blocked Arthur's sword strokes. "Did Isolde manage to kill Tristan before she sent you running to Camlann?"

"Do you really think that pitiful creature could murder a Knight of the Round Table? Tristan slew her!" A fresh bolt of rage shot through Arthur, and he cursed himself as his bastard's plot became blatantly clear. Mordred had sent Isolde to assassinate her husband, thinking Arthur would question her and she'd "confess" the details of the plan to destroy Camlann. When they rode to defend the town, Mordred's army would wipe them out through sheer numbers. And Arthur should have seen it coming, just from the nighttime attack alone. What intelligent commander would take the field in the damned dark?

"Ahhhh, too bad." Mordred smirked. "Either way, it worked. All that's left is shoving you into a hole and shoveling in the dirt."

"Don't start digging just yet, boy. Each of my knights is worth ten of yours." Unfortunately, they were too far away to do him any good, scattered over the battlefield protecting his loyal lords.

The only Table knight Arthur had kept with him was Lancelot, who had his hands full keeping the rebels from swarming the king. The champion's sword swung like a scythe in the moonlight, all stunning strength and an utter lack of mercy.

For his part, Arthur had to keep his attention on his bastard as Mordred probed for an opening in his guard. He was definitely better than he'd been when they'd dueled in June, faster, stronger, and certainly more battle hardened. Enough so, in fact, to keep Arthur on his toes despite the advantages he enjoyed as a Magus.

Arthur had the ugly suspicion that if he'd still been human, Mordred would almost certainly have killed him.

He wasn't human now, of course, but remembering Gwen's dream, he found himself wondering if even that would be enough to save him against odds like these.

Gwen had finally created a stable gate. But as she stared through it at the scene beyond, her heart sank.

"Saints and devils," Lady Lynet moaned, echoing her thoughts.

"Look how many of them there are! They'll kill us before we even find Arthur!"

"So we kill them instead," Iblis said grimly. "Enough fireballs and lightning bolts, and . . ."

Gwen's stomach twisted at the thought of the agonized screams of burning men. *Arthur was right. I could never have used a fireball on Mordred.* Aloud, she said, "We can't kill those men. Half of them are peasants."

"So?" Iblis demanded. "Forgive me, my queen, but given the circumstances, I don't see what difference that makes. Not when all our lives hang by a thread."

Gwen shot her a cool glance. "All lives on that field are valuable to their loved ones. We must think of a way to accomplish our goals without excessive loss of life, if we can. Besides, if we kill too many peasants, there won't be enough manpower to bring in the full harvest in the fall. Thousands will starve before spring."

"Well, we must do something," Morgana said, her eyes grim. "Otherwise they'll drag us from the saddle long before we reach Arthur and his knights."

Gwen's nails bit into her palms. Desperately, she stared into the gate, wracking her brain for a solution. She had to get to Arthur. Her head was so empty of ideas, she could swear it echoed.

She wanted to throw up.

How many of Arthur's loyalists had been overwhelmed by the sheer mass of Mordred's forces—and how could Gwen keep even more men from joining them? Frantically, she tried to come up with a plan, an idea, something.

Perhaps Iblis is right. Perhaps we have no choice except to ride through the gate and start shooting fireballs into the crowd . . . I can take Excalibur to Arthur in the light of screaming men burning like torches. He'll love that.

In that instant, the idea burst into her mind as if God himself had whispered it in her ear. *Fireballs . . .*

A broad grin spread across Gwen's face.

* * *

Come, my knights, my warriors!" Mordred bellowed. His green eyes met Arthur's, cold with vicious purpose. "Help me slay this monster who calls himself High King of Britain!"

They hit him in a wave of flesh and bone—fifty men, easily—half of whom Arthur recognized as Mordred's hangers-on, the pack the prince had once caroused with.

Sorry, you bastard, I have no intention of dying today. Bellowing, the king met them in a blur of sword and shield.

But it was going to be a close thing. Weapons probed and slashed at him, seeking to break through his guard. His Magus speed saved him as Arthur knocked aside spears, axes, and swords, using his shield and his blade simultaneously in furious sweeps. Sweat ran down his armored ribs, itching under the ringing chain mail, stinging his eyes and gluing his hair to his skull under the heavy metal weight of his helm.

If he were human, he'd be dead.

Mordred hung back, the coward, watching him fight for his life with calculating eyes and a snarling mouth. Arthur shot him a look of lethal promise that made his eyes flicker.

As he fought, the king was aware of Lancelot maneuvering until they were fighting back-to-back. Lance, his relentlessly loyal cuckolder, would defend Arthur to his last breath.

A trio of warriors lunged at him, three men who had obviously fought together before, judging by their precisely coordinated attacks. One man came in high, the second low, the third swinging left-handed from the opposite direction. Arthur swept his shield up and to the side, catching the first two blades and forcing them aside as he blocked the third with his sword.

Mordred, watching, spotted his opening and struck, snake quick, swinging his weapon at the king's head. Arthur brought his shield up and around with Magus speed, simultaneously twisting to drive his blade at Mordred's throat. Somehow the bastard raised his shield in time to block the blow. Arthur's sword struck it like a hammer.

And the king's sword shattered.

Chunks of steel cartwheeled away, glittering in the moonlight—and taking Arthur's last hope of survival along for the ride.

G wen's horse was on fire.

Blue flame licked along the white mare's neck like a mane, raced across her barrel and flanks, then burned down the beast's legs. Yet the horse didn't seem to feel the flames as she leaped through Gwen's gate.

The other ladies thundered after the queen on mounts blazing with the same heatless magical flame that left the animals untouched.

Morgana, bringing up the rear, heard the rebels cry out in superstitious terror at the sight of them. "Demons! God save us, they've summoned demons!" someone shouted, and others picked up the idea, repeating it until it became a chorus that menaced with its very terror. "Demons! They're demons, run!"

Men began to push and shove, trying to escape the women on their burning horses, trampling each other in their haste to flee the battlefield.

Just as Gwen had intended.

But listening to those screams, Morgana felt a chill. Yes, the queen had been right to focus on how to save Arthur while sparing the most life on the field. But looking beyond that, Morgana imagined what the world would think of Arthur if he did emerge victorious—if they believed he'd done so with the help of demons.

But before Morgana could come up with a solution to that problem, she heard Gwen's anguished scream.

Looking past the queen's shoulder, she saw something glitter over the hill ahead, flying through the air as a mob of soldiers shoved and fought beneath it.

For just a moment the crowd parted, and she saw Arthur Pendragon in the center of it, a shattered blade in his hand. There was nothing left but a jagged metal stub.

Then the mob surged, dragging him down under a wave of screaming men.

"It's my dream," Gwen shouted in a voice raw with anguish. "And we're too far away!"

G wen's dream was coming true, just as she'd been warning him it would for months.

I've been a fool, Arthur thought as the mass of soldiers smashed into him, their weight bearing him down into the mud with a thick, liquid splat. He bucked and fought, but men knelt on his arms and chest, pinning his thighs, his shins, and his feet, their victorious howls blowing the smell of beer and rotten teeth into his face. One son of a bitch actually had the gall to grab Arthur's helmed head, despite his snapping fangs.

"Give me room!" Mordred barked. The one who'd grabbed the king's head released him and backed hastily away. He must know Mordred would go right through him to kill his father.

Arthur looked up into his son's nasty grin as the bastard raised his sword, preparing to behead him. "Goodbye, old man! I'm finally going to get what I deserve!"

Then Lancelot fell out of the sky.

One moment Arthur was straining to throw off the mass of men pinning him as the bastard's blade flashed downward.

The next, du Lac crashed down on someone's back, smashing the enemy soldier flat and running him through. Mordred's blade hit Lance's shield with a thunderous clang, and the two began to fight, savage as badgers.

Arthur kicked men off him as he sought to rise and guard his champion's back, but more rebels crashed down on him, joining those who held him down. Strong as he was, he couldn't find the leverage to free himself of their suffocating weight.

So there was no one to watch Lance's broad back as he'd watched Arthur's. As the champion went after Mordred, the rebels hit him from behind, driving a dozen cowardly blades into his back, his ribs, his arms and shoulders, some deflected by his mail, most not.

A hauberk was not designed to withstand so many assaults. Lance's knees buckled. The knight gasped a curse as he went down, collapsing across the pile pinning Arthur before the rebels shoved his pierced, bleeding body away, kicking and cursing it.

With a roar of grief and fury, Arthur shifted, as he damned well should have thought to do to start with. Hauberk and armor vanished in a burst of magic, leaving him with four furry legs and a muzzle full of sharp teeth. Going for the nearest throat, he sank those wolf fangs deep, twisting his head to break the man's neck. Screaming, the rebels surged backward, trying desperately to get away from the devil king in their midst.

Then he was on to the next coward, and the one after that, and the one after that, ripping out throats and leaving dying men gagging and convulsing as he tore through the massed traitors. Some stabbed at him, screaming, but most turned and fled in howling confusion. They streamed down the hill, shouting about demons and a king become wolf.

But the one he really wanted dead was Mordred. Mordred, who'd just cost him his finest knight and dearest friend. Unconscious and bleeding, there was no way for Lancelot to shift and heal his injuries, and no time for a healer to reach him.

Mordred, surprisingly, didn't take the opportunity to run for his life. Arthur might have raised a lying traitor, but at least he wasn't a coward. The bastard's eyes were wide in the Y-slit of his visor, but they narrowed as Arthur gathered himself to spring.

"I always said you were a beast." He snatched up someone's forgotten spear out of an obvious desire to kill the king from as great a distance as possible. "I didn't realize you consorted with devils."

As he snarled at his son, a too-familiar voice shouted, "Arthur!" *Gwen!*

Horrified, Arthur jerked toward the direction of her voice—to freeze, staring in gaping astonishment. Even Mordred gasped.

His queen was mounted on a horse of fire.

Flames leaped and licked around her, a cool, unearthly blue brighter than the moonlight, illuminating the desperation on her face as she rode. Flames danced along the great sword she held in one hand as her horse charged across the battlefield at a full gallop. Men dove out of her way, clearing a path for her with panicked howls.

Arthur had never seen such a blade. It was so long and broad he was surprised his wife could heft it. Then he remembered that hers was no longer a woman's strength—as she, Lance, Merlin, and half the court had been trying to tell him. Now he could see it, just as he finally realized her strength was more than physical. She was charging through blood and gore and death—all the things he'd feared would haunt her—and all he saw in her eyes was a fiery determination to get to him. It was time for him to pull his head out of his arse and start to see her as a ruler in her own right.

"Arthur!" She hurled the sword at him like a spear. *"Excalibur,"* she told him in the Truebond. *"Her name is Excalibur."*

For a moment, it seemed everyone, foes and friends alike, watched the great blade's glittering flight through the moonlight. There was no way a woman could throw such a weapon so far. Hell, he doubted any man could do it. And yet the sword flew toward him in a high, flashing arc he knew had to be propelled by Gwen's magic.

Hands! He needed hands. Arthur shifted to human and flung up his right arm, magically garbed again in his armor. As if guided by God's own hand, the hilt of the sword slapped into his gloved palm hard enough to sting.

Whereupon the weapon almost knocked him right off his feet. Not from the impact, but the sheer boiling force of the magic that infused the great blade.

Steadying himself, Arthur spun—right into Mordred's attack. Excalibur struck the bastard's sword in midarc, cutting it in two like a sheet of parchment. The rebel jerked back just enough, and what should have been a mortal blow instead caught his throat with its razor point instead of the edge. He went down in an arcing spray of blood.

For a moment, Arthur felt a bitter relief as he looked down at the sprawled body, thinking his bastard was dead at last.

That hope died as Mordred grabbed his throat with both hands, trying to stanch the flow of blood. Arthur silently cursed, tensing for another attack. Arthur was bitterly aware of the way the scene echoed his previous defeat of his son all those months ago. This time, though, there would be no mercy for the treacherous little fuck. He'd learned his lesson.

Gwen slid her burning mare to a halt on the hilltop, now almost deserted save for Arthur, Mordred, Lance, and the dead. "Are you all right?"

"I'm fine, but Lance is hurt," he snapped. "See what you can do for him." Then he turned to deal with the bastard he'd only wounded.

Again.

Arthur was not surprised to see Mordred had once more shed his helm, normally something no knight with any sense would willingly do. Wounded, but with all the cunning of a viper, Mordred wanted his father to see his lying eyes.

Not this time, boy. Arthur braced his booted feet apart and steeled himself. Ordinarily, he'd offer quarter; killing a wounded man like this was a little too close to murder. But quarter demanded an opponent willing to abide by the rule of honor, and Mordred had demonstrated no such rule bound him.

Not honor, love, or loyalty. There's nothing in him but the scheming ambition to steal a kingdom he'd done nothing to build.

His son stared up at him, both hands fruitlessly gripping his throat. Blood streamed from between his fingers—but, curse it, not enough to kill him. Arthur was going to have to finish him off. The king raised

Excalibur, preparing to drive it downward and spit the traitor like a chicken.

"No, Father!" Mordred pleaded in a cracked, broken voice. "Please, I beg your forgiveness!" Tears tracked streaks in the battle dust caking his face.

A dark-haired boy laughed as his father tickled him into kicking squeals, green eyes crinkled in merriment. The memory stabbed Arthur like a dirk in the ribs, a bitter, grinding pain that made him ache all the way to the soul.

He met his son's gaze with an emotionless stare. Mordred was not the only one who could act as well as any traveling player. "I can smell your traitor's deception hanging over you like the reek of shit. Even if I couldn't, I'm not stupid enough to believe anything that comes out of your lying mouth." Coldly, Arthur eyed his bastard, ignoring the ache in his chest. "When did my son die? When did you kill my child?"

Mordred's face twisted in thwarted rage. "*You* killed him, Father! You killed him with your endless old-man droning about honor and duty!" Surging upward like a striking snake, he grabbed a sword from some dead man's hand and drove it at his father's groin in a murderous blur of steel and fury.

Arthur twisted aside and ran him through.

Excalibur sliced through Mordred's chain mail hauberk in one smooth stroke, pinning him in the mud. He dropped his sword, gasping, eyes wide and surprised as he stared at the great blade in his heart. His gaze went fixed, and he slumped back into the muck.

Dead.

The king jerked Excalibur from Mordred's chest, flicked off the blood with a practiced snap, and slid it into the empty scabbard at his hip. The blade was inches too long for it; the scabbard had been made for a shorter sword, and the weapon's width split the leather. He'd have to have the armorer make a new one. Arthur turned away, leaving Mordred dead and staring in the mud. *Damned if I'll grieve.*

In midstep, he stopped to stare in shock. His numb agony burst into flaming rage.

Lancelot lay with his dark head in his wife's lap, drinking from her wrist.

FOURTEEN

Arthur's hand curled around Excalibur's hilt, prepared to draw it. Prepared for one insane moment to kill them both, even knowing that because of the Truebond, he'd share Gwen's death. Just then, that was exactly the way he wanted it.

She looked up at him, her lovely face serene in the light of the moon. Showing no fear, though she knew full well what he could do— what he had done just now to his own child.

Why am I surprised? Gwen has never been afraid of me, even when my own knights flinch.

"I don't fear you because I know you, Arthur Pendragon," she told him in the Truebond. "Just as you know me."

And he did. His rage drained away, his hand relaxing its grip on Excalibur's hilt. Had it not been for Merlin's spell and his own cowardly abandonment, he knew Gwen would never have betrayed him with Lancelot, just as Lancelot would never have betrayed his king and childhood friend.

Mordred had just demonstrated what it felt like to truly be betrayed by someone you loved. Gwen and Lancelot had never done that.

Blowing out a breath, Arthur frowned, again becoming aware that the cries of battle had become a shrieking chorus of "Demons!" and "Fiends of hell!"

The king scanned the battlefield from his hilltop vantage point, and didn't much like what he saw. *"That's going to be a problem,"* he told Gwen in the Truebond. *"The Pope's going to excommunicate me. Again."*

"But he may mean it this time," Gwen thought, and he knew it was not something she'd intended to share with him.

He started to reply, but a cold, pure voice interrupted, ringing across the battlefield like cathedral bells. "Hold! Hold and heed me, thou faithless traitors to thy anointed king!"

Startled, Gwen and Arthur glanced around to see the voice's cry. The fleeing mob halted in their tracks to stare in a terror that quickly turned to wonder.

The angel's great wings spread wide as her robes whipped in the wind of her glowing horse's passage. Her halo blazed with a radiance that seared tearing eyes. "Heed me!" she thundered as her shining horse reared, dancing on powerful hind legs. "Heed me, oath-breakers and traitors! You dare make war on Arthur Pendragon, anointed of the Lord, thy God! You imperil your souls!"

Men cried out, falling to their knees in fear and wonder.

Arthur, gooseflesh spilling across his skin, damned near joined them. Could the Lord have actually chosen him in truth . . . ?

"It's Morgana, Arthur," Gwen told him in the Truebond.

He blinked and looked again, finally seeing the healer's features in the angel's blinding face. *"It's a trick. She's playing on their belief."* He recoiled, years of priestly exhortations ringing in his ears. *"Blasphemy . . ."*

"Perhaps, but if it saves Britain from war with the Pope, it's worth the price."

"Aye." He snorted. *"I suppose I'll just have to spend the rest of the night on my face on the cold chapel floor praying for forgiveness."*

"Or perhaps God really does favor us," Gwen told him in their bond. *"You just overcame the worst odds seen in combat in hundreds of years. Perhaps God's hand truly is upon us."*

Mounted on her glowing horse, Morgana made sure the rebels quit the field, the Knights of the Round Table providing steely encouragement to speed any stragglers along. Playing her role to the hilt, the Druid "angel" adjured them to pray for forgiveness for their treasonous sins. Hopefully all that prayer would keep the lot of them from considering rebellion for a very long time.

Lancelot groaned.

Arthur turned to watch as his friend realized whose lap lay beneath his head. Reddening, the champion scrambled to his feet, giving Gwen an uncharacteristically awkward bob of the head. "Thank you, my queen."

"You're welcome," Guinevere said, her tone desert dry.

Rolling his shoulders, Lance winced. "Sweet, infant Jesu, I felt like one of the queen's pincushions."

"And well, you should," Arthur told him tartly. "That was a fool's move—though I'd be dead now without it." Reaching out a hand, he grabbed his champion's forearm in a warrior's grip. "Thank you, my Lord Lancelot."

Lance gave him a tired smile. "Well, somebody has to run the country." His gaze flicked toward Gwen, and just as quickly away again. Making a show of scanning the mud, he spotted his sword and shield and picked them up, then flicked each to rid them of clinging mud and gore. "I'd best go help the others encourage the rebels' retreat." Turning, he strode off down the hill.

G wen watched Arthur watch his champion walk away. The king's back was straight, his shoulders unbowed, but she could almost feel his pain. He'd won a great victory—*they* had won a great victory—but Arthur would do no celebrating.

He'd had to kill his son.

Never mind that it had been necessary. Never mind that Mordred had given him no choice, and would have killed him given the chance.

Whether he wanted to or not, Arthur needed to mourn, even if it was only for the son Mordred had never been.

She knew that, though he'd blocked the Truebond again, as if to give himself privacy to grieve. Fortunately, there were ways for a woman to comfort her husband even without a magical mental link. Stepping up behind Arthur, Gwen slid her arms around him from behind. With a deep sigh, he turned in her arms and drew her close.

The smell of blood and death and battle sweat had ceased to bother Gwen almost two decades before; she scarcely noticed them now. Instead she stood on tiptoe and pressed her mouth to his.

For a moment his lips felt sealed and cool against hers. Then he dragged her hard against his powerful body, and his mouth crushed over hers in fierce, anguished need. Gwen gave herself up to him, kissing him back with all the passion she had in her, opening herself in the Truebond, should he reach for the comfort she offered. Arching her breasts against his chest, she pressed close until there wasn't room for so much as an eyelash between them.

"We won, Gwen," he told her in the Truebond. "We won . . ."

Though to his heart, Gwen knew, it felt more like a defeat.

They gathered on the hilltop—Arthur and his knights, Gwen and her ladies. The witches had burned the bodies of their fallen enemies with a spell that poured across the battlefield, wiping away all traces of blood and death.

The people of Camlann would be able to plant wheat in the spring.

Gwen watched Arthur with a wife's concern. He listened with apparent attention as Kay gave his report. The rebel lords were dead to a man, as were Varn and his lieutenants. There would be no more trouble from that quarter, particularly given Morgana's trick. Gwen suspected Kay did not entirely approve, but he wasn't about to argue with her success.

The Knights of the Round Table had made sure Arthur's loyalist lords had survived the battle, though more than one had suffered injuries that needed the healer's attention.

Now all that was left was mopping up, a routine familiar from countless other battles. Arthur would reward his loyal lords with the fiefdoms of the traitors, while granting knighthoods to those warriors whose bravery and service had been outstanding. Kay being Kay, he'd already compiled a list of names for the king's consideration.

Though Arthur seemed to be listening closely, Gwen sensed his seneschal had only half his attention. Opening herself in the Truebond, she could feel the weariness dragging at him. It was more than physical exhaustion; it was a deep ache of the soul.

And she had no idea what to do about it.

Glancing around the hilltop, Gwen saw she was not the only one paying close attention to one of the Knights of the Round Table. All of her ladies seemed intent on one or the other of them, cleaning the blood and sweat from weary Magi with a spell, or offering a cup of mead and the implied promise of a more intimate drink when they returned to Camelot.

She could see the deeper emotions that tied the Knights to the ladies, the bonds of more than blood that would potentially form over the years. If they were fortunate, perhaps some of them would find what she and Arthur had found.

The only exception to the mood of sensuality, it seemed, was Lancelot. He stood to one side, watching the byplay between the couples with a cynical twist to his mouth.

It struck Gwen yet again that she had done damage to the knight that would not easily heal. Unfortunately, she had done all she could; the rest was up to Lance himself.

But as she watched, Morgana approached him. The healer laid a hand on the side of his face and sent a wave of magic across his skin, wiping away the blood, sweat, and dirt of his struggle to protect his king. She gave him a smile and offered him a cup of mead. He accepted it and drank, eyeing her with a familiar hunger. Yet the sense of distance lingered. *There'll be no bards singing sweet songs about that pair.*

Still, Gwen was comforted that her friends would have each other tonight at least.

Morgana turned to create a gate with a gesture, then took Lancelot's hand to draw him through it.

"Let's go, my love," Gwen told Arthur, as she conjured her own gate. She knew just where they needed to go—and it wasn't the fortress.

*T*his, Arthur thought as he stepped through Gwen's mystical doorway, *is definitely not Camelot.*

Magic surrounded him, foaming over his skin, invigorating him when it had been all he could do to walk when he'd entered her gate. Arthur took a deep breath, feeling like a drowning man who had suddenly been granted a deep, life-giving breath. Strength flooded him, lifting the mood of despair that had almost sucked him down.

He glanced around. It was dark here, so much so even his normally acute night vision could make nothing out.

Gwen gestured. A fireball appeared in the air, shedding a golden glow over the soaring quartz walls of some kind of cave. The faceted stone threw back a thousand glittering points of reflection, illuminating the lake that dominated the cavern. A wide stone circle occupied its center, while a waterfall pattered at its other end.

God, Arthur longed to plunge under that inviting flow. "Where are we?"

His wife smiled, looking around the cavern in pleasure. "Nimue called it the Mageverse."

As she went on to describe Excalibur's creation, Arthur remembered the pain he'd felt in the Truebond about the same time. *She paid the magical price to get me that weapon, just when I needed it so badly.*

As she spoke, Gwen began to play squire as she so often did after a battle, first pulling off his helm and gauntlets before reaching for the sword belt's knot. He stopped her with a gesture.

And drew Excalibur.

Driven by some deeper impulse he didn't really understand, Arthur strode to one of the great boulders that lined the cavern. Lifting the sword, he plunged it downward, though he half feared the blade would break at as it slammed into the rock. Instead, the enchanted steel bit into the crystal as if sinking into a ripe melon—and began to glow even brighter, as if it was drinking in the magic of the stone.

Arthur studied it with satisfaction. "Better than a torch."

"What gave you that idea?" Gwen moved to join him.

Though in his human days, he'd have needed help to shrug out of the heavy chain mail hauberk, now he dragged it off over his head as if it weighed no more than a silk tunic. "Well, you did say it was unbreakable."

"Yes, but how did you know it would glow?"

Arthur hesitated, before giving her a sheepish shrug. "I don't know. Somehow I just . . . knew. As if it told me, though I realize that sounds like bollocks."

"Arthur, it's a magic sword. Who knows what it can do?" She gave him that cheeky grin. "Now, do you mean to get naked or not?"

Laughing, yet intensely aware of her admiring gaze, he pulled off the padded jacket, the boots, and the britches.

For a long moment, she did nothing, said nothing. Simply stared at his naked body while his cock rose under her passionate gaze. Not to mention the sight of her wearing that chain mail hauberk.

There was something about Gwen in armor that made him want to strip her out of it . . . and fuck until they both went blind.

Then he took a deep breath—and almost gagged at his own reek. God knew what had been in that mud. And yet she stood there and looked at him with huge pupils eating the light. He wondered what she was thinking. Though he had no desire to spill his dark mood on to her, Arthur opened himself in the Truebond. What he found in her mind made his heart beat faster.

Filthy or not, she loved the look of him. Reaching out, Gwen traced her fingers over the contours of his torso, the thick ripple of muscle and the jut of bone. Her gaze roamed his body, admiring and hungry.

She wanted him. That alone was enough to make his cock thrust at her in silent demand.

Gwen began to undress.

She did it slowly, untying her belt and dropping it to the stone, then reaching for the hem of her hauberk and pulling it off by seductive inches before tossing it aside. It rang as it hit the stone floor with a heavy thump. The padded jacket was next; she drew that off even more slowly, revealing her slim, glorious body one delicate inch at a time. The shins, the knees, the thighs. By the time she reached her sex, he was as hard as Excalibur's blade.

Gwen smiled at him, Eve with an apple in her hand, and pulled the jacket higher, exposing her soft stomach, narrow waist . . . and finally, her breasts, full, pale, and round, with deliciously jutting nipples.

As she dropped the jacket to stand naked before him, he gave her the smile that he knew aroused her, dark and sharp, with just a hint of fang. "God, I want a bite of you."

"And you'll get it, but not just yet." As she brushed her thumb across his lower lip in a slow caress, Gwen's wicked smile faded to something more serious. "You don't have to play a role for me today. You don't need your scary King Arthur mask. You don't have to flash your fangs."

He had to grin at that. She did know him so well. "But I *like* my scary King Arthur mask. And so do you."

She smiled then. "Well, yes. But you don't need it just now." Her fingers brushed over him, exploring the contours of his abdomen and ribs. For a moment he thought she'd take hold of his cock, but instead her fingers slid upward to brush over a pointed male nipple.

"Tease."

"You enjoy my teasing." She smiled at him, all wicked wanton. "Don't you?"

"God, yes, wench." She was running her fingers back and forth across his nipple until it was all he could do not to moan. Having her touch him like this, without his having to do anything except feel . . . It was so deliciously sweet. So exactly what he needed.

Gwen caught his hand and drew him toward the water lying still and dark in the center of the cave. Together, they waded into the water. It was deliciously cool, and it felt good to his battered body.

She smiled over her shoulder at him, a teasing flash of teeth as she led him deeper. The bottom dropped out from under their feet, and they both began to swim across the dark water.

Arthur picked up a flash of desire from her, a wicked little impulse. Obliging her, he paused to tread water as she ducked beneath the surface. Pale limbs flashed underwater as she swam around him, fingers brushing his body, effortlessly arousing. He treaded water, letting her tease him with delicate little touches to his arms, his back, his broad thighs.

And his cock.

Just the barest stroke, a whisper of it along his rising shaft. Delicately arousing. Gwen had always known how to drive him mad. He sensed what she intended an instant before she did it. Still submerged, she engulfed his cock for a quick suckle that made him jolt. She backed away, only to close long, tapered fingers around his balls, stroking the delicate sac and sensitive skin. Building his heat.

Then his cock was in her mouth again as she floated, treating him to the sensation of wet tongue and smooth throat working around the width of his shaft. He groaned, wrestling with the instinct to grab her head and drag her closer, tighter. *If I'm not careful, I'll drown her.*

She had to be using some kind of spell to stay under so long, he realized with what little brainpower he had left. He watched her graceful back, the bare curves of her lush arse and long, strong legs as she floated, licking and sucking.

The sight of her, combined with those vividly erotic sensations, aroused him beyond bearing. He vibrated on the verge of climax, fists clenched, head thrown back, fighting his lust.

Finally she broke away and surfaced, flashing him a little devil's grin before she turned and stroked rapidly for the other side. Arthur rumbled in feral male interest and swam after her, determined to give her a little taste of the same medicine. His feet hit the shallow end of the pool a heartbeat after hers, and he threw himself into a hungry lunge.

His snatching hand just missed as Gwen levitated out of the pool. Water streamed down her pale, glorious body as she floated in midair, giving him a taunting grin. His eyes narrowed, and he growled, preparing to spring up and grab her, but she waved an admonishing finger.

"Naughty," she chided. "Patience, King Fang. You'll get what you want in a moment—when I decide to give it to you."

He gave her a hot, menacing grin. "Of course, my queen. I would be delighted to wait upon your whim." His tone—not to mention the Truebond—told her just how far from submissive he really felt.

She lifted a delicate blond brow at him. "Would you like to be in chains again?"

His answering grin was downright feral. "I'd rather put you in chains. You look so good in them."

Gwen gave him a wicked smirk. "I could say the same of you, my king."

Arthur's grin broadened as he let himself imagine all the delicious things he could do to a Gwen spread-eagle and bound. Judging by the sudden bloom of heat in her smile, he'd scored a direct hit. He laughed wickedly. "You like the idea as much as I do."

"Unfortunately," she purred in a tone he suspected she'd learned directly from him, "I have other plans." She gestured at the waterfall pattering into the pool a short distance away. Her gaze softened. "Please, Arthur. You need this, and I need to give it to you."

"I've never been able to refuse you a damn thing," he grumbled and stalked over to the waterfall, knowing what she wanted and where she wanted him. Turning, he found her holding a jar of soap she hadn't held a moment before. She must have conjured it, judging by the flick of magic he could still feel in the Truebond.

Arthur watched her pour the soap into her palm as she stepped closer to stroke soapy fingers across his chest.

"You are so beautiful, my warrior," she told him softly. "You wear the blood and sweat of battle the way another king wears royal robes."

If anyone else had said it, he would have dismissed it as blatant flattery. But the Truebond told him Guinevere meant every word.

"Of course I mean it." She sounded a little offended that he'd think anything else. Despite her irritation, she went back to caressing him, her elegant hands stroking slow circles over his skin.

His cock stood every bit as high and hard as Excalibur driven into that stone.

Gwen rewarded his erection with a teasing brush of her fingers along the balls and up the shaft. And then, with a tiny, evil little smile, she started washing him again. Every time he was on the verge of losing control and grabbing her, she gave him a light push under the waterfall, which had the effect of cooling his considerable lust just enough so he didn't pounce on her like a wolf on a lamb.

Arthur could've withstood that kind of teasing when he was a mortal man. Now that he had a Magus's appetites, he was even less capable of patience. Especially with his balls drawn tight under his shaft and his cock pointing more up than down, despite its length and weight.

But just before he lost control completely, she shoved him under the waterfall, dropped to her knees, and took his long, hard shaft in hand. He caught his breath as she swooped down over it and engulfed it in the heat of her mouth.

There was something about kneeling at Arthur Pendragon's feet with his cock in her mouth that never failed to make Gwen's lust rise. Despite the cool water sheeting down over her head as she licked and suckled him, she could feel herself growing deliciously wet.

God, it felt so good. He felt so good. She stroked both hands up and down the length of his brawny thighs, cupped the weight of his balls in one hand, running the other along his shaft in a tight practiced grip. And all the while she worshiped him, swirling her tongue over the elegant mushroom head of his cock, angling the big shaft upward so she could nibble down its length from the sensitive rim and along the snaking veins to the balls. Sucking each in turn into her mouth, she gave them both swirling licks that wrung a deep groan from him. As powerful as he was, for all his Magus strength and feral intelligence, she loved that her mouth had the power to make him quiver like a horse run hard.

"Speaking of horses, you'd better mount me soon," he told her, his voice a growling rumble. "I don't know how much longer I can last."

In the Truebond, she replied, "*You underestimate yourself, my king. I'll make you rise again.*" She kissed him, lips pressing hot against his. "*And again.*" Another slow, burning kiss. "*And again.*"

Dropping to her knees, Gwen engulfed him again in one long breathless sucking swoop, taking him in almost to the balls. The tight grip of her fist on his shaft pumped once, twice, three times.

And he roared, flooding her mouth with salty jets of come. Swallowing, she felt him shudder against her body. His knees buckled, but he caught himself and straightened again.

"God," he groaned, "you're good at that."

She leaned over and bit one of the twitching muscles of his thigh. His knees almost buckled again, and she smiled. "I'm glad you approve."

"Oh, I more than approve." He bent, hooked an arm under her arse, and lifted her, straightening with effortless strength. Giving her a toothy Magus smile, he purred, "I mean to fuck you blind."

"Oh." She blinked at him, at those white fangs so very close, and felt her mouth go dry.

He laughed, and turned with her to shove her back against the cave wall behind them so that the waterfall tumbled over their heads again. His mouth fed on hers, a hot, delicious contrast to the water, and she moaned against his lips.

The stone behind her felt cool, worn smooth from uncounted years of pounding spray, and she shivered a little. Not that she was cold, not with Arthur pressed between her thighs, muscular and hot and kissing her like a demon, all dark seduction.

His velvet lips brushed and teased as his tongue swirled around hers, so sweet, so familiar, but with a deliciously alien edge provided by his fangs. One hand supported her rump as the other roamed her body, stroking breasts and belly and arse with wicked skill, pausing to squeeze and tug a nipple or caress the line of her throat in a dark I'm-going-to-bite-you promise.

As he toyed with her, cream flooded her sex, joining the slickness that had only increased since she'd started undressing him.

Lifting her with that abrupt, overwhelming Magus strength, he sucked one nipple into his mouth. The sensation of wet heat, the taunting swirls of his skilled tongue—all those gorgeous carnal pleasures were almost enough to make her come.

Almost.

What Gwen really needed was his cock. She could feel its smooth head brushing her pussy when he moved, so painfully erect it stood straight up, as if begging him to impale her. "Fuck me, Arthur." She let her head fall back against the stone wall. The waterfall cascaded onto her face, and she gasped into the spray. It didn't help a bit. "Please. I need it."

He lifted his head from her hard nipple to give her a Satanic grin. "No."

"If you want me to beg . . ."

"Please do." The grin broadened.

"Wretched man."

He closed his teeth over her nipple in a ridiculously arousing bite. "Well, it makes me so hard when you beg."

"Surely that's redundant at this point."

"True. I'd still love to hear you do it."

"Fine." She met his hot gaze. "Please, Arthur Pendragon. I need your cock. I need to feel you driving to the balls in my tight, slick pussy. I need your mouth on my tits. I need your fangs in my throat, drinking my blood. I need . . ." *Your forgiveness.*

She hadn't meant to say it. Not out loud, not even in the Truebond. Yet still the words hung there, seeming to glow with their intensity.

Your forgiveness.

The wicked humor banished from his eyes. *"You have it."*

Her eyes widened as the impact of those words hit her like a longbow arrow thunking into her heart. He meant it.

"Of course I mean it." Arthur sounded slightly impatient in the Truebond, as if he was stating something she should damn well know. *"What kind of idiot throws love away?"*

Someone who doesn't believe it was love at all.

"Gwen, we've been married seventeen years," he told her roughly. "I don't need the Truebond to know how you feel." He flashed that white fanged grin at her, anticipation lighting his dark eyes. "I sure as hell know how *I* feel . . ."

And he picked her up and drove her down on his cock, impaling her in a thick, hot rush. The sensation of being stuffed with him almost made her eyes cross. It also felt incredibly arousing, so deliciously pleasurable, she writhed helplessly in his powerful arms.

He rolled his hips as he tightened his strong grip on her arse, forcing her downward onto his shaft as he simultaneously thrust upward.

Gwen gasped, relishing his deep, grinding strokes, throwing her head back, enjoying the waterfall's cool patter striking her face.

A big hand tangled in her hair. Arthur's burning eyes met hers as his hunger blazed at her in the Truebond, as intense as the sensation of the cock probing her.

Dragging her head back, arching her neck, her husband sank his fangs into her throat.

Gwen groaned in pleasure at the heat of his velvet mouth, the sharp sensation of his teeth slicing her skin. He began to drink as his hips rolled and his hands lifted her up and down, grinding her onto his cock.

The hot pleasure of cock and fangs felt overwhelming and delicious as pounding sensation sent her flying.

"Jesu, Arthur," Gwen whispered. "It feels so good."

"*Then let me make it better*," Arthur said in the Truebond. And dropped every last psychic barrier he had.

The pleasure she felt became a ferocious storm of delight as Arthur's sensations piled onto her own. Gwen screamed, the sound rough with raw lust. Though the king's lips were sealed over her throat, his satisfied growl rumbled against her skin.

He'd been blocking the link so long, she'd almost forgotten the shattering power of a shared orgasm. It was so much more intense than any climax she'd ever had—a blinding sensory storm.

But the real impact hit when their blended orgasm at last began to fade. Gwen became aware of Arthur's mind. Not just his surface thoughts, but the deeper emotions and worries he'd been blocking for weeks. Carefully, he slid his fangs from her skin with a final satisfied lick. And faced her, drawing her close.

"I was wrong." He stared down into her eyes, his own steady and unflinching with honesty. "Wrong about refusing to let you fight. I'd be dead now if you hadn't brought Excalibur to me, if you hadn't asked Nimue to help you create the sword, even though it meant paying the price of its creation in pain."

He sighed and stroked her face. "I've seen war cripple men with fear and evil memories. I've lived with my own nightmares, my own bloody ghosts. I didn't want you to know that shadow on your pure soul." He hesitated. "But more than that, I didn't want to risk losing you. I couldn't stand the thought of watching you fall beneath Mordred's sword."

"But I didn't." She eyed him, wondering where he was going with this.

"No. I underestimated you. You're so much stronger than I thought a woman could be, not just physically, but mentally and emotionally, too. But I should have known better. You've always been strong throughout all the years of our marriage, despite war and miscarriages and everyone who wanted us dead, my son included. Hell, you're stronger than *I* am, come to that." Suddenly his mood shifted into lazy menace, dark eyes glittering. "Which doesn't change the fact that you disobeyed a royal order."

"Ah. Yes. Well . . ." Gwen's pleased smile faded into sensual alarm.

"You do know," he murmured, his lids dipping as he leaned close to whisper, his voice rough and erotic, "what happens to a pretty little witch queen who ignores her king's orders?"

"A spanking?"

He flashed those fangs. "Yes—as an appetizer. Unfortunately for you, I'm afraid it's going to take quite a bit more than that to satisfy me. One mere spanking just won't be enough."

She swallowed and licked her lips, her heart banging in her chest. "It won't?"

"I'm afraid that tight little arse of yours will be paying the price for your defiance."

Gwen returned his hot male smile with a sassy grin. "I look forward to it."

"We'll see just how happy you are when my hand starts reddening that pretty rump." His grin broadened. "And my cock starts fucking it."

But beneath that erotic anticipation was another set of emotions: relief that they'd survived despite the odds, despite the cost. "I love you, Gwen," he told her.

"And I love you, my king."

His strong arms drew her close, and she nestled against him with a purr of happy anticipation.

No matter what challenges the future held as they tried to save humanity from itself, Gwen knew she and Arthur would meet them together. And they'd overcome.

"Of course we will," Arthur said. *"Love does not back down."*

AFTERWORD

Many of the Knights of the Round Table who appear in "The Once and Future Lover" find happiness in my other published Mageverse novels and novellas, all of which are set in the present day.

Lancelot falls in love with Morgana's granddaughter, cop Grace Morgan, in "Seduction's Gift," a novella in *Hot Blooded*.

In "Galahad," a novella in the anthology *Bite*, Lancelot's son falls for a beautiful former teacher named Caroline Lang.

Gawain comes to love Tristan's granddaughter, Lark McGuin, in *Master of Swords*.

In *Master of Shadows*, Tristan finds court seducer La Belle Coeur impossible to resist.

Centuries pass before Arthur and Gwen have a son. In *Master of Fire*, cop and forensic scientist Logan MacRoy (whose last name means "son of the king") falls for a beautiful chemist named Giada Shepherd.

I regret to say three characters in "The Once and Future Lover" do not get happy endings. Sir Bors dies in combat in the course of one of the books, as does Lady Diera.

In a couple of the books, I list Sir Kay as among the current Knights of the Round Table. However, in two other Mageverse stories,

I state Kay died in action during World War II. (This contradiction is a result of both my rotten memory and the fact the series took a decade to write.)

While writing "The Once and Future Lover," I realized Kay must be dead, because he's too important as one of Arthur's advisors. If he were still alive, he'd be front and center, so he must be dead in the present day.

If you'd like to learn more about my books, please visit my website, angelasknights.com. You'll find a list of the Mageverse books in reading order there at angelasknights.com/books.html. (Note that several of the Mageverse books don't involve a Knight of the Round Table as the romantic hero. You may want to refer to the printable booklist if you want to read the series in order.)

Last but not least, there's the story of Morgana's 1,500-year obsession with Percival, Marrok, and Cador in "Oath of Service." That's right—there are three of them, God help me. Look for that one in *Love Bites*. You'll find an excerpt at the end of this book.

Best,
Angela Knight

BONDAGE,
BEAUTY
AND THE BEAST

The air was cold on my breasts, and my nipples tingled, drawn into tight, hard points. Staring into the darkness of the velvet hood, I tried not to shiver. I could hear the man pacing around me, inches away, moving so quietly, and yet there was an impression of size, of danger about him despite his silence. I was acutely aware of my nakedness.

"What do you think?" asked the precise tenor of my stepson. The whoreson bastard.

"Lovely," the man said. His voice was odd, a deep, rich rumble that vibrated pleasantly in my ears. He was behind me now. Suddenly hands engulfed my breasts, big hands, hard and callused, lifting the soft globes to pluck delicately at my nipples. I stifled a moan and would have tried to push him away, but my wrists were bound in front of me. "She has very responsive breasts," he said.

"Brianne's tits are her best feature," agreed Cedric. "God knows my lord father thought so. May he rot in hell. He must have been addled, marrying her as he did with one foot in the grave. My God, look at her. She's younger than *I* am."

"Yes," answered the rumble. The big hands moved, drifting down the bare, sensitive ripples of my ribs, testing the plane of my belly. I fought not to squirm. I would not give either man that satisfaction.

The hand drifted between my thighs, long fingers burrowing skillfully into the curls there, parting the lips that had gone so shamefully damp under the man's skillful caresses. I stiffened in outrage, but I knew a protest would only earn me a slap from Cedric.

He stroked slowly between the plump lips, taking his time, teasing shameful pleasure from my body. It seemed I felt a brush of fur against my inner thighs as he touched me, and I wondered if he wore gloves.

"Well," Cedric demanded. "Do you agree? Will you keep her here, in your castle . . . ?"

A very long finger found the opening of my cunt and slowly eased its way inside. "That depends," the man said. "I still don't understand why you want to sell her to me."

"Because otherwise I'll have to pay Brianne the share of the inheritance the old man left her," Cedric said with exaggerated patience. "And I don't care to do that."

A low, rumbling growl vibrated in my ear. I stirred nervously. It sounded far more like a wolf than a man.

When Cedric spoke again, he, too, sounded nervous. "I was going to kill her, but I remembered you and Edrea and all the games you used to play here before . . ." His voice trailed off.

"Before she cursed me." The voice was so cold with frigid anger that I flinched. He slipped an arm around me to hold me still. I felt fur and linen brush my naked flesh, and shivered.

"Ah, yes. Don't you see, milord? It's poetic justice. She seduced my father with her charms, she would have inherited a third of everything rightfully mine . . . but instead, she becomes your slave. Yours to torment, as you are tormented."

The finger probing me was joined by a second. The sensation was liquid, hot. Shameful. "Yessssss."

"She is, after all, nobly born," Cedric said, cajoling. "You won't often have a chance at such a beauty, thanks to Edrea . . ."

The growl was so loud I jumped. "True, curse you. But this one . . . this one won't refuse me. I won't allow it." He released my waist and cunt, and suddenly hands were prying my bottom cheeks apart. A finger stabbed up, forcing its way into my anus. I arched my back and gasped in pain.

"I'll take her whenever I want, however I want," the voice growled.

"So," said Cedric, voice vibrating with triumph. "It's agreed?"

"Not so fast. First I want to see her face."

Before I could even pull at the ropes binding my wrists, he whirled me to face him and snatched the hood off my head. Blinking in the light of the torches, I looked into the face of the one who would be my master. And felt my heart skip in shock.

The top of my head barely came to his breastbone, and his shoulders were wide as a sword over a chest roped in muscle. He wore a rich wine doublet, a fine linen shirt, and black britches that hugged his long, brawny legs. His boots were made of soft dark leather that clung to his strong calves.

In all, he had the sort of strong male form to make a maiden's heart beat faster—had it not been covered entirely in silky black fur.

His pelt—there was no other word for it—was as shiny and black as a panther's everywhere except on his head, where it lengthened into a magnificent mane that extended down his back. Great horns thrust through that silken hair, curving like a ram's on either side of his arrogant head.

Yet despite those animal features, his face was human. Indeed, there was raw masculine beauty in his high, broad cheekbones and square chin that not even fur could disguise. His lips were full and sensuous, though as dark as his pelt, and his teeth gleamed white as he smiled down at me, hungry and possessive.

"I'll take her," he told Cedric, his voice rumbling with lust. I fainted dead away.

*   *   *

If anyone had told me when I married the old earl that six months later I'd be naked on my hands and knees scrubbing floors, I would have called him mad.

But there I was, knees aching from the cold stone of milord's castle floor, my wet hands chill from the wash water.

Other parts of me were all too warm.

My breasts rubbed against the chains that looped from the slave collar down between my legs and up my back to my collar again. The links, warm from my skin, tormented my hardened nipples and clit even as they rolled against the openings of my sex and bottom. They tortured me, those chains, with little spurts of heat and pleasure and discomfort . . . almost as much as the eyes I could feel watching me from across the room.

My master's eyes.

Yet I did not dare stop in the task I had been given. I had learned my lesson when I challenged him as we rode to his castle.

"I will not be your slave," I'd told him then, trying not to lean against his chest as I sat across his lap in the saddle. "My father . . ."

"Sold you to the highest bidder," he said, in a voice somewhere between a purr and a growl, "Who sold you to me."

"Unlawfully," I said, lifting my chin.

The Beast shrugged. "Cedric is now the Earl of Darkcliffe. He can do what he wishes with you."

I swallowed. "It is *not* his right to sell me like some bondslave."

"Right is what you take," he told me. "And I have claimed the right to you." He lifted one of those human-looking hands from the reins and stretched his fingers wide. Inch-long claws extended from his fingertips.

So it was that I found myself scrubbing floors.

Now I dragged the scrub brush grimly over the worn stone. My chains still tormented me, but not as much as my bitter thoughts. By now Cedric had followed through with his plan to tell all and sundry that highwaymen had killed me. Thanks to his high rank, none would dare question him, not even my father, mere baron that he was.

I had no choice but to obey the Beast as I would a husband, or feel his fist. Or claws.

"Brianne," he said from his corner, and I started. His eyes shone green fire at me. "Come here."

My heart sank. I knew he wanted more from me now than playing the menial.

Wishing I dared stall, I stood and walked toward him, chains jangling softly. Folding my manacled wrists in front of me, I stood before him and waited, head bowed in galling submission.

"Down. On the floor," he ordered. "On your back."

Gnawing my lip, I lay down and looked up at him as he sat there in his massive carved chair. His booted feet were inches from my bare toes.

"Now rest your heels on the arms of my chair," the Beast said, his voice a deep, thrumming purr.

I obeyed. And swallowed, realizing that this pose spread my thighs, exposing me completely to those green eyes.

"Very nice," he said, leaning forward in the chair. "I like the way that red hair of yours pools around your face. And your nipples . . ."

He licked his lips, looking uncomfortably like a tiger anticipating a meal. Green eyes stared directly into mine, the irises vertical slits. "Caress yourself for me."

"What?" I squeaked.

"Your nipples," he growled, impatient. "Roll them between your fingers."

I thought about refusing, but a scratching sound caught my attention. He was extending and retracting his claws like a cat kneading a cushion. The tips raked the wood of the chair arm with a chilling *scritch scritch scritch.*

Biting my lip, I lifted both hands, listening to the chains clank, and caught my pointed nipples between my fingers. I could feel myself going bright red with mortification as I began to roll them.

"Stretch them upward," he ordered.

I pulled at the soft, pink flesh and tried not to groan at the curls of warm sensation that rolled through me.

"That's right," he said. Something hard and thick grew behind the tight fabric of his fawn britches. "Grab those pretty breasts. Lift them to me."

I obeyed, my fingers sinking into my own soft skin. "They're quite big. I wonder . . . Can you lick them?"

"I . . . don't know." I'd certainly never tried.

"Find out."

Reluctantly, I bent my head down, tightening my grip until the nipple pouted into range of my tongue. I licked. And squirmed as I caught my nipple in a glancing swipe.

"Oh, yes." The Beast's eyes were glowing like twin candle flames. "I thought you could. Now masturbate for me."

Heat flooded my face. But there was something about that hot green gaze that ripped away my will to resist. I reached down. My fingers threaded through cherry curls, slid between my lips.

And found, to my shame, that I was very wet. My fingers glided to my clit to begin a practiced circling.

The Beast's hand went to the buttons of his britches. I froze.

"Continue," he rumbled, even as he freed his huge, dark erection. Like his lips, his shaft was so black it was almost blue. And it was near as thick as my wrist.

Staring helplessly at milord's massive cock, I rubbed my clit, feeling something wet trickle furtively between my lips.

His hand, claws retracted, began to stroke up and down that menacing rod.

I gasped, unable to control my breathing, as one hand strummed my clit and the other rolled my nipple. Milord watched, his big hand working his shaft. His eyes glowed hotter, male and predatory. A sense of rigid restraint vibrated around him, as if he barely kept himself from falling on me like a starving lion.

I slid two fingers into my cunt. My hips rolled upward, but I managed to still them. I had to obey his orders, but I didn't have to be so obvious in my lust.

"Tomorrow, I think," the Beast said, "I'll show you the dungeon Edrea designed for our pleasure. I'd love to see you stretched out in chains there, writhing as I paint those big breasts with candle wax. I can't wait to watch that noblewoman's arrogance turn to helpless submission."

Eyes narrowed to slits, a lazy rumble in his throat, Beast stroked himself. I watched his hand move and wondered whether it was natural to have a cock of such size. The earl had not had half milord's length, even in his rare moments of rigidity.

My shame faded as my heat rose, and I couldn't seem to stop myself from burying my fingers deeply into my wetness, each gliding entry painting fire throughout my mound. My thighs twitched and I shut my eyes, gritting my teeth as I sought the climax that danced somewhere just beyond the next stroke of my fingers.

"Open your eyes!" Beast growled, and I snapped them wide.

He was on his feet now, astride me, looking down from his great height as he pumped his shaft. My own hand picked up its pace and I whimpered, twisting between his shiny black boots.

"That's it," he purred, "I want you to come. Come watching me. Come thinking about what I'm going to do to you. How I'm going to take you. Soon."

I groaned in mingled shame and helpless excitement, thrusting my hips upward at him.

And then, suddenly, the heat in my pearl exploded, thrumming through me in hard ripples that made me scream out with the raw, stark pleasure of it. Distantly, I could hear Beast's purring rumble, building in intensity toward a low roar.

Something wet splashed onto my upturned face, hot and white.

Gasping, I looked up at him, towering above me, and licked his come from my lips.

I stood close to the fire, savoring its warmth while I tried not to stare at my master. He sat at an elaborately carved dining table, eating with neat, precise movements of his knife. My stomach rumbled. I'd had no food since before my kidnapping the previous night, and I was more than ready to eat.

Milord put down his knife and leaned back, eyes going to me. "Come here," he said, and I stiffened at a wave of heat. I remembered all too well what had followed those words this afternoon.

But I also knew better than to refuse, so I padded across the stone floor toward him, feeling my silk skirts sliding around my legs as I walked. Milord Beast had allowed me to dress after our last heated encounter, though the gown was a thin white silk that barely veiled the pink of my nipples.

He spread his knees apart and pointed to the floor between them. "Kneel."

I bit my lip as my heartbeat accelerated. Obediently, I crouched between his boots, feeling the warmth from his muscular thighs bathe me.

Milord watched me as he reached out a long arm to the table in front of him. Then he held it out to me, holding a bit of savory meat like a man feeding a hound.

"Open for me," he said.

I parted my lips. His fingers, covered in satiny fur, slid into my mouth, touched my tongue, teased it with the bite. Greatly tempted, I managed not to lick them as they withdrew. I chewed the morsel, hot juices flooding down my throat.

Milord Beast looked down at me. His eyes glowed green with masculine pleasure at my submission as he fed me a piece of crusty bread dripping with butter. When a drop slid down one of his long fingers,

I automatically licked it away. And shivered at the hot male taste of him.

My eyes darted to his. He smiled slowly, showing white teeth. I stared up at him helplessly. My nipples drew tight and a delicious memory teased its way through my mind; milord's come splashing on my lips.

Next he presented me with a goblet of wine, upending it as I drank thirstily, feeling the tart burn slide down my throat.

So he fed me, and I ate from his hands, until he pushed back the plate and goblet with sudden impatience. "Time for dessert." His hands caught in the fabric of my gown.

Claws extended, he shredded it with one easy pull, leaving me naked. Before I could protest, his big hands closed over my waist, and I found myself on my back on the table.

"Milord!" I squeaked as his ruthless strength made short work of the last clinging tatters of my gown.

He ignored my objection, stepping back from the table to stare. His lips parted in a widening smile, and for the first time I noticed his fangs. They were as white and sharp as a wolf's. My heart leaped in fear, yet perversely, I could feel cream trickling between my thighs.

The Beast walked around the table and I watched as he circled, eyes fixed on me.

His gaze flicked to a small earthen jar. He reached over and picked it up, then dipped a spoon in it. When he held the silver utensil up to the light, a sluggish golden stream fell back into the jar.

Leaning over me again, he held the spoon above my breasts. As I watched, a stream of honey poured down to roll over my nipples and pearl on the full curves of my flesh.

Slowly, slowly, milord dribbled a stream of honey across my breasts, down the curve of my ribs, lingered to make a pool in my navel before painting my lower abdomen with shimmering gold. Then, finally, he poured the honey directly into the soft fur covering my mound.

At last he stood back and gave me that wicked, fanged grin again. "I have a sweet tooth."

I tensed as milord bent over me, nervously aware of those fangs. A long red tongue flicked between his lips and swiped across my nipple, which instantly began to strain upward in yearning. Delicately he rewarded it, closing his mouth over the pink bud and sucking it with such delicious skill, I whimpered.

Finally he released the nubbin, only to begin slowly licking the honey still clinging to my breasts, lapping them with long strokes, pausing here and there to suck or nibble gently. I tensed each time, but those fangs never did more than press softly against my skin.

When he started working his way down the length of my torso, the ticklish sensation made me writhe. He paused to tongue the honey from my navel, sucked deeply at it, then continued down my abdomen.

A different tension invaded me. I'd heard whispers from other noblewomen, tales of wickedly skilled lovers, but the earl had hardly been of that stripe.

So when Beast moved between my legs at last and lowered his head, I shivered in equal parts of embarrassment and curiosity. His first long lick made me jump as he tasted my curls, then tugged them gently between his lips. At length he deepened the movement, tongue swirling around my pearl, flicking at my lips.

Never had I felt such a rush of pleasure. Yet the sensation only intensified when he burrowed his seeking tongue even deeper into my sex, stabbing hard into my core. I gasped.

He lifted his head. "You're wet," he purred. "Evidently you enjoy the attentions of a monster more than you'd like to admit."

I writhed and moaned at his words. It was true, all true, and my shame scalded me. But then his tongue was at work again, licking my pearl, sucking it, and the pleasure drove every other thought from my head.

I looked down. He stared back at me from between my thighs. My sex hid half his face, but his eyes burned with triumph and hunger. Helpless, I threw back my head and cried out as lust blasted through me.

With a low, impatient growl of need, Milord Beast stood in a rush and began to unbutton his britches. At last his male organ had escaped to jut out at me. I swallowed, feeling my eyes widen as he bent closer to me, aiming himself.

In the back of my mind, I felt a flicker of disappointment; I'd been so close to climax, and now I knew he'd be through with me in a thrust or two.

But then he began to push into my body, his size stretching me in a way I'd never known. Even when I thought he'd reached his limit, he kept coming, and I whimpered in surprise.

"So big," I moaned, "so hot."

He grinned. "So *tight*."

Finally he stopped, all the way in me at last. I licked my lips, staring at him as he stood between my thighs. He caught my calves and lifted them to rest on his shoulders, and then he began to thrust. I twisted.

I was no virgin, of course, but the earl had been nothing like this. Such size . . . It was almost painful, being filled so deeply. I wished he would give me his mouth again.

But then, as I lay there, feeling the slow, careful stoking of his great rod, a strange pleasure stole over me until my hips rocked. He'd already gone on much longer than my husband ever had, and the pleasure to be found in his thrusts was a delightful surprise. My breathing rough-ened and I gasped as he circled his hips.

As if I'd given him a signal, he picked up his pace until he was lunging hard against me, grinding his hips into the cradle of mine, tormenting my pearl into a blaze. He leaned closer as he rode me until his face was inches from my breasts. Hungrily he licked at me, eyes locked on mine. Unable to stop myself, I threaded my hands into his mane, twisting them as his relentless thrusts seared through me.

"Give to me," he rumbled. "Come. Come with a beast's prick pounding in your cunt. Now."

And he rammed as deeply as he could go.

I screamed as the waves of my orgasm pulsed through me. He roared.

* * *

Putting my back into it, I hauled the bucket out of the well. The castle yard was abnormally quiet around me—but then, the entire castle was abnormally quiet for a structure of such size. The only servants in residence were a forbidding cook and a couple of timid maids, plus a very brawny footman who gave me looks I didn't care for.

Bucket in hand, I straightened to look out the portcullis. Beyond it I could see the long, rocky slope the castle sat upon, rolling down to the shadowed tree line of the forest. Suddenly I yearned for the still darkness out there with an intensity that made me grit my teeth.

But I knew better. There'd be no freedom for me. I'd take my bucket inside the castle and later I'd present myself to milord in his bedchamber where, once again, he'd shoot me to the heights of pleasure and the depths of shame. With my willing—nay, eager—participation.

I was no better than a slut.

I thought of the shame my father would feel if he knew, thought of the stain I brought to our family with my wantonness. I'd been raised better. Yet, when the Beast touched me, I forgot family and pride and God in the headlong rush to pleasure.

I grew aware that I still stared longingly at the forest. In that moment, a bitter need surged within me to rush out into the trees, to run from my own hunger and milord's too-skillful hands.

If I stayed here, I'd become his slave in spirit as well as fact.

I started running for the portcullis before I even knew what I was about, my slippers quick on the stones, the homespun skirts of my working clothes fluttering about me.

I knew I risked his rage, but I had no choice. I could not remain to become a whore to a beast, no matter now deliciously seductive.

* * *

Huddled against the rough bark of the tree at my back, I peered out into the darkness and suspected I'd made a huge mistake.

In my haste and impulsiveness, I'd neglected to bring food or money for the journey, and my thin slippers were hardly the shoes to wear on a hike. But it was too late to turn back now.

I sighed and tried not to think about what milord was likely doing at this moment. He probably knew I was gone, just as I knew he would not be pleased.

Crunch.

I lifted my head. Something moved through the brush. Something large. I fixed my eyes on the shaft of moonlight cutting through the trees and stared, my heart pounding. It was Milord Beast; I knew it. And he would be so angry with me.

Why did I find that thought intriguing?

A shadowed man-shape stepped out of the brush, moved forward into the light. Small, piggy eyes stared at me out of a whiskered face, and a grin gaped, revealing rotten teeth. "Well, lads," he said, "what 'ave we 'ere?"

As I stared at him in growing terror, three others stepped out of the darkness. All were dressed in mismatched rags, and all were dirty, with something vile in the eyes. It occurred to me that Cedric's story about my being killed by highwaymen might turn out to be more prophecy than lie.

I scarcely had time to scream before they were upon me. My world became a muddle of horror; hard hands, breath stinking of ale and onions, rough fingers digging painfully into my breasts, my thighs, my wrists.

Shoved flat on the ground, black shadows over me, hurting me, a hand clamped over my mouth to stifle my hysterical screams. Cold air on my lower body, my skirt around my waist, a hardness poking me between my thighs. I tried to scream but couldn't, couldn't even breathe . . .

And then suddenly there *were* screams, hoarse with terror, cut off sharply. Screams not my own.

The shadows around me surged and rolled. Yet I was left huddled alone in the chill leaves, forgotten and quivering as the air filled with a horrible snarling.

Wolves, I thought. I knew I should run, but in my terror, I couldn't move.

Finally I managed to drag myself to my feet. My attackers had vanished. I whimpered in relief and gagged at the thick, fetid stink in the air. I wondered what on earth it was—until I saw the black human shapes on the ground.

The brassy smell choking me was blood.

One of the shadows stirred and rose to glide toward me. I took a hasty step back, a scream clawing for my throat.

Milord Beast stepped into the moonlight.

A wave of relief broke over me and I felt a helpless grin spread across my face. I took a half step toward him, holding out my arms in welcome. "Milord!"

His lips peeled back from his teeth. "I don't know why you're so relieved," he snarled. "Before the night is over, you may find yourself longing for the company of these bastards."

H e'd brought chains.

"Apparently," milord growled as he snapped the slave collar around my throat, "I made a serious mistake in taking this off you to begin with. Without it, you don't seem to appreciate your position."

I had never seen his anger before that moment, and it terrified me. A growl rumbled continuously in his throat, and his movements were short and rough. I was acutely aware of how small I was against his brawny height.

I sucked in my breath and drew on my failing courage. "Thank you for saving me from those peasants, milord." I could barely hear my own voice, it had so little strength.

"I considered letting them have you," he snapped, "but I feared there'd be nothing left of you to punish."

With that, he turned and stalked off. Hands now chained behind my back, I stumbled after him, on the end of the leash he held. Somehow, I had to blunt his anger. "Please understand. I could do nothing else."

He whirled on me and I instinctively jumped back, almost falling as I hit the end of my tether. "I could have raped you," he said. "I thought about it. I could have fucked you without any consideration, but no, instead I saw to your pleasure before tending to my own. And you did experience pleasure, both times. Didn't you?"

I swallowed and told the truth. "Yes, milord."

"Indeed. The whole castle heard you screaming as you came. I thought we could . . . I even unchained you afterward. And how did you reward me? You ran for the woods. You're lucky I didn't let them kill you."

I couldn't take it anymore. "Milord, I couldn't let you treat me as a whore!"

"You have no idea how a whore is treated!" His eyes narrowed and an unpleasant smile crossed his lips. "But you will."

I stumbled after milord's broad back as he stalked into his castle, my leash held tightly in his hand. He headed into the main hall, his steps long and angry as I scrambled behind.

I frowned, suddenly aware of strange sounds coming from the hall—loud slaps and gasps. Milord stopped so suddenly I almost collided with him. Cautiously, I peered past the powerful bulge of his biceps. And drew in a hard breath.

The footman sat in milord's chair, his shirt and coat discarded over the back of it. The firelight painted his muscular torso as his arm rose and fell, broad hand descending again and again on the naked bottom of the woman draped across his lap. She squirmed, her rump reddening under his steady smacks. I could see the thick blond bush growing at the base of her belly, the lips of her vulva sprung apart by her bending posture.

Throwing her head back, she peered over her shoulder at the footman, her eyes bright, her cheeks as rosy as her bottom. "You've got . . . AH! . . . a hard . . . hand, Jack! Ease off . . ."

"My hand ain't the only thing that's hard, May."

The next smack seemed to echo, and she kicked and screeched. "Oh, please, have mercy!"

"As if you wanted it," Jack snorted, and stopped spanking her long enough to plunge two fingers into her. "HA! You're hot as blood pudding, you little tart."

Outraged, I threw a look up toward milord's face, expecting him to berate the lewd pair. Instead, he wore a half smile I didn't care for at all.

I huffed and tried to look away, but my eyes soon slid back to the footman and his all-too-willing victim. Despite her energetic squirming, it seemed she sought to make her bottom more accessible to her captor's ringing smacks.

"As much as I hate to interrupt this charming scene, Jack," milord purred at last, "I have another occupation for your hard hand—and no doubt even harder cock."

"Milord!" Jack gasped, and jumped to his feet, dumping the unwary May on the floor. Gasping in outrage, she shot him a glare as he hastened to explain. "I was just disciplining this wench for allowing your slave to escape."

"I know what you were doing," milord said dryly. "Come along, Jack. You too, May. I suspect I can find a use for you as well."

I struggled and kicked, writhing in the air, my protests muffled by the gag Jack had tied around my head. My ankles, circled by broad leather bands, were spread painfully wide and fastened to a long iron bar that hung from the dungeon ceiling. My wrists, similarly cuffed, were chained securely to the bands around my ankles.

It was a pose that bent me double and spread me open as I hung in the air, my mouth watering around the thick, cock-shaped gag that filled it. Knowing Jack and milord leered at my helpless nudity, I felt my cheeks burn with fury and shame.

To avoid those hot, lecherous eyes, I peered as best I could around milord's "torture chamber."

The room itself was quite large, and dark, with torches smoking and sparking in niches in the stonewalls. Yet it appeared crowded from the stocks, posts, and racks that stood in strategic spots, draped with chains and obviously ready for unwilling prisoners. Against one wall stood a long oak table that held sinister implements I strained anxiously to examine.

There was only one chair. More of a throne, really, big and padded in leather. Milord occupied it, sprawled with one long leg dangling over the arm. May curled submissively at his feet, as naked as I, her breasts pressed to his booted legs. His breeches were unlaced and she played with his thick male organ in a lazy way. He had grown hard watching Jack struggle to bind me.

The footman gave one of the buckles a last tug, then turned toward his master. "She's ready, milord."

The Beast smiled as he looked from my bound, helpless body to Jack's eager grin. "Indulge yourself, Jack. But remember, I want to hear as many moans of pleasure as cries of pain."

Jack's blue eyes widened and he turned to stare at me. "You're going to let *me* . . . ?"

"She needs to learn her place, Jack. And you're just the man to teach her."

My mouth went dry at the smile that spread over Jack's handsome peasant face. I tensed, bracing for his reaching hands . . .

Instead he turned away. As I watched anxiously, Jack walked across the dungeon to that table with its sinister collection. Evidently the footman knew what he was looking for. He picked out a few objects and carried them back to me.

Turning to milord, he held up a piece of small gold jewelry. "Edrea's enchanted pincers."

"Good choice," said the Beast.

Jack turned to me and let me inspect the device he held. At first glance, it looked like a tiny lion's head with an open, roaring mouth.

"Can you guess where this goes?"

I swallowed around the leather cock, very much afraid I could.

"Here's a hint." He reached toward my breast. I cringed back, but to no avail. He slid my pointed nipple into the lion's mouth. Instantly the tiny gold jaws clamped shut. I gasped.

"Edrea cast a spell on it," Jack explained, enjoying my reaction. "There ain't much in this castle that doesn't carry her enchantments."

"Including me," growled milord, and the footman winced at his blunder.

Then the tiny lion head began delicately chewing my nipple and I forgot everything else. Its teeth were not sharp enough for pain. Instead, a gentle glow of pleasure ignited in my breast.

Even as I shuttered my eyes in pleasure, Jack applied another pincer to my other breast. The footman licked his lips, eyes hot. "She's got pretty tits, don't she?"

"Yes," said milord. I looked up. His eyes, too, were locked on me. At his feet, May had taken his hardened organ into her mouth and was beginning to lick it in long, teasing strokes. The Beast's nostrils flared. I whimpered around my gag as the twin lions gnawed at their captive nipples.

Jack walked away to select among the objects on the table again. In a moment he returned with a small clay jar and a long, cylindrical object. Carved of wood, it was covered in soft leather except for its head, which bore a crown of knobs. "Now, milady, you've had your pleasure. It's time for the pain," he purred.

I realized the object he held was a phallus.

Jack grinned. "Ah, lady, don't fear. I'll oil you proper." He bounced the clay jar in his other hand.

As I watched with widening eyes, he tucked the dildo under one arm and began to unscrew the lid.

Naive as I was, I didn't realize where he planned to put that sinister cock until he slid his oiled fingers into my virgin anus.

I whined around the gag as one thick finger worked its way into the tiny opening. Though I jerked and struggled in my bonds, all my efforts won me was burning ache in my limbs . . . and molten stares from Jack and Milord Beast. I subsided sullenly, Jack's finger buried to the knuckle in my bottom.

"Don't stop now," said milord. "I do so enjoy the view—the way those long legs flex and that white rump quivers . . ."

"Oh, aye," murmured Jack. He gave the Beast a leering masculine grin. "Well, if it's struggles you want, I'll see she gives you plenty to watch." And with that, he jerked out of me to pour more oil on his long, thick fingers.

Again, I was subjected to the violation of my anus by his peasant hands, with two fingers this time. It was all I could do not to groan in pain and shame as he stroked them in and out.

"She's *tight*, milord," Jack said. "Seems to me if a man really wanted to tame her, fucking this little hole might be just the way to do it."

"It's occurred to me as well," said the Beast. "And that's precisely what I intend to do."

Jack's lecherous grin faded into disappointment. I realized he'd hoped to take me there himself.

I stared bitterly at milord, and he gazed back, eyes hard. Almost absently, he stroked May's blond head as she eagerly serviced him with her mouth. The sucking, smacking noises she made sounded obscenely loud in the sudden silence, and I longed to tell her to perform more quietly, until the absurdity of the desire hit me. As if there were a decorous way to perform such a lewd act.

Milord's eyes narrowed, and I realized he'd read the condemnation in my gaze. In the next breath, he made me pay for it. "Well? What are you waiting for, Jack?"

The footman instantly recovered his good humor and bent to peer at my bottom. I felt his rough hands spread my tender cheeks as he presented the knobbed phallus to my opening.

Then very slowly, he pressed the dildo into me, twisting his wrist so that the knobs stretched and scraped the tiny orifice. I writhed in pain, my body bouncing in my bonds as it entered inch by inch.

"Lick her," the Beast commanded.

Jack looked up the contorted length of my body and smiled into my eyes. Then he lowered his head and gave my pearl a long swipe of his tongue. I sucked in a breath.

Licking and nibbling my wet lower lips and hard pearl with wicked skill, Jack twisted the phallus as he buried it inside me until that knobby head tortured my back channel.

I moaned around the gag, caught between the pleasure of his tongue and the pain of the penetration. To add to my shame, the pincers still worked my nipples, casting a hot and evil spell on my helpless body. It hurt; God, how it hurt, and yet . . .

I should find no pleasure at all in this. None. No decent woman would. And yet Jack's mouth was skilled and warm, and the pincers opened and closed so gently, even as the knobbed phallus violated me in a place never intended for entry.

Desperately I sought to distract myself by turning my eyes toward milord. He had fisted one hand in May's hair and used the grip to guide her as she licked and nibbled at his great shaft. Her skin looked very white and naked against his black fur. Powerful muscles rippled up and down his torso as he rocked his hips against her face.

His organ looked so very long and thick, and I remembered his vow to occupy the space now being violated by the dildo. He was even thicker than its agonizing width . . .

"That's it, Jack," he purred suddenly. "Ream that white arse of hers. Make the highborn bitch plead for mercy. She thinks I treated her so badly—give her something to compare my kindness to. Fuck. Fuck. Fuck."

His handsome lips curled back revealing fangs as he grabbed May's head with both hands and held her still for his hard thrusts. His back arched and I gasped in surprise as she seemed to take every inch of him down her throat. The Beast roared out his pleasure . . .

Just then, Jack discovered the right place to tease with his evil tongue and I felt the first long ripples of climax begin deep in my body. The twin lions' heads bit down sharply, and the footman drove the phallus home with a single, brutal thrust.

And I followed my master into degraded ecstasy.

The room was still except for labored gasps. I fought to suck in enough air through my nose, the phallic gag still impaling my mouth.

Milord reclined, sated, in his seat as May caressed his furry testicles.

Jack was watching me with greedy eyes. A huge erection bulked within his tight trousers. He cast a wary look at milord before picking up the final toy he'd chosen from the table earlier. At first I took it for a bone hairpin until he slipped the U-shaped object around the hood of my clit.

I gasped and stiffened as the tiny thing began to tighten and release my sensitive flesh. *Another of Edrea's bewitched toys. Perverse bitch.*

Jack smirked into my eyes. Shooting our master a wary glance, he quickly began unbuttoning his trousers.

"Time for something else, I think," said the Beast. "Get the cane, Jack."

The footman's handsome mouth twisted into a grimace and he reluctantly rebuttoned his fly. I, however, was too frightened to gloat.

I had reason to be. Jack went back to the table against the back wall, and when he returned, he carried a light rod in one hand.

Eyes widening, I looked through my spread thighs at him. He grinned, set his booted feet apart, and drew back a muscled arm. The cane whistled as it arched down and slashed across the cheeks of my rump. I fought not to squeal at its bite.

"Oh, yesssss," said milord. "That was nice. Again."

Jack's blue eyes glittered as he stared at my bottom and took aim again. His second stroke made me bounce in my bonds. I heard my master purr in pleasure. The third blow was lighter than the previous two, barely a sting. Several more followed, similarly light. Light enough, in fact, that I became aware of the movement of the device around my pearl and the pincers that still nibbled at my breasts. And the Beast's green eyes, fixed on my twitching bottom.

Then Jack slashed the crop down hard enough to make me squeal behind my gag. The next one was barely a tap, and the next . . .

And so it went until I writhed in the air, caught somewhere between Edrea's magical devices and Jack's crop, delight and pain melding until I ceased to know which was which. All the while, Jack and Milord Beast watched me lustfully, and I could see their hungry organs lengthening, growing ever harder. At any moment, the footman was going to throw down that accursed crop and plunge his phallus into me . . . I gasped and whimpered, twisting.

The next blow painted fire across my buttocks, a flame almost as hot as the one burning in my core.

The Beast surged to his feet. "That's enough, Jack."

The footman threw him a bitter look, but his brawny arm stopped its descent.

"You've served me well tonight," milord said. "And I imagine you've worked up quite a lust doing it. Take May to your quarters and enjoy yourself."

A broad grin spread across Jack's face. "Oh, aye." He tossed down his crop, then strode over and grabbed the naked blonde by the forearm. "Come, my girl. I've got plans for *your* arse now." He swung her over his shoulder and sauntered for the stairs. The heavy door banged shut behind him.

Milord moved across the room on silent feet, where he paused to stare intently at my reddened bottom. "You know," he said almost casually, "I think Jack has the right of it. Fucking your arse is just the way to bring you to heel."

I stared up at my master, my breath caught in my throat. Edrea's infernal devices and Jack's ruthless crop had ignited a fire in me, and I would be more than happy to feel the Beast's thick shaft—anywhere but where he intended to put it. He took a step closer and I cringed.

He grinned at my instinctive fear, visibly enjoying my helplessness as I hung there with my wrists bound to my calves. He stepped in close, reaching for my cheeks to pry them apart with his strong hands. His fingers felt very warm against my skin, even still burning as it was from Jack's cane.

Idly, the Beast flicked at my pearl, causing Edrea's toy to pulse against it until I couldn't contain my whimpers. Milord smiled at the sound and reached for the laces of his breeches.

A moment later, his massive cock bobbed in the air, its single eye seeming fixed on my bottom. I tensed myself, bracing for his thrust.

Instead the Beast lifted his fingers from my pearl and traced them through my damp flesh, down toward the opening he lusted for. Claws retracted, he tickled it, then delicately began to work his forefinger into my anus, still well greased from the use Jack had put it to earlier.

I snorted in pain behind my phallic gag, but could do nothing to dissuade him as he continued to burrow up my tight channel. Finally, in up to the knuckle, he paused, then began stroking in and out. I swallowed.

"MMMmm," he rumbled. "I've been looking forward to this since Cedric stripped you in front of me." I made a protesting sound.

"Come now, Brianne. Surely you were expecting this." He pushed the finger in more deeply still, illustrating his point. "What's the point of owning a slave if you don't bugger her?" Smiling almost benevolently, he took his hand away and caught his organ with it. I moaned, remembering how Jack's artificial phallus had felt, the treacherous pain and pleasure of it.

Then the head of the Beast's big staff butted my anus, and I knew I was totally helpless to save myself.

Milord entered me slowly, ruthless and relentless. His green eyes glittered triumphantly down into mine, and he watched my face hungrily as he sank into my tight channel. I shivered, feeling how thick he was, how hot. It felt as though my bottom could not possibly withstand his assault.

Suddenly he reached up with one hand, and I cringed as his claws flashed. But he did nothing worse than cut the buckles that held my gag in place. I spat it out, my tongue feeling thick and dry—almost as thick as the huge shaft that filled me.

Milord paused, his hips cradled between my spread legs. "Care to plead?" He sounded almost pleasant.

"Would it . . ." I stopped and licked my lips. "Would it do any good?"

"No, but I'd love to hear it anyway." He began to withdraw with the same agonizing slowness he'd used to enter.

"Forgive me . . . if I don't oblige you," I grunted.

"Quite all right." He grinned, showing fangs that reminded me to watch what I said.

I subsided—and became aware of the pincers that were once more gnawing my breasts. Milord's pelvis rubbed Edrea's toy across my pearl, sending streamers of heat twining along my nerves. Arousal re-ignited in my core, stoked in some strange alchemy by the Beast's big shaft. I shifted under him and the movement teased my pearl, made his shaft torment my anus in a new and dizzying way. I gasped.

"That's it," said milord, watching me closely. "Give in to it. Learn to like it. Feel my cock in your tight little arse, fucking it. You can't stop me. You might as well surrender to it. Because you're mine whether you like it or not, and I'm going to bugger you whenever the mood hits me."

It felt good when he pulled out of me. There was something so arousing about it, about that big phallus withdrawing and driving deep. It hurt, yes, when he thrust his shaft into me; I felt so stretched, so stuffed . . . but when he withdrew, his cock sparked pleasure deep in my core.

So it alternated, shuttling me back and forth between agony and delight, faster and faster, as the Beast's nostrils flared and he began to ride me harder and still harder. Until he lunged against me in long, brutal thrusts as I bounced in the air, gasping at each buggering dig, at the endless upward spiral of ecstasy he'd caught me in.

Until I hit the top of it. Closing my eyes, I screamed out my climax.

"Oh, yessssss," said the Beast. And a moment later, he filled my bottom with his cream.

THE BEAST'S STORY

Brianne hung in her chains, the elegant white curve of her rump exposed to my appreciative eyes. How delicious it was, thrusting my hard flesh into the tiny clenching hole between her cheeks, feeling her helpless muscles fighting my advance. Her great blue eyes stared up at me as I forced my way deeper, wild with pain and fear . . . and the slow, hot spark of desire. Who'd have guessed such a haughty bitch capable of such passion? Of such complete surrender to a beast?

Unfortunately, that surrender is not enough. Not if I am to break Edrea's spell.

I can still remember the witch's taunting voice the day she laid her enchantment: "*You think yourself such a master of women. You think yourself too good for the likes of me. Well, see what luck you have without that handsome face. Only one way may you break my spell: by bringing a beautiful noblewoman to submission until she willingly embraces your mastery.*"

Typical of her. Edrea always was obsessed with slaves and masters . . . or mistresses.

When Cedric brought Brianne to me, I thought her a gift from the

God I no longer believed in. Then, after she responded to my caresses with such eagerness, I tried to free her from her chains, in hopes she'd prove her willingness to submit. I was a fool. Such a beauty will not yield herself easily.

Obviously, I must take more drastic steps.

I continued in my campaign to teach Brianne submission in the days that followed. To my delight and her discomfort, she proved a very good pupil. In time, she came to quiver with anticipation every time I pulled her across my lap for a spanking or chained her to the bed for a session of erotic punishment. Her body knew that each flick of pain would be followed by nibbles and caresses that slowly built, driving her irresistibly to climax. True, she fought her reactions, but the power of her own body overwhelmed her will. I saw her surrender a bit more each day.

But she wasn't the only one who surrendered. There was something addictive about mastering Brianne, about watching her react to my mouth and hands and cock. I made her wanton, even as she fought me. In time I was motivated less by a desire to break the spell than the need to have Brianne, over and over, in every way that occurred to me.

Then came the day I reaped what I had sown.

I sat in the great chair in my bedchamber with Brianne and Jack at my feet. Her wrists were bound to her ankles as Jack held her helpless in his arms, back arched, her full, pretty white breasts thrust upward. My slave's long, auburn hair cascaded across the footman's arms and over his thighs, and her eyes were closed, white teeth biting her full lower lip.

Staring into her face, I dripped another drop of candle wax on her nipples and she flinched. Yet I could see traces of arousal on her face and knew she reacted to the harness holding two dildos buried between her legs. The phalli, being enchanted, twisted and thrust inside her, bringing her ever closer to climax.

I grinned and tipped the candle again, watching as another molten drop joined the wax hardening on her nipples.

The wax wasn't the only thing growing stiff.

I tried to decide how to take her this time. I could smell her arousal, so I knew she'd be deliciously wet. On the other hand, I'd been making progress on teaching her to enjoy being sodomized. . . .

"Well," said an all-too-familiar voice, "I see you're diligently trying to escape my spell."

Looking up, I saw Edrea standing in front of the fire, her red hair blazing in its light, a snarl on her pretty lips. Her long black gown, sewn with astrological symbols, was cut to make the most of her small breasts.

"You're a beast, Ardolf Greycastle," she snarled, "and I'm going to make sure you stay that way."

BRIANNE'S STORY

One minute I lay pinned in Jack's arms while milord dripped wax on my hard nipples and twin enchanted dildos thrust inside me.

The next I stood halfway across the room, free and bewildered. The Beast now knelt in front of a tall, redheaded woman I'd never seen before. He was naked, and I saw with a shock that thick, silver chains bound his arms behind his back, wrists lashed to elbows.

"Edrea, you bitch . . ." he snarled, and I stared, realizing that the redhead must be the sorceress who'd enchanted him.

"Be still, Ardolf," the witch snapped, and milord's fangs snapped closed. He strained silently against his chains, but she ignored him, turning instead toward me. I fought the impulse to take a step back, and instead made a quick sign against evil.

"You're a pretty one," Edrea said, not sounding at all pleased. "I see why he's so besotted with you. And I see he's made you suffer these past days."

Automatically I started to deny it, then closed my mouth. Why should I defend him? He'd given me as much shame as desire, pain as delight.

She smiled thinly. "Indeed. Not only has he tormented you, he's made you enjoy it. And you a noblewoman, a lady from a distinguished line."

How did she know that? Edrea lifted a long finger and traced the gold embroidery covering her black gown. "I know a great many things, Lady Brianne. I know, for example, that you'd like nothing better than revenge."

I tossed back my hair. "And why should I not?"

Her smile was vulpine. "No reason, milady. No reason at all." She began to pace around me and I turned cautiously to follow her, keenly aware of my nakedness. "I could help you achieve that revenge you so crave."

I stared at her warily. "Why?"

"Blunt, aren't you? Because it suits me. You've been humiliated, as I have been humiliated. And we are both the victims of one man."

She paused and sent milord a long look. He peeled his lips back from his sharp teeth.

"What do you have in mind?"

Edrea turned back to me and one corner of her mouth kicked up in triumph. "Justice, my dear. An eye for an eye. You do unto him as he's done unto you."

I looked toward the Beast, who knelt by the fire, looking huge, handsome . . . and dangerous, despite his chains. It was, I admit, an interesting proposition. "What do you have in mind?"

"Why don't we start simply, Lady Brianne? He put a leash on you, so you may put one on him." And with that, she reached into one of her bell sleeves and pulled out a length of chain attached to a gold band.

I took it from her long fingers and studied it curiously. The little collar would obviously not encircle milord's powerful neck. "I don't think it will fit him."

She laughed, high and musically. "It doesn't go around his *throat*, you silly child."

The light dawned. "You jest."

"Indeed I do not. Would you like to put it on him?"

I looked back at him. For one of the few times I can remember seeing him naked, his staff lay limp between his thighs. "In his present mood, I doubt it will stay on him."

"Oh, that. I can remedy that situation." She traced a complicated sign in the air.

Milord's phallus began to lengthen. In seconds, he was as thick and hard as he'd been when Edrea put in her appearance.

I grinned wickedly and sauntered over to him. He bared his teeth at me and I stopped short, uncertain.

Edrea made another gesture. He froze.

Bending to him, I took the hard length of his staff in my hand, then slipped the golden collar around its dark head. Backing away, I pulled the chain taut. The Beast roared in startled pain, and I jumped.

Edrea had drifted up to my shoulder. "The collar," she purred in my ear, "has teeth."

I froze, eyes wide as I stared into the rage in his. Despite everything, I did not want to hurt him.

But he'd hurt me. And enjoyed it. Stiffening my resolve, I tugged again, but more gently. Milord, eyes blazing, heaved himself to his feet.

"Let's take him to the dungeon, shall we?" said Edrea. "Lead the way, milady."

Turning, I drew my master after me by his rigid cock.

So it was that I found myself back in the dungeon, but this time, I was to watch and enjoy.

I sat in the chair Milord Beast had so often occupied when I was punished. Jack crouched at my feet, stroking the inside of my thighs as Edrea had ordered. He looked fearful. I shifted in my chair as it occurred to me that, since the witch evidently meant to free me, I should get up and leave rather than participate further.

Then I saw my former master pulling at his chains, the muscles in his broad back working as he faced the wall he was bound to, and I settled back against the velvet cushions. I could not resist the opportunity to see him being forced to take the treatment he'd so often meted out to me.

"Ah, here we are!" said Edrea as she turned away from the wide table that held the toys and devices my master had used on me. She held a long, supple riding crop in one hand, slashing it in the air to produce an evil swish. The Beast threw a narrow, green-eyed look at her over his thick shoulder.

Grinning, I found myself wondering if perhaps Edrea would let me do the honors.

Evidently not. Edrea sauntered toward him, swaying her hips, trailing one finger down her cleavage. Without warning, she raised the crop and brought it down in a brutal swipe. It struck him with a muffled whap.

He didn't even jump, instead eyeing her hotly.

She rocked back on her heels and frowned. "I see that thick fur affords you some protection. Well, let's see how you do with this." And she gestured at the crop. Light flashed along its length and I blinked and looked closer. The crop had sprouted serrated metal teeth.

Edrea lifted it over the Beast's broad back. "*No!*" I gasped.

This time, he did jump as the crop slashed down across his spine, but he made no sound.

"Edrea, you're going to injure him!"

"Of course. He has to bleed." She threw me a narrow look, mouth tight with displeasure. "Nothing else gets through to him. Jack, give her something else to think about."

Instantly Jack pushed my legs apart, pressed his face to my sex, and began to lap between my lips, much as he had on other occasions. This time though, I felt no heat. "Stop it!" I hissed, pushing at his forehead as Edrea's crop bit into milord's back.

"Don't be a fool," Jack hissed back. "Do ye want 'er to turn *you* into somethin'?"

Eyes still fixed on my suffering master, I saw a movement down his broad back. Bright red, trickling through milord's black fur. Blood.

"No! Edrea, stop!"

She ignored me, her eyes blazing as she flogged him.

I watched helplessly, cringing at the steady swish and WHAP beating an evil rhythm until the fur on his wide back shone red and matted. I felt ill. Writhing, I fought Jack's hold, but he half crawled into the chair with me and bore his body down on mine to contain my struggles.

The horror I felt surprised me. Milord had enslaved me, chained and tormented me, sodomized and forced me, and yet watching Edrea beat him was agonizing. For looking into her set face, her fixed, cold eyes, I knew she meant to kill him, and the thought of his death left a great ache in me.

I knew I was a fool to feel that way. I should rejoice in his fate, in the prospect of freedom it brought me, but I felt no joy. Instead I remembered the pleasure he'd given me with his tongue, with his hands, the feel of his strong, hot body moving against mine, driving his shaft into my core with liquid strokes. And the look on his face at those times, the hunger that was more than sexual. As if he needed something from me even he didn't understand.

Even in his deepest rage, when I'd tried to escape him, he hadn't been able to bring himself to truly hurt me.

And now Edrea would certainly kill him.

Deep in my soul there rose a silent scream of protest as I saw his great body arch in agony under Edrea's vicious blows, before going limp.

The witch threw down her crop in disgust. "He's unconscious, the useless lout. Well, I'll get no pleasure out of him now. Jack, come here."

Such cold fear stole over the footman's handsome face, I felt a spurt of pity for him, though he'd never been my ally. Reluctantly, he pulled himself off me and went to meet Edrea.

"Down on the floor!" she barked at him, and he obeyed, a quiver of terror rolling through him.

Edrea tossed up her skirts and mounted the footman like a horse, grabbing his limp shaft with one hand and aiming it toward her opening. I heard her mutter a spell and he hardened even as she drove herself down over him.

Ruthlessly, the witch began to ride the hapless footman, grinding her pelvis hard against his, her face contorted with lust and hate. Her eyes, black in the torchlight, were locked on milord's bloodied back.

Edrea's rhythmic gasps and grunts filled the dungeon as she drove hard on Jack, seeking her climax ruthlessly. She shut her eyes, grimacing, and I saw my chance. Quickly I rose and slipped toward milord, hanging limp in his chains.

"Beast," I hissed. No response. "Master!"

He stirred, lifted his head at last. His great green eyes opened and fought to focus on me. "Brianne . . . Brianne . . . what're you . . . ?" His words were slurred, barely audible over Edrea's obscene grunts.

"Thank God!" I crossed myself and sidled closer. "I thought she'd killed you!"

"Give her . . . time." His lips twitched, then he sucked in a breath of pain.

I stole a look at the witch. Jack was arching under her, his hands clamped over her small breasts. "How can I help you, milord?"

"Get you . . . gone. She'll kill . . . you."

He was right. I knew that, knew I should slip away while she was distracted by Jack and the Beast. But it wasn't in me to leave him. "No. I can't let her kill you, milord. Isn't there something we can do?"

It seemed his eyes sharpened, focused for the first time since Edrea had begun to flog him. "You mean that. You'd help me?"

I lifted my chin. "Yes."

He studied me, blinking hard, obviously fighting the dizziness of blood loss.

"There is a way," said milord at last. "But it would be . . ." The Beast stopped to gasp in a painful breath. ". . . very dangerous."

"Anything is better than waiting for Edrea to decide to turn her magic on me," I told him stoutly.

He stared at me intently and I saw doubt and fear and hope do battle in his green eyes. Finally he nodded his great head and spoke, his voice low and harsh with pain. "Very well. In my library you will find a . . ." He stopped to gasp, battling pain. ". . . a small porcelain statue of kissing lovers. Turn it over and look at its base. You'll see a small raised square. Pry the square off. There's a vial inside the statue. That vial contains a potion that can strip a witch of her powers forever—if it is poured over an open cut in her skin. You must somehow inflict the wound and pour it on Edrea."

I frowned. "That's no small problem."

"No." He looked at Edrea, still fucking Jack. I watched the hope drain from his eyes. "It's too great a risk. She'll kill you, and I would not see you die. Leave me."

"And abandon you to be tortured to death? Nay." Ignoring his frustrated growl, I turned to watch Edrea, hoping she'd still be engrossed in Jack. Indeed, she looked on the verge of coming. I knew I'd have no better chance and slunk toward the door.

"Lady Brianne!" It was the witch's voice, sharp and hard.

I stopped and bit back a curse. "Milady?"

"Where do you go?" She gazed at me suspiciously, frozen on top of Jack.

Could she read my mind? No, else I'd be dead. Still, I told part of the truth. "The library, milady. There are . . . belongings of mine there I wish to retrieve."

Beneath her, Jack stared at me, then flicked a look at milord. His eyes widened in comprehension and I realized he knew about Beast's enchanted potion.

One of his hands moved up to Edrea's buttocks and pinched her viciously. "Ride, woman! I want to come!"

Instantly, the witch forgot me and snapped a glare down at Jack. He whitened. "You forget yourself, peasant," she purred, and rose from him. "Evidently, you need a lesson in keeping your place."

I slipped up the stairs while she chained him to the wall.

As I climbed, I heard Jack's first scream. Cringing, I began to run. I couldn't let his sacrifice go to waste.

The glass vial was exactly where milord had said it would be, and I was soon on my way back down the dungeon steps with it clutched in my hand.

I found Jack writhing in chains, a horrible, strangled sound bubbling between his lips. Edrea was lashing a riding crop across his loins, paying especial attention to the cock she must have been keeping erect by magic.

Licking my dry lips, I wondered how I was going to cut her. How deep did the wound have to be? Could I scratch her with my nails? Was there something at the table I could use?

Cautiously I edged toward it, fighting to ignore the footman's cries. The table was a massive affair built of sacred oak, and its surface was littered with various whips, clamps, gags, dildos, and other things I had no name for.

My attention was caught by a phallus in a leather harness that was apparently intended to hold it around the wearer's hips. The dildo was made of wood and leather, like others I'd had used on me, but unlike them, it was studded with short spikes. I imagined the lethal agony the device would inflict, and shuddered in horror.

"Well now—that's an idea," the witch purred in my ear.

I jumped and stared at her wildly. She still held the crop in one hand. Behind her, Jack hung limp in his bonds, unconscious.

Edrea picked up the harness and its demon phallus. My flesh went icy as I wondered if she intended to use it on me.

"He fucked you up the arse, didn't he?" the witch asked suddenly. I blinked at her numbly as a roaring sound filled my ears.

She smiled a terrible smile. "How would you like to return the favor?" And she held up the spiked dildo.

"No!" I backed away, shaking my head.

"Oh, come now, Lady Brianne," Edrea said, following me with the demonic phallus held by the harness. "Surely you haven't lost your taste for vengeance."

"Milord may have tormented me, but he was never vicious. And he saw to it that I found pleasure in what he did." I stopped, surprised to hear myself so defending him. But it was true. I had enjoyed it on some dark level. Even the pain. For a moment I felt a spurt of shame. Pushing the emotion away, I lifted my head. I had to save my Beast.

Edrea's lush mouth tightened and she made a sweeping gesture.

And the phallus was harnessed around my hips. I stared down at its lethal jut in horror. I reached for the straps, meaning to unbuckle them.

"You realize, don't you," the witch said coldly, "that if I so wish it, you will fuck him like a rabbit. It would be much better for you if you do it of your own will."

I stared at her, wondering sickly what horrible punishment she'd inflict on me if I didn't obey her. But ultimately, that made no difference. I couldn't participate in this horrific crime against milord. "No." I had to fight to keep my voice level.

"I'd never have guessed you such a coward, Edrea," said the Beast, his voice clear and cold.

She forgot me, whirling to stalk over to him with narrowed, snapping eyes. "You dare call me a coward? You, who were too afraid of Jovas to marry me?"

The Beast's lips moved in a sneering smile. "I didn't fear Jovas. I just didn't like the ugliness in you."

Her eyes widened. Then she whirled toward me and threw her arms out, and I knew, with gut-knotting horror, that she was about to bewitch me into sodomizing milord with the dildo.

But Edrea miscalculated. One long hand flew out past the Beast's face as she gestured. Quick as a blink, he sank his fangs into her wrist.

The witch howled in agony, grabbing her forearm and staring down at the wound in shock. I flew toward her, seeing my chance. "Here, let me help!" She allowed me to take her forearm.

And I broke the vial over it, spilling the scarlet potion over it like blood.

"*Bitch!*" Edrea screamed and threw me away. "I'll see you burn for that, you highborn trollop!" And she drew a complex sign in the air.

Nothing happened.

The Beast laughed. Suddenly the air was full of smoke and light, and I heard a high, hopeless scream that could only be Edrea's.

When the smoke cleared, a tall blond man stood beside my master. He was handsome and broad-chested, and there was such an aura of power about him that I longed to drop to one knee.

"Well met, Ardolf Greycastle!" the man said, grinning wolfishly at my master.

"And you, Jovas," milord said, smiling back with all his teeth. "I gather you've come for your new property."

The blond turned his lupine smile toward Edrea, who cringed from him in horror. "Indeed I have." He moved toward her, stalking, and she backed away. "So, witch . . . I hear you've been very, very bad. You know what happens to naughty little girls, don't you?"

"Bastard!" screeched Edrea, which was exactly the wrong thing to say.

Jovas laughed and grabbed her hair in one big hand, then snatched her nose to nose with him. She screeched again as she rose on her toes. "Now, that's no way to talk to your master, little slave."

"No!" She flailed at him. "I'll be no slave!"

"Oh, yes, you will. You've no powers to protect you now; your shield is gone. You're mine." Those last words were delivered in a purr to rival milord's. Jovas's big hand tightened, forcing the witch to her knees. Then he looked up toward my master. "This is a grand day, Ardolf Greycastle. One I've hungered for. Would you care to savor it with me?"

The Beast's smile made my blood chill. "Oh, aye. I would, at that." Jovas gestured, and for a moment I was blinded as light burst in the room.

When my sight cleared, Jack and milord were free, and thankfully, uninjured, their wounds healed.

That done, the sorcerer turned and dragged Edrea toward milord's great chair. He fell into it and dragged her across his lap.

Over the sound of tearing fabric as Jovas did away with Edrea's gown, I asked my master, "Who is he?"

"A very great wizard," said milord, sounding darkly pleased. He moved up behind me and took my breasts in both hands. "He's had a yen for Edrea for years, but she would never yield to him. And he is hardly the sort to submit to a woman's whim. She managed to keep him from her with a magical shield, but when you doused her with the potion, the spell collapsed. Now she's at his mercy."

And it was rapidly evident he had none. As we watched, the wizard began to pound her bottom with his broad, hard palm. She kicked and screamed, cheeks reddening under each hard smack, the firm, rounded flesh shuddering.

Jovas watched her naked rump quiver and bounce with lustful eyes, a wide grin on his face. Jack slinked over to watch, his eyes burning with cruel enjoyment of his tormentor's punishment.

My master squeezed my nipples and I gasped, feeling my own arousal grow. I began to understand why the Beast took such delight in spanking me as I watched her squirming kicks.

I wasn't the only one who appreciated the view. Milord's cock grew thick and hot against my back with every smack.

The air rang with Edrea's howls of protest, the sound competing with the loud slaps of Jovas's hand. Her naked breasts quivered against his legs.

Whatever punishment Jovas intended, I knew he'd be merciless with her. My own hot anticipation astonished me almost as much as the quiver of envy I felt.

My master rolled and squeezed my nipples, and I groaned, watching as Jovas pounded Edrea's bottom. I could see her sex, red, furred, and pouting, flashing as her long legs kicked.

Suddenly, Jovas stopped and jerked Edrea to her feet. I felt a twinge of disappointment that the display was over.

My disappointment vanished as Jovas pushed her to the stone floor and pounced on her, sucking and nibbling her nipples. She pounded at his shoulders, but he ignored her struggles, squeezing her breasts, reaching down between her legs with the other hand to find her sex. Edrea cursed and bit at him, and I saw him lift his head to murmur something. A spell, apparently; light flared, and when it faded, the witch was still, as if wrapped in invisible chains. Milord slipped a hand down and began to caress my dampening flesh.

Jovas's tongue looked very long and red as he licked the witch's nipples until they grew into blushing points. His hand, stroking steadily, slid along her petals with increasing ease and speed, as if she grew wet under his demanding attentions. He murmured again and his robes disappeared in a flash of light, revealing a body as long, muscular, and hard as any knight's.

I stared in fascination at his muscular rump as he lifted himself and pressed his body between Edrea's slender legs. His hips lifted, slid downward, and for a moment I could see his thick staff as he sheathed it in Edrea.

Jovas went to work over her, his muscular body rising and falling on her white, helpless one. Sweat rolled between his shoulder blades. I grew very hot.

Suddenly he rolled, bringing Edrea on top of him without missing a stroke. He craned his head around to look at us, then grabbed the witch's bottom and pulled her cheeks apart in lewd invitation.

Instead of answering Jovas's inviting gesture, milord grabbed my shoulders and turned me to face him. Applying gentle pressure, he forced me to my knees. Knowing what he wanted, I grinned and took his staff into my mouth, rolling my tongue over it to coat it thoroughly in saliva. He thrust his hips against my face and I moaned, knowing what he intended to do to Edrea once I had his organ well lubricated.

It occurred to me as I sucked him that I shouldn't be participating with such enthusiasm in the witch's humiliation. Then again, I also knew what she would have done to me if we had not defeated her, and I could not escape the feeling that she was getting no more than she deserved. I sucked my master even harder.

At last milord pulled free of my mouth and strode toward Edrea and Jovas. Between her legs, I could see the wizard's organ moving in and out of her in long strokes. I swallowed.

Then milord covered her, and I could see only a tangle of legs and the Beast's black furred rump, rising over them. I heard a long, feminine groan and knew he'd entered Edrea's anus.

I licked my lips and cut my eyes toward Jack, feeling such desperate hunger that I wanted to beg the footman to take me. Instead, he left my side and crossed to the tangle of bodies. I saw him kneel facing them, then lift Edrea's head by the hair and aim his phallus for her mouth. His fist tightened, dragging her onto his cock.

Rolling his head on his shoulders in pleasure, he used his grip on her head to guide her back and forth as he fucked her throat.

My nipples burned, and I could feel a steady trickle of wetness filling my core. It was too easy to imagine what she felt, filled by the three cocks of her captors, the smooth burning strength of each of them thrusting in and out of her. I wanted one of them to take me. Now.

But they were too busy revenging themselves on the witch, so at last, in frustration, I went to milord's throne and threw myself into it. Hooking one leg over the arm, I began to caress my own wet flesh.

From where I sat on the throne, I could see how they held her helpless between them. Jovas arched under her, forcing her to ride his grinding hips, even as my master covered her, thrusting against the taut curve of her rump. Edrea shuddered as they pounded into her, but she couldn't protest even if she wanted to with her mouth stuffed with Jack's shaft.

Holding her head immobile with both hands now, he hunched against her face, fucking her throat ruthlessly. I wondered if she could breathe, but judging from the flare of her nostrils, she was evidently managing it somehow.

I shivered and stroked my own breast with one hand, slipping the other down between my legs. It was incredibly arousing, watching them take her. My cream slid hot and thick between my lips.

For a moment it occurred to me that I had fallen far under milord's ownership. He'd made me forget my high birth and ancient name until I cared for nothing but the heat he made me feel.

But in truth, it was not as if my blue blood had ever done a damn thing for me but get me married to a doddering old man with a greedy son. This was pleasure. It was, in fact, more than most women ever found.

As I watched, swirling a forefinger through my soaking heat, I imagined milord's huge shaft sliding out of Edrea's helplessly open bottom, then plunging in again. I remembered the way it had felt when he'd taken me that way, and gasped, pinching my nipple hard in a spasm of desire.

For a moment it seemed she was trying to fight them—white flesh surged against strong hands—but they quelled her rebellion with no particular effort and went back to impaling her again. Their bodies slapped against hers harder now, faster, and I could almost feel three thick shafts ramming in and out of me. I plunged three fingers into myself as deeply as I could, strumming my pearl with my thumb.

As I watched, I heard her begin to moan around Jack's cock. The sound held more delight than suffering.

It seemed the witch had embraced her punishment.

Suddenly the Beast roared out that distinctive sound he makes when he climaxes, and he stiffened, driving deep. At almost the same moment, Jovas's spine arched, lifting both Edrea and my master clear off the ground. Edrea made a muffled sound around Jack's organ, and the footman gasped.

The tangle of sweaty sex that was Edrea, Jack, Jovas, and milord collapsed. Bare strokes away from my own climax, I groaned in frustration.

Milord was the first to pick himself up from the huddle, one hand going to the base of his spine as he stretched his back. Jack was next up, grinning with the satisfaction of his revenge.

Then at last, Jovas stood, lifting Edrea and slinging her over his shoulder, naked and limp. He gestured, and for a moment the dungeon was illuminated in a blaze of light. When it faded, he was dressed in his robes. Edrea, however, was still naked . . . except for chains and a slave collar such as I had worn on more than one occasion lately.

The wizard held out a hand to milord, who took it, careful of his claws. "My thanks for your assistance, Lord Greycastle," Jovas said, very formally for a man who'd just helped his host rape a witch.

The Beast grinned at him with an astonishing number of teeth. "Believe me, it was my pleasure. I trust you'll keep your slave well punished?"

Jovas grinned back, showing teeth of his own. "Count on it, Ardolf." He hesitated. "I wish I could break the bitch's curse for you, but I'm afraid she set it too well."

The Beast shrugged. "I know. You certainly gave it your best effort those months ago. On the other hand, the potion worked. I'll have to be satisfied with that."

The wizard's eyes slid to me as I sat, decorously bolt upright, in milord's chair. "Perhaps you'll be able to break your spell another way, milord."

The Beast looked at me, then glanced away. "I don't think so." His jaw tightened. "Punish the bitch well, Jovas."

The wizard leered. "Oh, I will. I'm feeling . . . inspired."

Edrea lifted her head and I saw the flash of helpless acceptance on her face just before they disappeared.

"I hope," said Jack, "he whips the ass off her."

"I doubt it," said the Beast, sounding a little bitter. "He was always soft where she was concerned. That's why he didn't leave her with me."

Jack shrugged. "Too bad. Still, I'm sure he'll keep her busy . . ."

"No doubt. Get some sleep, Jack. I'm sure you need it." The Beast waved the footman toward the door and he lost no time finding it. The thick wooden slab slammed shut, leaving me alone with my master . . . and a burning need deep in my core.

I stared at the Beast hungrily, my nipples tingling, feeling a hot trickle deep within. Would he want to take me now, so soon after the witch? I thought it likely; he'd often astonished me with his stamina in the past. "Milord," I began softly, taking a step forward.

He looked away. "We'll get your clothes. I will provide you with a full purse for the road and summon some of the village men to provide you with an escort. You needn't worry about Cedric. I'll take care of him. And I'll see he gives you your inheritance."

I blinked, feeling I'd been dunked in ice water. "You're sending me away?"

"I'm freeing you."

"But . . . but why?"

He looked at me, full on. There was pain in his eyes. "You saved my life tonight at considerable risk to your own. I can't continue to hold you."

I stared at him. Free. I'd be free again. Free to go back to my own castle, to my women and my tapestries. Free.

Free to be wedded again against my will to some old man. The young ones, after all, look for wealthy widows or pretty young virgins, and I was neither. "No."

"What?" he asked, astonished.

"If you feel any gratitude at all for me, you won't make me leave." I looked at the high, muscular arch of his chest, the width of his arms.

"I took you." Confusion and guilt filled his eyes. "I enslaved you. Beat and sodomized you."

"And I loved every last moment of it." I remembered the feeling of his broad shaft sliding into me, his tongue flicking over my nipples . . . even his hard hand hitting my rump. "You've given me more pleasure than I have ever known. I'd rather live as your slave than be free without you."

And he roared.

I jumped back as his back arched, then twisted like a gigged fish. He began to glow and it seemed his fur ignited.

I screamed in horror. I had killed him. This was the witch's revenge and I had somehow triggered it.

Fur crisped, burned, dropped away in hunks as he clawed at the air. His horns disappeared in a curl of flame and his claws went incandescent and disappeared. I began to scream for Jack, knowing he could do nothing, screamed for Jovas, knowing the wizard couldn't hear.

And then the flame was gone and the Beast fell to his knees. "Milord?"

He moaned. I rushed to him, but hesitated, reluctant to touch him. His skin looked so . . . pink. But as I examined him, I realized there were no burns marring it.

"Beast?" I whispered.

He lifted his naked face and looked at me from eyes that shone with joy. "My name is Ardolf Greycastle," he said.

The fur had blunted the sharp, clean lines of his features, blurring his male beauty. I stared at him in wonder.

Then Ardolf stood up in a rush of hard muscle and human flesh, and I saw him for the first time truly naked. The sight made my mouth go dry. He looked a little shorter without the mane that had bulked around his head, but my head still came no higher than his breastbone. He was every inch the knight, powerful with thick muscle bred by swinging a sword and riding a warhorse.

His laugh was deep music as he snatched me against his chest. He felt so hard without that cushion of fur around him. "That's twice I owe you, girl. Once for my life, again for breaking the spell."

The spell was broken? I brushed a cautious hand along his ribs, feeling bone and muscle and velvet skin. It was true. He was a man again. "Are you going to set me free?"

His eyes were just as green as I remembered, though they no longer glowed. "Not likely, slave. In fact, you have some atoning to do." His attempt at a growl was spoiled by his grin.

"Atoning?" I squeaked as he picked me up and carried me toward his throne.

"Aye. You dared put a leash, by God, on your master." He dropped into his chair. "And you wanted to see that witch take a crop to me. If anyone gets punished around here, girl, it's going to be you."

I sighed in pleasure, then lost my contentment in a screech as his broad, furless hand descended on my rump in a stinging slap. Minutes later, I was bucking and cursing, heartily regretting my submission, as he continued to spank me with wicked, lustful enjoyment.

At last, when my bottom was blazing, he stayed his hand, rose from his place, and went down on his back on the stone, lifting me up over him. With barely a pause, he brought me down on his eager cock and sheathed it with a twist of his hips. I braced my hands on his chest and glared at him as he began to thrust with smooth strength.

But he felt so good in me. Each long dig of his organ in my wet cunt ignited my lust, until soon I was meeting his thrusts, forgetting my fiery rump in the pleasure of it.

In seconds, my pique was replaced by desire, and I twisted and shivered around his burrowing shaft as he pinched my nipples mercilessly. I climaxed with a scream. His own cry echoed it, sounding almost as loud as his old roar.

We collapsed together in the afterglow, damp and contented.

"You realize, don't you," he said at last, "that you're going to marry me."

"As milord wishes," I sighed.

And we lived happily ever after—with frequent visits to the dungeon.

A QUESTION
OF PLEASURE

Rose Carson slipped back around the corner of the high stone wall as Major Alan McReynolds opened the wooden gate. Heart in her throat, she waited. A moment later, McReynolds strode past, tall and handsome in his Union uniform, dark head held high. With a lover's keen awareness, she knew he felt troubled. Something in the line of his broad, muscled shoulders spoke of disquiet.

He'd be even more disturbed if he knew the woman he loved was a Rebel spy sent to play on his well-known taste for beautiful women. That she'd inadvertently fallen in love with him would be no comfort at all.

Well, Rose thought, setting her mouth in a tight line, this was the last time. Once she got her hands on that list, she'd be free of her obligation to the Confederacy, content in the knowledge that she'd done her duty. Alan would never have to know what she'd done. But if he ever found out . . .

Well. That didn't bear thinking about.

Enough time had passed to allow Alan to turn the corner on his way to army headquarters a few blocks away in the heart of Washington. Quickly, Rose moved out from around the corner of the garden wall and along the walk toward the gate. Without hesitating, she pushed it open.

For a moment, she allowed herself to scan her lover's property. There was the apple tree they'd exchanged fevered kisses beneath, and there, the thorny, bloodred beauty of the rose bushes whose scent had perfumed so many passionate encounters.

And the house. The elegant two-story brick town house had been the backdrop of some of the happiest moments of her life. How many times had she lain in the canopied bed upstairs, writhing under Alan's skillful touch as his mouth sipped and nibbled? How many nights had she curled against his big body as he slept, her eyes burning with love and guilt?

But no matter what they'd done, no matter how Rose felt about it, she had duties she couldn't ignore. Steeling herself against the bite of her conscience, she walked up the stairs to knock on the finely carved door. Taking a deep breath, Rose folded her hands against her dove-gray skirts and waited for one of Alan's servants to admit her.

There was no answer.

Rose frowned. She'd concocted an explanation for needing to visit Alan's library, something about a forgotten book he'd told her to recover for him, but it looked as though the trip was for nothing. Impatiently, she tried the door. To her surprise, it swung open.

She rocked back on her heels and considered the house's dim interior. This was a stroke of luck.

Quickly she slipped inside, heading for the narrow stairway at the head of the hall. Gathering her skirts in one slim hand, she ascended.

Alan's library lay off to the right of the stairs, a dark, masculine room lined with heavy mahogany bookcases and row upon row of books. Rose, however, only had eyes for the massive desk. Just last night, she'd caught a glimpse of a list of names on the desktop—and several of those names belonged to men she knew to be Confederate spies. If she could just get a look at that list, find out who was in danger of detection and arrest . . . She rustled behind the desk and began opening drawers.

Ah, there it was. In the top drawer, of all places. She frowned. Bad hiding place for such an obviously important piece of intelligence.

"I'm disappointed in you, Rose. I thought you'd be harder to trap."

Rose's heart leaped into her throat and she jerked her head up.

Alan stood in the doorway, his handsome face hard, a fine muscle ticking in his rigid jaw. He held a pistol pointed right at her head. She froze as he slowly advanced into the room, the weapon unwavering. Rose had the feeling that if she so much as blinked, he'd shoot her.

"I've suspected you for some time," he said, his tone almost casual. "You were just a little bit too fascinated by things you should have no interest in. But still, I couldn't quite bring myself to believe you could hide a viper's treachery behind such a sweet face."

Her knees threatened to buckle under her. She caught herself against the desktop. "Alan, you don't understand . . ."

"Oh, I understand too well." His dark eyes were bitter. "I understand you're a spy and a traitor. I understand you used my passion for you to play me for a fool."

Instinctively, she held up a terrified hand to ward him off. He grabbed her wrist and snatched her against him, close enough to see the cold intention on his face. "And I understand," he purred, "that you're going to tell me the name of the spy master you report to, and every bit of intelligence you've ever collected."

Rose's spine stiffened in outrage. "I'm not going to tell you any such thing!"

"Sweet, by the time I'm through with you, you'll be begging to reveal every secret you ever knew."

She lifted her chin, outraged that he thought her so lacking in spirit as to believe such a ridiculous threat. "You're bluffing."

"I assure you, I am totally serious. There are any number of techniques I can use . . ."

Enraged, she barked out a laugh. "What sort of fool do you take me for? The Union army doesn't torture female prisoners!"

His smile was ugly. "No. The army doesn't." His grip tightened on her wrist until she gasped. "But I'm not the army."

Ruthlessly, Alan dragged Rose to the bedroom, the gun in his free hand. With a powerful wrench of his shoulder, he propelled her into the room. She whirled around and stared at him wildly, her skirts swinging around her like a bell.

Deliberately, Alan walked to the armchair he'd brought in and sat down in it, keeping the gun trained on her the whole time. Fear and defiance blazed in her wide brown eyes and he felt a twinge of pity for her. Just a twinge, though, easily fought down. She'd betrayed him. Besides, this wouldn't take long.

"Strip," he growled.

She pulled herself to her full height. "I will not!"

"You were eager enough last night."

"You were acting like a gentleman last night."

"While you were busy whoring yourself for your Rebel masters. Strip."

Damn her. But he knew that the prospect of being naked in front of him—at least under these circumstances—would make her surrender. She'd start talking soon enough, then, and there would be no need for the other preparations he'd made.

She tilted her chin and glowered at him. "I shall not!"

He cocked the gun. "Strip or talk."

"Shoot me, then. I'll not do either."

His mouth pulled into a grim smile as he took the pistol off cock. "Well. You seemed to have called my bluff." Alan put the gun aside.

And pounced. Rose kicked and fought, but her struggles did her no good against his determined hands. He dragged her to the bed and roped her hands to the overhead supports of the canopy with the cords he'd tied there earlier. Then he drew a penknife from his pocket and went to work, cutting the buttons off her gown, slicing through the laces of her corset, dragging relentlessly at the fabric until it gave, until she wore nothing but her stockings and tiny black slippers.

By the time he was done, they were both panting, she glaring at him in rage, he frustrated and furious.

Now, dammit. Now she would talk.

"All right," he said.

"It's nothing you haven't seen before," she spat.

True. But on the other hand, he thought, as awareness of the situation burst upon him, she hadn't been tied before. Her white, pretty breasts hadn't trembled with every breath, her brown eyes brilliant with wrath, her slim torso twisting as she fought the cords that held her. She hadn't looked so . . . tempting.

"Don't you realize the position you're in?" Alan growled, fighting his own heady reaction to her. "Nobody knows you're here. I've dismissed the servants. I can do any damn thing I want to you. The only thing that can stop me is you. Telling me everything. The name of your spymaster, what you told him, everything. Now."

Her lovely dark eyes narrowed and she bit off every word. "Do . . . your . . . worst."

Looking at her naked vulnerability, Alan wondered if she'd be so quick to dare him if she knew how much he *wanted* to do his worst— or just how bad his worst could be.

Rose tugged on the cords that bound her wrists to the canopy supports and stared in uneasy fascination at Alan. He glared back, his features sharp with a strange combination of predatory hunger and baffled rage. She could feel his eyes on her bare breasts, almost like a physical touch. Despite the situation, despite the anger between them, a slow coil of hunger curled in her belly.

He took a step closer to her and his lids lowered. "Are you sure you want to issue rash challenges to me? Particularly considering your present . . . situation."

She lifted her chin. "You won't hurt me, Alan. No matter how much you might want to."

Anger flared in his eyes before he concealed it. "A dangerous delusion. I assure you, I will hurt you. And enjoy it, particularly after the way you betrayed me." He paused, then said almost casually, "I think you deserve anything I care to do to you."

He was not going to terrorize her, damn him. "What will you do, then?"

Alan's jaw tightened, and she saw that her challenge angered him.

"That's a very good question, actually. I've given it a lot of thought." He walked over to the nightstand beside the bed, opened a drawer, and pulled out a long white candle. "I'm hesitant to damage that pretty white skin permanently, particularly since I intend to make use of it. But I think I've hit on a compromise."

Reaching into a pocket, he drew out a wax packet of sulfur matches. As she watched nervously, he lifted his boot and struck the match on the sole in a swift, violent gesture. A flame flared to life, and he applied it to the candle.

Eyeing the burning taper, Rose felt a twinge of fear. It was daylight and quite bright in the room. What did he mean to do with that?

He turned to her, a demon's smile curving his sensuous mouth, and moved closer until the candle shed a yellow radiance over her pale skin. "Such lovely breasts, so round and smooth and tempting." He reached out with his free hand and caught one of them, a rough thumb brushing over the nipple until it tightened, grew plump and hard as heat flooded her. Leaning closer, he bent and flicked his tongue over the pert tip. She jumped at the sharp stab of pleasure.

Delicately, he took her beaded flesh completely into his mouth, suckling until her breathing roughened and her strength and anger drained into a dangerous sensuality.

Rose had never felt more naked in her life, more vulnerable and hungry than she felt now, bound and helpless for him. And he'd never looked so big, so deliciously male. An erotic barbarian determined to make a conquest of her tight and creamy flesh.

He slid his arm around her back and forced her to arch over it, pressing her breast hard against his mouth.

"Alannnnn," she moaned.

He raised his head and smiled at her—just as he tilted the candle over her other breast. A molten drop fell, splashed onto her nipple. She arched with a gasp at the fiery pain. Instinctively she tried to jerk back, but the powerful arm around her waist wouldn't let her escape.

"Stop!"

He merely smiled and began to nibble and lick her left nipple again—even as the hand that held the candle dripped wax on her right.

Alan listened to her gasps and whimpers, felt the way she arched and struggled in the tight grip of his arm. His cock was hard as a sword against his belly, and he badly wanted to plunge it into her.

Swallowing, he took a deep breath and tried to master himself. He hadn't expected that it would go this far, hadn't expected to actually have to drip the wax on her hard little nipples.

And he certainly hadn't expected to enjoy it. In fact, when he'd come up with this particular interrogation method, he'd almost discarded it for fear that he wouldn't be able to do such a thing to her. He'd had no idea of the temptation he'd find in her pretty breast brushing his face, her lithe body surging against his, her moaning whimpers. He couldn't have anticipated the look on her face, the desire, the flashes of pain, the secret, appalled pleasure.

Against all expectation, she found his torment of her as arousing as he did.

He was losing control of this. He was supposed to be interrogating her, gathering information vital to the safety of the Union. But God, she tempted him . . .

Alan gasped, feeling his heart thundering in his chest. He wanted to plunge into her, feel her wet heat closing over him . . . And she *was* wet, he realized. He could smell the musk of her arousal.

With a groan, he jerked away, gripping the candle hard in his fist. "What's the name of your spymaster, Rose?"

She hung there, blinking at him as if stunned by the past heated minutes. Slowly, she licked her lips, her small pink tongue flicking out to trace the rosy fullness of her mouth. He almost attacked her again. "Alan, I . . ."

He crouched, tensing against the urgency of his lust. "Tell me and I can take you. Let me end this."

Rose whimpered. "No, please, don't make me . . ."

"Yes!" he roared.

Her eyes were brown and deep. "I can't." He snarled.

As Rose watched with a combination of fear and desire, Alan lifted the candle and blew it out in a single violent gesture, then threw it to the floor. The slim length of wax thunked against the carpet and rolled.

He began to unbutton his uniform shirt, his fingers so impatient that one of the buttons popped off to sail across the room. He didn't seem to notice. In a moment, his shirt fell open to reveal the tight, hard musculature of his chest.

His hand dropped to the fly of his trousers and worked the buttons with a series of rough jerks. Freed, his organ immediately sprang out to jut at her. Deliciously thick and hard, angled slightly upward with the violence of his lust, it was a silent testament to his intentions.

Remembering how it felt thrusting into her, Rose closed her eyes and moaned.

"Rose."

She opened her eyes and looked at him. He'd stepped closer, so close his cock almost touched her. She felt a violent need to caress it, and clenched her bound hands. "Alan, let me go. I want to . . ."

"Tell me what I want to know."

Rose gritted her teeth in frustration. "I can't, damn you! I've got a duty to . . ."

"So have I," he growled. He caught his big phallus in one hand. "Do you have any idea what I could do to you? What I want to do?" Almost unconsciously, his hand began to move, stroking the thick shaft. "You look so lusciously helpless, hanging there like that. I want to throw you down and fuck you."

She started; he'd never used that word to her before. Mesmerized, she stared at his slowly moving fist. His own eyes were fixed on her breasts, on the nipple that still wore a coat of wax. "I didn't expect to like this," he growled. "I didn't think I'd love listening to you gasp and whimper when that wax hit your pretty little nipple." His hand began to move faster and his face tightened.

Rose swallowed, taking in the way he looked standing there with his shirt hanging open, his pants unbuttoned to reveal the big cock he fisted in long strokes, his polished boots set wide.

"I think I'll go out and get a strap for that tempting ass of yours. Tie you spread-eagle . . . and watch your bottom turn pink . . . as I give it lick after lick with that strap—and my tongue." He grimaced through set teeth. His back arched, and she could see his thighs begin to tremble. "I wonder if . . . I'll love that as much as using that candle . . . And then . . . And then I'll fuck . . . ARRRRRRGHH!"

As she watched in dizzy hunger, a jet of sperm shot from his cock to splash on her belly.

Aftershocks of climax still sparked along Alan's nerves as he walked to the drawer and took out a long rope. Going back to her, he pulled his penknife. Two quick passes of the blade freed her wrists, but before she could get away, he forced her back on the bed.

"Alan, what are you . . . ?"

"I've got business to attend to, and I'm not going to leave you running loose."

As he looped the rope around her chest to bind her arms to her side, he noticed how the cord caught under her nipples. Alan licked his lips and wound the rope around her again so that the rosy little crests were pinched between the lengths of hemp. She squirmed in discomfort as the fibers tormented the delicate flesh.

He made a few fast passes around her wrists to tie them off, still eyeing the saucy tilt of her nipples imprisoned in the rope. Looking up, Alan found her dark eyes locked on his face, wide with a combination of desire and fear.

Unable to resist investigating the depth of her passion, he reached between her smooth thighs, smiling at her gasp. She was very wet.

Nostrils flaring, he thought about leaving her tied in a way that would maintain that sexual excitement. Maybe with something buried deep in that creamy little pussy . . .

He remembered the candle. It lay on the floor next to his boots. Alan bent to pick up the candle and gave it a frowning look. It was too long for the task he had in mind for it. With an easy twist of his big hands, he broke the taper in two and leaned over her again. His fingers parted her, and the tip slid into her wet flesh easily. He smiled and drove it in and out.

"Alaann," she moaned. "Don't. That's humiliating."

His mouth pulled tight, and he removed the candle. "So is the way you used me."

Come to think of it, he owed her a little humiliation.

In the nightstand was a bottle of oil he'd used the day before to massage her slender back. Now he used it on the second half of the candle, intent on giving Rose a lesson in shame she wouldn't soon forget.

She yelped in alarm when he rolled her over and spread her cheeks to gain access to the tight little hole between them. Ignoring her protests, Alan presented the blunt end of the candle to her anus and bore down. He had to use force to drive the candle into her exquisitely tight ass, particularly when she began to groan and struggle against her bonds. "Damn you, Alan!" she gasped. "Stop that!"

Involuntarily, he imagined what it would be like to shove something even larger into her tight rear opening. His spent phallus stirred and lengthened. Perhaps after he got back . . .

Inserting the pointed taper into her creamy vagina, Alan passed the end of the cord up between her cheeks and lips, making sure that the cord pressed her clitoris while trapping the candles within her. He looped it once around her hips to keep it there, then dragged her ankles up and roped them together.

Finished binding his prisoner, he straightened and looked down at her. She looked delicious, her nipples pouting around the tight bite of the rope, her sex wonderfully spread and stuffed.

"You," she told him, glaring up at him with snapping dark eyes, "are a bastard."

He grinned at her. "Yes, I am. Maybe you'd better keep that in mind."

Whistling in satisfaction, he turned his back on his pretty captive and sauntered out.

Rose writhed as the twin candles rubbed together inside her vagina and anus. What a clever, vicious bastard Alan was, knowing just how to tie her to drive her mad.

And to stand there and caress himself while she watched, dying for him . . . She gritted her teeth and tried to ignore the hemp gnawing at her tender breasts. *Just think about something else, Rose,* she told herself. *Don't remember the way that hard phallus feels when he pushes it into you, don't think about his mouth and his tongue and his hands.*

An escape plan. That's what she needed, a way to escape. Maybe the ropes around her wrists . . . Rose pulled and twisted her arms, hoping Alan hadn't been as careful as he should be.

All she got for her trouble was the rasp of the harsh rope over her aching clit. Growling, Rose subsided. Her sex felt so swollen, so engorged with blood, so hot and aching that just squirming made it worse. If only she could free herself. She wouldn't run. She'd lie in wait for that bastard, Alan, and then she'd . . .

. . . Tie him spread-eagle on the bed and impale herself on his massive organ until they both screamed in pleasure.

Dropping her head back against the mattress, Rose moaned.

Alan strolled down the street, ignoring the curious stares of passersby no doubt wondering why he wore his uniform overcoat in such warm weather.

It concealed his huge erection.

He kept picturing the tiny dark opening of her anus spreading around that candle. He'd ordinarily never consider sodomy, but now it seemed ideal, a sweet punishment to torment Rose while sating his need to drive his cock hard and deep into her. Over and over.

He knew Rose's erotic hunger was one of the best weapons in his arsenal. If he could keep her trembling on the edge of orgasm, sheer frustration might loosen her tongue where no amount of torture ever would.

On the other hand, a little torture couldn't hurt, either. He had several things in mind that should prove very effective in bringing Rose to heel. All he needed were a few tools. And he knew just where to get them.

Robinson's was a tack shop that catered to wealthy gentlemen, but it sold a lot more than saddles to those savvy enough to know about the store's back room. Alan had never felt a need for its stock, but he'd heard rumors about it from various dissipated sorts with adventurous mistresses. Now he was glad for that knowledge.

Walking into the shop's expensive interior, Alan took a deep breath of air, scented with leather, and walked over to the proprietor. "I'd like to see the stock in the back, please."

Robinson, a rotund little man, shot him a single sharp look and came around the counter to escort him through a heavy oak door in the rear of the room.

To Alan's surprise, he found Captain Michael Taylor looking over a selection of light riding crops. The captain, a tall, muscular blond, quirked a brow at him in surprise. "McReynolds. Somehow I never expected to meet you here."

Alan's smile was dry as he moved over beside the other man. "I've recently acquired a mount who needs a firm hand."

Taylor grinned, his handsome face taking on a deeply masculine expression of anticipation. "Yes, I have one of those myself. It can be very rewarding." He paused delicately. "Is this the first occasion you've had to discipline a . . . filly?"

"As a matter of fact, yes." He eyed the crops and frowned. "These seem a little heavy. I don't want to cut her."

Taylor nodded at Robinson, who stepped behind a counter that was a replica of the one in the front. Bending, the shopkeeper pulled out a long narrow box and flipped it open.

"This should be more what you want," Taylor said, gesturing at the box. Alan, moving closer, saw that it held a series of light whips with lashes made of woven silk. "They won't inflict any real damage, but the reaction from your mount should be highly satisfactory."

Alan nodded and selected one. Turning, he propped a foot on the lower rung of a chair standing to one side, brought his arm up, and slashed the whip hard across his thigh. It stung, but he thought Taylor right about its relative harmlessness.

"This should do nicely," he said, and he handed the whip to Robinson. "At least for a start." He cocked a brow at Taylor. "This particular filly is a bit difficult."

"If you find that further discipline is called for," Taylor suggested delicately, "I can suggest several devices that may accomplish your ends."

"Oh?"

Taylor nodded at Robinson and the man reached behind the counter again.

* * *

Rose moaned, feeling the candles torment her as she shifted. God, she wanted Alan so badly, longed to feel that thick, hard organ digging into her eager flesh. Unfortunately, she knew that he would never give her what she wanted unless she told him everything *he* wanted. And she couldn't do that. People would die if she gave in; Alan would see to it.

Frowning, Rose clenched her fists. She had to maintain her silence, no matter how her lust tormented her. She wouldn't be responsible for those deaths.

The bedroom door creaked open, and Rose twisted her head around as Alan strolled in with a long brown paper package tucked under one arm. He dumped it carelessly on the leather armchair and walked toward her, hands busy on the buttons of his coat. "Miss me?" he asked, grinning down at her.

She was tempted to say something unladylike, but bit her lip. "Nothing to say? That's not very wise of you." He settled a hip on the bed beside her and reached for the thatch of soft curls between her bound legs. She gasped in outrage, but there was no way to keep him from worming a finger between her thighs and probing at her candle-stuffed sex. "MMmm." His smile was slow and wicked. "Poor Rose. So hungry. So wet. Would you like to come?"

Her eyes flared wide, then narrowed in suspicion. "I thought the idea was to keep me hungry."

He reached into a pocket and pulled out that penknife again. "Well, yes." Taking her bound ankles in one big hand, he sawed carefully at the rope until it began to drop away from her in loops. "But I think maybe you could use a little relief. Not much, though." The curve of his smile deepened. "Just a taste."

Her feet sprang apart as he released them, tingling, though he hadn't tied her so tightly as to block circulation.

Before she could move, he took her ankles in his hands and dragged them over his shoulders. With a hungry growl, Alan buried his face against her sex, pushed aside the coil of rope that still trapped the candles, and began to lick. She gasped. The sensation of his long, hot tongue rolling skillfully over her wet flesh seared her right to the bone. Her thighs jerked, the muscles beginning to spasm almost at once. She'd been so hot for so long. Helplessly, Rose began to pump her hips against his face, twisting at each talented tongue stroke, each lingering suck. She was going over . . .

He stopped.

Her hips strained upward against his powerful grip, but Alan had withdrawn, lifting his head to watch her with eyes that burned.

"What's the name of your spymaster, Rose?"

"BASTARD!"

"I'm sure he is, but I doubt he answers to that. What's his name?"

Fighting a wave of rage and desire, Rose spat, "I'm not telling you anything, you Yankee son of a bitch."

Even in her present mood, she found his smile chilling. "Interesting choice of words, Rose. I think it's time you found out just what we Yankees do to pretty little Rebel captives."

So hard he thought he'd burst, Alan stripped out of his shirt as he stared at his prisoner's lifted ass. She'd given him a hell of a fight when he'd cut her free of the ropes and bent her over the rail at the foot of the bed, but she might as well have saved herself the effort. There was no way she could stop him from tying her ankles to the frame, lashing her wrists together and tying them to the head of the bed with a three-foot length of rope until she was stretched hard across the bed. Then he stuffed three pillows between her stomach and the rail. It was a deliciously arousing pose, one that spread her sex and displayed the rosy little hole he was dying to stuff. He took a half step toward her . . .

Clenching his fists, Alan managed to stop. Later. Right now, he had to do his job. He veered toward the paper package he'd left on the chair and ripped it open with shaking hands. Several objects fell out, but it was the whip that interested him. He picked it up and turned to her.

She was watching him, brown eyes wide in alarm. "What are you going to do with that?"

"What do you think?" His voice sounded more husky than menacing.

Rose jerked, lifting her head and shoulders off the bed, but she couldn't free herself. "No! Alan, you can't!"

"And I won't." He smiled. "All you have to do is tell me what I want to know."

Her eyes flickered in search of an escape that was nowhere to be seen. "Alan, please. Don't you understand? It's not just me; people will die if I give you that information."

"People will die if you don't." Jaw tightening, he moved up behind her. "Union soldiers, betrayed into ambush by the spies you shield. I can't afford to ignore this, Rose. If I could, you wouldn't be here. You'd be free, or you'd be in jail." He lifted the cat. "Now. Who is your spymaster, Rose?"

"Go to hell."

"Not without company." And he slashed the whip down hard across the curve of her rump. As the lashes of the cat bit into her smooth skin, she yelped, twisting.

For a moment he hesitated, eyeing her bottom anxiously. It had been a hard slash, but to Alan's relief, he saw no mark except a slight blush. His mouth curved into a grim smile.

He brought the whip down again, laying a diagonal slash across her pretty bottom. His next strokes were rapid and hard, one after the other until she writhed, the sweet uplifted bowls of her ass clenching and jiggling.

His breathing roughened as her struggles alternately displayed and hid her sex and puckered rosette. He'd probed that tiny hole earlier when he'd freed her, and he knew it was still oiled from the candle. Ready for his use.

For a moment he pictured her lying voluptuously vanquished in the aftermath of a long, slow buggering, her anus swollen from his hard thrusts, dewed in his sperm.

He grinned and snapped the whip down across her tempting cheeks again.

Rose yelped as the next cut fell on her bottom, slashing a line of fire across her skin. She couldn't believe he was doing this to her.

Yes, she'd known he would be dangerous if he ever found out. She'd even wondered a time or two if he would kill her. But this . . . She hadn't expected to be subjected to this kind of erotic torment, this sensuous humiliation.

Anxiously she twisted around until she could see Alan in the mirror across from the bed. His muscle-knit chest shone, sweat-burnished, rippling as his arm rose and fell with each merciless stroke. His face looked tight and feral with hunger, hot eyes locked on her bottom. She tried to suppress the bucking and twitching that seemed to incite him to flog her even harder, but each flaming stroke of the whip defeated her determination.

Alan flung the cat down and reached for her rump, only to arrest the movement in midgesture. Jaw tight, he strode around to sit on the bed in front of her. Slipping a hand under her chin, he lifted it and forced her to meet his eyes.

"This has to stop," he growled. "Now. Your spymaster, Rose."

"I can't!" she wailed.

"Damn you, you'd better!" He set his jaw, his eyes burning. "Don't you see what's happening to me?"

"Forgive me, but I'm more interested in what you're doing to *me*."

"So am I." His nostrils flared. "I'm utterly fascinated by every twitch of your ass, every gasp and moan and whimper. It makes me hard, Rose. It makes me want to fuck you."

Staring up at him, she found she couldn't speak, couldn't move, half hypnotized by the dark lust she could see blazing in his eyes.

"It's almost beyond my control, my sweet," he said, his voice low and growling. "If you keep resisting me, if you refuse to submit, I can't guarantee my actions." He stood up in a rush of male power and reached for the buttons of his breeches. A second later, she was confronted by the hard thrust of his rod. "It's up to you."

She looked up at him and licked her dry lips. "Oh, no. You can't escape responsibility by saying it's all my fault, that I drove you to it. If you're excited by torturing me, the fault lies with you."

His head jerked up and a startled flicker of self-awareness pierced his lust. "You . . . have a point. No gentleman would do to you what I've done."

Alan got up from the bed and moved around behind her. Rose took a deep breath, relieved that he'd come to his senses at last. She'd known the man she'd loved couldn't do such things to her. As for the flicker of disappointment she felt . . . well, she'd ignore that.

Suddenly his hard hands gripped her bottom, parting her cheeks. "I suppose," Alan grated, "this means I'm no gentleman." To Rose's shock, the broad head of his shaft pressed against her anus.

"ALAAAAAAAANNNNNNN!!!"

A tight, feral smile cut Alan's face as he leaned into her. Slowly the big head of his cock penetrated the muscular ring of her anus, sliding relentlessly inward despite her desperately clamping muscles. Her asshole was well-greased, and the power of his hips insured she couldn't keep him out.

Fighting every inch of the way, he drove the width of his organ deeper, then deeper still, breathing in harsh gasps. She babbled threats and pleas in a voice high with anxiety, but he ignored her protests and burrowed deeper.

Finally he was in to the balls. He stopped, eyes narrowed as he fought not to come on the spot, her conquered rectum massaging his massive cock with its oiled, silky walls. He'd known reaming her would be delicious. Why else had he been imagining this moment since he'd impaled her ass on the candle?

"You're hurting me," she said breathlessly.

He grinned. "I know." Slowly he began to withdraw, savoring the feeling of his cock sliding along the tight channel that felt so slick and hot. Rose sucked in a gasp.

Alan set his feet to gain purchase and pushed, biting his lip in delight. "If you submit to me, it will get better."

She whimpered. "It . . . can't. You're too . . . big."

He suspected his answering smile must have a demonic cast. "All the more reason to submit, then." But the going was getting a little easier now, as if she had begun to adjust to the invasion despite herself. Sweating, he began to pick up the pace, stroking in and out.

"What if . . ." She hesitated and sobbed out a breath. "What if I agree to tell you what you want to know? Will you spare me?"

"No." The word was out before he could reconsider it, but it was just as well. He was not going to abandon his conquest now. He wasn't going to stop until he'd come in the depths of her ass.

With a growl, he began to ride her faster.

Rose twisted at the fiery shaft bisecting her bottom. She knew she deserved it for her disloyal impulse to betray her country.

Each long, merciless thrust bounced her against the bed rail as his pelvis ground against her sex. Yet the pain no longer felt like a knife in her ass. He was right that surrendering to his phallus made the penetration easier.

Turning her head, she saw him in the mirror, hunched over her in his breeches and boots, reaming her, his face twisted in predatory hunger. She felt a curl of arousal as she watched him, a spurt of pleasure rising through the pain and shame of his invasion. A strange delight rose at each withdrawal as his big shaft slid from her, only to torment her again on its return.

Alan looked up and his eyes met her in the mirror. He smiled slowly. Reaching between her thighs, he found the hard bud of her clitoris. Slowly he stroked it as he buggered her. She caught her breath as the pleasure strengthened, swirling up from her pearl like a kindling fire. She whimpered.

"Why, darling," he gritted, driving the next stroke with such power that her breath left her lungs, "is that desire rising in your eyes? Can it be that you enjoy having your ass reamed by a Yankee bastard?" She twisted and gasped.

"Well, I don't mind telling you, I love ramming your Rebel asshole. What a sweet, tight little butt you've got."

Rose pressed her eyes closed. The fire aroused by his skillful fingers met the painful blaze of his buggering cock, and the two seared her with lust.

"Get used to it, darling," he purred, leaning over her until his breath stirred her hair. His fingers swirled over her clitoris. "I'm going to be fucking you this way frequently. You're just too tight and tempting to resist."

She squirmed. The desire she'd felt all day now leaped hot again, and the smooth, even strokes of his shaft drove it higher. "Thick," she whimpered. "You're so cruelly thick."

He growled. The pace of his hips had picked up, grown erratic and urgent as he buggered her. Her thighs quivered with each stroke of his fingers. She began to shiver in waves.

"That's it. Come on my Yankee cock. Let me feel that little asshole squeezing me." His voice was a deep, velvet drawl. She shuddered helplessly.

Without warning, he shoved so brutally deep, she jumped. She could feel his phallus jerking deep in her bottom as he groaned in pleasure. "Take it," he rumbled. "Take it all!"

Her orgasm crashed over her like a wave, washing away pain and shame and duty, leaving nothing but the raw delight of Alan's cock pulsing out his cream in the depths of her ass.

R ose sat on the velvet seat of the closed carriage, wrapped in the folds of her cloak. She wore nothing more, and she squirmed at the feeling of the red silk lining rubbing over her breasts and thighs.

Flexing her bound hands, she wondered what she'd do if the cloak slipped.

A silly concern, really. Considering the hard expression on Alan's face as he sat across from her, she might do better to worry about where he was taking her and what erotic torment he'd prepared for her tonight.

She'd been his captive for a week now. Seven endless days of exploring aspects of herself she'd never imagined—and would have rather remained ignorant about. The leap of her passions as his hard palm slammed down on her bottom, the way she grew shamelessly wet when he screwed tiny clamps onto her nipples, the excitement of wondering when he'd break, when he'd throw her down and ride her in a frenzy of hunger.

It was no wonder she'd been able to resist his torture, she thought, twisting her bound hands in her cloak. She loved what he was doing too much.

But tonight . . . tonight he'd stripped her and wrapped her in her cloak, slipped a feathered mask over her face, and hustled her out to his coach. And she had no idea where they were headed.

Had he decided to turn her over to the authorities? No, surely he'd have dressed her first . . .

The carriage lurched and stopped, rocking on its springs. Alan opened the door and stepped out, nodding the coachman away. As he reached in and helped her out, he wrapped one arm around her to make sure she stayed modestly concealed by the cloak. Rose felt perversely grateful for his consideration.

Stepping down, she found she stood in front of a huge, very stylish house with peaked gables and gingerbread fretwork. Alan put his hand to the small of her back, urging her forward. She approached the staircase on dragging feet.

As they climbed the steps, one of the house's double doors swung wide, revealing a tall, handsome blond in a Union uniform. The blond smiled and waved them inside.

"Alan, what . . . ?" Rose murmured as their host closed the door behind them, leaving them in a wide foyer.

"You're in no position to ask questions."

"Up the stairs, Major," the blond said, nodding toward the winding staircase off to the left. Alan tightened his grip on her waist and urged her toward it. She couldn't fight without giving the blond a tempting view, so she set her teeth and went where he directed.

On the third floor, they found a carpeted hallway lined with doors, all firmly closed. The blond moved around them and led the way to the third door on the left. Producing a key, he opened it and stepped inside.

Rose followed him in, her chin tilted to hide her fear.

It was only when the blond moved to relock the door from the inside that she realized Alan hadn't followed.

Rose took a step back as the big blond turned to her with an unholy smile. "What . . . what's going on? Where's Alan going?"

"He's left you to my care, sweet." He began to move toward her slowly. "He believes he has taken too gentle a hand with you, and he's entrusted me with the task of bringing you to heel."

Rose backed away, eyes widening. "Who are you?"

"You," said the blond, reaching for her cloak, "may call me Master Taylor."

Alan watched through the hidden spy hole as Taylor bound Rose's hands and flipped the end of the rope through a hook in the ceiling. She was half bent over a padded bar, but the way her wrists were tied arched her so that her breasts and ass thrust out as if begging for attention. Attention Alan was quite sure they'd get, if he knew Taylor.

And he did, which was precisely why he'd insisted on watching. He wasn't sure he trusted the captain not to hurt Rose for the sheer pleasure of doing so.

And what a pleasure it was. That, Alan knew from his own experience.

A slight, cruel smile curving his mouth, Taylor walked over to a small japanned casket that sat on the mirrored vanity. He drew out a ceramic jar and Alan tensed in anticipation. Taylor had told him of the cream that jar held, described the effect it would have on Rose. And the idea filled Alan with a combination of lust and jealousy.

Slowly Taylor pulled on a pair of leather gloves and carried the jar back to Rose's stretched and helpless body.

"I imagine you must be pretty curious by now," the captain said, dipping two fingers into the cream. "Perhaps you even feel a bit betrayed that the major would turn you over to me."

Rose tossed her head and eyed him haughtily from behind the feathered mask. "I'm sure I'm no longer surprised by anything the major does. He takes a positive delight in cruelty."

"Of course he does." Taylor walked around behind her and paused, contemplating the white, delicately rounded curves of her bottom. "Nothing stiffens a man's cock quite like having a lovely, helpless woman at his mercy. His to torment. His to fuck."

Leaning forward, he pressed his cream-covered fingers deeply into Rose's sweet sex. She jumped in her bonds and gritted out, "I imagine such things would be arousing—to a sadist."

"To any man, Rose." He dipped his leather-sheathed fingers into the jar again. "Men have a need, an instinct, to dominate. And the conquest is all the sweeter when it's a beautiful woman who is forced to submit."

Taylor paused and contemplated her pouting sex, then began to work the cream inside. His smile was slow and hot. "Her cries of pain and surrender heat his blood until his rod is as hard as a sword."

He dug his fingers into the jar again, scooped out a generous portion, and, before she could move, thrust them deeply into her anus.

Alan growled in rage, the sound drowned out by Rose's startled yelp.

"Oh, come now, Rose," Taylor said, grinning as he screwed his fingers more deeply into her. "I'm quite sure Alan has made use of this little hole already. How could he resist? Your pain was his pleasure, your submission, his victory."

Briskly he drew his fingers out of her and turned to the rack of whips hanging on the wall. Alan tensed, but Taylor abided by their agreement by choosing the lightest silk cat-o'-nine-tails for the next phase of the punishment.

Rose watched him saunter toward her, flicking the cat. Her brown eyes were bitter. "I've been whipped before. That toy will do you no good."

Taylor's smile stretched, slow and deadly. "It will," he purred, "where I'll use it." Drawing his arm back, he laid the silken lash hard, right across her rosy little nipples.

She cried out in rage and pained surprise, bouncing on her toes. Taylor's second strike caught her before she had time to recover from the first, making her generous breasts jiggle. She writhed, throwing back her head until the long tendons of her throat slid and worked.

Taylor stopped and deliberately began to unbutton his breeches. Alan noted with surprise that he wasn't totally hard yet; apparently such scenes were common enough to him to lose some of their erotic impact.

Alan himself was hard as a rifle barrel.

"I want you to watch what flogging your big, pretty breasts does to me," Taylor said softly. "Watch, and know how little mercy you can expect."

WHAP! WHAP! WHAP!

Rose's shoulders worked, her torso twisting as she fought to get away from the burning sting of the little whip, her nipples swelling and flushing. The captain's cock lengthened, slowly going a deep red as it hardened to impressive proportions.

WHAP! WHAP! WHAP!

She was crying out now, in high, gasping yelps of pain.

"That's right, sweet. Sing for me," Taylor crooned, his massive organ swinging with every stroke.

Suddenly he arrested his hand in midair and looked closely at Rose's face, her eyes screwed shut, her teeth clamped in her lip. "It's taking effect, isn't it?"

"What?" she gasped without opening her eyes.

"The drug in the cream," he said, running a hand over his big shaft. "The drug that makes you crave cock."

R ose gasped. Her breasts burned, her nipples swollen from Taylor's relentless whip, but that pain was negligible next to the fire blazing in her sex and rectum. An image floated through her mind: Alan, looming over her, shafting her in long, skillful strokes. She whimpered, wishing desperately that he was here now. He'd take her, he'd put the fire out . . .

"How," said Taylor seductively, leaning closer, "would you like to feel my cock sliding into your tender little quim?"

Her eyes flared wide and flew to the big phallus that thrust from his unbuttoned britches. She licked her lips. It looked so hard . . .

He smiled slightly, sliding a hand over the object of her fascination. "Just imagine, Rose. It would be so hot . . ."

She couldn't. She didn't even know him. It would be wrong. It would make a whore of her. It wasn't like with Alan, the man she loved and once dreamed of marrying . . .

But she was burning, itching for a long shaft driven deep, and Alan wasn't here.

"You need this, Rose," Taylor told her, his voice seductive, tempting as Satan's.

"Yes," she whimpered, deeply ashamed. But the hunger in her didn't care about shame. It cared only for his cock.

"I wonder," Taylor said with a smile she found chilling even in her present mood, "just how much you do need it. Would you like to find out?"

She struggled to concentrate past the flames licking her core. It was so hard to think. "What do you mean?"

"You'll see." Moving closer, Taylor pulled a folding knife from his pocket. A few passes of its sharp blade and Rose could straighten from her bent pose over the rail. Her back ached savagely, but not as much as her sex. She braced herself against the rail and tried to catch her breath.

"Well," Taylor said abruptly. "You're free now. What are you going to do?"

"I don't . . ." she began, and stopped, rubbing her abraded wrists. She couldn't think. Her sex felt twice its normal size; her every breath tormented her clitoris.

Then, as she watched in bewilderment, Taylor walked to the door, inserted the key, and twisted it. With a flourish, he swung the wooden portal wide.

"There, Rose. You're free. You can go."

She blinked at him suspiciously. "Go?"

"Yes. You're not a captive anymore. I'm releasing you."

Rose took a step toward the door—and groaned as the fires leaped. Her hand flew to her sex before she could stop herself. Involuntarily her eyes slid to Taylor's big phallus, jutting so temptingly as he stood by the doorway.

He smiled and moved closer. "I wonder which you would rather do: leave—or kneel at my feet and suck my cock."

Outrageous suggestion. She wished her head would clear enough to let her tell him so. The very idea that she would go to her knees and take that big, plum-shaped head between her lips, caress the thick shaft, swirl her tongue around it until he grew so hard with lust that he would fling her to her back and drive to her depths in a deep, pounding fuck. Of course she wouldn't do any such thing.

Rose directed her feet to take another step toward the door. She was quite surprised when her knees gave out and dumped her in front of Taylor's massive prick.

She was even more astonished when she felt its great plum head slide seductively between her lips.

Alan watched in angry jealousy as Rose's sweet mouth engulfed Taylor's cock. He knew it served him right; he'd brought her here to be punished, and now he'd been hoisted on his own petard.

But that self-aware thought vanished like smoke as Taylor's prick began to slide deeper between Rose's full, moist lips. Her lashes fanning her cheeks, she closed her eyes and suckled him with desperate force. Taylor leaned back a bit to watch her, smiling a purely male smile of triumph that made Alan want to punch in his teeth. If she was to kneel submissively at anyone's feet, it should be his.

"That's it, girl," Taylor purred, wrapping a big fist in her long, dark hair. Slowly he flexed his hips to shove his cock deeper down her throat. "Come on, sweet, I know you can take more of it than that." Rose widened her mouth obediently and forced her head closer to his belly, making a little choking sound of distress at his width. After moments of fruitlessly attempting to engulf him, she drew back and eyed the big shaft a moment as if trying to come up with a strategy of attack. Then, delicately, she put out her tongue and began to swirl it over the sensitive head. Her tongue looked long and pink, describing an erotic curl as it went to work.

One small hand came up and reached into Taylor's breeches to fondle his heavy balls. Her fingers appeared very white against the dark, wrinkled skin with its thick pelt of wiry blond hair.

Taylor shuddered, his eyes sliding shut as his head rolled back on his shoulders. With slow, even thrusts, he worked his dick against Rose's eagerly laboring tongue.

She looked up at him, her dark eyes shining with a feverish kind of hunger. "Do you want me?" she breathed, and licked at his organ again.

"Ohhhhh. Oh, yes. Suck me, you little bitch."

Rose darted her head forward and took him in again, sucking so vigorously that her cheeks hollowed. Taylor's knees buckled, then straightened again.

She pulled back again and looked up at him, one long hand holding his cock in a possessive grip. "I'm so wet, Taylor, so hot. Wouldn't you like to . . ."

Damn her! With a snarl, Alan whirled away from the spy hole and strode for the door. His booted foot hit the wood and it bounced open, making Taylor and Rose jump.

"Any fucking you get, you slut," Alan snarled, "will be done by *me.*"

R ose squealed, kicking, as Alan's hard, callused hand descended again and again on her bare bottom.

"She's pinkening nicely," observed Taylor in a tone of polite interest in direct contrast to the size of the bulge she could see in his uniform trousers.

"I know. It's such a lovely shade."

"Bastard!" Rose spat, struggling desperately. But her legs were clamped between Alan's thighs as he gripped her wrists in one hand. There wasn't a damn thing she could do to save herself from his violently stinging blows. Worse, the spanking made the heat in her belly flame even higher.

"You know," Taylor said, "technically speaking, it's not her fault. We *did* drug her with that cream. Otherwise she would never have been so willing to wrap that sweet mouth around my cock."

"I know that." But the burning impacts of his hand didn't slow. "I'm beating her ass for the sheer satisfaction of it."

"I know . . . OOOW! ALAN! . . . something you'd like . . . OW! . . . even more, you Yankee son of a . . . AH!"

"If it's punishment you've got in mind, it occurs to me that a bit of fucking might do the job nicely," Taylor said.

"Didn't you hear her?" Alan continued to pound. "She wants it."

Rose glanced up and froze at the slow, sadistic smile spreading over Taylor's face. "Perhaps she should be more careful about what she wishes for. I think the sensation of two cocks sliding into her tight little holes might be . . ." he hesitated, and the smile widened, "an embarrassment of riches."

A lan rocked back on his booted heels and watched Rose squirm in the harness that held her suspended from the ceiling. The leather straps circled her waist and shoulders, and her knees were drawn up to her chest and clipped to the straps. Her hands were lashed together and bound over her head to the same ceiling hook that held the harness.

The position left her pink sex spread wide and ready below her kicking calves as she writhed in the harness—a tight, delectably helpless package, ready for male pleasure. "Inventive rig," he commented.

Taylor eyed their struggling captive with satisfaction. "Yes, it does solve a multitude of problems. She can be penetrated any way that suits with a minimum of awkwardness. And, of course, she can be flogged just as easily."

Rose's dark eyes glittered at them over her gag; Alan could almost feel the burn of her rage. She'd been so bitter and vocal in her objections that Taylor had buckled a length of leather over her mouth to silence her.

Frowning, Alan moved closer and reached to probe between her thighs. Despite her earlier complaints, the delicate lips felt slick and dewed with desire. He felt his cock pulse in lust. Slipping a finger deeply into her channel, Alan lifted his head to meet her dark eyes. They looked vague and hot with hunger. Suddenly she jumped, a muffled sound escaping from the gag.

"I've always loved a tight female ass," Taylor said from behind her. "I don't know about you, McReynolds, but I am more than ready to begin."

Alan swallowed. "Yeah. So am I." He reached for his fly.

Breathing hard through her nose, Rose watched Alan free his beautifully erect cock. The harness put brutal pressure on her armpits, and her doubled pose made it difficult to breathe, but her drug-induced desire was so great, she didn't care. The need to feel Alan thrust into her devoured Rose.

Eyes glittering, her lover stepped between her wide-spread thighs. Staring into her face, he touched her sex with the broad, smooth head of his organ, then dragged it back and forth through her desperate slit. Her core seemed to open and clench as if reaching for him. Unable to help herself, Rose made a muffled, pleading sound behind her gag.

Alan smiled slowly. Then, with a skillful twist, he drove into her. She caught her breath at the feeling of her needy tissues spreading hungrily around his hard satin organ. He drew in a hissing breath and his eyes slid closed. Big hands closed over her hips, holding her still as he began a forceful hunching. She wanted to reach for him, but her bound hands could only clench at one another.

With a greedy growl, Alan buried his face in the curve of her throat and nibbled and sucked at the taut flesh as he gored her in long strokes. She quivered helplessly as his big shaft sated the hunger that had tormented her since Taylor had anointed her with that demonic cream.

A pair of broad hands closed over her hard nipples to pluck and twist them. "MMmmm. Nice, eh?" Taylor purred in her ear. "All that cock in your hungry little cunt. But what about your ass? As I remember, I greased your tiny bung pretty thoroughly, too . . ."

His hands tightened painfully on her breasts, immobilizing her. Something blunt and smooth probed at her anus. "Luckily, I've got just what you need."

Rose whined behind her gag as his massive length began to penetrate her. Alan paused, buried deep, to allow Taylor to complete her impalement.

Slowly the Union captain drove his organ deeper into Rose's asshole until, at last, she was completely stuffed with hard male flesh. She gasped helplessly, unable to breathe, trapped and gored.

With a single violent gesture, Alan reached up and dragged at the buckle of her gag until it fell free and she was able to suck in a grateful breath.

"God, she's tiny," the captain grunted. "I don't think I've ever had such a tight asshole." Slowly he began to withdraw, his organ sliding along her well-greased channel. Rose squirmed, finding something almost satisfying about the feeling. The deep, relentless burn of the cream he'd used was soothed by his hard, ruthless cock.

He stroked inside again as Alan withdrew. Rose felt the two thick shafts pass each other in her helplessly spread body. She could only writhe. "Nooo," she moaned, though she'd die if they stopped.

"Yes." Alan dipped his head and found her swollen lips, kissing her with hungry intensity. Taylor's thick fingers caressed her nipples again, plucking and rolling even as he fucked her ass with lingering strokes. At the same time, Alan's pelvis ground into her clit, his rod shuttling back and forth in her wet sex.

Rose tossed her head, feeling surrounded by male muscle and bone. There seemed to be far more than four hands on her, and she felt plugged to the throat with cock. It should have hurt. Instead, she felt only a voluptuous pleasure that grew with every stroke.

"I envy you, McReynolds," Taylor growled suddenly. "Having a tight, luscious little captive like this to bugger and fuck. No wonder you haven't told headquarters."

Alan's hands tightened on her rump. "They'd just put her in some dark little hole of a jail. Much better to . . ." He drove in a hard, deep thrust. ". . . take care of her privately."

"And so piquant to have a Reb spy at your mercy." He circled his hips and she whimpered as his organ tormented her rectum.

"Yes." Alan's eyes blazed down into her. "Bound and helpless." His voice roughened, his face darkening. "Ready for . . . whatever I want . . ." He groaned.

They were driving into her quickly now, merciless in hunger. Each stroke stretched and tormented her, stuffed her, jolted her with a blend of delight and pain.

Taylor came first, freezing with his organ buried to the balls in her ass, growling like a wolf. The feeling of his big cock impaling her provided a painful counterpoint to Alan's last pounding lunges, his hips digging into her clit.

Rose convulsed with a scream as the pleasure exploded through her in a long, pulsing eruption. Even as her orgasm crested, she heard Alan's triumphant bellow.

Alan's hot mouth closed over Rose's clit. Gently, relentlessly, he began to suck as her thighs twitched with the first pulsing waves of orgasm. Catching his dark head close, she came, keening and twisting as though with a seizure. And still he drew on her button, driving her higher, harder, until she fell back, limp and sated, her thighs spread on the cool sheets.

Dimly, Rose felt him draw away, heard the creak and shift of the bed as he moved up to lie beside her. And, even in her satisfaction, she found herself wishing that he'd entered her, ridden her hard instead of simply bringing her to ecstasy with his mouth.

A niggle of dissatisfaction pierced her pleasure. Two weeks had gone by since Alan and Taylor had taken her together, and nothing had been the same.

As if realizing that he'd gone too far that night, Alan hadn't touched her for three days afterward. Rose hadn't minded at the time; she was so sore from the violent fucking she'd gotten that she was hardly up to anything more.

But as time went on, she realized things had changed. True, sometimes he still took her almost ruthlessly, but for the most part, he'd treated her like spun glass. He hadn't tied her, hadn't spanked her, hadn't buggered her. Hadn't even questioned her.

It came as a nasty shock to Rose when she realized she wished he would.

There'd been something so violently arousing about those times, about her helplessness, about watching his control slip until at last he had no choice but to take her. She might have been his prisoner, but he'd been a captive, too.

Now all that seemed to be over. Had he gotten bored with her? Was he keeping her out of some sense of duty or guilt or some combination of the two?

"Rose," Alan said, "there's something I've got to tell you."

Frowning, she looked at him. He met her eyes, then looked away. Rolling off the bed, he paced to the window as if he couldn't meet her eyes.

Was he about to send her to prison? Was he going to let her go? And why did she suddenly feel this sinking fear—not of incarceration, but of never seeing him again?

"What is it, Alan?" Rose heard the steadiness in her own voice and was relieved. At least her desolation didn't show.

He braced a muscled forearm against the window frame and leaned against it, his back rippling. "There's something I've been keeping from you. Something important."

The last of her sensual languor disappeared. "What? What's happening?"

"Lee surrendered two weeks ago." Stunned, Rose could only stare.

Alan laughed, a short, harsh bark of sound. "The day after Taylor and I tortured you, as a matter of fact."

She licked her lips and found her voice. "Why didn't you tell me?"

His broad shoulders rounded a moment, then straightened with a jerk. "Because I knew you'd demand I let you go. And I didn't want your last memory of me to be my brutalizing you with that bastard Taylor."

She should be angry. She knew that. So why did she feel this perverse leap of joy?

No, she knew why. It meant Alan still loved her, even knowing she was a spy. He hadn't wanted to let her go.

"I've made arrangements to get you a proper gown," he continued, sounding almost matter-of-fact. "I had to do some fancy lying to your landlady to explain why you disappeared for so long, but I think I've pulled it off. You'll want to bathe and dress first, but I'll take you home as soon as you're finished."

"What if I don't want to go home?"

Alan's head jerked around toward her as his eyes widened. "Not go home? Why?"

Rose stared at him searchingly. "Why did it matter so much that the night with Taylor was not our last together?"

He pivoted to face her, both hands going behind his back, feet bracing until he stood at parade rest. "Because it was wrong. I had no business taking you to him like that, letting him . . ." He stopped and swallowed, looking away. "The other things I did were bad enough, but allowing Taylor to sodomize you . . . I don't know what I was thinking. When I saw you sucking him, I . . ." He drew in a hard breath. "You don't do things like that to the woman you love."

"Love." The bloom of joy she felt burst wide into wonder. "But I'm a Rebel spy, Alan. I lied to you. I . . ."

"You were serving your country."

"So were you. You had to get me to talk."

His mouth twisted into a bitter line. "That wasn't patriotism. That was lust. That was something dark and . . ."

"Exciting."

Alan looked at her, caught between shame and defiance. "Yes, it was. It was wrong. You said yourself, I'm no gentleman to do such things and enjoy them."

"Then I'm no lady. Because there were times . . ." Rose broke off and took a deep breath. "There were times I enjoyed them, too. It was exciting, being at your mercy, feeling your hunger. Even the punishments . . . I don't know why I felt that way, but I did. I do." She clenched her fists. "And I don't want to leave."

His eyes flared with something hot and dark. Then he looked away. "You can't stay."

"Why not?"

"It wouldn't be wise."

"When have we ever been wise?

"Rose," he exploded, wheeling toward her, "there are times I want to take you like that again. I dream about you tied up and helpless, squirming under that damn silk whip. I dream about buggering you, about making you get down on your knees, making you suck me the way you did Taylor. You've got to get away from me."

"What if," Rose said carefully, heart pounding, "I have the same dreams?"

"How can you?" Disbelief and despair vibrated in his voice.

"How can I go back to being a proper Southern belle, all cool and distant and painfully proper?" She took a deep breath. "How can I do that when I remember what it felt like to be at your mercy—and love every minute of it? I can't, Alan. And I don't want to."

Deliberately she moved between the canopy supports of the bed, turned her back to him, and lifted her hands, grabbing the overhead rails.

Slowly, disbelieving, he took a step toward her, then two. Then he turned away and strode toward the bureau. He reached into the top drawer and brought out a length of rope and a bottle of mineral oil.

Five minutes later, Rose was roped securely to the bed frame, whimpering as Major Alan McReynolds drove his cock into her ass in long, violent digs. But even as her rectum burned under his assault, she sighed in pleasure and relief. She was still his captive.

And he was still hers.

Turn the page for an excerpt from

OATH OF SERVICE

Appearing in *Love Bites*,
Angela Knight's new anthology
of erotic vampire stories

The dominant hauled his pretty companion across his lap and flipped up her short PVC skirt to reveal lacy stockings, a garter belt, and no panties at all. Despite her protesting yelps, he proceeded to spank her in hard, ruthless swats.

Morgana Le Fay tensed, her first instinct to feed him a magical blast that would put him through the nearest wall.

That was not, however, the kind of thing one could do in the middle of a nightclub in front of half the population of New York. Especially when the "victim's" moan sounded far more like pleasure than pain.

Morgana sent a tendril of magic into the little blonde's mind to discover she'd been deliberately bratting—whatever that was—to goad her boyfriend into just that response. Judging by her hot arousal, she was thoroughly relishing every stinging impact of his broad hand.

As for the man, a probe of his mind revealed he knew his lover had been trying to manipulate him. It gave him the excuse to pretend an anger he didn't feel, while meting out a punishment they both enjoyed.

Well, really, Morgana, what did you expect? It is a BDSM club . . .

Morgana watched the girl's long legs flash, kicking in mock protest.

Those creamy buttocks were going nicely rosy, much to the obvious enjoyment of the male patrons who'd turned to watch.

The Maja looked away, trying to ignore her own flare of heat. *Keep your mind on the job, witch. Somebody's killing these people . . . and using magic to do it. You don't have time for nasty fantasies if you want to stop the bastard.*

She scanned the area, keeping her gaze casual, though it was anything but. The Whip Hand was one of New York's most exclusive clubs, whether devoted to BDSM or more vanilla activities. The membership leaned toward upwardly mobile—if kinky—professionals: doctors, lawyers, bankers, stockbrokers, a celebrity or two. The place accordingly had an air of expensive seduction, between the long, massive bar and the surrounding tables and chairs, all of them dark oak carved with crosses and writhing nude bodies. The bar was surrounded by "dungeon" rooms equipped with St. Andrews crosses, spanking benches, and other assorted gear designed for tying people up and doing painfully erotic things to them. The overall effect was a sense of sensual menace, rather as if Torquemada had decided to run a bordello between torturing alleged witches.

Adding to the atmosphere of sensuality, smoky jazz filled the air instead of the usual deafening rock du jour that made hearing a luxury at other clubs. Given Morgana's sensitive Maja hearing, she approved, though the overall witch-torturing theme made her twitch. She'd come entirely too close to getting hanged by a fanatical priest once. It hadn't been erotic at all.

Though if Percival had been doing the torturing . . . *Stop that.*

Involuntarily, her gaze flashed across the bar to the rear booth where her team sat. They were dressed in The Whip Hand's idea of proper attire for dominants: expensive tooled-leather pants, boots, tight black T-shirts. Thanks to their enchanted scabbards, the long swords they wore diagonally across their backs were invisible. Guns would be of little use against the monster they were hunting.

Looking at them lounging around that table like a trio of lions on the veldt, Morgana felt a spurt of heat. She knew better, but she was still human—more or less. If a woman didn't feel a tingle at the sight of Percival, Cador, and Marrok looking ready to break all Ten Commandments, she needed to check her pulse.

Someone who didn't know them would probably register Marrok first. He looked the most menacing of the three, being six-five and brawny as a bull, with a broad, stubbled jaw, deep-set brown eyes, and a long Roman nose over a lazily sensual mouth. Despite the faint air of brutishness, in reality he was a laughing, genial soul who often played peacemaker between his hot-tempered and lethal teammates.

Which made what happened if you managed to truly anger him all the more shocking. On those rare occasions, his berserker rages could make even Arthur Pendragon step softly.

Then there was Cador. At six feet tall, he was shorter than the others, but that only made him look more muscular, with the sculpted brawn a man built when he spent hours a day swinging a long sword.

If that wasn't enough to make a woman's heart beat faster, Cador had shoulder-length hair, which, in combat, he wore tightly braided to his skull. That curling mane would have drawn the eye regardless, but the effect was intensified by its color, a rich, dark auburn.

His features were utterly perfect, as if God had calculated every angle for maximum impact on the female eye. Thick auburn brows dipped over laughing eyes the striking turquoise blue of the Caribbean. His nose was a perfectly straight and knife-blade narrow, while his wide, mobile mouth was prone toward deceptively charming smiles.

Deceptive, because Cador had a sadistic streak as broad as the Thames. He was not the kind of man you wanted to meet in combat, particularly if you'd done something to piss him off. He made no secret of his dislike of Morgana, though he was chivalrous enough to manage cool civility most of the time.

Last—but hardly least, since he was the trio's leader—there was Percival. At six-three, he was a bit leaner than the others, with all the muscular power, explosive speed, and hypnotic grace of a jaguar.

He had a long, starkly masculine face, with prominent angular cheekbones, a hawkish nose, and a sensualist's mouth. He wore his thick honey-gold hair just long enough to curl, and his gray eyes were cool and watchful. There was something about him that suggested a kind of erotic cruelty Morgana really shouldn't have found intriguing.

Any one of the three men could make any woman stare. All three of them together posed a safety hazard to any female in their collective orbit. Morgana wasn't surprised when a passing well-endowed redhead walked right into the chair in her path.

Marrok caught her before she could fall on her face. Lifting her to her feet, the big man leaned down to speak to her, probably asking if she was all right. Then he turned and headed back to the booth, apparently unaware of the longing look the girl shot his mile-wide back.

Technically speaking, he shouldn't have rescued her. He'd had to react far faster than humanly possible to catch her before she hit the ground. Morgana also knew he couldn't help himself; Marrok *was* one of the Knights of the Round Table. Though come to think of it, Percival hadn't even budged. Cador had probably considered it, but Marrok had beaten him to it. Besides, Cador would have gotten the girl's cell number, sexual opportunist that he was.

"Mmmm." A woman purred to her companion off to Morgana's right. "Wouldn't you love to be the meat in that sandwich?"

"They're probably gay."

The woman snorted. "Not the way they keep watching that chick in the red corset."

Morgana was wearing a red corset.

"The one in black leather looks like he'd like to take her into one of the scene rooms and chain her to a St. Andrews cross."

Percival wore black leather, though she hadn't noticed him watching her. The idea that he had been sent another wave of heat through Morgana that only intensified at a female scream. The sound was more suggestive of a really good orgasm than pain.

For a moment, Morgana could almost see it: herself, naked, chained to one of the X-shaped bondage crosses as Percival stalked around her, a leather flogger in his hand . . .

Don't be ridiculous. Percival probably would like to flog you, but it would have nothing to do with sex. Like most of the witches and vampires in Avalon, he seemed to consider Morgana a cold-blooded, manipulative bitch.

And he was right.

A girl strutted past, a pair of clamps swinging from her generous breasts. They looked damned painful, judging by the swollen red condition of the nipples they gripped.

"God, I'd love to put a pair of those on Morgana," Marrok murmured, saying exactly what Percival was thinking.

Snorting, Cador took a swig of his Corona. "She'd geld you with a fireball."

"Yeah, but it would be worth it."

As the clamped girl jiggled past Morgana, the witch's eyes slid down to the clamps, then flicked directly to Percival's face. Her vivid green eyes darkened with lust. His cock hardened in a searing liquid rush.

In the middle of a fucking mission to keep a werewolf from eating more women. Percival's temper began to steam. It burned all the hotter because he was as angry at himself as he was at her.

Passing his thumb over the signet ring on his right hand, he activated the spell that allowed them to communicate during missions. *"Get your head out of your cunt and on the fucking job, Morgana. If one of these women dies because of you, I swear to Saint Michael I will bend you over the Round Table and whip the ass off you!"*

"You forget yourself, Lord Percival. I am leading this mission!"

"Then lead it," Percival snarled, *"and quit turning it into fucking amateur hour."*

A white-hot stiletto of agony stabbed between his eyes, so savagely intense it almost tore a gasp of pain from his mouth. He bit it back.

"*Goddammit Morgana!*" Marrok growled in the link, "*Cador and I didn't do anything. Why hit us?*" Morgana's spell must've caught the pair as it traveled through their spelled rings. Morgana made no reply; she'd evidently closed the mental link.

"Sorry," Percival growled.

Cador grunted and took another deep swallow of his beer, auburn brows dipping in a frown. "I don't like the way this is going. She's too distracted. I've never seen her this off her game."

He was right. They'd worked with Morgana for centuries now, and Percival knew she normally maintained an icy focus on the mission at hand. That, plus her magical power, intelligence, and ruthless dedication meant they rarely failed to achieve their objective.

What's more, Morgana never admitted defeat. She'd do whatever it took to succeed, refusing to yield to physical or mental exhaustion. She pushed herself so hard that she'd won the respect of all three knights, even Cador, who personally disliked her. Percival had seen her keep casting spells to defend the team when she was so badly wounded he was surprised she was even conscious. Again and again, she'd proven she was willing to die for them—and they, in turn, would die for her.

Which didn't mean she couldn't royally piss them all off. Today's little psychic zap was hardly unusual behavior for her.

Which was why he'd had more than one fantasy of turning her over his lap for the spanking she'd been asking for.

Among other things . . .

Cador returned to his favorite topic. "So when are we going to look for another Maja partner?"

Marrok glowered at him. "When you can name one with as much raw power as Morgana Le Fay."

"Well, it doesn't have to be just one Maja," Cador pointed out. "Two or even three . . ."

"Might be equivalent to Morgana's power, but not of her experience or talent for magical combat strategy." Percival rattled the ice in his glass impatiently. "Nobody is as good in a magical duel as Morgana. Except maybe Kel, and he's a shape-shifting dragon."

Cador pursed his lips, considering. "Gwen's pretty damn good."

"True, but Arthur is hardly going to let us have Gwen, is he?" Marrok leaned in, his jaw taking on a familiar stubborn jut.

As the two knights began arguing about which Maja would make a better addition to their partnership, Percival's gaze drifted back to Morgana. He'd known the witch fifteen centuries now, years of desperate combat, furious arguments, and steely friendship.

Centuries ago, the four of them had been among the first twenty-four people to drink from Merlin's enchanted Grail. The potion it contained had magically changed them all, transforming the twelve Knights of the Round Table into vampires, or Magi, while twelve women, including Morgana and Queen Guinevere, had become witches, or Majae.

In the centuries since, those twenty-four had become ten thousand, as their descendants joined them in the battle to protect humanity against its own self-destructive impulses. Collectively they were called the Magekind, sworn to use their impressive abilities to hunt those like the magical killer who was their target tonight.

Today they all lived in Avalon, an enchanted city of immortals located in the Mageverse, a parallel universe where magic was a universal force like gravity or electromagnetism. That universe's version of Earth was also home to everything from fairies to dragons and elemental gods.

Mortal Earth, meanwhile, remained home to werewolves like the one they were hunting today. He was a nasty bastard. Over the past two months, seventeen women had vanished from nightclubs around the country, only to be found the next day as piles of gnawed bone.

He'd evidently *eaten* them.

The human authorities had yet to put all the pieces together.

Which was fortunate, given the questions that particular realization would raise.

Because the victims' bodies had been reduced to skeletal remains so quickly, the mortal authorities assumed they'd been dead much longer than they were. Thus they'd excluded individuals who had been missing less than a month. All of which made identification much harder, since police needed some idea who a victim might be in order to obtain dental records to compare skulls to.

Unlike the police, however, Percival and his team had Morgana. Last night the witch had a vision that some kind of magical predator was abducting, murdering, and eating women. Women who'd been taken from nightclubs.

Merlin's Grimoire—an enchanted talking book that was a cross between Watson the IBM supercomputer and something out of a Harry Potter movie—had found newspaper articles from around the country detailing skeletal remains believed to be the victims of animal attacks.

Morgana had told Grim about a flash of an image she'd seen in her vision: a hand holding a whip outlined in red neon. The book had identified it as the logo for a New York club called The Whip Hand.

Which explains why the most powerful witch on the planet was dressed in red corset, a thong, lacy stockings, and high heels. It was a costume that displayed every gorgeous inch of her elegant body, long, toned legs, and full breasts.

In other words, she was dressed like a submissive—just the kind of woman the killer liked to hunt. Morgana was playing the bait to the hilt, prancing around on those crimson stilettos, drawing the eyes of every straight man in the place, whether dominant or submissive.

Percival couldn't blame them. Morgana was an exquisitely beautiful woman, with that long-boned, elegant face, a narrow nose, full lips, and delicately chiseled cheekbones. Her large eyes were a green so vivid, they reminded him of spring leaves, and her black hair fell in a silken waterfall of ebony curls to the small of her back.

All of which should make her an irresistible target for the killer.

Which was why the three of them were occupying a table, pretending to be sexual dominants. If the killer was a werewolf, as Morgana believed, she'd need the backup. Werewolves were not only eight feet of fangs, fur, and claws, they were invulnerable to magical attacks. With no way of defending herself, she'd be almost as helpless as the mortal victims had been.

True, Morgana was stronger than human, not to mention good with a sword—given fifteen hundred years of experience, she should be—but that might not be enough to let her fight off a monster. Percival, Marrok, and Cador, with their vampire strength, would more than balance the scales. Considering what the killer had done to those seventeen women, he deserved everything they could dish out.

Nor could he claim to be a victim of animal instinct. Unlike the movie version, real werewolves were no more driven to murder than real vampires. This fucker was just a furry serial killer who liked to butcher women.

"Morg's got another nibble," Marrok said.

Percival tensed as the strange dominant approached Morgana. He was a handsome man, tall and blond with blue eyes so piercing, the color was evident all the way across the room. Dressed in black jeans and a blue polo shirt, he looked broad-shouldered and muscular as he loomed over Morgana. The bastard had to be six-one, six-two. He leaned down to speak to her, his expression hooded, sensual.

Under the table, Percival's hands curled into fists.

Morgana looked up at the man, her glance assessing.. She said something and turned away, her body language dismissive.

The big man froze, his face going expressionless. Then he nodded stiffly and walked away.

"Aaaaand he goes down in flames," Cador said with a cynical grin. "Morgana Le Fay—body of a Victoria's Secret model, personality of a rabid polar bear."

The witch glanced toward their table, then hastily away. Her cheeks colored.

Cador straightened in astonishment. "Did she just blush?"

"Appeared that way to me," Marrok drawled.

Both men turned and looked at Percival, who glowered back. "What?"

Cador put down his beer bottle with a thump. "You know what. If we're not going to get a new partner . . ."

Marrok snorted. "Fuck that."

". . . You need to address this thing you've got going with her."

"What thing?" Percival gritted his teeth so hard, they creaked.

"Don't play stupid," Cador snapped. "You can't pull it off."

Marrok leaned forward and directed a cool, level gaze his way. "She wants you, Percival. She's wanted you for a long time."

"She wants a goddamn giant lizard." Percival curled a lip and sipped his drink, only to grimace as he realized it was nothing but half-melted ice. He gestured their waitress over. "I'm afraid I don't measure up."

"Soren's not her lover." Cador sprawled back in the booth, eyeing him. "Soren's just her scaly, shape-shifting fuck buddy, and you well know it."

He was also Dragonkind's ambassador to the vampires and witches of Avalon. The pair had been on-again, off-again lovers for the better part of a decade.

Yet a decade wasn't long at all by the standards of the Magekind; Percival, Cador, and Marrok had been Morgana's partners a hell of a lot longer than that.

She'd also been cutting Percival off at the knees for most of that time.

As the waitress refilled Percival's scotch, his mind flashed back to the earliest of those galling encounters . . .

It had begun when Morgana, Percival, Marrok, Cador, and a young Maja named Sebille had ended up in a fight with thirty-eight Saxon raiders. The Magekind were normally more than a match for human warriors, but those odds were pretty bad however you sliced it. The five had had their hands full, but in the end, they'd managed to drag victory from the bloody fangs of defeat. By the time it was all over, four of the five of them had been in the mood to celebrate their survival, despite the rain pounding on the leather roof of the tent Morgana had conjured.

Marrok and Cador had wasted no time seducing Sebille out of her clothes. Cador had found an excuse to spill the little redhead across his lap for a brisk spanking while Marrok toyed with her pink nipples, plucking and rolling them into hard peaks. Both men were savagely erect.

So was Percival, for that matter, but his focus wasn't on the lush little redhead. The woman he wanted was Morgana Le Fay.

The dark-haired witch was trying unsuccessfully to ignore the laughing trio and the scent of arousal that filled the tent. She hadn't been as brittle in those days, or as inclined to give the team those nasty little jolts.

But Percival had been just as fiercely attracted to her as he was now. There had always been something irresistible about all that beauty, intelligence, and raw magical power.

He wanted her. What's more, his acute vampire senses told him she was aroused by what Cador and Marrok were doing to Sebille. Her green eyes kept flickering toward the Maja's pinkening arse as she giggled and yelped under Cador's carefully measured spanking.

Recognizing his cue, Percival rose from his place across the fire from Morgana and moved to sit beside her. The scent of her need teased his nose and made his cock buck behind the laces of his britches.

"If they're going to fuck her," Morgana growled, "why don't they just do it?"

"Because spanking her arouses them all. It's foreplay." Deliberately, Percival let his voice go low and deep. "Would you like to try it?"

Her head snapped toward him, and her green eyes widened. She recovered quickly, giving her chin a regal tilt she must have copied from Queen Guinevere. "Absolutely not."

"Are you sure?" He gave her a slow smile. "Because I'd be willing to . . . accommodate you. I'd love to see that lovely arse bare across my lap."

Her pupils expanded, her lips parted, and she swallowed audibly. But a moment later, she stiffened, eyes going hard. "I said no."

Percival's first instinct was to keep pushing, explore the vulnerability he sensed, but he knew the witch well enough to recognize when she'd dug in her heels.

It was Morgana, surprisingly, who refused to let it go. "Her submission to this . . . to being spanked like a child . . . It's beneath a Maja."

The girl evidently heard, for she shot Morgana a wounded look and went still over Cador's lap before trying to rear up and regain her feet. The knight flattened a palm on her back, stilling her as he gave Morgana a narrow glare.

Knowing his friend was a heartbeat from giving Morgana herself a spanking—welcome or not—Percival intervened. "Don't discount the importance of submission, Morgana. Everyone submits to something, whether it's men, the law, or the will of God. You submit to the king, do you not?"

"That's hardly the same thing," she scoffed, but her eyes flickered. Something in her expression made him wonder about her one night with Arthur, when, as a nineteen-year-old girl, she'd conceived Mordred, Arthur's illegitimate son. The seventeen-year-old king hadn't known Guinevere at the time, and neither of the lovers had been aware they were half siblings. According to Merlin, Arthur's father, Uther Pendragon, had taken Morgana's mother by force following an attack on her Druid temple.

Following a hunch, Percival gave Morgana a cool look. He'd been commanding men—and women—for years, and he knew a vulnerable spot when he saw one. "Perhaps before you insult and humiliate a fellow Maja, you should know what you're talking about."

"I don't think . . ."

"That much is obvious." Rising, he crouched behind her, caught her shoulders, and turned her to face the trio. She tried to turn away, but his hands tightened on her upper arms, and she stilled. "Watch."

Cador had gone back to spanking the girl, but now both he and Marrok knew they had an audience. There was a reason the two were Percival's partners. They had a way of sensing his intentions and giving him exactly what he wanted.

Cador smoothed a hand over the curves of the girl's lovely arse. They'd used leather cords to bind her arms and legs. He slid a finger into the girl's sex. "Mmmm," he purred. "She's slick as fresh-churned butter and tighter than a nun."

The girl whimpered, a tiny, helpless sound that made Percival harden even more—and he already could have pounded stakes with his dick.

"Sebille's little nipples are nice and hard," Marrok told his partner. He'd draped the girl's upper body across his own lap as he sat beside his partner, teasing the hard peaks.

Morgana made a low, rough sound.

"What was that?" Percival asked, knowing damned well she'd almost moaned before she bit back. Apparently their witch liked a little hot talk.

For a moment there was a charged silence filled by the soft, wet sounds of Cador's fingers working the girl's pussy, her helpless moans, and the two knights' low rumbles of approval.

The lush scent of sexual arousal teased Percival's nose—coming not least from Morgana. "Look at them," he purred, his mouth barely an inch from the rapid rabbit beat of the witch's carotid. "Sebille's so hot and ready . . . and small as a doll between them, bulls that they are." He pulled her into his lap, letting her feel his erection. "She's helpless. At their mercy."

"No." That definitely sounded like a moan.

"Would you like to be at mine, Morgana?"